SO-CWT-084

Kay Wasn't Afraid Anymore. . . .

"I've wanted to be with you ever since I saw you that morning," he said. His voice was choked and yet soft. He turned over, encompassing Kay's body with his arms and pressing her lips apart as he slipped his tongue deep into her mouth. Her breath was warm against his face as she uttered a sigh of satisfaction. She slid her arms around his muscular neck and responded avidly. . . .

Kay gasped. "Fred, Fred, you're so right for me, *so very right.*"

Later Kay would remember her first intimate experience with a kind of wonder. She recalled thinking it seemed as if her body was no longer her own, but an extension of his. She had never imagined that such warmth, such closeness could possibly exist between two people. And yet in that act of joining she experienced a freedom of self that would forever change her life. . . .

ACTION PAPERBACKS
1722 West Harrison
Olympia, WA 98502

Dear Reader:

We trust you will enjoy this Richard Gallen romance. We plan to bring you more of the best in both contemporary and historical romantic fiction with four exciting new titles each month.

We'd like your help.

We value your suggestions and opinions. They will help us to publish the kind of romances you want to read. Please send us your comments, or just let us know which Richard Gallen romances you have especially enjoyed. Write to the address below. We're looking forward to hearing from you!

Happy reading!

Judy Sullivan
Richard Gallen Books
8-10 West 36th St.
New York, N.Y. 10018

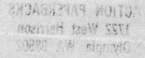
ACTION PAPERBACKS
1722 West Harrison
Olympia, WA 98502

Star Quality

LEILA LYONS

PUBLISHED BY RICHARD GALLEN BOOKS
Distributed by POCKET BOOKS

Books by Leila Lyons

Pillars of Heaven
Star Quality

This novel is a work of fiction. Names, characters, places
and incidents are either the product of the author's imagination or are used fictitiously, and any resemblance to actual
persons, living or dead, events or locales is entirely coinci-
dental.

 A RICHARD GALLEN BOOKS *Original* publication

Distributed by
POCKET BOOKS, a Simon & Schuster division of
GULF & WESTERN CORPORATION
1230 Avenue of the Americas, New York, N.Y. 10020

Copyright © 1981 by J. C. Conaway

All rights reserved, including the right to reproduce
this book or portions thereof in any form whatsoever.
For information address Pocket Books, 1230 Avenue
of the Americas, New York, N.Y. 10020

ISBN: 0-671-43558-2

First Pocket Books printing October, 1981

10 9 8 7 6 5 4 3 2 1

RICHARD GALLEN and colophon are trademarks
of Simon & Schuster and Richard Gallen & Co., Inc.

Printed in the U.S.A.

To Stacy, who has it

One star differeth from another star in glory.

1 Corinthians 26:41

Prologue

Raina

The alarm clock landed in the wastebasket. Its harsh buzz was muffled by a snow drift of tissue. Raina Pendleton groaned with the effort of having thrown it into its usual place of interment and sank back into bed. Her head throbbed and her thoughts were muddled. Damn Coy Winston! Damn stingers! Damn mornings! Raina fumbled for a cigarette, lit up a Salem and dully admired the Florentine gold finish of the Cartier lighter.

A sharp rap on the door caused her to jerk her head, increasing the dull throb.

"Come on, Raina," cajoled a voice as rich and dark as apple butter. "You've got to get going."

It was Jessie Johnson, the Pendletons' black cook and leading opponent of Raina's sybaritic life style.

Raina reached for the alarm clock, and realized that she'd already thrown it into the wastebasket. "Go 'way," she groaned and threw a pillow at the door.

"Time to get up, Raina . . . past time. Your name's going to be Miss Mud if you don't pull it together and get yourself on the road to New Hope."

"Oh no," exclaimed Raina. "Today can't be the twelfth."

From the other side of the door: "It is unless the *News* has decided to lie about the date as well as everything else. Now are you getting up or am I getting a bucket of ice water?"

"I'm getting up."

"I'll be fixing your breakfast."

2

"Oh gross! No breakfast, just coffee."

Ordinarily Raina would have ignored Jessie's wake-up call, and would have stayed in bed until her hangover had been slept away. But today was different. It was Monday, June 12, 1966, and she was leaving her home town of Harrisburg, Pennsylvania—she hoped forever.

Raina had aspirations; she wanted to be an actress. Of course she already considered herself quite a successful one and had many high school awards to prove it. The previous spring at the Pennsylvania High School Drama Festival, Raina had shared the best actress award with a student from Scranton named Jana Donatello. To everyone's surprise the two liked one another and admired each other's work. Another young woman, Kay Kincade from Bethlehem, won the best costume design award that year. The trio joined forces and became fast friends, causing their jealous peers to sarcastically dub them "the White Supremes." The three had this in common: they were very attractive, extraordinarily talented and were driven in their desire to succeed. They soon discovered that they had each applied to the famous Playhouse in New Hope as summer apprentices, and vowed that if by some wonderful quirk of fate they were all accepted, they would share an apartment.

Three days before the date of their respective graduations, Raina, Jana and Kay each received an affirmative answer from the Playhouse. The letter stated that they were expected to be in New Hope for a meeting at ten o'clock, June fifteenth. For the minimal salary of fifty dollars a week they were expected to perform apprentice duties willingly and efficiently. This would entail all aspects of theatre production from scene painting to scene stealing, from ticket selling to selling tickets, from stitching costumes to putting an audience into stitches. The final paragraph reminded them that they were apprentices and that rarely, if ever, did apprentices get a chance to design a show or appear in a major role. The letter was signed with a flourish by Clay Jordan, the director of the Playhouse. The young women phoned one another immediately. Each was sure that this opportunity was the positive start of a brilliant career.

As soon as her letter from the Playhouse arrived, Raina had climbed into her red Thunderbird. It was a four-seater complete with stereo and whitewalls and was a graduation gift from her absentee parents. Skipping her high school graduation, she'd set off for New Hope to secure an apartment for herself and her two new friends. Raina was familiar with New Hope; armed with a fake I.D., for the past year she had made many excursions to the various nightclubs of that lively area.

She'd found a charming apartment complete with three bedrooms on the second floor of a post-Civil War building. It was located on the corner of Mechanic Street and Nye Alley and overlooked the canal. The rent was a hundred dollars more than the trio had agreed upon, but Raina had decided to make up the difference and say nothing to the others. Raina could afford to be generous; she was the only child of an extremely wealthy Harrisburg family.

Raina's father was Adam Pendleton, the frozen food magnate. Five years earlier he had established a line of frozen pies, cakes and other sweet treats, distributed under the homey title "Aunt Lucy's." Adam was currently in New York City negotiating for the distribution of Aunt Lucy's to Puerto Rico, Alaska, Hawaii and Mexico. Her mother, Amanda Pendleton, a successful decorator, had deigned to marry Adam and leave her lucrative job at W.J. Sloane's in New York City. Amanda brought to Harrisburg not only her decorating talents but also an unparalleled snob appeal that insured her success with the well-heeled families. Amanda was in Arizona cashing in on the current vogue of American Indian decor. She ran from reservation to reservation, buying blankets, baskets, and an assortment of clay pots. Amanda persuaded her clients that they would be "doing their own thing" by redecorating their homes like teepees. The only thing she didn't buy in Arizona was the sunset. According to decorating flacks, Amanda was quoted as saying, "I've already used that color scheme."

Raina stared at her nude figure in the mirrored door that led through to the dressing room and bath. Even in disarray Raina Pendleton was a young goddess. Her skin glowed with a tawny hue as if her veins flowed with honey. Though she was very tall and lithe, Raina had high full breasts and long supple legs. A veil of silver-gold hair streaked lighter by the sun and frequent applications of lemon juice shaded Raina's remarkable face. It was narrow, but her wide cheekbones and generous mouth kept her from appearing hard. Her eyes were huge, slightly almond shaped and a curious green in color. Flecked with blue and gold, they resembled the wings of a dragonfly. Her nose was patrician with an insouciant tilt at the tip, and her sensuous mouth was framed by tiny lines like tender parentheses.

Raina ran her fingertips over the pale blue circles beneath her eyes, and muttered, "Damn Coy Winston!" Then she kicked open the dressing room door. The room was stacked with wicker baskets that served as suitcases and garment bags bloated with clothing. Jessie had done Raina's packing for her.

Raina dug two aspirins out of her medicine chest and washed them down with water. She stepped into the chilling shower and, after emitting a banshee scream, began to bathe.

Raina used the blow dryer until she could no longer stand the noise. Then she slipped into a dressing gown, a heady confection of amber chiffon trimmed with matching ostrich feathers. Stepping into a pair of inexpensive rubber flipflops, she descended the back stairs to the kitchen.

Jessie looked up from the stove where she was frying bacon. She was dark as a burnt tree stump and shaped like a lima bean, but her broad face was humorous and lit by twinkling eyes that shone as brightly as polished stones.

"You better eat something. You'll feel better."

Raina, paling at the sight of the wriggling bacon strips, went directly to the freezer, and retrieved a raspberry popsicle.

"There's not quite enough preservatives in bacon, Jessie. This morning I need all the preservatives I can get." Raina poured a great mug of coffee, sat down at the large oak table and finished the popsicle. She stirred the coffee with the red-stained popsicle stick and drank it down. "Thanks for packing my things."

"I'll get Lemuel to pūt 'em in the car." After Jessie had finished the bacon, she said, "Well, honey, I've got to get going." She stuck a floppy black straw hat on her head. "I've got some errands to run." Jessie looked around the room and sighed. "Seems like somebody ought to be here to see you off."

Raina, consumed by a rush of affection for Jessie, hugged her and kissed her cheek. "I'm fine on my own, Jessie. Haven't I always been?"

The cook offered no comment, but kissed the young woman in return. Tears misted her eyes. "Take care, Raina."

Raina, her hair brushed dry, dressed in low-cut denim bellbottoms, a halter top made of a tie-dyed material and sandals. She hooked a pair of hooped earrings through her pierced ears and, after putting on a selection of expensive rings, decided that she was ready for New Hope. The items as well as most of her "with it" wardrobe had been purchased at Carnaby Street the previous summer on a tour to London—another gift from her parents to celebrate her starring role in her high school play, which neither had attended.

The luggage had been loaded into the car along with a stereo and a great raft of records—mostly rock with a few original cast albums. Raina hurried about her room checking her drawers one last time to see if there was anything she had left behind. She opened the lid of her makeup case and scooped the clutter from the top of her dresser inside. As she was going down the steps, the telephone rang. Raina stopped and caught her breath. Perhaps it was her mother or father calling to wish her a *bon voyage* on her new adventure.

She frowned. It was Coy Winston, his voice thick with sleep and alcohol. Coy was the boringly handsome son of a wealthy Harrisburg family, and due to his social standing, was a sometime playmate of Raina's.

"No, I haven't left yet, Coy. How else could I be answering the phone? No . . . no, I don't want you to come over and see me off, Coy. No, *really*. You should stay in bed and recuperate. Why on earth did you let me drink stingers? . . . We what? Nude swimming? That's funny, I don't even remember. Look, Coy, I can't talk any longer. Jessie is waiting for my final instructions. . . . Yes, of course I'll write. . . . I can't recall it off hand but I'll send you the address. Then you can come visit. . . . Yes, Coy, yes. Now I've got to go. Kisses, kisses." Raina's forced smile slid from her face as she hung up the phone. "Nude swimming! Why, I could have caught a cold."

Without a backward glance Raina slipped behind the wheel of her Thunderbird and flipped the radio to a hard rock station. Seconds later she was speeding down the highway toward New Hope, Pennsylvania.

Jana

Jana stood in the center of her room and cried in exasperation. "God in Heaven! The place looks like it's been ransacked." She spun around in a circle and sat down on a stack of cardboard cartons. Every closet door was open, every drawer was pulled out, and every available space—chairs, cabinets and bed—was covered with an assortment of clothing, possessions and tissue paper.

"I don't *need* all this junk." She picked up a pad that was headed "Things To Take" and began striking through the long list with a blunt pencil.

At eighteen, Jana Donatello was a striking young woman. She was not tall—only five foot, three inches —but her perfect proportions made her appear taller, whether on stage, in photographs, or in person.

Jana's Italian heritage was apparent in her features. Her shoulder-length hair was so black and glossy it looked kissed by moonlight. Her skin was the color of a ripened peach and her eyes the color of the deep blue Mediterranean. At first glance, Jana was called wholesome and healthy-looking, which indeed she was. But upon closer inspection, one could perceive an emerging sensuality. A heavy fringe of eyelashes cast feathery shadows across her sculpted cheeks; flared nostrils gave the indication of temper and passion; and lips full and slightly pouting were meant for kisses and sweet secrets.

Jana finished the process of elimination and, pleased

with herself, carried an armload of discarded clothes back to the closet.

"Goodness, Jana. What*ever* are you doing?" Barbara Donatello had entered the room. An older version of Jana, she looked more like an elder sister than a mother. Although she was in her mid-forties, Barbara showed remarkably few signs of aging. Her body was still solid and limber and her face, except for spiderweb lines around the eyes, was completely free of wrinkles. The resemblance ended there. With her sleek hair pulled back into a tight bun, and dressed in drab conservative clothes, Barbara resembled a modern nun more than the mother of an eighteen-year-old girl. Her face was devoid of makeup except for light lipstick.

"Mother, I can't take all this stuff. There's no point in packing a lot of clothes I never wear anymore." She held up a plaid wrap-around skirt. "Look. Practically everything's out of style. The kids today are wearing kicky clothes. Not all this conservative Catholic school stuff."

Pursing her lips, Barbara sat down on the edge of the now visible bed. "Jana," she recited wearily, "you know I do the best I can on the small pension that is allotted me. I simply can't afford . . ." It was an old excuse, a litany as familiar as the one taught at school.

Setting her mouth in a straight line of discontent, Barbara went on. "I suppose you want to wear glass beads, moccasins and those horrible fringed leather vests." Barbara rolled her eyes heavenward. "I brought my daughter up to be a squaw."

Jana sighed and turned away. There was no point in arguing with Barbara or trying to explain her feelings; there never had been.

"You're not taking that jumper?" Barbara exclaimed. "It looks so cute on you."

"Cute," groaned Jana. "Mother, I don't want to look *cute*. Little girls look *cute*."

"I suppose you want to look like those straw-hatted sluts with the tinted glasses and no underwear."

"Oh, mother. We'll never understand each other."

Barbara sniffed and launched into a lamentation on single-parenthood that Jana had heard countless times before. "I've done the best I could, Jana, since your father was . . ." Here her eyes invariably became moist. "Suddenly—I was . . ." a meaningful pause, *"a . . . woman . . . alone."* She whined on and on, bemoaning tribulations that had long since become more a matter of habit than anything else. As her monologue wound down, she sniffed loudly. "A woman alone is not a woman," she concluded.

The recital over, Jana said softly, "Mother, why don't you go down and watch your programs while I repack my things?"

Her mother looked relieved. "All right. I'll just do that." She glanced at her watch. "Oh, dear, *Search for Tomorrow* has already been on for five minutes." She hurried downstairs.

Jana danced around the room, relieved that for once her mother had not given her an argument. A half an hour later she appeared at the bottom of the stairs carrying two large suitcases and a canvas bag slung over her shoulder. She had changed into a pair of jeans, a loose-fitting Mexican blouse and sneakers. Her mother glanced up from the television set and scowled. "It's going to be a long drive," Jana said, justifying her outfit. "I thought I might as well be comfortable." Barbara glanced in exasperation at the blown-up photograph of her late husband, James Donatello, that had been hand tinted and brush stroked to make it look like an oil painting. The picture hung in an ornate gold frame over a fake fireplace that held the TV set. Then she snapped off her program to punctuate her disapproval.

"Look, Mother, since I have so little luggage now, why don't I take the bus to New Hope?"

Her mother's response was swift. "James would never forgive me if I let you take a bus all by yourself to that . . . that *artists' colony*. Besides, I want to see where you're living. You certainly can't get much for fifty dollars a month."

"Raina said it was lovely and that we'll each have

our own room. The apartment overlooks the canal and the house is post-Civil War."

"I hope the plumbing works. Well," Barbara conceded, "if Raina Pendleton made the selection it must be all right." Barbara had read of the Pendleton family in the society pages of the Pittsburgh *Press.* "I must say I'm certainly glad for you to be acquainted with a young woman of such an impeccable background. But who is this other girl?"

"Kay Kincade," Jana supplied and grinned. "Kay, why she's the Star of Bethlehem."

Barbara frowned. "You know I don't like blasphemous talk, Jana."

"She's a wonderful girl," Jana plowed on. "Bright, funny, quite pretty, really, and very, very talented."

"But what of her family?"

"I got the impression they were poor . . . like us."

"Bite your tongue! We could never be called poor. No one would dare call us that, despite our circumstances. I've managed to keep up quite a good front."

"Yes, mother," Jana replied. "On that I can agree with you. Shall we go?"

"Very well, dear. You check the doors and windows while I turn off the lights and turn on the radio. Scranton has had its share of burglaries."

The two women climbed into the car, a '60 dark green Chevrolet sedan. As Barbara released the gear she admonished her daughter, "Now, don't badger me, Jana. You know how I hate to drive, and forty miles an hour is fast enough for anybody." Jana settled back in the seat and prepared to endure her mother for the length of the long and tiring trip.

On a rainy Saturday night in April 1958, the Donatellos were returning from one of Scranton's movie houses. They had taken Jana to see *Gigi,* the MGM musical extravaganza starring Leslie Caron. Little Jana was very much impressed with the French actress. Stretched out in the back seat, she dramatically informed her parents that she wanted to cut her hair

short and take ballet lessons. Her father, a gruff man
with limited perception, scoffed at her. He was feeling
his wife's knee and thinking of their Saturday night
love-making. He understood things of the flesh and
little else. Suddenly they were blinded by the unex-
pected appearance of car headlights. The driver of the
car, impatient to pass a beer truck, crashed into the
Donatellos. Barbara was thrown clear and suffered a
concussion and a severed artery in her arm. Jana was
shielded by the front and back seats and sustained only
minor bruises. But James Donatello was killed out-
right, his chest crushed by the steering wheel.

Barbara was devastated. She had lost not only a
kind husband and a good provider but a potent lover
as well. For a long time she resented her child because
Jana had lived. Barbara would rather have had a sur-
viving lover than a daughter.

Barbara became morose. She cared little for her appearance and rarely left her home, choosing instead to
remain in her room with only her memory and her
despair as companions.

Jana, not understanding her mother's feelings toward her, became moody and withdrawn. The condition
persisted for nearly two years until a perceptive rela-
tive, Barbara's younger brother, realized what had been
happening between mother and daughter and the cause
for it. He talked to Barbara and she listened to him,
and Barbara agreed to seek psychiatric help for both
herself and Jana. The brother would be paying the
expenses.

When the psychiatric sessions ended, Barbara and
Jana had formed a sort of truce. Jana loved her mother, but from a distance. That was the only way Barbara would allow it. And Barbara renewed her concern
for her daughter's education and welfare. It was a
workable relationship, but one that did not encourage
sentimentality, understanding or even displays of affection.

*   *   *

This trip seemed interminable to Jana. Not only did she have to endure her mother's driving and her self-indulgent reminiscences about her father, she also couldn't play the radio. Barbara couldn't stand "all that noise." Jana concentrated instead on the trees and vegetation lining the roads, which were heavy with late spring's green promise of fulfillment. Finally, a sign half-hidden by the emerald tresses of a willow tree said that fifteen miles ahead was New Hope, Pennsylvania.

Kay

The sunshine could not penetrate the thick cover of smoke hovering over Bethlehem, Pennsylvania. The sky emitted an unearthly gray glow that muted the shadows and caused everything to resemble an over-exposed photograph.

"Even the Greyhound bus station looks pretty this morning," Kay Kincade remarked, more to herself than to the *others*.

The *others*—her family—were overrunning the interior of the drab waiting room, examining the junk food machines and trying each in turn. Cups of bubbling sodas, packets of cheese crackers, bars of chocolate candy and bags of pre-buttered popcorn were selected and then voraciously consumed.

Kay stared at them in hopeless resignation. They just didn't have any class and never would have. Thank God, she was getting out, or she could see herself a few years hence. She'd be just like her mother, married to a man just like her father and producing an odd assortment of children who would grow up only to repeat the ghastly process. She glanced at her older sister Effie, married to a mechanic and pregnant for a second time. Effie was eating a candy bar and staring into space from eyes as dull as a cow's. Kay shuddered, not only with revulsion, but with the thrilling knowledge that she was not going to turn out that way. Being an apprentice at the Playhouse was only the first step in her oh-so-right direction.

*   *   *

It seemed like Kay had been brought up with her own Ali Baba's cave, only in this case it was the refrigerator. Instead of sparkling jewels inside, her cave contained prodigious amounts of ice cream, pastries, cheese spread, soda, bread, olive loaf, mayonnaise and chocolate syrup. The instant gratification of it all fairly enchanted the young girl.

The Kincade family was closely knit. Because Mr. Kincade owned some property on which there were gas stations, he was considered "self-employed." The family rarely left the house except to visit the grocery store.

It wasn't until Kay started school that she realized that everybody wasn't fat. The teasing began immediately. At various times she was known as "Fat, Fat Water Rat," "Lump," and "Tubby." Kay was completely unhappy with her new environment. Her classes bored her. Anything bored her that lasted longer than half an hour and wasn't in black and white. She always sat in the last row in class, and occupied her time by poking holes in her swollen lunch bag with a pencil. Then using her fingers she would dig out furtive amounts of heavily iced cake or peanut butter and banana sandwiches. When the last class was over at three o'clock she rushed home to the ramshackle Victorian house on Walnut Street flanked by the family owned gas stations. The house appeared to lean forward, the paint was badly chipped, the shutters hung at peculiar angles and the small yard was overgrown with a variety of weeds. But once she opened the front door, to be greeted by the wonderful aroma of her mother's cooking, Kay immediately felt better. The food, combined with the casual and convivial atmosphere of her home life, temporarily made her forget the horrors of her school day. Evenings were spent before a flickering TV screen surrounded by folding trays piled high with caloric delights.

When she entered the third grade, Kay fell in love with something besides food and television—her art class. The teacher, Miss Ledoux, recognizing Kay's instinctive talents, let her design the class's morning glory hats for an Easter pageant. They were constructed out of poster board and purple crepe paper and the results were somewhat remarkable. Despite the hats, Kay's peers remained unimpressed.

Junior high school was even worse: owing to boys and gym class. The male members of her class who had previously taunted her without mercy now simply ignored her. The girls in gym class made fun of Kay for her lack of coordination and her appearance in the regulation clothing. One pretty little thing remarked that Kay resembled a grape with legs.

During this period Kay's tastes changed. She found that the usual TV fare bored her and she began taking herself to the films. Alone in the darkened theatre she watched the glamorous ladies of the screen go through their emotional paces in an array of spectacular costumes. Kay soon developed an interest in designing clothes and taught herself to sew on her mother's sewing machine. She began creating her own clothes. Most of her early designs were ill-chosen. Running to horizontal stripes and elaborate ruffles, her dresses only provoked more caustic comments from her classmates.

Kay developed difficulty in breathing. She was taken to a doctor and the appalled man ordered the girl to go on a diet. The doctor gave Kay the support she needed, and under his strict supervision she switched from marshmallow topping to cottage cheese. The weight loss was slow but was accompanied by her gain in height. To sustain her diet, Kay stayed away from her family as much as possible. She spent her evenings at the library poring over costume books and chronicles on film and the stage, or at the movies watching her favorite actresses model the clothes that she herself would soon be able to wear.

Locked away in her room, Kay sketched from memory or imagination. Her English instructor urged Kay to design and sew costumes for the Thespians, the high school drama group. By the middle of her junior year in high school Kay was designing all the shows.

The costume room beneath the auditorium became her haven, and while her other classmates were experimenting with drugs and sex, Kay was experimenting with fabrics and trims.

"Want a bite?" demanded her twelve-year-old brother Terry, who thrust a melting ice cream sandwich at her. Terry was already on his way to becoming obese.

"No," snapped Kay. "Go over there and drip."

Now at eighteen, Kay's stringent dieting and exercise had given her a body that still surprised her. She was not yet what anyone would call slender; fashion purists would say that Kay needed to lose ten, perhaps fifteen, more pounds. But in the Kincade family she was gently chided as "the skinny one."

Striking rather than beautiful, Kay's most arresting feature was her great mane of wavy auburn hair—a gift from her mother. Her skin was pale pink and shone like glazed porcelain. Her eyes, huge and blue, resembled fully opened flowers. Her nose was short, slightly upturned; her mouth was wide, sensuous lips always parted in breathless anticipation or curling slightly at the corners, barely concealing her enormous sense of humor. She wore clothes a trifle too faddish for her still full figure. The long dress had puffed sleeves and was made of a nubby pink fabric, block-printed with tiny flowers. Kay had made the dress herself based upon a picture she had seen in a fashion magazine. Her feet were encased in a pair of high button shoes circa 1917—a thrift shop find.

Kay chewed on her ragged cuticles and checked the time on her watch. The bus was late by nearly fifteen minutes. She fumbled in her red beaded purse—another thrift shop purchase—and withdrew a Winston, which, using three matches, she managed to light. As she was lighting her cigarette, a paperback copy of Dr. Joshua Priestly's self-help book *Do It Now* fell to the coral and grey tiled floor. Quickly retrieving it, she tucked it back into her bag. Along with her new figure, Kay had acquired a passion for self-help books aimed at improving every aspect of her life. She had studied Yoga and meditation, and had learned how to say no when she meant no.

Of course she longed to say yes to the right person, but no one had asked her. Kay was still a virgin and not at all happy about it. When she first entered high school, Kay's peers had put her into a slot. The label read "fat, ungainly and poor."

Even though Kay had completely changed her appearance, and had cultivated her considerable talent, it hadn't made any difference to her classmates. She continued to be ignored by all, and had gone through high school without friends or confidants. Now, leaving Bethlehem, Kay felt that at last she would be leaving all her bitterness behind. She had read somewhere that the most popular students in high school were usually underachievers in life, and that those introverts with strange and quirky life styles sometimes went on to become famous. *Famous.* She whispered the word to herself, rolling it over her tongue like a piece of hard candy.

"Kay, Kay, come quickly." It was her mother, a redhaired, shapeless repository for cellulite.

Kay unwillingly abandoned her reverie. "What is it? Has the bus come?"

"Yes, it's just pulling in now."

The entire Kincade family—mother, father, aunt, older sister and three younger brothers—clamored around Kay, shoving, kissing, patting and in general making a commotion. The other passengers had queued up. They and the bus driver stopped to stare at the incredible send-off. Kay was beginning to wish that the bus had run over her.

Mrs. Kincade, her mouth reeking of artificial chocolate and preserved coconut, pressed a shoe box into Kay's arms. "Here, darlin'."

"What's that?" groaned Kay.

Her mother smacked her lips. "Fudge and fried chicken."

Kay felt a wave of nausea sweep over her. "For

heaven's sake, Ma. It's only a three-hour bus ride. I'm not boarding a tramp steamer to Timbuktu."

"Take! Eat! You're lookin' more like that Twiggy every day."

"Ma, I don't want the food. I've given up food, remember?"

"Don't insult your Ma's cooking," warned Mr. Kincade, a barrel-shaped, balding man whose interests were limited to the Pittsburgh Steelers, home cooking and his bowel movements.

"All right, all right," groaned Kay, snatching the greasy box from her mother's fingers. Feeling slightly delirious, she backed away from her advancing family toward the open door of the bus. Her eyes stinging with tears of embarrassment, she stumbled into the bus and quickly found a seat on the side opposite her family. She sat down and pressed her face against the window. If only she could disappear through the pane like Alice Through the Looking Glass. Her eyes widened in horror. Her family had run around the bus and were jumping up and pounding their fat fists on the window pane. Kay could fairly feel the bus rocking.

Kay crouched down in her seat and mercifully the bus began to lurch forward, leaving the Kincade family shrouded in a cloud of noxious fumes.

A few miles out of Bethlehem, the other passengers lost their interest in Kay and the young woman regained some of her composure. She slid the shoe box under her seat, opened Dr. Priestly's book and read to herself: "Some wise sage once said that one should live his life as if each day was his last. Now, if that were the case, what would you do? Settle into that easy chair and watch your favorite TV program? Or would you spread your wings and soar above the unexplored mountains and hidden valleys of your very being?"

Kay closed the book and smiled smugly to herself. "That's just what I'm doing. Leaving the mundane behind, starting a new life with hope, as in New Hope, Pennsylvania!"

Part One

Chapter One

Kay sat dejectedly in front of the doorway of Number 9, Nye Alley. The Greyhound bus carrying Kay and all her cardboard boxes and tied-up suitcases had arrived at twelve forty-five. It had taken her several trips to bring her possessions to the apartment, only to discover that the door was locked. Not knowing what else to do, she was simply waiting for one of the other girls to arrive. She was beginning to get discouraged when she saw a red Thunderbird pull into the narrow alleyway and heard a familiar voice call her name.

"Kay, are you the first one here?"

Kay jumped up. "Raina, I'm so glad you're here! I was afraid I had the wrong address, or maybe even the wrong town."

Raina got out of the car, ran to Kay, and embraced her. "What a drag. I've got the hangover of all time. Come, let's go somewhere and get a drink."

"Shouldn't we put our stuff inside?" asked Kay.

"Oh, look," exclaimed Raina. "There's an outdoor restaurant right next to the canal. Perhaps we can get a drink there. Just leave your things here, we won't be gone long."

The outdoor restaurant was called The Open Pit. The food was cooked over a barbeque grill and there were tables shaded by brightly colored umbrellas next to the canal.

"The Open Pit," groaned Raina. "It sounds like something out of Dante's *Inferno*."

The young women sat down at an outside table

overlooking the canal. A giant willow tree dipped its verdant tresses into the yellow water. The sky above was a dazzling blue and as empty as a clean sheet of paper. Nearby a fence of hollyhocks was tended by a mass of bumblebees. The somnolent buzz added a lazy orchestration to the warm sounds of that day in June.

In a few moments a waiter with shoulder-length hair and a greyhound's face, thin and ascetic, appeared to take their order.

"I want a bloody mary with two shots of vodka and lots of Tabasco," said Raina.

"I'll have the same," echoed Kay somewhat uncertainly. Her experience with drinking was just about zero.

When the waiter departed, Raina lit a cigarette and turned to Kay. "I'm sorry you had such a long wait," she said. "Perhaps I should warn you that Sylvia Oglethorpe, that's our landlady, is a little bit eccentric. She hardly ever gets up in the daytime. I had a helluva time waking her in order to see the apartment."

"But I thought you said she runs that gourmet shop in the front of the building. How can she open the shop if she doesn't get up?"

Raina shrugged. "I haven't a clue. Perhaps it's just a front for some sort of drug ring."

The waiter, who had been eavesdropping, grinned as he served the drinks. "My name is Sonny. Glad to have you in the neighborhood." He lowered his voice. "Listen, I can get my hands on really great grass. Maybe some night you'll ask me up. I'll help hang your drapes or something."

Kay opened her mouth to respond enthusiastically to this overture, but a glance at Raina, whose face had become as expressionless as an oyster, checked her. "Maybe," she replied noncommittally. The waiter, disappointed by the rebuff, sauntered away. Raina then offered a toast.

"Here's to New Hope and new friends." They clinked their glasses together and drank.

"What did you do last night?" asked Kay with interest.

"I went out with Coy Winston, that guy I told you about. We got terribly drunk on stingers and went nude swimming in the country club pool."

A hint of envy crept into Kay's voice. "Nude swimming? Both of you . . . *nude?*"

"Both of us."

"Did anything happen?"

"If you mean by 'did anything happen' did we have sex, I can't honestly remember," Raina replied blithely. "Come, we'd better go open up the house of blue lights so that we'll be able to let Jana inside. I hope I'm able to get Sylvia up. I don't have keys either."

Together they walked down the alleyway toward the gourmet shop that occupied the front of their building. Raina bounced up the steps to the porch and peered inside the shop. "It looks like today's one of those days that Sylvia didn't get up."

Kay stared through dirty windows at the cans of dusty gourmet foods imported from all over the world, strange and exotic teas, and French ironware beautifully hand painted by expert craftsmen. "Very fancy," she muttered. "I'll bet the prices are fancy, too."

"Let's go look around back to see if she's in. Her apartment is on the first floor. Look here. There's a walkway right beside the canal." They walked down the grassy path that edged the ribbon of ochre-colored water.

A wrought iron gate cast a shadow across the courtyard like a spiderweb spun by a giant spider. It creaked on its hinges as it opened. Weeds grew through the flagstone patio like decorations on a patchwork quilt. They noticed a saucer of milk with a thin film over it sitting beside the door.

"Well, it looks as if Sylvia's cat didn't get up either," Raina remarked, and looked into the window of the Dutch door. It was completely dark inside. She pressed the button and a bell with a churchlike quality rang out.

"It sounds like Notre Dame Cathedral," giggled Kay.

"Nobody could sleep through that. I don't suppose our landlady has a hunched back."

"No," laughed Raina, "but a hump would make a nice finishing touch. Hmmmm. I'd better ring again. The bell is tolling for thee, Sylvia Oglethorpe!"

After the seventh ring they heard micelike movements inside the apartment and a musical voice sang out, "Just a minute . . . whoever it is."

Raina glanced at Kay with a relieved expression on her face. A few moments later the top half of the Dutch door opened and Sylvia Oglethorpe appeared. She was disheveled and wore a chenille robe that was soiled from many a past repast. Her face was small and round, her features tiny. Atop a sharp nose were a pair of thick glasses that magnified her watery eyes. Her hair —dull brown flecked with grey—was a mass of untidy curls. Her small hands were constantly in motion, fluttering like caught birds. Sylvia stared intently at her "early" callers like a clairvoyant looking into crystal, then asked brightly, "Who is it?"

"It's me, Raina Pendleton. I rented the apartment upstairs, remember?"

Sylvia smacked her lips together. "Is it June already?"

"The twelfth," Raina informed her, suppressing a snicker.

"Would you be so kind as to excuse me just a minute?" she asked and shuffled away. Her stockings hung like concertinas around her ankles in accordian pleats.

Kay looked at Raina. "It seems our Miss Oglethorpe is a drinker. *That's* why she doesn't manage to get up in the daytime."

Moments later Miss Oglethorpe was back. She had run her fingers through her hair and had used a strong mouthwash. She stepped out onto the patio explaining: "I'd ask you in, but my maid is ill," her musical voice rose and fell as if she were searching for the correct note, "and didn't come to clean this week." It was an obvious lie but a pathetic one.

Raina introduced Kay, and the landlady nodded grandly. The self-proclaimed queen of her own world, Miss Oglethorpe chatted away, spreading herself equally among all who were her subjects. Regally she led Raina and Kay around the back of the building to the whitewashed wooden door that opened onto the steep steps leading to the porch of the second floor apartment.

They reached the porch, which was overhung with grape ivy. Kay, impressed by the heavy oak door that had a small window panel in the center, remarked, "It looks very safe."

Miss Oglethorpe fumbled with the keys for an interminable amount of time before managing to open the door. The main room of the apartment was large and sunny, and the ceiling was decorated with a profusion of baguettes, ogees, friezes, cornices and other stucco embellishments. Everything was painted white with the exception of the floor, which was covered with a heavy wooden planking of dark walnut. It was sparsely furnished with an odd assortment of pieces. Among other things, there was a white plant stand with carved elephant heads—the trunks forming the legs—a gilded piano stool, and a couch made from three heavily labeled and obviously well-traveled steamer trunks with pillows thrown on the top. There was a player piano in one corner with a large embroidered scarf hanging over the side. Opposite was an ornate rattan screen.

"All the pieces are props," explained Miss Oglethorpe. "They're bits and pieces from the various plays I've done over the years at the Playhouse. It makes for a rather charming room, don't you think?"

"I love it," exclaimed Kay.

"I feel like I'm on stage already," added Raina.

Off the living room was a small, pine-paneled kitchen with a window overlooking Nye Alley. The bathroom was old-fashioned. The tub was one of those great claw-footed antiques, but was equipped with a shower. The window was made of green and yellow stained glass which Miss Oglethorpe explained had been done by one of the local craftsmen. Further on, three doors opened off to three small bedrooms, each containing a wrought iron bed and a walnut bedstand. Covering the walls were posters from past productions at the Playhouse. Some of them were autographed by the different actors and actresses who had stayed in the apartment.

"Well, my darlings, I hope you'll be happy here." She looked puzzled and counted the two girls. "There are only two of you. I thought there were going to be three."

"There will be, Sylvia," explained Raina. "Jana will be arriving some time later."

"Jana, Raina and Kay. What a delightful combination. Oh, you must visit my gourmet shop sometime. I'll bring you up a basket of goodies later. I have some marvelous watercress soup from France. Just serve it well chilled. Oh, I almost forgot. Here are the keys."

After Miss Oglethorpe left the apartment, Raina asked Kay, "Well, what do you think of it?"

"I'm really surprised. It's lovely and quite charming for the rent."

"I love it. I just love it. Now, let's get things out of the car and go exploring."

Suddenly there was a loud commotion and Raina and Kay ran to the window to see what it was. A mule drawn barge containing a Dixieland band and a party of twenty or so people passed by. Several of the party waved to Raina and Kay. "How often does that happen?" asked Kay.

"I forgot to tell you," bubbled Raina. "Just one of the little extras that comes with the apartment. A bit of New Hope's past."

Kay smiled, "We'd better keep our shades drawn."

Raina and Kay carried their things up into the apartment and dumped them in the middle of the living room. They sat and had a cigarette, hoping that Jana might turn up, then decided not to wait any longer. They left the door to the apartment unlocked and tacked a note on the downstairs door telling her that they would be back shortly.

The young women made their way down Mechanic Street, which had become crowded with tourists and colorful locals. Most of the young people were dressed in the uniform of the day—frayed jeans, extravagant shirts, mountaineer dresses, and period costumes.

"You know, Kay," said Raina as they crossed the bridge on South Main Street, "they say that the hippie movement started in New Hope, not Haight-Ashbury."

"I'm glad my parents never saw this place. They might never have let me come."

They crossed the bridge and made their way through the parking lot next to the famous theatre. The Play-house had been converted from a very old grist mill into a summer theatre. They raced over the gravel lot and stood on the steps of the rustic building. They threw their arms around one another and jumped up and down in excitement.

"I can't believe we're here," cried Kay.

"We are," pronounced Raina, "and this is just the beginning."

They walked to a stone wall overlooking a pond situated right next to the theatre. "Look!" said Raina, pointing to a large sign that hung beneath the rustic letters identifying the theatre. It read:

SUMMER SEASON—OPENING SOON

"That's us," she squealed. "That's us!"

The main door of the Playhouse suddenly opened and a man emerged into the bright sunlight. Both women started. He was the most beautiful man they had ever seen. Not handsome, but beautiful and per-fect. He was tall, magnificently proportioned, and car-ried himself with an ease that came from knowing his own worth. His hair was the color of wheat and a pair of deep dimples scored his otherwise flawless face. He could have been anywhere from twenty-five to forty, but his physical movements bespoke youth.

He saw the two young women and flashed them a dazzling smile. His teeth were as white and even as sugar cubes. He hurried down the steps and skipped across the parking lot where a beige Jaguar sat waiting. Without bothering to open the door, he vaulted inside, shimmied into the seat and seconds later was speeding away.

"Did you see him?" gasped Kay.

"I'm not blind yet," replied Raina.

"Do you suppose he's one of the actors?"

"Let's find out," suggested Raina. "Come, the box office is open. Perhaps we can ask there."

An old woman whose face was a nest of soft wrinkles asked how she could help them. They explained that they were apprentices and were wondering about the identity of the man who had just left the theatre. "Why, that's Mr. Clay Jordan," the old woman smiled knowingly. "He's the director of the Playhouse."

Chapter Two

"The Director of the Playhouse. I simply can't believe it," said Raina. "He makes every guy I've ever gone out with look like a clod. I wonder if he's straight?"

"Straight?"

"I mean whether or not he likes girls. Straight as opposed to gay," Raina explained.

"Oh, please God, make him straight," intoned Kay. Then to Raina, "He looked at us as if he were straight."

On their way back across the bridge, they encountered a friendly group of long-haired young men who quickly clustered about them. Each of them eagerly shouted out his name. Kay was a little disturbed, but Raina was quite unflustered. When asked, she told the young men where their apartment was. They asked if there was anything they could do to help get the young women settled in. Their offer seemed genuine.

"Well, we could use some plants," announced Raina. "Our living room is rather barren."

"We could also use some more chairs, if any of you see any decent ones that are being thrown out," added Kay.

"Now we really must go. We're expecting our third roommate."

"Wow! A third," cried one of the young men. "Is she as pretty as the two of you?"

"Prettier," smiled Raina, and signaled to Kay that they should be leaving. The young men were still waving good-bye to them as they turned the corner up Mechanic Street.

The girls stopped to light a cigarette and Kay asked, "Why did you do that? They're liable to show up."

"Would that be so bad?" Raina laughed. "They were awfully nice and one of them was quite good looking."

"He was also very well built."

"I noticed you noticing."

When they reached Nye Alley they saw the dark green Chevrolet parked next to the door leading to the apartment.

"Jana's here!" cried Kay.

"We'd better put out these cigarettes. Remember what she said about her mother." They ground them under their heels and sprinted toward the staircase.

Jana and her mother were sitting on the couch. Barbara was saying, "I hope this isn't a habit. Imagine leaving the front door unlocked. Why, we might have surprised a burglar."

"Really, Mother. It was just a thoughtful gesture on Raina's part. She knows I don't have a key yet.

"And did you see those characters wandering around the streets? The place looks like some sort of drug haven, like those pictures you see of San Francisco." She was about to ask her daughter if she had ever taken drugs when Kay and Raina came bursting into the room. The three girls hugged one another, then squealed and jumped up and down for what seemed to Barbara a full five minutes.

"Goodness," she smiled wanly. "You'd think you were all long lost friends instead of three girls who barely know each other."

Jana looked at her friends apologetically, then turned to introduce them to her mother. Barbara's eyes appraised each girl. She neither liked nor approved of what she saw. But she knew there was no way she could take Jana back with her. Indeed, she didn't want to. Her daughter had always made her uncomfortable. And now, finding herself very much a fifth wheel, Barbara decided it was time for her to go.

Jana walked her mother to the car. They brushed

cheeks. As the car drove away, each of them was profoundly relieved.

When Jana returned, the three girls started squealing
and jumping up and down once again.

"It's too much!" cried Kay. "To be on our own. It's
just too much!"

"I can't believe it," sighed Jana.

"I'll drink to that," said Raina. "Drink! God in
Heaven, we haven't even christened the place properly.
Let's get straightened out here. Then I'll go shopping.
I can't imagine getting through the night without a bit
of booze in the house. How could we celebrate without
it? Now I suppose the first thing we ought to do is
select our bedrooms. It makes no difference to me
which one I take, but I warn you both, I'm very noisy."
She grinned. "Particularly when I'm not alone."

"I'd like to be closest to the john," said Kay. "I
tinkle a lot. I take diuretic pills, you know."

Jana and Raina agreed that Kay should have the
bedroom nearest the bath. They flipped a coin to decide
who would get each of the other two rooms. After carrying their clothes into their respective bedrooms, they
looked through the kitchen.

"There are a few cleaning things here, at least enough
to get started," said Jana. "Why don't I start cleaning
and you two can shop."

"I can manage the shopping by myself, if that's all
right," said Raina. "I do know the area. Let's just make
a list of what we want. I'll get cleaning supplies, some
food and some liquor." She turned to Kay. "Unless you
want to come with me?"

"I'd rather not do the food shopping," said Kay. "I'm
still drawn to the baked goods section."

"Don't worry about that," said Raina. "We all need
to watch our figures. I'll buy lots of healthy, thinning
things and an absolute minimum of junk food."

The girls sat down and made out a list. Their tastes
in food were agreeably similar and Jana and Kay, who
hardly drank at all, had no preference in liquor.

"Then I'll select the things, my dears," said Raina. "I know what's good and what isn't. Thunderbird is definitely out."

Raina put on an oversized pair of sunglasses and got her bag. As she opened the front door she nearly tripped over a large wicker basket filled with tins of gourmet foods—smoked oysters, pickled ears of corn, spiced eggplant, artichoke hearts, baby shrimps, smoked salmon, escargot, sardines, and several jars of black caviar, plus a note from their landlady. "Welcome. I thought these might come in handy in case you decide to entertain. Sylvia."

"Isn't she a dear," said Kay. "But we don't know anybody."

"We soon will," smiled Raina. "Tell Jana about our director."

"You met him?" queried Jana eagerly.

"No, but we saw him," groaned Kay. "You won't believe how gorgeous he is. You just won't believe it." She eyed the basket. "I wonder if it's still edible. After all, she never opens her shop."

"Caviar never goes bad," Raina tossed over her shoulder as she left.

While driving down Mechanic Street, Raina spotted a liquor store, quickly slammed on her brakes, double parked and rushed inside.

"Do you have chilled champagne?" she asked the clerk.

He eyed her suspiciously. "You don't look old enough to buy liquor. Do you have any proof of age?"

With a perfect affectation of amused unconcern, Raina produced her fake I.D.

After giving it a close scrutiny, the clerk handed it back and said grudgingly, "Yes, miss. What kind would you like?"

"Mumm's, if you have it. Four bottles. You do deliver, don't you?"

"Yes, I could arrange that. Are you far?"

"Just up on Nye Alley." Raina breezed through the liquor store selecting half gallons of vodka, scotch, rum, and bourbon. She couldn't abide the taste of gin. She also bought ten bottles of moderately priced wine —five chablis and five burgundy. She wrote a check and pre-tipped the delivery boy, instructing him to tell her roommates to put the champagne and the white wine in the refrigerator. Then she left the store.

A policeman was about to give her a ticket.

"Oh, officer, I'm here. I only stopped for a moment."

The cop looked up, his heartbeat quickened, and his pulse gained sudden strength in his throat and temples. His tongue felt thick and he heard himself straining for air.

"Uh, is this your car, Miss?"

"Raina Pendleton. Why, yes it is, and what is your name?"

"Uh, Travis McCafferty. You're, uh, not supposed to . . ."

"I just moved here with two lovely roommates," Raina interrupted blithely. "I have a wonderful idea, Officer McCafferty. Why don't you come by tonight, say around nine? We'll be warming our apartment." The officer returned the unwritten ticket to his pocket. Raina appraised him. He was handsome in a coarse kind of way, about thirty years old, and had an earnest expression on his face. His hair was an aggressive auburn and his broad nose was spattered lightly with freckles. His powerful body threatened to burst the seams of his clothing.

McCafferty suggested that he might check the security on the apartment, since they were three girls living alone.

"How very sweet of you, McCafferty. Till tonight then."

McCafferty watched Raina as she exceeded the speed limit down South Main.

The delivery boy arrived at the apartment carrying three cartons of liquor and wine. He accepted another tip from Jana and after he had gone Jana exclaimed,

"I don't believe this! This is enough liquor to last us all summer."

"I hope so," said Kay. "There must be a hundred dollars' worth here. We'd better put the champagne and wine in the fridge, and what say we set up a bar on that funny looking side board?"

"That's a great idea," agreed Jana.

They carried the bottles of liquor over to the side board, a curious piece constructed of burnt bamboo with brass fittings—a sort of bastard Brighton design.

Later they looked around the living room and surveyed the cleaning they had done.

"I think it looks really nice," said Jana. "Perhaps some plants or some flowers . . ."

"And some drapes," Kay interposed. "We'll select some nice bright material and I'll make some café curtains. God knows we'll need them with that canal boat going by practically every hour."

"Well, shall we tackle the bathroom?" Jana wondered aloud.

"Thank goodness nothing's really dirty, just dusty. I guess Sylvia hasn't rented the apartment in a while."

"I wonder how she lives. I mean, she obviously doesn't act anymore. And she *can't* make any money from that gourmet shop."

"Not if she never gets up." Kay looked serious. "You know, I bet she was one helluva good actress. Sorry—my mother says I have a mouth like a truck driver. And Raina's isn't exactly that of a nun."

"Four-letter words don't bother me," replied Jana. "I think the only really vulgar things in this world are poverty and war."

"You sound like a hippie." Kay assumed an "adult" tone of voice.

Jana shrugged and was thoughtful for a moment. "Well, I think they have some very fine ideals. Even though I don't approve of their drug taking and promiscuity."

"You don't?" Kay was surprised. "I intend to try everything this summer, and I mean *everything!*"

"You mean like grass?"

"Grass, too, but I was mainly thinking of sex." Kay struck a dramatic pose. "I intend to lose my virginity this summer."

"Kay!" Jana was shocked. "You *can't* mean that."

"I do and I shall. That is, if anyone asks me."

"That shouldn't be any problem. Goodness, I get asked all the time."

"You would. I went through high school without even so much as a single date, let alone a proposition."

Jana turned to face her friend. "I can't believe it. You're so pretty."

Kay glanced at the floor self-consciously. "I told you I was very fat until three years ago when I went on a diet. I don't think I ever told you how fat." She paused and bit her lip. "I was a hundred and seventy-five pounds fat."

"I can't believe it. How did you manage to lose it?"

"It wasn't easy," Kay replied bitterly. "I can tell you that. My whole family is blubber oriented. They used to laugh at me every time I brought cottage cheese or melba toast into the house."

"Well, you're very well built now," offered Jana. "But I don't know why you hide your body in such a voluminous dress. You should wear something that shows off the new you."

"I still feel fat. I guess that's why no one ever asked me out, even after I lost weight. You know how high school is. You're put in a category and by God you stay there. I guess everybody else continued to see me as a blimp." Kay suddenly looked panicked. "Don't tell Raina."

"Tell her what?"

"About not dating in high school and . . . that I'm a virgin."

"What possible difference could it make?"

"She's not, you know."

"I gathered that. Still I don't see . . ."

"I just don't want her to know. She was so popular in high school and everything. I mean, she never said so, but you can see that, can't you? The way she carries herself, the clothes she wears. Her whole manner."

"Kay, you mustn't envy Raina." Jana took Kay's hand. "Don't envy anyone. I meant it when I said you were pretty. You are. You've just got to start *feeling* that you are."

"I suppose I am, but I can't get used to my new self." She gave a little laugh. "Would you believe that I felt more secure under those layers of flesh?"

"I read somewhere that's one reason why people overeat. Anyway, we'll watch our diets this summer and we'll be working like anything at the Playhouse. Why, you won't have a chance to put back any weight. You'll probably lose some more."

A voice from the front of the apartment called out in a suburban matron's voice. "Yoohoo, welcome wagon!"

Kay clutched Jana's arm. "It's Raina. Promise you won't say anything."

Jana smiled. "Of course, I promise."

Raina was surrounded by brown bags overflowing with purchases. Slung over her shoulder, military fashion, were a mop and a broom. "Cheers, dears," she greeted. "God, I feel like Helen Housewife. Come, help me put all this junk away, then we'll have champagne and caviar to celebrate."

A short time later Kay, contemplating an English cracker loaded with caviar, announced, "I've got a confession to make. I've never had caviar. Or champagne."

"Neither have I," echoed Jana.

"Then it's time, my loves. Don't worry, Kay. Caviar is very low cal. And champagne is the best thing I've found for soaring the spirits." She raised high her jelly glass brimming with champagne. "Well, everybody, here's to us."

She looked around the room. "Hmmm. Everything looks perfectly divine. And yet it does need something."

"Drapes," said Kay.

"Plants," said Jana.

"And candles," added Raina. "By the way, I have fake I.D.s for both of you." The girls looked perplexed. "So we can get served in bars, of course. It's the best way to meet men."

"Raina," Kay asked suddenly, "are you on the pill?" Raina laughed. "Why, of course. Isn't everybody?"

"Why, ah, I'm not, and I was wondering . . . Do you think if I went to a doctor here in New Hope he'd prescribe them for me?"

"I don't see why not," answered Raina. "But if you get them, you must take them regularly. God, I'm so forgetful I had to tape signs all over the house to remind me."

"Your parents approved?" queried Jana.

"Goodness no. I wrote 'take your vitamins' on scraps of paper. It was like a personal call to arms. Everywhere. On the refrigerator, my bathroom mirror, even on the dashboard of my car. Take—your—vitamins!"

Raina's remark, combined with the effects of the champagne, caused the girls to break into a fit of laughter. When at last she caught her breath, Raina said, "I've got a great idea. Look, it's nearly six o'clock. Why don't we finish hanging up our clothes, shower, get dressed in something smashing and I'll take us all to dinner at Chez Odette. It's supposed to be the best restaurant in town."

"Raina, we can't let you do that," protested Jana.

"No, we can't," agreed Kay.

"Of course you can. My treat. To celebrate our first night in New Hope. Besides, look at all the work you two did on the apartment. I didn't lift a finger. What do you say?" Jana and Kay looked at one another and nodded their heads in delicious anticipation.

An hour later the three were ready to go. Raina, her hair loose and flowing, glowed like spun metal. She wore an emerald green gown. It was backless and the bare minimum of bodice was held by a thin strap wound around the neck. It was ankle length and a slit up either side revealed Raina's shapely legs. She wore a pair of evening sandals, the leather dyed to match.

Her only jewelry was a pair of large gold hoop earrings.

"You look smashing," squealed Kay. "You look like you're not wearing any underwear."

"I'm not," replied Raina. "What a charming outfit that is. Don't tell me you made it?"

"I make everything I wear. Do you really like it? You don't think it's too busy?"

Kay's dress was also long. It had great puffy sleeves and a scoop neck surrounded by an immense ruffle. The material was a finely woven cotton of cerulean blue printed with tiny white flowers.

"If you wouldn't mind one suggestion?" ventured Raina. Kay shook her head. "Why don't you remove the ruffle? It would simplify the dress and show off your bustline. Could you do that without harming the dress?"

"Of course, I'm a seamstress *extraordinaire*." Kay unzipped the dress and pulled it over her head. Then she sat down near the light and, using a seam ripper, undid the thread and released the ruffle. Kay was a careful seamstress and the material beneath had been finished off. She put the dress back on and looked at herself in the mirror. She agreed that it was an improvement.

Jana was the last to make her appearance. When she emerged from her bedroom wearing a dress of Chinese red silk she looked breathtaking. Jana had an inborn grace that turned even the most common act into a brief piece of theatre. She seemed to be unaware of her beauty, and this humility was perhaps her most alluring asset.

The skirt was mini length, daringly low cut with a halter top. "Do you like it?" she asked her friends.

"Fantastic!" cried Raina.

"It's beautiful, Jana. But I can't believe your mother let you get away with it."

Jana stuck out her chin. "I never told my mother I bought it. If she ever saw me in something like this she would throw me into a nunnery."

Suddenly the room was bathed in the tangerine of sunset. The girls rushed to the window overlooking the canal. The water looked like a bed strewn with glittering gold coins and the high grass seemed as though it had been crafted from bronze. A flock of thrushes swooped and soared over the water, finally coming to rest in the nearby trees, whose leaves were also gilded by the sunshine.

The trio drove slowly through New Hope's streets, which were bustling with tourists who had come from far and near drawn by the charm of the village and the shops that exhibited and sold paintings, handicrafts, antiques and jewelry. A short time later Raina turned off South Main into the parking lot of Chez Odette. The restaurant was a rambling white building that had been founded by Odette Myrtle, a charming actress of another era.

The maître d' led them into the main dining room. As the young women walked through the restaurant, every male looked up in admiration and every female looked askance with jealousy. They saw Raina—slender, silver-blonde, and exotically beautiful; saw voluptuous and vital Kay with hair redder than the evening sunset; and Jana, radiant beneath a cloud of silky black hair.

They were definitely a striking and formidable trio.

Chapter Three

When the young women emerged from Chez Odette, night had come to New Hope. A silver moon, full and scarved in clouds, moved lazily across the sky like a solitary ship on an endless voyage. A billowing fog was rolling in from the river and everything seemed to be wavery in the hazy light. Long plumes of mist swirled around the girls' legs as they crossed the parking lot to the red Thunderbird.

When they reached the apartment they had a surprise. The long-haired young men whom Raina and Kay had met that same afternoon were waiting for them, sitting on what appeared to be gilt ballroom chairs and holding great potted palms and delicate lacy ferns in their laps. The acknowledged leader, one Hamish Feather, stood up and saluted them from behind a palm frond.

"Good evening, lovely ladies. I see you have been joined by a dark-haired beauty of the night."

"What is all this?" laughed Raina.

"You said you could use some chairs and some plants. So here they are—chairs and plants."

"But where did you get them?" asked Kay suspiciously.

"Ask me no questions, I'll tell you no lies," grinned Hamish, a striking young man with shoulder length ash-blond hair and a well trimmed beard to match. His eyes were grey, but in the moonlight appeared to be as yellow as a cat's. "Our story is not for the neighbors' ears. Perhaps you'll ask us up. If you have some wine, we have some grass."

Raina glanced at Jana and Kay, whose expressions were dubious. "What harm will it do?" she whispered. "Even if it turns out to be troublesome, I'm expecting a policeman to stop by later."

"A policeman!" exclaimed Jana and Kay. "What did you do?"

Raina smiled sweetly. "I didn't get a parking ticket."

"Come on, let's have an impromptu housewarming party. It seems the least we can do for our generous guests." Raina parked the car beneath the willow tree next to The Open Pit. Then the three girls, followed by the five gift-bearing young men, ascended the staircase to the second floor.

After the plants were placed along the canal side windows and the young men were each seated in the gilt chairs, Raina asked, "All right, not a drop of wine until you tell us where you got those items."

Hamish stood up, bowed, and stage whispered, "We stole them from a funeral parlor over in Lambertville."

The girls sat in stunned silence. Jana was the first to speak. "You stole . . . these chairs . . . from a funeral parlor?"

"Hey, the little lady is not only beautiful, she has groovy hearing."

"How did you manage that?" asked Kay, more curious than shocked.

"Quite easily," bragged Hamish. "You see, there was a funeral going on and nobody was in the outer waiting room. That's where we got the plants, too."

Raina was the first to start laughing. Kay joined in, snorting and giggling and holding her sides. Jana, who could not help being caught up in her friends' mirth, covered her mouth with her hands and bent forward on the couch. Finally she offered a comment, still choking with laughter. "I . . . don't suppose . . . that the customers . . . will miss them!"

Raina broke away from the group and staggered into the kitchen still holding her sides. She opened the re-

frigerator and produced a gallon bottle of chilled wine.
She called into the living room. "Kay, Jana, come help
me." The girls quickly responded. "Kay, go put some
records on the stereo. Jana, how about opening some
of the cocktail stuff that Sylvia sent up? And I have a
couple of cheeses in there. These boys look like they're
hungry."

"I don't think it's for food," replied Jana. "Have we
got enough glasses?"

"I picked up some plastic cups at the supermarket.
Oh, isn't this fun, our first party!"

"It'll be some scene for your policeman friend if he
drops by," murmured Jana as she unwrapped the
cheese.

The flickering candles cast furtive shadows against
the white walls of the living room. The eight people sat
in a circle in the middle of the floor sipping wine and
listening to the music. Hamish Feather, the renegade
son of a Pennsylvania Dutch family, was using an
album jacket to clean his marijuana and roll joints.

Jana watched him with uneasy fascination. She whispered to Raina who was on her left. "What will I do?
I don't think I want to smoke grass."

"Either pass it by or don't inhale."

"This is good stuff," Hamish intoned. "My sister
grows it herself up in Lambertville." He sprinkled a
generous amount onto each waiting square of paper,
deftly rolled them and sealed them with his tongue.

"He's licking them," whispered Jana.

"Shhh," admonished Kay.

Jana excused herself and slipped unnoticed into the
bathroom. She gargled mouthwash, hoping to kill any
germs she might encounter from the proffered joint.
When she returned, the "cigarette" was being passed
around the room. She watched Raina as she deeply
drew on the tightly rolled tube. After sucking the smoke
into her lungs and holding it, Raina offered the joint
to Jana. For a moment Jana stared at it. Then, making
a decision, she gamely followed Raina's example. The
smoke burned her throat as she fought to hold it down.

Tears blurred her eyes and she coughed. Jana blushed with embarrassment but no one said anything. Each was intent upon his own thoughts and was drifting along with the Beatles. Eagerly Kay took the joint from Jana.

"Ouch. It's too short."

"Wait, I've got a roach clip," said Hamish, who was perceptive enough to realize that the girls, at least Kay and Jana, were inexperienced with grass. "Here, I'll show you." He sat beside her.

Kay was immediately aware of the warmth of his body and the tangy masculine smell that emanated from him. He was easily the best of the bunch. But unfortunately Hamish was interested in Raina.

Another joint and another record. Kay and Jana were watching one another.

"Do you feel anything?" asked Jana.

"With all that champagne and wine, who could tell?" responded Kay. "I thought colors were supposed to get better, but nothing looks better except Hamish, and he looks better and better."

Jana, too, had noticed how well-built Hamish was. She looked over the five. The other four were almost interchangeable in appearance. Her anxieties ate at her, despite the fact that none of the young men had made advances or sly innuendos to any of them. They seemed content to lie on the floor, listen to the music and watch the slow-motion shadows dance across the ceiling.

Above the music a loud and steady knocking came from downstairs. Raina was slow to react. Then she exclaimed, "God in Heaven! That's Travis McCafferty!"

"Who?" asked Hamish.

"A policeman." The men began to scramble for cover. "Wait, wait. Take it easy. This is a social call. He's not going to ruin our evening. After all, he didn't give me a ticket for double parking."

Nonetheless, Hamish gathered up the joints and stuck them in his pocket.

"Just a minute," Raina called down. She turned on a lamp and, as composed as ever, swept down the stairs. When she opened the door, Officer McCafferty was leaning against the door frame. He was wearing his civilian clothes—a tight fitting T-shirt and equally snug jeans.

"McCafferty! I was afraid you'd forgotten our party." He stepped inside. "I hope you're . . . off-duty."

"Don't worry," he grinned. "I could smell the grass down here. Hey, I brought some of my own." He produced several joints from the back pocket of his jeans and held out a bottle that had been concealed behind his back.

"We have liquor."

"Probably not Jamison's Irish Whiskey. And I like that the best."

When they entered the living room, the five men were sitting stiffly in the chairs. Someone had put on the original cast recording of *My Fair Lady*. McCafferty looked around.

"Hey, everybody relax. I'm with you." After pouring himself a drink he settled next to Raina on the sofa and offered her a joint. "Try one of mine. Pure Acapulco Gold." The hippies cast uneasy glances at one another. "Come on," said McCafferty. "There's no paddy wagon downstairs. I swear it." He lit up and passed it to Raina, who, after smoking, passed it to Jana.

"Why not?" Jana took two long drags and began noticing things about the others she hadn't seen before. Their skin seemed to glow as if it were lit by a black light. Everything in the room blurred into a bright whirling kaleidoscope of color. The waving arcs and shards of color expanded and retreated with the vibrations of the music.

"Come on, Jana." The voice pulled her from her reverie.

She opened her eyes. Hamish was leaning over her, the others were dancing. He gripped her wrist. "Come on," he breathed, "let's join them."

Jana had never before danced with such total abandon. Her body moved easily, giving her a certain looseness, a new freedom. Kay danced with the other four, who took turns swinging her about.

Raina and McCafferty were dancing apart from the others. They were not keeping time with the music, but had created their own rhythm. And that rhythm, slow and undulating, fused their bodies together in a tight embrace, an almost total blend of two entities. A short time later they danced toward the hall, then disappeared into Raina's bedroom.

Jana lay staring at the ceiling. Shafts of sunlight pouring into the room coupled with the vibrant noises of Mechanic Street had awakened her. Her clock read ten minutes past noon. She sat up, afraid for a moment she had missed the meeting at the Playhouse. But wait, it was only Saturday. They were not due until Monday. She climbed out of bed, stopped short as she remembered the previous night, and sat back down with a groan.

Everything came rushing back to her. The wine, the hippies, the grass and the music. She shuddered. For a moment she could not remember the end of the evening. Then, as the pieces of her memory fell into place, she sighed with great relief.

Sometime after McCafferty and Raina had gone off together, Jana and Kay slipped into the kitchen and decided to gently ask the five young men to leave. Even though she was high, Kay had decided that she wasn't ready to offer up her virginity just yet, at least not to Hamish or any of his four pleasant but nondescript followers.

To their relief, the young men left willingly and without protest. After many friendly kisses and hugs had been bestowed on both girls, they promised that they would return.

Kay and Jana cleared up the debris before going to bed. Neither was willing to acknowledge that Raina was not alone in her bedroom—Jana out of embarrassment, and Kay out of envy.

Jana closed her shutters against the light and noise of the street. After putting on her robe, she went into the kitchen to make coffee. Kay was already there.

"How do you feel, Jana?"

"Everything's just a little hazy, but strangely enough, not bad."

"That's probably because we ate everything in sight as we were cleaning up. My poor waistline. I had heard, but I had no idea how hungry grass can make you."

"Hmmm. You're making fresh coffee."

"Yes. I hate that instant drek."

Jana inclined her head in the direction of Raina's bedroom. "Did the policeman stay the night?"

"I think so. I thought I heard them stirring about. Anyway, I've made a large pot of coffee."

She filled two cups and they went into the living room and sat down at the small rattan table in front of the windows overlooking the canal.

"You know," said Kay thoughtfully, "I think I'm going to love New Hope."

"I think I already do," replied Jana.

Raina watched the sleeping form of Officer McCafferty beside her. In the warm, sunshine glow of the room he looked unreal, as if some Italian master had sculpted him from apricot marble. He slept very soundly, his broad chest slowly rising and falling. His eyes were closed tightly against the sun and tiny squint lines ran from either corner almost to his hair line. Raina realized now that her previous sexual experiences had been with enthusiastic but unseasoned young men. McCafferty had made her reach heights she had never reached before, indeed never known existed. He made love to her again early that morning. He was like an adventurer who had discovered a new continent. He explored the mountains and the valleys of her body as well as the hidden crevices. Raina responded fully and without inhibition, as she did whenever someone offered seemingly genuine affection.

Raina ran her fingertips through McCafferty's hair. He stirred slightly as she bent down to kiss his eyelids. They opened slowly beneath her touch. "I'm sorry to wake you, McCafferty, but do you have to work this afternoon?"

"No," he replied huskily. "It's Saturday. I've got night duty."

She snuggled close to him. "Right now you've got morning duty."

"Again?" he grinned. "You're insatiable." Raina slid her hand down his flat stomach to where his soft reddish hair grew in profusion.

"You don't seem exactly averse to the idea," she whispered.

Chapter Four

The apprentices sat in the darkened auditorium of the Playhouse. The stage was cluttered with bits and pieces of scenery, props and furniture from past productions. There was a mock Louis XVI chair, a backdrop depicting a vaulted cathedral ceiling, a hat rack with several feather boas hanging from it and a lucite steamer trunk.

Clay Jordan appeared. The director was wearing a faded blue workshirt, undoubtedly from Saks Fifth Avenue, a pair of snug white ducks, and a jaunty red scarf tied around his neck. He turned on the work light and bowed to his captive audience. Then he spoke in a rich, melodious voice.

"Welcome to the Playhouse. The Playhouse has endured for twenty-seven years, making it older than any of you here." He smiled. "Myself excluded. Since its opening, the Playhouse has been among the most famous regional theatres in the United States. You now share a theatrical heritage. Our greatest actors have trod these boards. Our foremost playwrights have had their plays produced upon this stage. And here our best designers have cut their teeth and gone on to glory . . . not to mention Tony Awards." Jordan paused and stepped closer to the edge of the stage. "This is a place of history, yes, but it is also a place of magic. Can you feel it? The past merging with the present? Of course you can, because each of us belongs to a very special group, a very unique fraternity whose product

transcends the barriers of language, religion and politics.
We belong to the theatre."

The assemblage broke into spontaneous applause.
Jordan gracefully acknowledged it and continued.
"Each of you has an artistic obligation to give yourself
completely, heart and soul, to this great Playhouse.
With your efforts we shall continue the magic that was
started when this theatre opened. The public has come
to expect no less than the finest from us, and we shall
give it to them. I know that this summer will be one
that you will remember the rest of your lives." Jordan
scanned his audience. "Do any of you have any questions?" Kay held up her hand and he nodded in her
direction.

"I was wondering, Mr. Jordan, if this season has been
selected and if so, what it is."

"We will be opening with *The Fantastiks,* which as
you all know, is presently running in New York's Greenwich Village. Then we'll do Neil Simon's *The Star
Spangled Girl.* From there, we're going to do a revival
of Cole Porter's *Anything Goes.* It has a delightful
book and a fantastic score. After that we're going to
do N. Richard Nash's *The Rainmaker*—one of my
favorite plays. The second to the last production will
be *Stop the World, I Want to Get Off.* Hoping that our
audience is going to be a bit tired of the lighter weight
stuff by the end of the summer, we're going to end the
season with Tennessee Williams' *Suddenly Last Summer.*"

There were murmurs among the audience. He held
up his hands for quiet. "I have put together this season
with as much thought and care as I could possibly
muster. One of my considerations was that each play
can be done with one basic set. As you may not know,
the Playhouse, for all its fame and loving planning, has
godawful offstage space." There was a burst of laughter. "On that note I should like to end our little meeting, and if you will gather here beside me, I will give
you a personally guided tour of the Playhouse and
grounds." There was more applause.

"He's a bit much, don't you think?" whispered Kay.

"Shhh," replied Jana. "I thought he was inspiring."

"He got to me," admitted Raina.

Kay flashed her a knowing smile. "He got to all of us. I was referring to the speech."

The three, like most of the apprentices, were profoundly disappointed at the cramped quarters and lack of offstage space. The theatre seemed not glamorous at all. And the basement where the dressing rooms and work rooms were located was even worse. The areas were badly lit and smelled of must and old greasepaint. However, their disappointment faded when the three young women entered the ladies' dressing room and saw the signatures of the female stars who had once appeared at the Playhouse. They were written across the walls in a variety of scripts. It was like a very oddly patterned wallpaper.

"God!" said Kay, scanning the names. "Practically everybody who's anybody in the theatre has worked here."

"It gives you a funny feeling," said Jana. "Almost awe-inspiring. Mr. Jordan was right about it being a place of history and a place of magic."

"Someday we'll be famous too," remarked Raina. "And someday three young novices just like ourselves will be standing here staring at our signatures."

"So why wait?" suggested Kay. "Let's sign in now." She picked up an old eyebrow pencil that lay on top of a makeup table and wrote her name in an available space. Then she passed it to Raina who did the same. Finally to Jana.

"I don't feel right somehow," said Jana. "I don't feel I've earned the right as yet."

"Go on," urged Kay. "It'll bring good luck. I know it will."

Jana hesitated, then boldly signed her name, even larger than the others. "In case any of the future apprentices are nearsighted."

Just then a plain-faced girl in grubby attire stuck

her head into the dressing room. "Hey, you all, Mr. Jordan wants to see us outside."

Jordan and the group gathered at the back of the theatre on a large grassless patch of land overlooking the Delaware River. Here he gave them their assignments and their locker numbers, and told them what to expect. "You already know the pay is low. Well, the hours are going to be long and grueling. You're going to work harder than you ever have in your life. By day you'll be constructing and painting scenery, hanging lights, making costumes, props, doing publicity, the whole ball of wax. By night you'll be rehearsing or performing. And, as I've stated so bluntly in my letter to each of you, please don't get your hopes up for getting a starring role. As you know, most of our leads are actors imported from New York City. They're not necessarily names, but they are professionals. However, those of you who are interested in the acting aspect of the theatre will get a chance to show me your stuff. I want you to know that I'm not averse to putting any of you in a starring role, but I have to make damn certain you can handle it. We've got a reputation here at the Playhouse to live up to. And I intend to see that my productions are the very best that have ever been seen here. Now, if you'll break up into your specific groups, your group leaders will further explain your duties."

The three girls had each been given different assignments. Kay, of course, was to assist on costumes and would be working under the auspices of the designer, Meg Franklin. Jana was given over to Saul Silver, the set designer. And Raina would be working directly with Clay Jordan as a member of the publicity staff.

Jana and the others on set design met on the stage. Saul Silver was already there. He had set up a strong light over a large table on which were stacks of sketches and a model of the Playhouse stage. Silver, a studious-looking man in his mid-thirties, began his talk without preamble or greetings. "This, as you can see, is a model of the stage. In comparison to the more modern stages being built and in use, it's not a very workable area. But it has somehow worked for all these past twenty-some years. Now if you would like to gather around I will show you the preliminary sketches I have made for the summer productions."

Despite Silver's ascerbic personality, he was a fine designer and craftsman. His sketches showed imagination, flair and a certain uniqueness. And, unlike many set designers, he was also an accomplished sketch artist. When they reached the sketches for *Suddenly Last Summer,* Jana caught her breath. Silver's depiction of the fantastic, primeval garden where the action of the play took place was as unrealistic as the decor of a dramatic ballet and captured the terror of Williams' play. Jana could fairly visualize herself standing in the middle of the set acting her heart out.

"They're wonderful," she blurted. "They capture the very essence of the play."

Silver was about to respond in his usual caustic manner but, noting Jana's sincere enthusiasm, not to mention her beauty, changed his words before they left his mouth. He rearranged his face into a smile and replied, "Thank you, Miss . . ."

"Jana Donatello," the young woman supplied.

Silver went through each play with his apprentices, explaining his concepts and freely answering questions. By the end of the session he was totally disarmed by their interest. It seemed to him that this season at the Playhouse was going to be more interesting and rewarding than his other assignments had been. He credited Jana's enthusiasm for this minor phenomenon.

The four costume apprentices, including Kay, who would act as assistant costume designer, were cramped into the small, airless sewing room. Meg Franklin eyed them with some trepidation. Meg had a round, well-scrubbed face completely free of make-up. Her black hair, prematurely flecked with grey, was worn in a

French gamin fashion. She wore a man's shirt, bib overalls, and scuffed moccasins.

Meg Franklin was a militant lesbian. She was also
the daughter of a prominent local resident who sup-
ported the Playhouse with massive amounts of money.
Her appointment as costume designer was a political
maneuver. Meg was ill-equipped to handle it, for her
talent was modest and she had difficulty getting along
with people, particularly men. She did have sketches,
but they were sloppily drawn and poorly realized. Kay
was dismayed. She felt, and rightly so, that she was
this woman's superior, at least in terms of talent.

Meg cleared her throat and began her talk in a brisk,
no-nonsense manner. "We'll start on the costumes for
The Fantastiks as soon as it's cast, which will be next
week. There are things that we can do to occupy our
time until then. Obviously, this costume room is a
goddamn mess. We ought to clean it out, paint it, and in
general put things in goddam apple-pie, order. Wear
your oldest clothes; it's going to be a dirty job. Are
there any questions?"

Before anyone could ask anything, a young man appeared in the doorway. Everyone looked up. His name
was Fred Spangler. He was twenty-two years old, and
by current standards handsome. His hair was light
brown, shoulder length and smooth as paint. He sported
a mustache that was intricately curled and a beard
cropped close to his flesh. His eyes were large, brown
and as warm as a puppy's. His smile was ingenuous.
He was dressed in a pair of jeans so worn that they
looked as if they might disintegrate at any moment. A
handmade denim vest decorated with, among other
things, peace symbols and astrological signs partially
covered his shirtless torso. His chest and arms were
massive, and glistening with perspiration. He was out
of breath. "Pardon me," he puffed. "I'm late for the
meeting. Could any of you tell me where I can find
Saul Silver, the set designer?"

Meg scowled at the young man. "Pretty late I'd say.
It's already eleven-fifteen."

"I didn't ask for the time, lady. I asked for directions. Now, can you tell me where he is or not?"

"They're up on the stage," Kay volunteered. Meg gave her such a withering glance that she wished she hadn't.

"Thank you," replied Fred, his eyes pausing long enough to appreciate Kay's appearance. He winked and said, "I'll see you later." He made it sound like a promise.

The box office was a large sunny room located at the front of the Playhouse that did double-duty as Jordan's office. He showed Raina and his other assistant, a dynamic young man named Jeff Kramen in, admonished the two young people to call him by his first name, then poured each of them a cup of coffee from an electric percolator. After they were seated, Jordan leaned against the edge of his desk and sipped his coffee before beginning. "Without good publicity we might as well not put on a show. As far as I'm concerned, your work is just about the most important thing that will go on here at the theatre. I chose the two of you to assist me because you're both smart, energetic, attractive young people and I think you can handle the job."

"What exactly will our duties be, Mr. Jordan—I mean Clay?" asked Raina, who decided that Clay Jordan was even better looking close up than he was at a distance.

Looking directly at her, Jordan replied. "We're going to put our heads together and see what exciting and off-beat ideas we can come up with to help publicize *The Fantastiks*. I take it you're familiar with the play." They both nodded. "Well it should be very popular. This will be the first production done in this area outside of New York City." Jordan stood up and flexed his legs. "What say we all put on our thinking caps, take a break for lunch, and meet back here at one-thirty." The two young people started to leave. "Oh, Raina, would you wear something a little more appropriate around the theatre?"

"Appropriate in what way?"

"Something a little less St. Tropez and a little more hayseed summer theatre."

Raina took the rebuff in good humor. She cast him a flirtatious glance and replied, "I'll show up this afternoon looking like Daisy Mae."

Chapter Five

The restaurant was situated on the crest of a hill. It was a circular building of white painted wood. Surrounding it was a parking lot and a line of picnic tables crowded with young actors, technicians and apprentices, not only from the Playhouse but from the Music Circus and the Delaware Players. Dressed in pseudo-hippie mode, they were an animated lot noisily conversing between bites about the great love of their life—the theatre.

As the girls waited in line for their lunch they were appreciatively looked over by those males present who were straight. The females either feigned disinterest or buzzed with speculation about the attractive trio. Jana, Raina and Kay carried their trays to a whitewashed picnic table and began their lunch—steaming bowls of fish chowder and tall glasses of iced coffee. Had they not been so deeply immersed in conversation they would have been approached by the more daring young men, but their camaraderie discouraged even the most ardent admirer.

"Where Clay is concerned," Raina was saying, "we should make a vow."

"What's that?" asked the others.

"Well. I think it's fairly obvious that Clay is interested in all of us. However, we don't want men storming through our little encampment like Grant through Richmond. I think we ought to strike an agreement that when one of us sleeps with someone then that someone should be excluded from the others' beds."

"Then you mean it's hands off for whoever gets a man first," translated Kay.

"Exactly."

"It certainly would keep things uncomplicated," said Jana. "But of course I don't think that's going to be any problem since I'm not planning on sleeping with anyone."

Kay and Raina looked at Jana incredulously. "But what's the point of being on your own?" argued Kay.

"It's all part of growing up," added Raina.

Jana shrugged her shoulders. "I wouldn't feel right about it. I suppose it's my Catholic upbringing." Seeing her friends' disappointment, Jana decided to take a lighter approach. "Hey, I'm not planning to join a convent or anything like that. It's just that I don't consider my virginity a burden."

Raina grinned. "Oh, it'll happen when it's time to happen."

Then Kay mentioned as casually as possible, "By the way, girls, did you see *him?*" They were puzzled. "That mountain of muscle with the face full of hair."

"Oh, you must mean the lighting designer," said Jana. "His name's Fred something or other." She pursed her lips. "I suppose he is attractive in a primitive sort of way."

"Who'd I miss?" exclaimed Raina. "Tell, tell!"

"Just the sexiest hunk of manhood in town. I did a little snooping around. His name's Fred Spangler." Kay toyed with her straw. "I wonder how I can get transferred from costumes to lighting."

"Oh, don't you care for Meg Franklin?" grinned Raina.

"Not only is she a dyke," said Kay, "but she's untalented to boot. My God, she can't even draw, let alone design. And if that wasn't bad enough, I have a feeling she's got her eye on me."

"Oh, noooooo!" squealed the others.

"Miss Well of Loneliness can just stay lonely," declared Kay. "This girl ain't going that route."

"Hey," said Raina. "We've got to get going. I'm

going to drop you two at the theatre first, then I'm going back to the apartment to change into something Tom Sawyerish."

Sunbeams filtering through the shutters of Raina's room appeared to be solid shafts of yellow light. Raina unconsciously walked around them as she trailed from closet to chest putting together an appropriate and provocative outfit. Finally she made her selection and stood admiring herself in her mirror. The corners of her mouth tilted, her eyes shone. Raina was now wearing very short denim shorts, a halter top constructed of two red bandannas, and a pair of red canvas sneakers.

"Hannah Hillbilly. Who said blondes shouldn't wear red?" Raina grinned at her reflection, then decided that the outfit needed something else. She added a pair of large gold hooped earrings, knowing that they appealed to most men. She hoped Clay was one of them.

•   •   •

A summer rain, warm and gentle, fell briefly over New Hope before wending its way across the Delaware. It did not dampen the earth any more than it did opening night spirits. Trees sparkled with fine drops and strings of lights were blurred in the soft mist the rain had left behind. Brightly colored umbrellas blossomed like flowers over the theatregoers as they hurried across the parking lot. The jewelry worn by the ladies rivaled the glittering drops that still clung to the foliage. The sports coats and summer suits worn by their male companions outshone the technicolor bulbs. Light chatter, subdued and witty, soon filled the auditorium and penetrated the heavy act curtain.

The stage was a flurry of activity as last minute wrongs were being righted. A loose hem was stitched into place, a mysterious handprint covered by quick drying paint, a torn sheet of music taped together. Clay Jordan delivered an inspiring speech to those assembled. Muted whispers of "break a leg" were whispered to the cast. The house lights flickered and then were brought down as the overture began.

The opening night of the Playhouse had arrived, and Kay, huddled in the back row with the other apprentices, was apprehensive. She felt, as many did, that Meg Franklin was inept and was incapable of meeting the demands of the show. Jordan, too, was dissatisfied with Meg's designs for *The Fantastiks*. Since the director and the costume designer did not see eye to eye, Jordan had given Kay leeway to improve the costumes as best she could; this had caused further friction between him and Meg. In a last-minute effort to give the costumes a sense of fantasy, as well as to disguise their poor design, Kay had added ribbons to everything. Gatherings of sleek pink satin bows adorned the dress of the ingenue and untidy clumps of ragtag ribbons accentuated the comic seediness of the Old Actor and Mortimer. The effort was successful. The characters took on an added dimension, resembling performers in a carnival or a traveling masque. It was to Jordan's way of thinking very much in keeping with the spirit of the play.

Jana, tingling with nerves as she watched the actors speak their opening lines, had spent many sleepless nights working at the theatre alongside Saul Silver and the other apprentices. With paint and brushes they created magic to the accompaniment of an all-night rock station from Philadelphia. Single-handedly Jana had executed a leaf drop made from a piece of green painted canvas, which she had cut at the edges to simulate foliage. Over this she had pasted three-dimensional leaves made of fabric, tissue paper, and green foil. She plaited strips of material to simulate vines, and after every piece was securely in place, expertly shaded the entire thing. Although Jana complained that she would never be able to remove the paint from beneath her fingernails, it was a spectacular piece of work and she was justly proud of it.

Publicity had exceeded Jordan's wildest hopes, Raina

reflected as she avidly watched the play in progress. She and Jeff Kramen had been ingenious in their tireless efforts to bring attention to the Playhouse. Using Raina's car they had distributed posters as far north as Farmington and as far south as Philadelphia. Raina had cajoled the local radio station into presenting a series of interviews with the actors involved in the production. She had further managed to get free advertising space from the newspapers and a banner hung over South Main Street. Her feat of feats had been to get the approval of the city fathers to let the company stage the Rape Ballet in the Playhouse parking lot a week before opening night. Tourists and townspeople drawn by the somewhat shocking title of the number came in droves. The ballet, expertly choreographed, turned out to be not about a sexual rape at all but about a comic abduction. The onlookers were both relieved and delighted by the antics of the actors. And everybody wanted to see the play itself. Opening night tickets were sold out three hours after the box office opened.

Now as the first performance came to a close, everyone from the stars to the lowliest "go-fer" knew they had a hit on their hands. Near the end of the eighth curtain call, Clay Jordan, sartorially splendid in a white linen suit, came onstage. The audience grew quiet and, smiling radiantly, the director delivered an impromptu speech. "All of us here at the Playhouse are heartened by your response to our first production of the season. But this is only our first effort. There are five more to come." He quickly rattled off the names of the forthcoming plays, then smiled sincerely, humbly, at the audience. "We vow to you, our audience, that we will make every effort to assure the continued quality of the upcoming season. We hope that you will be with us again and again to further judge our endeavors." Jordan stepped back and allowed the performers one last thunderous curtain call.

Chapter Six

The cast party was to be held at Clay Jordan's rented house on Ferry Street. The house, a late Victorian structure of brown stone and oak, had been decorated with summer flowers and outfitted with four bars and a small rock band. Everyone connected with the Playhouse had been invited, as was each Playhouse patron who had given time as well as money to the continuance of the famous theatre.

Jana, Raina and Kay returned to their apartment and were in the process of getting ready for the prestigious event. In two short hours all the tensions of the preceding weeks had disappeared and the trio was eagerly looking forward to an evening of complete enjoyment and relaxation.

Jana, wrapped in a cloud of steam, emerged from the bathroom. "I never thought I'd get my nails clean," she cried in triumph and held her hands up for the others to see.

"I know how you feel," said Kay. "I thought this Bertha the Sewing Machine Girl was going to be permanently crippled."

Raina was sitting at the rattan table painting her nails. "I woke up in the middle of the night and found that my right hand was flexing and unflexing as if I were stapling an imaginary poster on a tree trunk. I never had any idea it took so much work to put on a show."

"The result was worth it," said Jana. "The production was—well—fantastic!"

"I hope Fred's at the party," groaned Kay. "Since we've met I've barely had a chance to talk to him. I'm always in the basement bent over a sewing machine and he's always up on a ladder adjusting the lights. I'm not even sure he's seen anything but the top of my head. I don't think he knows I've got a face."

"Oh. he's seen you all right," said Jana. "I've been watching him. Every time you come on stage, he lights up like a kleig light. Now if you can only shake off the attentions of Meg Franklin."

"Oh, she isn't too friendly with me these days. Not since I usurped her position, as she sees it."

"If Clay were smart," said Raina, "he'd fire that diesel and put you in charge."

"I wish he would. She's too neurotic to handle her job. I actually think she gets a thrill when things go wrong." Kay shrugged. "Well, I can be thankful for one thing—I haven't gained an ounce. As a matter of fact, I think I've lost three or four pounds."

"I think you have too," responded Raina. "Why don't you wear that peacock-blue dress of yours tonight. the one with the plunging neckline and the slit up the side."

"Don't you think it's too plain?"

"Not if you let me loan you something smashing to go with it."

"What did you have in mind?" asked Kay.

"My feather boa. It's emerald green. It would look great with your hair and that dress."

"I thought you were going to wear it."

"Oh, didn't I tell you? When I went to Philly last week I got a new outfit just for the party. It's white crepe and fits like a dream."

"It'll show off your tan," said Jana.

"That's one good thing about driving around putting up posters. I got some good color. Now if I can only get me some good director."

"Nothing's happened between you and Clay?" asked Jana.

"Nope, he's been all business. Still, I catch him, when

he thinks I'm not looking, giving me little glances. He's interested all right, and tonight I'm going to find out just how interested."

The muted rock music served as a background to the theatre conversations, some of which were more brittle than the ice clinking in the high-held glasses. A quartet of waiters—young men hired from a local college— moved swiftly through the crowd dispensing drinks and hors d'oeuvres.

Clay Jordan checked his watch for the third time in ten minutes. His famous smile was frozen. He was worried that Raina might not show up. Jordan was not a man to be sustained by flirtations. Sooner or later there had to be a culmination of those subtly expressed feelings and he was hoping that tonight was going to be the night.

The girls were sorely missed and everyone was looking for them. Fred Spangler stood leaning against the bar that had been set up in the outside garden. Patiently he watched the doorway for some sign of Kay. He hadn't wanted to come to the party. Parties weren't his thing, but Kay had insisted with a flickering promise of romance in her eyes. As Jana and Raina suspected, Fred had been attracted to Kay since the first morning he'd seen her. He sensed her vulnerability and appreciated her hard work, dedication and talent, as well as her sensual good looks.

At the opposite end of the bar Meg Franklin downed another bourbon and contemplated her situation. She knew that Jordan was not happy with her work. But Meg was one of those people who questioned her superior's right to criticize her. Her eyes scanned the undulating throng of elegantly dressed guests while her mouth grew more and more set, her lips thinning to an invisible crack. Meg was itching for a scene, although she was hardly aware of this. Had she been accused of it, she would have denied it; but she thrived on confrontations, particularly with men.

Saul Silver sipped his martini and half listened to an

apprentice ramble on about the virtues of expressionism when applied to the art of scenic design. Saul was anxiously awaiting Jana's arrival and had been looking forward to spending some time with her outside the atmosphere of the theatre. He knew that Jana admired him, but wondered just how far that admiration went.

The girls arrived at five minutes past eleven. Kay entered first wearing her peacock-blue dress and Raina's emerald green boa. Her hair framed her glowing porcelain face with thick auburn curls. She was followed by Jana, who was wearing a pink silk "slip" dress which Kay had miraculously found time to make for her. The dress was set off by a collar of jet beads she had found in a local shop. Raina entered last. Her skin was tanned a tawny golden brown and that color was further heightened by her white crepe dress. The only jewelry she wore was a pair of emerald drop earrings, antiques that had been left to her by her grandmother.

Jordan hurried to greet his stunning guests and led them to the garden bar for a drink. The trees were bright with colored lanterns and next to the bar an ornate fountain gurgled where a dozen goldfish furtively played about.

Meg turned away when she saw the trio. Such displays of femininity—their hair, their makeup, their pretty clothes—repelled and excited her at the same time. She thickly ordered another drink from the bartender and grunted her begrudging thanks as it was served. The girls easily outclassed the two New York actresses who had been imported to play the leads in *The Fantastiks* and *The Star-Spangled Girl*. Anyone observing the scene would surely have supposed that Jana, Raina and Kay were full-fledged actresses and not merely summer apprentices.

As Kay was sipping her white wine she saw Fred standing in the shadows of the garden and went to him. "Fred! I was afraid you wouldn't come."

He grinned boyishly. "I was beginning to think you'd stood me up."

"Never. I just wanted to shower and change for the party."

"You look so fantastic I'd like to light you."

She smiled. "Use plenty of surprise pink."

He smiled in return. "Always." He took her hand and gently pulled her behind a flowering bush, then kissed her. first on the tip of the nose, and then on the lips. Kay kissed him in return, softly at first and then more passionately. Fred smelled of clean perspiration, and to Kay at the moment it was the most sensuous scent in the world.

"You got dressed up for the party," she said at last.

"I put on a shirt."

"I almost wish you hadn't," Kay breathed against his cheek. "I like seeing your bare arms. That was the first thing that attracted me to you."

"Not my face?"

"That was the second thing."

"And is there a third thing?"

Kay giggled, "Good things come in threes."

Clay Jordan gazed at Raina with open admiration, an admiration he had until now been keeping to himself. She stood silhouetted against the dark blue night sky and her face, a little flushed, positively glowed. The emeralds dangling from her ears sparkled a green fire that was rivaled by the light in her eyes.

"Do you suppose," she asked suddenly, "we'll make love tonight?"

Beads of perspiration broke out on the director's upper lip. "I've been anticipating it," he replied softly, not wanting his answer to be overheard. "Another drink?" He took her empty goblet and thrust it at the bartender who refilled it with champagne. As he passed it back to her his fingers just brushed hers and he felt himself go hot, even though the night was surprisingly cool.

"I'm pleased," Raina breathed over the edge of her glass, "I don't like to be turned down."

*   *   *

Saul saw Jana enter with her roommates. He immediately dumped the remainder of his martini into a
potted plant, brushed aside his boring companion and
made his way to the garden.

He stood in the center of the French doors for a
moment admiring Jana. She had been surrounded by a
cluster of eager young men, actors and apprentices, all
anxious for her attention. A quick assessment and Saul
dismissed them. They were younger than he was, perhaps sounder of body and more poetic of face, but in
the short time he had known Jana he had come to
realize that younger men bored her. She was a wandering girl-child in search of a father figure, and he
was more than willing to play the part.

Saul planned to get what he wanted—Jana Donatello. She seemed to be completely made of soft textures and deep rich colors. There were no hard surfaces
—only silk melting into flesh, flesh melting into silk.

Jana saw him, took leave of her theatre friends and
rushed to Saul, clasping his hand in both of hers. "I
was afraid you'd already gone. We were late getting
here."

"It was worth the wait. You look lovely, Jana."

Jana, unused to such direct compliments, blushed
and turned away.

"You don't have a drink," observed Saul. "Shall I
get you one?"

"I did, but I left it on the bar—a glass of white
wine."

"I'll get it for you," he replied eagerly.

The local rock band was stationed between the garden and the library. The musicians' blank faces and
glazed eyes gave testimony to their affection for marijuana. Despite their insistent and twangy beat they were
as unanimated as mannequins. Taking his cue from
Jordan, the leader switched from bouncy rock to a
moderate version of "Since I Fell For You."

Taking Raina's glass and setting it aside, Jordan
eased her toward the makeshift dance floor made from
sheets of smooth plywood borrowed from the Play-

house. Raina was pleased but not surprised at their "fit," and knew that their physical empathy would extend to the bedroom.

Saul looked at Jana. "I'm not much of a dancer," she said quickly.

"Let me be the judge of that."

Kay gently pulled Fred away from the garden and they joined the other couples on the floor.

Meg's red-rimmed eyes matched her mood. She stared angrily at the happy twosomes. "Give me another drink," she ordered.

The bartender frowned and hesitated. Jordan had given him certain instructions. "I'm sorry. I'm not supposed to serve inebriated guests," he said uncomfortably.

"Inebriated," Meg mimicked in a high-pitched voice. "Listen, you creep, I want another drink . . . now!"

Even though he was intimidated, the bartender nonetheless cut the bourbon with water. After serving it he retreated to the opposite end of the bar with a sulky expression on his soft, pretty face.

When Kay and Fred danced by the bar, Meg grabbed Kay's arm and stopped them. "Aren't you going to say hello?" she asked harshly, ignoring Fred. "What a groovy dress." An edge of sarcasm crept into her voice. "Did you make it yourself?"

"Yes, I did," replied Kay evenly. "And I see that you've put on a fresh pair of overalls for the party." Meg regarded Kay with the blank outrage that some people feel when another person rejects their sexual advances. The band stopped playing and took their break. The people who had been dancing started toward the bar. Meg was caught in a lull between music and conversation. "You're not going to take my job, you conniving bitch!" her voice rang out gratingly.

Kay swung around. "Why don't you join the roller derby and leave costuming to those who have the talent?" She smiled sweetly at the bartender. "Another glass of wine, please."

There was a smattering of laughter. Meg unsteadily

got to her feet. The muscles in her face were twitching with offense. She glared at Kay, blinking and blinking again. She pulled back her arm intending to strike. The empty glass was still in her hand. Jordan caught Meg's wrist in a bruising grip, the glass fell and shattered on the flagstones. "Come on, Meg, you're leaving the party . . . and the Playhouse. I've had it with you."

Meg began to scream and kick. Fred calmly took her other arm and the two of them whisked her through the house and out the front door, her feet never touching the floor. Meg was still shrieking. Jordan shook her roughly, sobering her somewhat.

"You'd better go quietly, Meg. I'm running a summer theatre, not a psychiatric ward."

"Fuck you, Jordan," she hissed.

The director grimaced and replied blithely, "My dear, what a revolting thought."

When Jordan returned and the band began playing, "It's My Party and I'll Cry If I Want To," the mood of those who had witnessed the ugly scene was gradually lightened. Kay whispered to Jana. "I'm going to take Fred back to the apartment tonight. I'm getting myself deflowered."

Jana smiled and wondered if she would ever be so happy with the prospect of losing her virginity. "Are you sure?"

"Sure, I'm sure. Just look at him. He's so solid. No one in my family ever looked like *that*. He's magnificent."

"Have fun," replied Jana and meant it.

Kay saw Jordan motioning for her to come to him and she quickly responded. He was smiling but his words were very serious. "Kay, I want you to take over Meg's job, starting immediately. Do you think you can handle it?"

Kay thrust out her chin. "You bet I can, Mr. Jordan."

He clasped her hands in his and gave her his most sincere look. "Please call me Clay."

Kay could barely restrain herself. She immediately

gathered Raina and Jana around her and told them the news—that she had been given the job of costume designer of the Playhouse. The girls began squealing and jumping up and down as they always did when they were excited.

Clay left to greet some of his late arriving guests. Kay turned to Fred. "Come on, Fred. Let's go back to the apartment and celebrate."

He grinned. "Just the two of us?"

"I don't think Raina's going to come home tonight and I asked Jana to stay at the party as long as she could stand it."

Together she and Fred hurried from the party. The night was warm but Kay was shivering as Fred placed his arm around her shoulder.

"Are you cold?"

"No, just nervous. I'm not as experienced as I seem."

"Just how experienced is that?"

Kay stopped and turned to look into Fred's eyes. "Fred, I haven't had *any* experience and I'm as nervous as hell. What are you grinning about?"

He ran his hand through her hair. "Don't be nervous. We're going to be just fine."

Kay unlocked the door to the apartment and they went inside. She put on some music and poured them some wine. Fred lit a joint, smoked deeply, and passed it along. Kay began to relax. She felt safe and secure with Fred. He would not hurt her. He would not leave her. Fred, sensing her feelings, comforted her with his fingertips and lips. Then he stood up and began taking off his clothes.

"I need to take a shower," he said softly. "I didn't have a chance between the show and the party."

Kay watched in utter fascination as he slowly and methodically removed his clothing. The moonlight swam in through the window and coated his body with an almost celestial light.

"You're beautiful," she breathed.

"I was a tub of lard as a kid," he confided. "When I was fourteen I got so sick of being 'Fat Fred' I started working out." He turned so that his back was toward her and pushed down his shorts. His buttocks were muscular, deeply indented on either side and covered with a film of fine hair. When he turned around he was smiling.

"Come talk to me while I shower." He walked on the balls of his feet with an almost feminine grace; his powerful calf muscles flexed and relaxed with each step that he took. Kay followed him without protest. She sat down on the clothes hamper, her eyes fixed on the transparent plastic shower curtain. Slowly Fred began soaping his body. At first he washed his face making blubbery noises as the water ran over his mouth. Now and again he would part his lips, catch some of the water, gargle noisily and spit. Then he started running the large cake of soap over his shoulders, down each arm and back up to his armpits. After washing his back, he bent over and scrubbed each foot in turn, and his calves and thighs. Then, after scrubbing his chest, he began to slowly, gently wash his genitals.

Kay had never seen a pornographic film in her life, but she couldn't imagine anything more erotic than what she was seeing at that very moment. She became aware of her nipples thrusting through the material of her dress. They were hard and they ached. Then the curtains parted slightly and Fred stuck his head out. "It's a sticky night. Come on, Kay, join me."

Nothing on earth could have stopped her. She hurriedly tore out of her dress and removed her panties. When she stepped inside Fred wrapped his great arms around her, pulling her close. He rubbed his chest against her breasts and undulated his groin against her hip. Striving to temper his emotions, he picked up a cake of soap and began to bathe her. He stepped back, pulling her with him until they were out of contact with the water. Kay's skin tingled beneath his touch. His soapy fingers played over every inch of her body, beginning at her neck and trailing down her shoulders, turning her around to scrub her back and glide down her buttocks, then turning her again to give special attention to her breasts and stomach. Nor did he stop there, but continued lathering her until she was completely coated with a film of soap, even in the most intimate places.

After rinsing, they dried one another, marveling at the sweetness of their shared intimacy. Fred spotted the various shaped bottles that lined one of the shelves.

"What are all these?" he asked.

"Colognes, body oils."

He removed the stoppers and sniffed several, inhaling their heady odors deeply, and selected one he liked, a scent combining a variety of floral fragrances—tuberoses, freesia, and lily-of-the-valley. He dabbed a bit on Kay's shoulder, pressed his cheek against the wet spot, then rubbed a bit of it into the hair of his chest. "I like sweet-smelling things, particularly flowers. It's so spiritual." Fred sampled each bottle in turn and in doing so thoroughly drenched himself and Kay. Then he picked Kay up in his arms and carried her into the hall. "Which one is your bedroom?"

"That one," she gasped.

He lay her down on the satin coverlet and stretched out beside her, pressing his body against hers. The room was filled with the overpowering odor of the combined fragrances and the sound of their rapid heartbeats. Fred raised himself to one elbow and examined the delicate curves of Kay's lush, womanly body. Her skin was shining with an alabaster whiteness that accentuated the deep pink of her nipples and the small, dark triangle between her thighs. She lifted her arm and touched him. He jerked convulsively. Then she slid one leg across his and nestled her head against his shoulder. Her hand rested lightly on his chest as she settled against him, delighted by the delicious feeling of their bodies meeting. It was like two pieces of a jigsaw puzzle coming together.

Kay wasn't afraid anymore. She only wanted to please him . . . and herself. She moved her hand over

Fred's chest, curling the profuse hair in her fingertips and rubbing his nipples with the palm of her hand. Fred tingled as fiery sensations were ignited in every nerve in his body.

"I've wanted to be with you ever since I saw you that morning," he said. His voice was choked and yet soft. He turned over, encompassing Kay's body with his arms and pressing her lips apart as he slipped his tongue deep into her mouth. Her breath was warm against his face as she uttered a sigh of satisfaction. She slid her arms around his muscular neck and responded avidly, sucking and biting his tongue. She surged against him, instinctively wrapping her legs around his hips and pulling herself to him.

The need for air forced their mouths apart. Kay gasped. "Fred, Fred, you're so right for me, *so very right.*"

Later Kay would remember her first intimate experience with a kind of wonder. She recalled thinking it seemed as if her body was no longer her own, but an extension of his. She had never imagined that such warmth, such closeness could possibly exist between two people. And yet in that act of joining she experienced a freedom of self that would forever change her life.

As they shared a cigarette, Fred told Kay about his anxieties.

"I'm twenty-two now and prime meat for Vietnam. Time's running out. I've been expecting a call from my mother any day telling me that I've been notified."

"Not before the end of the summer!" exclaimed Kay. "They've simply got to let you have that."

He smiled at her indulgently. "I'm afraid the government doesn't take into consideration my interests at the moment."

"I've never understood what it all meant. You see, my brothers aren't old enough to be drafted and," she lowered her eyes, "since I didn't have any boyfriends in school, I've never been able to comprehend what one feels when friends or loved ones are sent away to that awful place." Kay paused, her voice broke. "Now I know. Oh, Fred, what are you going to do?"

"I don't believe in war, and particularly this one. My family didn't raise me that way. They stopped believing in all that gung-ho bullshit a long time ago. My dad was in World War II and he's still got shrapnel scattered all over his body. His two brothers—twins—died in that war. It's always been a source of worry to my mom that their bodies were never returned to the States. I guess there wasn't enough left to return. And then there's my Uncle Fred, I was named after him. He's mom's younger brother. He lives with us. He can't do too much except help around the house and yard and wake up screaming two or three nights a week. You see, he was captured by the Japanese, and I guess you know what they did to the G.I.'s during that war. So it goes."

"What will you do?"

His face hardened. "I don't know yet. I—I may even go to Canada."

"Aren't you afraid of being called a coward?"

Fred flexed his muscles. "Anybody calls me a coward and I'll beat the shit out of them. I won't be conned or intimidated by asshole politicians or flag waving warmongers. My parents are behind me no matter what I decide."

"So am I," said Kay and kissed him tenderly upon the eyelashes. Fred set the ashtray on the floor and took Kay in his arms.

"You want to do it again?" she asked. Fred shook his head and she looked perplexed.

He laughed and kissed her. "Not the same way. There are so many things we haven't tried yet."

It was nearly two o'clock and most of the guests had departed. Jana decided that she had given Kay and Fred as much time as she could. She was extremely tired and wanted nothing more than the comfort of her own bed. Staying on at the party had caused a problem for her. In remaining, she had inadvertently encouraged Saul Silver. She stared wearily at the rock band, now so high on a variety of pills washed down with alcohol and periodic breaks of smoking grass in the garden that they barely knew what they were playing. Several of the lanterns had burned out. The ice had melted in her glass and she had become increasingly bored with Saul's bombastic and lengthy viewpoints on designing for the theatre. She couldn't remember ever having been so bored by a man.

Sleep, beautiful sleep. That was all she could think of. She stood up, stifled a yawn, flexed her tired legs and turned to Saul. His eyes were closed but he was still talking.

". . . then I said, 'I think Cecil Beaton's settings are frivolous, gaudy, superfluous even. But the settings of Boris Aronson become an integral part of the play. They are in essence an added character.'" His eyes clicked open. "Don't you think so, Jana?"

"I've always said that . . . definitely superfluous. Really, Saul, I think it's time I should be getting back to the apartment."

"Has the party come to an end?"

Jana smiled thinly. "It ended about two hours ago."

"Let's have just one more drink. A nightcap. One for the road. A final toast."

"Saul, I'm really very tired. I haven't had a proper night's sleep in a week. I'm standing on my nerve ends."

He seemed not to hear her. "Bartender, two more." The bartender sleepily mixed Saul another martini on the rocks and gave Jana another wine.

"Now where was I?" Jana glanced at Saul sideways.

"Where you always are—in the middle of a stage set." She stood up and slammed down her glass. "Saul, I'm going."

He caught her elbow. "But you must let me come home with you."

"Aren't you married?"

"So?"

"I feel sick."

"Too much wine?"

"Too much you."

The set designer stiffened. "All this time you've just been leading me on."

Jana was incredulous. "Leading you on? I've been polite. Listening to one boring story after the other. Is that leading you on?"

"But I assumed . . ."

"You assumed what? That anyone who listens to you talk will go to bed with you? Then try the bartender. He's had to listen to you all evening, too."

Saul smiled at her crookedly. He didn't believe her. He downed his martini in one gulp and lifted his finger skyward, a signal that he was about to make a pertinent observation. Then he threw up all over the bar.

When Jana entered the apartment, she was immediately struck by the overpowering scent of flowers that rushed forward to greet her. Perplexed and sniffing she went into the bathroom where she saw two wet bathtowels on the floor and the opened bottles of scent. Jana smiled wistfully as she recapped the bottles and hung the towels over the shower rod.

When she finally got into bed, Jana snuggled her head against her pillow and thought of Kay and Fred, Raina and Clay. Sadly she wondered whether she would ever have a relationship.

Clay Jordan watched Raina as she performed solo on the dance floor. Her eyes were closed and her arms outstretched as she undulated her torso to the monotonous beat of the fading rock band. A sleek film of perspiration covered her flesh, making it appear as if it had been varnished. Her thick eyelashes were beaded with the mist of the night and her hair had lost some of its buoyancy and hung over her face like a limp hood of silver cloth. The white crepe dress, damp with perspiration and the night, clung to her shapely body like a second skin.

The waiters and bartenders were moving about the garden and the main floor of the house emptying ashtrays, gathering glasses and cleaning up in general. Jordan glanced at his watch, a thin sliver of gold. It was ten past three. Touching Raina on the shoulder, he said. "I think it's time to send everybody home."

"Everybody?"

"Present company excluded. By the way, you dance very well."

Raina's manner changed. Now she was all business. "I've had eight years of ballet, four of modern dance, and three of tap. I can hoof my way around Ann Miller and I can belt better than Rocky Graziano. So don't you go hiring any new actresses to play Reno Sweeney in *Anything Goes* until you see me strut my stuff."

Ordinarily Jordan was put off by young actresses jockeying for parts. But he was secure enough to know that Raina was truly attracted to him and her direct approach amused him. He replied nonchalantly. "I'll try you out next week. I haven't cast the part yet."

"I'm very pleased," Raina replied, affecting the same amount of nonchalance.

While Jordan presented his hired help with already written checks and extravagant tips, Raina retired to the bathroom to repair her makeup. After shutting and locking the door, she pressed a towel over her mouth and screamed with joy. She was confident that Jordan would like her interpretation of the evangelist turned nightclub singer. Humming "Anything Goes," Raina freshened her makeup, and when she returned, everyone but Clay was gone.

"Would you care for a nightcap?" Jordan pointed toward the bar and the bottle of champagne set at a jaunty angle in a heavy silver bucket. Raina smiled and nodded. Jordan worked his thumbs around the champagne cork and it flew away with a resounding pop. He filled two exquisite cut glass goblets and handed one to Raina. "Wait," he cautioned, "perhaps a little something to go with it." He reached into his pocket and extracted a vermeil pill box. Raina looked inside.

"What are they? M&Ms?"

Jordan laughed. "You got the initials right anyway. Mescaline. It's great with champagne. And I promise you that it'll make you see and feel things you've never even imagined."

Raina took a red pill and popped it into her mouth. After clinking her glass against Jordan's, she washed it down her throat.

As he sipped his champagne, Jordan undid his tie and unbuttoned his shirt to the waist. Then he took Raina's hand and pressed it against his tanned flesh. She wondered how he retained his color, for he always seemed to be at the theatre.

"Feel my heart. The beats are increasing, are they not?" Raina nodded. "Shall we go upstairs?"

They left their glasses behind, but Jordan carried the nearly full bottle of champagne. On their way up the narrow stairway, he explained, "My landlord indulges my taste in decor." Raina wasn't sure what he was talking about until he opened the door to the bedroom—then she knew. The room was not large, perhaps no more than sixteen feet by sixteen feet. Except for a low cabinet containing a stereo, a miniature refrigerator and a series of drawers, there was no furniture. The three walls were draped in apricot satin, and the fourth wall was very nearly covered by a giant mirror in the gilt rococo frame. The floor appeared to be four mattresses, each covered with fitted satin sheets matching the draperies. A track of lights bisecting the center of the ceiling blanketed the room with the iridescent glow of black light. "Far out," breathed Raina as she kicked off her heels and stepped inside.

"There are two rules in this room," said Jordan. "Clothing is forbidden and . . . anything goes."

Raina began singing and whirling around the room as she obligingly stripped. When she turned to face the director he, too, was nude, his clothes lying in a pile near the doorway. His body was more perfect than she had imagined. She knew that he was not a young man —his credits attested to that—but he was in peak physical condition.

"You're very beautiful, Raina."

"So are you."

He moved toward her and he seemed to be floating. She lowered her eyelids and welcomed the enveloping warmth of his flesh. Jordan pulled her down to the bed/floor as music—exotic savage rhythms—filled the room. Jordan did not talk much during love-making; he didn't want to waste words. His technique was a revelation to Raina. The variations were endless and a continual astonishment to her. Just when his feathery caresses and agile maneuverings had teased her into such a sensual fever that it seemed her flesh would sear, Jordan employed the cool champagne. She felt a trickle between her breasts, down her abdomen, and over her pelvis. The champagne was not wasted, but was licked off by Jordan's insatiable lips and tongue.

Later he opened a drawer and produced a small yellow box containing ampules of amyl nitrite. He broke one beneath Raina's nose and her rush was immediate. Flinging her head from side to side as she boldly straddled him, Raina watched herself in the mirror. She suddenly became aware that Jordan was watching her watch herself. It was like having another couple in the room. Raina's excitement was heightened by Jordan's remark: "Pretend they're not really us," he whispered. "They aren't, you know. They're two other people."

Jordan bucked his hips upward, ravishing her with long, pounding strokes. Raina clamped her arms around her breasts and thrust downward. As she approached her climax, Jordan reached out with one hand, took another "popper," and put it between her teeth. As she broke it and inhaled its acrid scent, her movements accelerated. A long deep groan burst from her throat like a bird fleeing the night. She knew that in all her experience, she had never known such infinite release. Jordan continued thrusting until he, too, joined her on that intoxicating plane. They did not part, but remained joined as man and woman. Raina slid down on top of him, and in that position they both drifted into sleep.

Chapter Seven

Raina and Jordan had been lovers for exactly six days when he decided to give her the leading role in *Anything Goes*. Then, as always, Jordan lost interest in his current affair when the young woman in question was cast in one of his plays. He simply ceased to see her as a sexual partner once she stepped onto his stage. Raina was thrilled to win the coveted part of Reno Sweeney, but totally dismayed when she found that Jordan's personal interest in her was over. Not only was her pride badly bruised, but she sorely missed his sexual shenanigans and doubted if she would ever be satisfied with "normal" sex again. Even McCafferty, her law enforcement fling, was on vacation, and there was no one else who held her interest.

Jana's feelings for Saul Silver remained as cool and guarded as they had been before the party. Evidently he did not remember, or chose not to remember, his behavior on that occasion; in any event, he simply acted as if nothing had happened between them. Jana had been asked out by nearly every actor and every man on the technical staff, and had politely but firmly refused. She was not interested in any of them, and indeed had little time for socializing since becoming Saul's assistant. She was encouraged by Raina's being cast as the lead in *Anything Goes,* and hoped to win the role of Catharine in the final play of the season, *Suddenly Last Summer.* She realized, somewhat anxiously, that her main competition was going to be Raina.

Kay and Fred's liaison had deepened into a love affair. Even though neither of them had yet confessed it, they knew that they were in love. They were completely enmeshed with their work on the show and with each other. But Fred's impending draft notice permeated their lives like an illness, clouding their peaceful existence.

Kay's work on the costumes of the thirties' musical consumed sixteen hours of her day. Besides being a talented designer, Kay was a remarkable organizer and delegator of work. The other costume apprentices held no animosity toward her. They respected her talent and worked under her with enthusiasm.

Every minute not spent in the costume room Kay willingly gave to Fred. Never before had she known such complete acceptance from another human being. Fred was everything she had ever dreamed about in a lover. He was strong, tender, bright and humorous. He was the very embodiment of her high school fantasies.

At a five-minute rehearsal break, Raina hurried off stage to find Jordan, who earlier had been watching her from the wings. He was nowhere in sight. She unhitched the cumbersome wings that were part of her costume for a number entitled "Heavenly Hop" and wiped away her perspiration with a much used towel. Then she sipped on a Coke that she had left behind at the beginning of rehearsal. It soothed her throat, which to her dismay was becoming somewhat sore with the strain of frequent rehearsals.

A flat was moved into position and behind it Clay Jordan and a young woman, a sophomore from a nearby college who had been cast in the chorus, appeared to be in deep conference. Raina smarted. The girl was flighty and pretty and Jordan was obviously interested in her.

Jordan saw Raina approaching and quickly concluded his talk with the chorus girl. Arranging his face into an easy smile, he said, "Good work, Raina. It's going to be a show-stopping number. However, you should save your voice for the rest of rehearsal. It's getting a bit ragged. Are you gargling, taking tea and all that?"

Raina regarded him narrowly. "Maybe I just need some relaxation."

Jordan glanced nervously around him. "Raina, not here."

"Why not here? You seem to be lining up your next piece here. Isn't she just a little bit common for you?"

Grabbing her by the shoulders, the director said through clenched teeth, "Raina, we had our little fling, but now it's over. Look, you got what you wanted—the lead in the show." He shrugged. "And I got what I wanted. But now I don't want it anymore. Can't you understand?"

Raina stared at him incredulously. "But, Clay. It was so good."

"It's *always* good for me, Raina."

Raina was further irritated by the differences in their appearance. Here she was, her hair stringy with perspiration and every vestige of her makeup worn away. Jordan, on the other hand, appeared cool and pristine. Not a hair was out of place and his shirt and slacks displayed nary a wrinkle.

"What's wrong, Clay? You don't look at me anymore except as a director. You don't touch me. Have I suddenly turned ugly?"

"Not at all, Raina. I'm just . . . not . . . interested."

"Nobody dumps me," growled Raina.

"Just think of it as part of your learning experience. Now let's end this conversation. This isn't the time or the place for it."

"But, Clay . . ."

"Look, I had you and you had me. And you got your part. We both got what we wanted. Isn't that enough?"

"I didn't go to bed with you for the part!" Raina cried.

"I know that. I didn't cast you because you had. Now, let's act like professionals and get back to work."

"Clay Jordan, you're a bastard!"

"That," smiled Jordan, "is the first time you've ever been trite."

Jordan strode off stage, leaving Raina shaken. She hurried back to her watery Coke and quickly finished it, wishing it were laced with brandy.

Jana, sitting on her bed, worked at composing a letter to her mother. It wasn't easy finding things to say, and she knew that her letters were forced and full of false conviviality.

". . . *Anything Goes* was a smash," she wrote. "Raina was terrific and Kay's costumes were wonderful. You probably remember the play, Mother. It was made into a movie. I tried out for the role of Lizzie in *The Rainmaker*. Mr. Jordan was very complimentary but told me I was too beautiful for the part. It didn't make the rejection any easier. I hope I'm not counting on too much, but I have a good chance at the lead in *Suddenly Last Summer*. Naturally, I'll keep you posted.

"I hope that you will be able to visit before the summer ends, for I doubt that I will be returning to Scranton before the three of us leave for New York. Uncle Ted's check will come in very handy for initial expenses. He always seems to save the day. I wrote him a thank you letter . . ."

Fred was asleep on his stomach and Kay was writing her weekly duty letter to her family, using his back as a desk top.

". . . and so, family, I am now the official costume designer of the Playhouse, *with* a hefty hike in salary, and I'm loving it. I'm sending you a review of *Anything Goes*. I underlined in red comments referring to me. The critic called the costumes "absolutely delicious." I hope you have been watching the news and have some understanding of the war in Vietnam. The guy I've been seeing may be drafted, and I hope he refuses to serve. It's Johnson's war. Let *him* go in Fred's place. Please, Mom and Pop, write your Congressman and protest this senseless war. I'm not asking for me but for my

brothers. If this terrible insanity continues, they'll surely be taken away and killed . . ."

Kay put down her pen. "I'm wasting my breath. Who
the hell am I fooling?" she muttered. "They won't even
know what I'm talking about."

Raina sat in a tub full of hot water and bath salts.
The warm water relieved the aches in her body but
didn't do anything to assuage the pain in her heart. A
writing tray was balanced across the edges of the tub.
She sighed heavily and continued her letter to her
parents.

> . . . I'm sorry you weren't able to make it to the
> opening. I did very well. Do you think there's any
> chance you could make it before the end of the
> run? It continues until August fifteenth.
>
> Jana, Kay and I are getting along famously.
> Did I tell you that Kay was elevated to costume
> designer and that Jana is painting scenery like an
> old hand? After *Anything Goes* is over, I'll be
> back in the publicity department, so I imagine this
> show is the high point of my summer. Do try to
> come. It's really very good. Not like those things
> in high school. I promise you I won't embarrass
> you. My director Mr. Jordan tells me he thinks I
> should do very well in New York City. I hope so.
> It's a big step from Harrisburg, Pennsylvania, but
> I think the shock will have been lessened by my
> summer here at the Playhouse.
>
> I'm enclosing a clipping of the local critic's re-
> view. Of course, he's not Brooks Atkinson, but I
> think his evaluation is very astute. The audiences
> liked the show, too, and we're practically sold out
> until the end of the run. So if you think you can
> make it, please call or send a telegram and I'll ar-
> range for tickets.

Raina set the writing tray aside, closed the shower
curtains and rinsed. After drying, she slipped into a

silk robe and went into the kitchen to get herself a brandy. She sat down at the table next to the windows overlooking the canal, lit a cigarette and thought about everything that had happened to her: her brief affair with Clay, her opening night triumph, and her unaccountable depression. From the window she watched with fascination as an apparition floated out of the mist. A white form stepped out of the fog looking like a creature that rose at night to menace the living. Raina slammed down her glass in shock and stared wide-eyed as the form came near. Then she saw that it was Sylvia Oglethorpe roaming through the night looking like a deranged Lady MacBeth. She staggered past the house and down the tow path, her full length nightgown trailing through the wet grass by the edge of the canal.

Raina doused her cigarette in the glass of brandy and pushed it aside, promising once again to rid herself of her destructive habits. Sylvia was a walking advertisement for abstinence.

Chapter Eight

Dressed in a sweatsuit and eating a peach yogurt, Kay danced into the living room. "I say," she said in a syrupy voice, "where *has* the summer gone? Lord! If I hear that phrase one more time down at the theatre, I think I'll barf."

"Uhhh ... still, it's true ... uhh," groaned Jana.

"Uhhh ... *très triste* ..." agreed Raina. "Aren't you going to ... uhhh ... join us?"

Jana and Raina, also in sweatsuits, were lying on the floor going through their morning exercise routines.

"In a minute, in a minute," replied Kay. She set aside the yogurt and joined her two roommates on the floor. "What did I miss?"

"Just the tummy flattening exercises," panted Raina. "And I shouldn't worry if I were you—you're screwing yours away."

Kay glanced down at her own flat stomach and solid thighs and smiled happily. She lay down on the floor and asked, "What's next on the beauty agenda?"

"Stretching," announced Raina. "Good for keeping the old tits high."

"Tits," laughed Jana. "What tits? God, I wish I had breasts like you, Kay."

Kay shrugged. "What's to want? But listen, I think it's the birth control pills. If you took the pill like Raina and I do, I bet you'd get bigger, too."

"I don't trust them," responded Jana. "They're not natural."

"Who do you think you are—Doris Day? Now not having sex, that's what's not natural," said Raina.

Jana looked first at Raina, then Kay. "What can I tell you? Someday he'll come along, the man I love. *Then* I'll take precautions."

"Precautions!" squealed Kay. "I thought you were Catholic."

"Catholic? Who could be Catholic living with you two? Come on, let's do another set."

Raina reached for her diet soda. "It's true, you know."

"What's true?" the other two said at the very same time.

"Where has the summer gone? I mean, we open the second to the last show of the season tomorrow night. It's all a gigantic blur, a marvelous, whirling kaleidoscope of comedy and drama. But, my dears, it's coming to an end."

"Thank God for my new position," said Kay. "I might not have had the money to go to New York."

"And my Uncle Ted's check," added Jana. "At least that will get me started."

"And here's to Aunt Lucy!" cried Raina. "Long may the United States of America and all her possessions continue to eat that sugary frozen junk."

"All right, guys, back to the exercises," said Raina. "Now that going nude onstage is all the rage, we'd better get it into shape."

"The first thing I'm going to do when I get to New York is to go see *Hair*," announced Kay. "I want to see all those naked men."

"Getting bored with Fred?" asked Raina.

Kay threw a pillow at her. "Never! I just happen to like to look at naked men. Is there anything wrong with that?"

"Hear, hear," agreed Raina.

The three young women lay back on the floor and began their stretching exercises, Kay grunting, Raina cursing, and Jana puffing. Ten minutes later, gasping in unison, they broke for a cup of coffee.

"I really can't stand it black," complained Kay.

"Think of it this way," explained Raina, "if you had cream and sugar, you'd have to exercise for twenty more minutes."

"Black it is. Lord, I feel like my body's one great big varicose vein. You know, I can't believe everything is done for *Stop the World*. I had the costumes finished three days ago. I love small casts." Kay picked up the half eaten container of yogurt. "How can people eat this stuff? It tastes like library paste."

"I've learned to like it," said Jana.

"And wheat germ, and bean sprouts," laughed Raina. "I'm beginning to feel like a salad. Now if only somebody would toss me."

"What about McCafferty?" asked Kay. "Isn't he back from vacation?"

Raina scowled. "He came back married." She took Kay's yogurt container and toasted. "What the hell, here's to him, and here's to Clay, and here's to all the fine young men who have crossed my path and rumpled my bed."

"I don't know if you have enough toasts for that," teased Kay.

Raina's laugh stopped abruptly. She looked at Jana. "Well, kid, tryouts are this afternoon for *Suddenly Last Summer*. Good luck, I mean it."

"Good luck to you, Raina. And I mean it too."

"Hey, no matter what happens, let's not get frosty," said Kay. "After all, one of you is bound to get the lead, now that Jordan realizes you each have more talent than a dozen under-employed New York actresses combined. It'll still be in the family."

Raina stood up and flexed her legs. "Maybe neither of us will get the part. I understand a *lot* of imports are coming down from New York to try out. It's funny how success breeds success. This season has been a financial smash. Clay must be rolling in his own ego. But, of course, he has to deal with the pressure. Each show has to be better than the last. I frankly don't think he'll cast either Jana or myself. He'll get some little miss

nobody on hiatus from a soap, a semi-name, and give
her the part of Catharine. It doesn't matter to him that
we've given blood, sweat and tears all summer to help
make the Playhouse a success. Oh no, did I really say
that?"

The girls each had another cup of coffee along with
granola fortified with wheat germ, natural honey and
raisins.

"All this grain," grumbled Kay. "Now you tell me
why cows don't have sexy bods."

"Well, they must turn on the bulls," Raina said. She
glanced uneasily at Jana. "I suppose there's no use
prolonging it. We might as well get ready and go down
to the Playhouse for the tryouts."

"We who are about to die salute you," said Jana
with forced brightness.

Kay stood up. "Hey, you two. Come off it. There's
no reason to get uptight just because you're trying out
for the same part. Hell, that's competition. You think
that won't happen in New York? Look, I know you're
torn up because you both want the part and yet you
both want the other one to have it. Well, as Meg
Franklin would have put it, that's goddam show biz.
Now go down there, do your best and don't worry
about the outcome. Do you think that if one of you
gets the part the other isn't going to be able to deal
with it? That's a crock. We're all too close for that,
and you know it. I'm going down to the liquor store to
buy a bottle of their best champagne. Tonight we're
going to have a celebration for whoever wins." Kay
grinned. "So long as it's one of you two. Now, shake
hands and come out fighting."

Rosemarie Paradise, a Playhouse volunteer who had
long since become a permanent fixture, set her lips in
disapproval and opened the doors of the box office to
allow for cross ventilation. Charlotte Kenyon, the college sophomore who was Jordan's latest amour, was
sitting at the director's desk answering his correspondence. Although she had been in the room for less than

a quarter of an hour, the entire place was permeated with her perfume. Rosemarie disliked the flippant young woman and deeply disapproved of her relationship with Clay Jordan. But then Rosemarie, herself the widow of a pillar of propriety, had never been particularly tolerant of the whims of men. Additionally, Charlotte called Rosemarie "Mrs. Paradise," instead of "Miss Rosemarie," as everyone else affectionately referred to her. The intention was not to show respect —which would never have occurred to Charlotte—but to make plain the enormous gulf of years that yawned between them. Charlotte seemed to think it was a positive achievement to be young.

Charlotte looked up from her stamp licking. "The air conditioner is on, Mrs. Paradise."

"I know that," Rosemarie replied a little more sharply than she had intended. "But it seems stuffy in here, don't you think?"

Charlotte sniffed. "I think this rotten old theatre stinks. It's nowhere near as much fun as I thought it would be. It absolutely reeks of age and decay."

Although this was said straightforwardly, Rosemarie knew that Charlotte was giving voice to her disapproval of old things in general.

Clay Jordan entered, started to kiss Charlotte, saw Rosemarie, and quickly made believe he was just checking an address on one of the envelopes. "Afternoon, Miss Rosemarie. How are ticket sales going?"

He smiled so warmly that Rosemarie could not help forgiving him for his latest peccadillo. Besides, she reasoned, Charlotte wouldn't last. Her kind never did. "Just lovely, Mr. Jordan."

"Why don't you take your lunch, Miss Rosemarie? Charlotte and I will look after things."

Leaving Charlotte in charge of "things" did not suit Rosemarie, but out of deference to Jordan's wishes she said that lunch sounded like a good idea. After all, she could be back in half an hour. Even Charlotte couldn't do much harm in that short amount of time.

As soon as the door was closed, Jordan exacted his

kiss from Charlotte. "Thanks for taking care of my mail."

Charlotte screwed up her face. "Why do you keep that old woman around? She gives me the creeps."

"She's very good at her job, my dear. And besides, she volunteers her time."

"Humph. Likely as not someone will come up to the ticket window and find her slumped over dead."

Jordan laughed. "You're terrible. Now have you got all of the girls' résumés?"

"Yes, here they are." She touched his arm. "Clay, you wouldn't really consider casting Jana, or that Raina? They're just beginners."

"They're also very good, my dear. You have to admit that Raina was smashing in *Anything Goes*. I have no doubt that either one could play the part, but being the fair director that I am," he grinned, "I'm going to cast the best."

"But not Raina."

Jordan's face clouded. "I've told you. She's nothing to me. She never was. And I've also warned you, Charlotte, *never* interfere with my decisions as a director. Don't even dare to suggest how I run my theatre."

Charlotte smiled weakly. "I'm sorry, Clay. I'll make you some coffee and bring it in to you."

Jordan kissed her and wondered briefly why he preferred her to Raina. But he knew why. He liked Charlotte's dependence on him. Raina and so many of the others had been too independent for his special needs. He preferred a woman he could dominate . . . in all ways.

Chapter Nine

After making a thorough examination of all the cardboard boxes, Sylvia Oglethorpe's huge ginger cat stretched out on the topmost one and presented himself to the warming rays of the sun. A U-Haul-It wagon had been attached to Raina's red Thunderbird and was stuffed with containers filled with the clothing and possessions of Raina, Jana and Kay. The trio was upstairs going through the apartment one last time checking for things they might have forgotten. Kay emerged from the bathroom triumphantly.

"Hey, you'll never believe this, but we left our toothbrushes." She waved the technicolor wands of plastic about like a majorette leading a parade. "Come on, let's get this show on the road. New York City awaits us."

Jana and Raina, tooting an imaginary trumpet and beating a phantom drum, fell in step behind Kay. They tromped downstairs and paraded around the car and the wagon. The ginger cat lifted its head and, quickly bored by the procession of silly humans, went back to sleep.

Then the young women proceeded down the alley to Sylvia's shop. They knew she was up for they had heard her earlier banging about and talking to herself. They were greeted by an unusual sight. The doors to the gourmet shop were flung open and Sylvia, puffing like a long distance runner, was hauling baskets of tinned food onto the porch. A sign tacked over the window proclaimed that she was having a sale. They watched her as she took a ladylike sip from a nearby bottle of brandy and surveyed her arrangement of baskets.

"Sylvia," ventured Raina.

The landlady swung around. When she saw all three girls, she immediately thought something was wrong.

"I hope I didn't wake you by clattering about?"

"No, not at all," said Jana. "We're just getting ready to go and we wanted to give you the keys and thank you for your kindness."

"Go, go?" repeated Sylvia. "Is it Labor Day already?"

"Nearly," answered Kay.

"Where has the summer gone?" wondered Sylvia. The three young women stifled their laughter. "I'm so sorry we couldn't get to know one another better, but I've been so . . . occupied. Where are you going?"

"To New York," said Raina. "We're going to get an apartment together and try our luck in the professional theatre."

Sylvia tilted her head toward the sky. The strong sun faded the deep lines on her face and for a moment she looked almost young again. "Go and persevere. You see, you *must* make it." Sylvia smiled wistfully. "For all of us . . . who didn't."

The girls each embraced her in turn and hurried away, as if sensing that further contact with the pathetic old woman might somehow impede their ambitions. Sylvia stood on the porch and watched as they drove away, hoping that they would turn around and wave one last time. They did.

The swarming streets of New Hope were overrun with tourists who had descended upon the community for the Labor Day weekend. As they passed the Playhouse, Kay burst into tears. This touched off a reaction from the other two and soon they were all sobbing.

"Don't look back," Kay sniffed loudly. "We mustn't ever look back." She emitted a hoarse laugh. "Besides, we're liable to turn into pillars of salt, and salt makes your body retain water."

They crossed the bridge to Lambertville and Route

202. Jana passed around tissues, Raina flipped on the radio, and the Beatles were playing. They wiped away their tears and settled back for the three-hour ride that would take them to New York City.

The countryside became a blur of green and tan. As the miles raced by, each young woman became lost in her own thoughts concerning the final events of the summer. . . .

Jana had been summoned to the Playhouse by Clay Jordan. She found him sitting in the center of the stage, the lights ablaze, his back toward the audience. He turned as he heard her approach.

"I have chosen you to play the part of Catharine Holly." Jana started to speak, but he held up his hand, and said, more to himself than to her: "All of the characters in Williams' plays fall into categories. That is, all but one—Catharine Holly. And she is the rarest specimen in Williams' entire literary jungle. She's a normal human being. A decent, intelligent girl, neither oversexed nor frustrated. She's a girl with a passion for truth-telling. Even though she can recognize truth, after witnessing her cousin Sebastian's horrifying death, she has sense enough to be shocked into schizophrenia. Jana, this is the key to her character. She has the strength and practicality to survive and recover her sanity. I usually do not cast according to type, but in this case I did. I feel that you are not unlike Catharine Holly. If you experienced a great trauma, you would call upon your inner resources and you would survive." He paused for her expected response.

"Mr. Jordan, I don't know what to say. I'm so thrilled. I promise to make you proud of me."

"I'm already proud of you, Jana. Now go to my office and have Charlotte give you a script, and I'll see you in rehearsal tomorrow morning at ten. By the way, your scene painting duties are hereby terminated."

Jana ran all the way back to the apartment. Her heart was so full of joy that she was afraid it was going to explode. Then, just as she reached the bottom step, her elation turned to concern. What about Raina? She would be so terribly disappointed. When she finally mustered the courage to push open the door and enter the apartment, she found Raina and Kay waiting for her. While she had been gone they had blown up scores of balloons which literally filled the living room. Raina waved an open bottle of champagne and Kay saluted her with another. They ran to Jana, hugged and kissed her, and the three of them began jumping up and down and squealing.

Kay was remembering the day Fred burned his draft card. It was the second Sunday in August and a group of draft resisters converged upon the state capitol at Trenton, chanting, "Hell no, we won't go!" Fred was prominent among them. Later, in an orderly fashion, the resisters formed a line and one by one threw their draft cards into a giant trashcan. Several impassioned speeches were made by the leaders of the rally. And Kay, who had accompanied her lover, applauded with many of the other spectators who were kept cordoned off from the display by the police. A small but noisy faction jeered the resisters and their ceremony. For a time Kay was afraid that violence might erupt. However, the Trenton police, to their credit, kept the peace between the two opposing groups.

Afterwards, while driving back to New Hope in the Thunderbird borrowed from Raina, Fred told Kay the news she had been dreading to hear. "My parents called me last night." Kay closed her eyes and held her breath. "My induction notice arrived."

"No, no!" Kay cried. "It's too soon. It can't happen. It *can't!*"

"I'm afraid it has, Kay, but I cannot, of course, comply with the government's wishes."

"What are you going to do?" Kay asked hollowly.

"As soon as I've set the lights for *Suddenly Last Summer,* I'm going to leave for Canada."

"So soon. . . ."

"I've been in touch with a friend of a friend and at least I'll have a place to stay in Montreal."

"I . . . I guess it's good you've had French," Kay feebly improvised.

"Yeah, sure is. . . Look, don't cry, Kay. We'll work something out." He was trying to spare her some measure of his own near-panic and distress.

"I'm not crying," she protested, but she was.

Fred stayed on until the opening night of the Tennessee Williams play. He was not only reluctant to leave Kay and the theatre he had come to love, but he wanted to be there to applaud Jana on her extraordinary interpretation of Williams' ill-fated heroine. Neither Fred nor Kay attended the opening night cast party. Instead, Kay went back to Fred's room at the Logan Inn to help him finish packing, and there they made love for what, for all they knew, might be the last time.

The bus departing for Trenton at midnight would take him to New York City. From there he would take a plane to Montreal. Raina offered Kay the use of her car, but Fred did not want to prolong their parting.

A short time before midnight, Kay walked with Fred to the bus station. The night was hot and paper dry. The streets were littered with couples from all walks of life intent upon enjoying themselves. Laughing and conversing, they moved from one bar to the next in search of pleasure. Kay looked upon them with a mixture of envy and contempt. Didn't they realize what was going on in the world? Weren't they concerned about what was happening? As if reading her mind, Fred clasped her hand, kissed her on the cheek, and said by way of explanation, "People who are not committed are just taking up space. I feel very lucky that I'm not one of them, and luckier still that I found you."

The station was like every other small town bus station—dirty, harshly lit and depressing. An elderly woman clothed in rags sat in the corner and rocked back and forth as she hummed a strident melody. A soldier, young and slightly drunk, sat opposite her smoking cigarette after cigarette.

Fred embraced Kay. "You have my address."

"Oh yes, yes, I'll write to you. And when we get to New York and find an apartment, I'll send you my address." Kay glanced through the glass doors. The New York bus was already loading. She clenched her teeth, determined not to cry.

"The bus is waiting, Kay."

"Yes, I know." She forced a smile. "You'd better go." She saw that Fred's lower lip was trembling, and she kissed him until the trembling stopped.

"I'm going now." He kissed her again and walked away. Kay watched him push through the doors and take his place in line. He disappeared into the dark interior of the Greyhound bus.

Raina stared at the road and recalled another night when the white line had not been so straight, but had wavered and fluttered like a ribbon caught in the wind.

Attending the opening night party for *Suddenly Last Summer* was a duty Raina would have liked to forgo. After witnessing the play, Raina's emotions were confused. She thought that Jana was touching in the lead and she had great happiness for her success, but at the same time Raina felt anger rising within her like bile in her throat. She knew that she could have played the part better. At first she blamed Jordan for his irrevocable decision, but in her heart Raina knew his reason for not casting her had to do less with her talent than with her lack of discipline. Her drinking was beginning to get the better of her, and she had begun to occasionally rely on tranquilizers and amphetamines to manage her increasingly brutal hangovers. Raina knew she was headed for deep water, but she couldn't admit it. And as the irresponsible often do, she punished herself for her errors by committing even more.

The final cast party of the season was held at the estate of Mr. and Mrs. Simon Newlander, wealthy patrons of the Playhouse and owners of an internationally famous fur company. After forcing herself to go backstage and congratulate Jana, Raina made an excuse about wanting to change her dress so that she wouldn't have to drive Jana to the party. She didn't think that she would be able to cope with being alone with Jana at the moment. Fortunately Jana did not seem to notice her friend's mood. Raina's feelings filled her with guilt. She stopped off in Lambertville at a small hotel bar to have a drink and try to compose herself before arriving at the party. The bar was appropriately named Wit's End, and was located on the main floor of a recently reconstructed nineteenth-century building. It was decorated in an art noveau style, complete with copies of Tiffany lampshades and a delicately curved mirrored bar.

The bartender sucked in his breath as he saw Raina enter. She was wearing a strapless full length dress of beige crepe. The material clung to her body and the color matched her tawny skin. In the dim light of the bar Raina appeared to be completely naked; as she came forward the bartender sighed with relief and disappointment. Raina slid onto the bar stool and opened her purse to make sure she had brought money with her—like a lot of wealthy people, she often forgot it. She smiled sweetly at the bartender who, despite the air-conditioning, was starting to perspire. He could feel it trickling down the inside of his arms. When he opened his mouth to speak the words caught in his throat. He cleared his throat and asked, "How can I help you, Miss?"

"A tequila, please, on the rocks with a twist of lemon."

As the bartender served Raina her drink, she noticed his appearance for the first time. He was rough and somewhat stupid looking, but the sleeves of his shirt were rolled up to reveal magnificently muscled arms lightly marbled with blue veins. She smiled once again. "I didn't know this bar was here. It's quite attractive." Her expression and tone were flirtatious. The bartender began to sweat more profusely.

Raina quickly finished her drink and ordered another. She hoped it would lift her spirits and rid her of the hostility she felt toward Jana. She knew that for their friendship's sake it was imperative that she get over this funk. And she would, by whatever means were available to her.

This time she sipped her drink slowly, savoring the tangy bite of the liquor. Things were beginning to come into focus now. It didn't matter that Jana had gotten the part. No one who really counted had seen her anyway. New Hope was past tense. New York and its challenges loomed before her. And after all, wasn't Broadway what really mattered, not some tacky little summer theatre in a hick town in Pennsylvania! She could afford to be generous because she was going to become a star. She knew she possessed that certain quality that set her apart; a special commodity that transcended talent and beauty.

The bartender, his face glistening, reappeared. "Another drink, Miss?"

"No, thank you," she replied languidly. "I'm off to a party. You wouldn't like to come, would you?"

"I'd love to, but I can't," he said, hardly knowing whether to take her seriously or not. "I'm on duty until two."

"Pity," Raina said idly as she placed a crisp twenty-dollar bill on the bar. "Perhaps another time."

Gravel flew from the back wheels of the Thunderbird and sprayed across the front of the hotel. Raina lit a cigarette and tore down the highway toward the party. The Newlanders' home was an ostentatious copy of a French chateau and sat on a hill overlooking the Delaware River. Raina zoomed into the parking lot, causing several guests to scatter. At the front door Raina was greeted by a stiff butler.

"Good evening, Miss."

"My God, what an absolutely lovely home. Where's the john?"

The butler blushed and murmured, "Upstairs, Miss. The first door on your left."

Her makeup freshened and her spirit fortified with the false security of alcohol, Raina joined the party.

Everybody was there; she was the last to arrive. Well, wasn't that the way it should be with a rising star? She made her way through the crowd, nodding, smiling and exchanging brief pleasantries as she sought out the bar. She was soon to find that there was a bar in every room and one at either end of the swimming pool. Save for the foyer and the bathrooms, there was a bar at every turn. After collecting a tequila, she found Jana surrounded by a crowd of admirers. Jana's face lit up when she saw her friend.

"Raina, I was afraid something had happened, that you weren't coming."

"I went back to change my gown," Raina lied, "but must have misplaced my keys. They're probably in the car somewhere."

Jana took Raina to one side. "Did you really like my performance?"

Raina smiled thinly. "I really liked it," she replied in truth. "Now I must find Clay and congratulate him on his excellent direction and, of course, his astute casting." Jana understood. She knew that not getting to play the coveted role must have hurt Raina deeply.

It took Raina about fifteen minutes to check out the male possibilities at the party. There were none. She was at poolside drinking another tequila when Charlotte came up to her.

"Why, Raina, you *did* come. I'm quite surprised. I was just telling Clay that I didn't think you'd have the courage to show your face."

"Why not? You've had the courage to show yours."

"Sweet, sweet."

"And where is our brilliant director? Knocking off a piece in the bathhouse?"

Charlotte thrust out her lower lip. "Clay and I are going together. He wouldn't look at another woman."

"How *did* you do it, Charlotte?" Raina drawled.

"You're just jealous because he threw you over for me."

"Charlotte, to tell you the truth, I've never been jealous of bad taste. You can have your pink flamingos on the lawn, your musical toilet paper holders, and your nauseating perfume that smells like ten nights on a troop train." She tossed her head and said with mock sincerity: "You really ought to do something with your hair, Charlotte. It looks like you've rinsed it in stale coffee. Perhaps some vitamins . . . And you know a really good astringent might shrink those pores. Funny, I remember Clay saying one night . . . during sex . . . that if he had enough poppers, he could make it with an orangutan . . . and here you are!"

Charlotte, shaking with anger, raised her hand to slap Raina. But Raina, anticipating her, quickly ducked out of the way. The unfortunate girl lost her balance, staggered backwards and fell into the pool. Sputtering and gasping, she swam to the edge and started to pull herself out. A crowd gathered. Raina walked over to where she was hanging on and calmly stepped on her hand.

"Just remember, Charlotte, it may start with a bang, but it ends with a whimper."

Raina ran into Jana as she was leaving the party. "What happened? Who fell into the pool?"

"Nobody of any importance. Look, Jana, I'm going to get out of here. I'm bored as hell. Will you be able to get back to the apartment all right?"

"Oh, yes. I can get a ride with somebody. But where are you going?"

Raina laughed and began singing, "There's a small hotel with a wishing . . . *well!*"

The hotel sign was dark and Raina was afraid the bar might be closed. She stopped two inches short of running into the back of another car and hurried toward Wit's End. The doors opened and there were still four or five customers scattered in the dark corners of the room. The bartender was washing glasses and didn't notice Raina until her perfume, rich and heady, seared his nostrils. Startled, he looked up and then smiled easily. It was evident he had been sampling his wares since Raina's departure.

"The party was dull," she said bluntly. "I was hoping I might find a little excitement here."

His eyes didn't leave hers as he asked, "Another tequila, Miss?"

She nodded. "Call me Raina. And you're . . ."

"Rafe."

"Nice name," commented Raina. "It suits." He had thick black hair, worn full and long, dark slanted eyes and high cheekbones.

"Are you part Indian, Rafe?"

"Yes, Miss."

"What tribe?"

"Can you guess?" She shook her head. "Delaware," he grinned. "One-fourth to be exact. Why, are you interested in American history?"

Raina laughed. She liked playing the game. "I understand that Indians don't have any body hair."

"Just a bit and it's . . . concentrated." Rafe put the drink down on the bar. Raina started to pay him but he held up his hand. "No. It's on the house."

"I'll drink to that."

Raina continued drinking until the bar was closed. Rafe matched her drink for drink. By the time the tables were stacked and the register was closed, they were both very high and full of sexual expectations. Rafe, who had a small room in the hotel, wanted to take Raina upstairs, but Raina wanted to go for a drive. After locking up, they climbed into Raina's Thunderbird, and sped away.

Despite the alcohol she had consumed, Raina thought her perceptions were startlingly clear. After crossing the bridge, they passed through New Hope in a flash.

Rafe gazed at Raina with preternaturally bright eyes and asked, "Where are you taking me?"

Raina threw up her arm and exclaimed, "To the wide open spaces!"

The moon was a smoldering, crimson knot in the sultry sky. The breezes conjured up by the speeding car cooled the flesh of the occupants but not their passion. Raina glanced at Rafe. It was amazing how much better looking he had gotten in the last few hours. Rafe stared back. The sharp breeze fanned her hair, spreading it apart into a golden aureole. In the vermilion moonlight her eyes looked fathomless. Except in the movies, Rafe had never seen such a beautiful young woman. He felt his hands go clammy and as inconspicuously as possible he wiped them on his pants.

With a jolt Raina turned off the main highway and onto a dirt road. The dust rose before the headlights like released spirits and then dust gave way to tall green stalks which surrounded the car like a forest.

Raina turned off the engine and sat up in her seat. "We're in a cornfield! What is this, the Road to Oz?"

"Let's find out," said Rafe with remarkable self-control.

They sat on the hood of the car sharing a bottle of tequila taken from the bar and watching the red moonlight as it turned the cornstalks into fingers of flame. A slight wind came up and rustled the leaves. "Listen," said Raina. "They're whispering about us."

"And what are they saying?"

"They're saying that we're about to do something outrageous."

"Are we?"

Raina lay back, her brilliant hair spilling across the hard red metal of the car. Rafe tossed aside the bottle of tequila and turned to look at her. She undid the zipper on the side of her dress, unfastened a hook, and the wrap-around dress opened like a cape.

"You didn't wear any underwear," he said hoarsely.

"It was too hot."

Rafe licked his lips as he cupped his hands over Raina's beautiful breasts. He massaged the flesh and felt the nipples grow hard under his touch. Then he slid his hands over her narrow waist, further and further down over her swelling hips, the perspiration from his palms leaving trails of moisture. He pressed his palms over her pelvis. Raina offered no resistance, but gave herself over to him for his complete exploration. Rafe's mouth went dry and his breath came in short gasps. He felt feverish, as if he were going to pass out at any minute. He swung around until he was positioned between Raina's outstretched legs. Then, using his elbows, he pushed her legs apart and moved his face closer. Her warmth burned his face like a recently stoked fire. . . .

They remained in the cornfield until the sun came up, filling the sky with a hard hot light and bringing with it the promise of yet another stifling day.

The late afternoon sun disappeared behind a mountain ridge. Raina removed her sunglasses, then glanced at her two friends. "Come on, guys. We're going to New York. How about a little team spirit."

"I brought the team spirit," announced Jana. "And since we're . . ." she glanced at a road sign, "almost there, I think it's time to break it out." She produced a large aluminum object from her oversized purse.

"What in the hell is that?" asked Kay. "A giant baked potato?"

Jana peeled away the aluminum, revealing a bottle of champagne. "I wrapped it up in tinfoil to keep it cold. I thought we'd drink it when we first saw New York."

The turnpike rose, carrying them to the crest of a hill. Suddenly the steep rock cliffs melted away and there, spread out before them like a gift, was New York City. The sky was rapidly deepening to violet, feathered with flamingo red. The buildings, now in silhouette, began flickering their lights.

After checking the rearview mirror, Raina pulled off the highway so that they could savor the breathtaking sight. Jana opened the champagne and filled three plastic cups she also had hidden in her bag. They sipped their champagne and stared at the magnificent panorama.

"I can't believe it," whispered Kay. "I simply can't believe it."

"I've never seen anything so beautiful in my life," said Jana.

Raina drained her glass. "I thought I was past being impressed."

"All those lights," said Kay. "You know, if you squint, you can almost imagine they're spelling out our names. Look, Raina, there's yours. And further right, Jana, see? J-A-N-A. And up above, flashing on and off like my heart must be at this very minute, if that doesn't say Kay then I'm crazy. You know, kiddos, I don't think we're in Kansas anymore."

Laughing, the young women began singing, "Follow the Yellow Brick Road" as they drove on to meet their respective destinies.

Part Two

Chapter Ten

The apartment building, located on Riverside Drive and Seventy-fourth Street, was sixteen stories high and occupied one-quarter of the block. It had a dowdy but not at all shabby grandeur and had survived the shifting economics of New York City since the turn of the century.

Clustered over the entranceway was a fanciful grouping of gargoyles, who stood sentinel despite the soot and the rudeness of the pigeons. They gave the observant resident or visitor a sense of security. The lobby, a conglomeration of marble, mirror and mahogany, gave testimony to the solemn nobility of another age. The four elevators, which had been converted to automatic some fifteen years ago, resembled giant gilt birdcages. The building was further watched over by a coterie of doormen. Their uniforms were shiny with wear, their epaulettes somewhat tarnished; nonetheless, these elderly gentlemen lent an air of continuing elegance to the faded majesty of the building.

The apartment on the fifteenth floor occupied by Jana, Raina and Kay was a real bargain. It was rent controlled and cost just two-hundred and sixty-seven dollars per month, including utilities. Raina's father had used his influence with a New York businessman friend who also controlled a certain amount of real estate on the West Side. The man put his private secretary to work on finding an apartment in one of his buildings that would be affordable to three struggling young actresses and also of a size to allow each of them

privacy. Raina had emphasized to her father that for
the sake of appearances the rent must conform with
the possible earning power of Jana and Kay and she had
insisted that each have her own bedroom.

The secretary made a thorough examination of her
employer's properties. An enormous apartment on Riverside Drive had become available through the recent
death of a widowed and once wealthy opera singer who
had lived there since 1931. The young women, even
though they were unaware of the apartment situation in
the city, were ecstatic with "their" find. The apartment
was freshly painted white throughout, new appliances
were installed and, unknown to Raina or the others, her
father had spent over a thousand dollars on tubs, trees
and shrubberies which were brought in to decorate the
terrace. The three young women naively assumed that
the service had been provided by the owner of the
building.

The rambling apartment consisted of a huge living
room, dining room, kitchen, three bedrooms, three
baths and a wraparound terrace which overlooked the
Hudson River.

The bright days of autumn and the solemn nights of
winter rushed by Jana, Raina and Kay as quickly as
time ever spent. Their appointment calendars were
crowded with reminders to send résumés, pick up pictures, meet so-and-so for lunch, attend auditions. Whatever free time was left Jana and Kay used for job hunt-
ing, Raina for dating. Jana found a job first—as a waitress in the famous theatrical restaurant, Joe Allen's.
Soon Kay was employed as a seamstress at the Eames
Costume House. And by the end of October Raina had
already gone through three lovers.

On Thanksgiving Day Jana made a duty call to her
mother. Kay had the operator trying to reach Fred in
Montreal the entire day, but with no success. Raina
pretended not to think of phoning her parents, who
hadn't bothered to call her either. That evening the

three treated themselves to Thanksgiving dinner at Luchow's mainly because the apartment, except for beds, was barren of furniture. A short time later another actress told Kay about "midnight shopping," a device many young theatre hopefuls employed to furnish their apartments. On Wednesday nights the people of the West Side put unwanted pieces of furniture out on the street. These items were collected during the night by the city sanitation men, but first they were thoroughly perused by the midnight shoppers. Kay had a difficult time convincing Jana to help her. Jana was embarrassed by midnight shopping. It meant putting on dark rain-coats and scouring the neighborhood for any worth-while pieces of furniture that had been discarded. Raina steadfastly refused to accompany them. Not only would dragging furniture off the street humiliate her, but also, as she declared, "There are rats as big as Buicks out there!"

By Christmas the apartment was on its way to be-coming an agreeable home. It was still sparsely furn-ished, but those pieces that Jana and Kay had so loving-ly repaired, refinished and recovered defied their orig-ins. Raina, who had come to recognize the inadvis-ability of blatant displays of financial largesse in the face of such efforts, deigned not to notice the gradual metamorphosis. But she secretly was happy to have a sofa to sit on and a table to hold her plate—without having to compromise anyone's pride.

New Year's Eve was a time for celebrating. Although Jana and Kay were working at jobs they hated, in the scheme of survival they did not dare think about that. And Raina had managed to get herself an agent. Their New Year's resolutions were short and typical of the makers.

Jana said: "This year I'm going to become a working actress and I'm going to get my Equity card."

Kay pronounced: "I'm going to get my own show to design and I'm going to go to Montreal to see Fred."

Raina vowed: "Seriously now, I'm giving up having affairs with men who can do nothing to further my career. After all, it's just as easy in a Cadillac as it is in the back of a Winnebago."

As strains of "Auld Lang Syne" drifted through the apartment, they held each other and cried. Although not one of them would admit it, they were still a little bit afraid of New York, their resolutions and the future.

Spring of 1967 came to New York several weeks before its scheduled date of appearance. Five days of cleansing rain preceeded the event, leaving the city washed and wrung out to dry. The clear blue sky, whimsically patterned with white clouds rimmed in gold, resembled a gigantic piece of freshly laundered material. Bright spots of green suddenly appeared on the barren trees of Riverside Park and tufts of grass pushed their way up through the sodden earth.

Kay, a gardening book in hand, rushed in from the terrace. "They're coming up! Almost all of them—my very own crocuses! Or is it croci?"

Jana, dressed in jeans and a large comfortable shirt, was in the process of stripping multiple layers of paint from a small oak table they had found on the street. She had a kerchief tied around her head and another around the lower part of her face, so she somewhat resembled a very young bandit. "What? What is it, Kay?"

"Come look. My flowers are coming up!"

Jana followed her friend onto the terrace and made the expected compliments over Kay's latest project. Tiny shoots were beginning to appear in an almost even line along the outer edges of redwood boxes containing privet hedges.

"I hope we don't get another spell of cold weather," said Kay. "The poor little things will freeze."

"Crocuses are pretty hearty. They've been known to grow right up through the snow."

"How's the table coming?"

"If I don't asphyxiate myself first, it's very nearly done. Once it's dried, I'll rub it with oil to preserve the wood."

Kay admired Jana's work. "It looks like the whole Playhouse experience wasn't in vain."

"If I can't get work as an actress, I can always take up furniture refinishing."

Kay looked at her friend with concern. "Don't worry, something will happen soon."

"Oh, I'm not complaining, really I'm not. I didn't expect it to happen overnight." She smiled. "But I also didn't expect so much competition. Every time there's an audition, hundreds of actresses show up . . . and I'm not even Equity yet. I'm talking about Off-Off-Broadway stuff."

Kay nodded. "I know, I know. Hell, I could design an Off-Off-Broadway show every week if I wanted to do it for free. But dammit, I've got to pay the rent. You really did a beautiful job on the table." Kay chewed her lower lip before asking carefully, "You didn't hear anything from La Mama?"

Jana shook her head. "No. They didn't even call me back."

"I thought the director liked you."

"He did until I told him I wasn't about to run around the stage in the altogether. Besides, it wasn't much of a script, just one of those anti-Vietnam things." Jana was immediately sorry for her remark. "Oh, Kay, I'm sorry. I didn't mean . . ."

"Forget it."

Jana sat down on the floor, put on a pair of stained rubber gloves, and began removing the rest of the blistered paint from a table leg. "Have you heard from Fred recently?"

"No," Kay replied sharply. Then, more softly, she added: "It's been almost three weeks now. What the hell, you can't carry on a romance through the post office. Letters never come on time. Besides, he can't come down here and I haven't been able to save enough mony to go up there. Even if I could get the time off from work."

"Kay, I told you I have a little money put aside . . ."

"No, Jana. I couldn't. I know that you're saving that

up to get more pictures taken. Besides, as I said, there's no way I can take off. I haven't been working there long enough." She sat on the couch. "Lord, if I thought I had nowhere to go but Eames Costume House, I'd kill myself. They treat us like a bunch of illegal aliens, wetbacks. I thought sweatshops were outlawed during the last century."

Jana turned to Kay. "I'm sorry, Kay. It must be very frustrating for you."

"No more so than you working at Joe Allen's as a waitress. I don't think I could do that."

"Well, at least I get to meet a lot of actors and producers. Of course, they all seem to have a one-track mind and it doesn't seem to have anything to do with my talent."

"Speaking of one-track minds, I take it Raina hasn't come home yet," Kay said as casually as possible. Then she picked up a dust rag and began dusting the random pieces of furniture scattered around the living room.

"Not yet," replied Jana, trying not to sound disapproving. "She must have stayed all night at Tony's."

"Undoubtedly she's working on getting free photo sessions for all of us," said Kay with a touch of sarcasm.

"Well, I hope she does. Tony Monteleone is one of the best photographers in town." Jana grinned. "I'd almost go to bed with him myself for a shooting."

"Don't talk dirty." Kay looked around. "Hmmm, there's nothing left to dust. We need some more furniture. We'll have to go 'midnight shopping' again." Jana scowled. As if reading Jana's mind, Kay said, "Get over it. None of us are famous yet."

Jana laughed. "It's just that . . . I keep thinking what my mother would say."

Kay looked around the room. "All in all, I think we've gotten some great bargains. A few more trips and we'll have the apartment completely furnished with all the latest antiques. Thank God you're handy at refinishing and I can sew and upholster."

"Yes," Jana conceded. "I must say that the pieces

don't look bad at all. Besides, I have to admit that
sometimes it's kind of fun.

"I just wish Raina would stop referring to the decor
as 'Early Salvation Army.' "

"Forget it. That's simply the way she is. Besides, she
contributes her share. All those expensive little things
she picks up at Bloomingdale's certainly give the place
a touch of much-needed class."

The big ginger cat that had been lying on one of the
window seats lifted his head. Deciding it was time to be
fed, he jumped down and did a turn around the floor,
rubbing first Kay and then Jana. When the girls had
arrived in New York they realized that they had "kidnapped" Sylvia's cat. They tried to call her several
times, but never got an answer. Then they unanimously
decided that he would be better off with them anyway.
Not knowing his former name, Kay christened him
Farouk after the fat, spoiled and self-indulgent former
king of Egypt. The name suited and the cat responded
to his new name immediately.

"Nothing for you, Farouk," said Kay affectionately.
"The way this cat eats, one of us better become a star
soon."

Farouk, finding that he wasn't going to get fed,
flipped his fat plume of a tail disdainfully and returned
to his place in the sun.

Kay sighed. "I'm so glad it's Saturday. If I had to
look at a sewing machine today, I think I'd take a dive
off the terrace." She asked Jana, "Do you have to work
tonight?"

Jana frowned and nodded. "I shouldn't gripe. Saturday night's the best tip night of the week. Did I tell you
I waited on David Merrick last Saturday?"

"Really? Did he ask about me?"

"Uh uh. He didn't ask about me either."

The telephone, a gold and white French model from
Bloomingdale's, began ringing. Kay cleared her throat
and answered in a brisk, businesslike fashion: "8684
. . . Miss Pendleton? . . . This is her answering service.
May I take a message?" Kay grabbed a pencil and be-

gan writing furiously. "Yes . . . yes, I have that . . . certainly, Mr. Gerard. I'll give her the message. Thank you." Kay slammed down the phone. "I don't believe it! That was Bradley Gerard, Raina's agent. He wants her to call him when she comes in. Maybe it's about that play in the Village she tried out for."

"It probably is," sighed Jana. "Raina seems to have all the luck. And she doesn't even try very hard."

"How did I sound as the answering service?"

"Very official. Maybe next month we can afford to get a legitimate one."

"And ruin my fun? Suppose Neil Simon comes up with a play about a telephone answering girl. I'll need the practice."

Jana removed the rubber gloves. "I'm afraid it's already been done. Don't you remember Judy Holliday in *Bells Are Ringing?*"

Kay snapped her fingers. "Well, I hope nobody's told Neil."

"Do you feel like some lunch?" Jana asked.

Kay nodded enthusiastically.

"What do you feel like?"

"Anything but yogurt."

Just then Raina entered the living room wearing a chocolate brown gown and looking very overdressed for that time of day. "Good morning, everyone."

Kay jumped up. "Raina, you just got a call from Bradley Gerard! He wants you to call him back."

"It's probably about that revue in the Village. I'll call him as soon as I've had some coffee. Is there any made?"

"I made some earlier this morning," said Jana. "There's plenty left."

Raina did a sixty-degree turn and surveyed the living room, which she seldom saw since she was rarely at home. "Well, isn't this precious . . . loving hands at home." She walked over to the table Jana had been working on and scowled. "Now *where* did you get this? W. J. Sloane, perhaps?"

Kay frowned. "Knock it off, Raina. Jana's worked

hard on that table and I think it looks fine. Can't you understand anything that doesn't have a price tag on it?"

Raina's eyes flashed. She opened her mouth to reply, but Jana interceded. "Uh, how was your evening, Raina?" she asked over-eagerly.

After making a show of brushing off the couch that Jana and Kay had hauled from Amsterdam Avenue, Raina collapsed. "If I see *Hair* one more time, I'll scream. Afterwards we did go to dinner at Sardi's and Tony introduced me to several people in *Cabaret*."

"Who, who?" the others demanded.

"I don't remember. I haven't seen the show yet. But Tony promised he'd take me as soon as he can get tickets. And if he can't get tickets, who can?"

"I was just about to make lunch," said Jana. "Would you like some?"

"No thanks, honey. I ate like a pig last night at Sardi's. I'm probably going to have to fast for three days just to get my figure back. Oh, I brought something for Farouk." She dug into her purse, withdrew a foil-wrapped packet, unfolded it and set in on the floor. "Shrimp, Farouk! I couldn't eat them all so I asked the waiter to give me a kitty bag."

The cat, drawn by the scent more than by Raina's attentions, hurried across the floor and began eating voraciously. "That's it, baby, gunge out! Maybe now you'll lay off the plants."

Kay brought Raina a cup of coffee. "Here. Hurry up and drink it. We're both dying to know what news Bradley has."

"Thanks, Kay." Raina lit a cigarette and sipped her coffee. "I've been thinking of dropping Tony for Brad. But don't worry, not until he takes pictures for our portfolios."

"Why, what's the matter?" asked Jana.

"Matter? There's nothing the matter. I'm just getting a little bored with him, that's all."

"Throw him my way," said Kay. "I think he's a hunk, an absolute hunk. Did you pick up the mail, Raina?"

"Nothing but a bill from Bloomingdale's. No letters from Canada. Well, I might as well call Brad and see what he wants." Jana and Kay clustered around the phone. "Hello, Brad? This is Raina. I just got the message that you called . . . Really? . . . They liked me? . . . Oh, I thought I was terrible. My throat was hoarse and you know how bad I am at cold readings . . . They really want me?" Raina clamped her hand over the receiver and whispered, "I got the part." Then: "What? What's that, Brad? Tonight? Yes, I did have plans but I can cancel them. What did you have in mind? *Hair?* No, I haven't seen it and I'd love to . . . Uh huh, Sardi's bar at seven-thirty. I'll see you then. And, Brad, thanks for everything. I'll try to think of some way to show my appreciation." Raina hung up the phone and burst into a scream of joy. "I got the part! I got the part!"

"The Off-Broadway show?" asked Jana.

"The one that's opening at the Village Barn. It's called *Bare Essentials.*"

"Isn't that the nude revue?" asked Jana.

"That's the one. Now I'll really have to go on a diet. Do you realize that this means I'll be able to join Equity?"

"Just for showing off your tits?" grinned Kay.

"First base, second base, the whole ball park!"

"Won't you be self-conscious?" asked Jana. "I mean going nude in front of all those people?"

"If I keep going the way I have, sooner or later most of the eligible bachelors of New York will have seen me in the raw anyway. Brad's taking me out tonight to celebrate. Oh no, now I've got to call Tony and make up some excuse to get out of our date. Let's see . . ."

"Why not tell him the truth, or at least part of it," suggested Jana. "Your agent wants to take you out to celebrate your getting the role. He should understand. It's business."

"Why, I never thought of telling the truth," grinned Raina.

*   *   *

Overhead the sky rumbled like the empty belly of a beggar. Lightning bounded across the New Jersey horizon and its sulphurous tang filled the night air.

A dark figure emerged from the alleyway between the buildings, and after looking first to the left and then to the right, stepped back into the shadows. After a few moments the person reappeared dragging a bulky form.

Kay stepped into the light puffing and pulling a rolled up carpet behind her. She eased it onto the sidewalk and attempted to hoist it onto her shoulder, but it fell and rolled open across the sidewalk. "Son-of-a-bitch!"

"Can I help you?"

"Gaaaah!" Kay screamed, and whirled around to face a strapping young man clutching a Sunday New York *Times*.

"Well, I—I—"

"Here, hold my paper." The young man bent over, rerolled the oriental rug, and effortlessly hoisted it to his shoulder. "Wait a minute! I should have asked where you live. You don't want me to carry this to the Bronx or somewhere, do you?"

Kay laughed. "Not at all, I live around the next block. Follow me."

When they passed the next streetlight Kay assessed the good deed doer. He had thick brown hair which was parted in the center and fell past his slightly prominent ears. His eyes were hidden by aviator-style glasses of a brown tint. His nose was broad, liberally sprinkled with freckles, and his chin pugnacious. His build was chunky. He was not unlike Fred. The young man caught her looking at him and he smiled, and that smile transformed his face to near handsomeness.

"I'm Alex Stafford."

"I'm Kay Kincade. I was just wondering whether I should invite you up for coffee. You don't look like a mad rapist."

"We mad rapists never do."

As they were crossing the street, a bag lady came shrieking out of the night. "That's my rug, you creeps! Where are you taking my rug? Give back my rug!"

Kay and Alex increased their speed to a trot, out-distancing the foul-mouthed harpie who stood in the center of the street cursing and screaming at full volume.

"Can't say I like your neighbors much," said Alex.

"She's harmless. Come on, it's in here. Hurry before she catches up to us." Kay opened the front door.

"Hey, this is a great old building. I tried to get an apartment in here but there's a waiting list."

"I didn't know that. Chalk up another one for Raina's dad." While they were going up in the elevator Kay told Alex about herself and her roommates and how they had come to get the apartment.

"And this is how you're furnishing it?"

"Sure thing. We've gotten our best pieces off the street."

Alex grinned. "I won't touch that line."

Kay and Alex sat gazing at the rug, which now lay on the living room floor. "I just can't fathom people throwing out a perfectly good rug," said Kay. "Except for that stain in the corner, it's in great shape. And after I clean up the whole thing I'll set a plant on that spot. Would you like coffee, or would you prefer beer, wine, or a drink?"

"I'd appreciate a beer. Hauling rugs is hot work."

As Kay handed Alex the beer she bluntly asked, "How come you're not in the war?"

Alex frowned. "You make that sound like an accusation." He removed his glasses and Kay clearly saw the small network of scars that surrounded his eyes like premature laugh lines. "I was there."

Kay lowered her gaze. "I'm sorry."

"Don't be sorry for me. I'm back. Be sorry for those poor bastards who're still there."

At that moment Kay knew that she was going to let Alex make love to her.

As Jana cleared the table her eyes searched the blue and white checkered cloth for some sign of a tip. She discovered it neatly hidden under a coffee cup. She picked it up and muttered an unseemly curse. The table of four had stayed over two hours and had left her a two dollar tip on a bill of thirty-one dollars and change. That wasn't even ten percent.

The bartender at the service bar noted Jana's sour expression and commented, "Tourists are always lousy tippers, Jana."

"How did you know they were tourists, Chris?"

"Who else would order Bloody Marys *after* eating?"

Jana regarded the young man and manufactured the expected smile. The bartender continued his conversation as he mixed a stinger. "So what's happening with your career?"

"What career, Chris? I'm doomed to be forever cast as a waitress. I'm beginning to wonder whether I'm ever going to get a show."

"You aren't Equity yet, are you?" She shook her head. "That makes it tough."

"Are you?"

"Yeah—Equity, SAG and AFTRA—the whole kaboodle. And here I am bartending in Joe Allen's."

"One of the girls said you were just in a show. Couldn't you be collecting unemployment?"

"Unemployment bores me. I've got to keep busy. Besides, I make better money here and it's a good place to make connections."

"Mmmm, that smells good. What is it?"

"A stinger—brandy and creme de menthe. They're lethal. Don't go away, I'll be back in a minute."

Jana watched him as he delivered the drink to a patron seated at the middle of the bar. Chris Callahan seemed to be the only male Jana had met lately who hadn't come on to her. Always pleasant and cheerful, Chris made Jana feel as if he truly liked her and not just her body. He was twenty-eight years old, tall, and goodlooking in a young matinee idol way. His résumé attested to his appearance as well as his talent: he'd been a dancing waiter in *Hello, Dolly* on Broadway, played the part of Patrick in the national tour of *Mame*, and Curly in the Music Circus production of *Oklahoma!* These were listed at the head of his credits.

Chris returned to Jana and picked up where he and her observations had left off. "I've had walk-ons on soaps, been in a Pepsi commercial, and I'm still waiting to be discovered. I'm a triple threat, but since the advent of *Hair* no one's looking for clean-cut types anymore. You've got to look very Haight-Ashbury. Ah, what the hell. This hippie thing will blow over and they'll want yours truly again . . . the boy next door!" Chris laughed. "Hell, we can't all go getting jobs. If every bartender, waiter and waitress in the Times Square area suddenly got lucky, it would be self-service time for the tourists! Say, Jana, why don't you come to a party with me after we get off?"

"I don't . . ."

"Don't say no yet. A lot of the kids who work in the neighborhood slinging hash and mixing drinks while they're waiting to be discovered will be there. It's a good place to meet people. You can pick up tips on stuff—what auditions are worth going to, who to avoid at the acting schools, where to get the best classes for the least money—that sort of thing." Chris leaned across the bar and smiled engagingly. "Besides, I'd like to get to know you better."

"It's already so late, Chris."

"Late? The night's just beginning. Jake will close out and I can leave at one-thirty. You only have one more table to see to and they're on their after dinner drinks." He gave her a hangdog expression. "If you don't come Vonda, the blonde bombshell in the coatroom, will be all over me. She wants my innocence, and I'm hanging onto that. Like any other all-American boy, I'm going to save myself for marriage."

Jana looked helplessly around the bar. Several waiters standing near the kitchen were watching her intently. Apparently they knew that Chris had been planning to ask her to the party. She wasn't about to let him lose face. "All right," she said finally. "I'll go, but only if you promise to protect my innocence as well as your own."

*   *   *

Despite urging from her agent, Raina declined to have anything more than cherrystone clams and a Russian vodka.

"Brad, if I'm going to be romping around stage in the nude I have to lose five pounds."

"Where, for God's sake?"

"Here, there, everywhere. I'm sitting on most of it."

"There's nothing wrong with your figure," Bradley argued. "At least have a steak. That's not fattening."

"No, Brad, I'm fine, really I am. Be a sweetheart and order another vodka for me while I repair my makeup."

An attentive waiter pulled out the table for Raina. Bradley watched his beautiful client as she walked through the main dining room at Sardi's, and he watched the people watching her. Ongoing conversations were forgotten and new ones started: Who was she? Almost everyone present was sure they had seen her somewhere before—on the cover of a magazine? In a Broadway show? Raina, tanned from lying on her terrace, was wearing a dress of rose silk. It was from Henri Bendel and featured a fringed stole and an uneven fringed hemline extending from mid-thigh to mid-calf.

Let them guess, thought Bradley. The girl will be a star soon enough. A nobody didn't walk with that kind of grace and self-assurance. Raina was meant to startle, not only with her beauty but also with her surprising talent.

Bradley had no illusions about *Bare Essentials*. It was a crude and tasteless show, but he believed it would run and make money. The main draw would be the public's current fascination with viewing their actors in the nude. Regardless, it was going to be a sensational beginning for Raina. Bradley was already negotiating with the producer to get her picture on the poster.

As Raina reappeared and approached the table he studied her. She looked as if she were about to accept a Tony Award. When she sat down, he moved closer to her until their thighs were touching. It was for the benefit of their audience as well as for himself. Raina smiled in mock surprise and Bradley felt that the time had come to mix business with pleasure.

"I've got Russian vodka at my place," he said softly.

"I thought you might."

Raina appraised her agent and dinner companion. Bradley Gerard was not a tall man, but few made remarks about his height. Having grown up on the lower East Side, Bradley had learned how to take care of himself both in business and on the street. He was sharp-featured with thick auburn hair and deep-set blue eyes that were never tranquil.

Raina sipped her drink and wondered if going to bed with Bradley would be a wise move. Then, casting caution aside, she decided why not? She was attracted to him and if things didn't work out she could always find another agent. Good lovers were at a premium and agents were not.

Raina said, "You're married, aren't you, Brad."

He looked at her with surprise. "How did you know?"

"You smell married. You'd never pick out that cologne for yourself. What is it? White Shoulders?"

He laughed. "The family lives in Connecticut. I maintain my own apartment here in town and, frankly, I was wondering if you'd like to engage in a sordid little affair."

"I was hoping you'd ask."

"In anticipation of your positive response, Russian vodka and a tin of Beluga caviar await your pleasure."

"The pleasure," Raina replied softly, "will be all yours."

Chapter Eleven

Within six weeks, every New Yorker and practically every tourist had seen Raina's much publicized face and form on the *Bare Essentials* poster. Twice a week they were pasted up in subways, on kiosks, telephone poles, construction fences, and across the windows of abandoned buildings. It was executed in warm colors and the artwork was in the psychedelic style of Peter Max. Raina was positioned in the center of the layout wearing nothing but a sheet and an insouciant expression. She was posed looking over her right shoulder, eyes looking directly at the camera and thus the viewer, her marvelous hair wind-blown by the photographer's fan. She held up behind her a pink satin sheet that fell just below the crests of her buttocks. Her right arm covered the tip of her right breast. The photographer had used backlighting so that her shapely form was silhouetted against the material. *Bare Essentials* had been painted on the sheet in hot red letters outlined in black that caught the public's eye nearly as quickly as Raina did. The poster wouldn't win any art director's awards but it did grab more attention than any other theatrical poster of that season.

The posters were sold at novelty stores, head shops, and penny arcades throughout the city. Even T-shirts were printed up and were worn by many people as an act of defiance against the "Establishment." The *Bare Essentials* posters were eventually exported to the major cities of the United States and became as important to collectors as those announcing popular rock concerts.

The poster, as well as the show, was denounced by an impressive number of clerics who couldn't come to grips with the current notion of nudity on the stage as a prerequisite to entertainment. But the publicity did not adversely affect the lines at the box office.

The producers of *Bare Essentials,* knowing full well that the critics would blast the production, kept the show in previews, which meant that the critics could not review the show until there was an official opening night. This added to the notorious publicity of the musical and tickets were sold out months in advance.

A few critics did manage to slip into *Bare Essentials* and their reviews were scathing. While they mentioned that the cast was certainly game and attractive in the buff, they denounced the sketches and songs, all of which dealt with sex in one form or another. The vapid numbers paid homage to everything from masturbation to group sex, and never used a euphemism for a four-letter word. Some members of the audience were shocked, others were outraged. Refunds were demanded and as long as the incidents were reported by the show business wags, the producers were only too glad to comply. Despite the fact that the show had never officially opened, productions were planned for Los Angeles, Chicago, Las Vegas, and four foreign countries. In brief, *Bare Essentials* was a smash hit.

Because of Raina's importance to the show, she was signed to a six-month contract with an option for six more.

Raina, unused to the discipline of performing eight shows a week, as well as the boredom of playing the same part over and over, became discontented after two months and wanted out of the contract. The producers were adamant about keeping her in the cast and Bradley advised her that there was no way he could sever the agreement. As headstrong as ever, Raina dropped her agent/lover and began looking for other means to get out of the show.

The same summer, using a contact of Chris's, Jana was auditioned for an Off-Broadway show entitled *The*

Games of War. It was an antiwar musical and boasted a rock score by the popular writer and performer Eric Jacobson. The story concerned a patriotic college girl who falls in love with a radical who is the head of the SDS on campus. Using her love as a lever the heroine turns the boy around and convinces him to join the service. When he's killed, her beliefs in the validity of the war are shattered.

As soon as Jana read the script, she knew that it was poor. But it was her chance to be in an Off-Broadway show, and thereby get her Equity card. And that meant she could take a most welcome leave of absence from waitressing at Joe Allen's.

Because of Eric Jacobson's reputation, the show had an unprecedented Off-Broadway budget of one hundred thousand dollars. But as soon as rehearsals had started it was clear to everyone concerned that the show was in trouble. New script writers were brought in and a string of directors were hired and fired in rapid succession. Choreographers were switched as well as scene and costume designers. During all this pandemonium Jana kept her spirits of professionalism, even though she was handed new songs and new scenes daily. Near the end of the rehearsal period she couldn't honestly say whether or not the production would be successful since it had changed so many times since she'd first read it.

Throughout this trying period, Jana's friendship deepened with Chris. She had little available time, but that which she did have was spent with him. Their relationship was more a platonic friendship than a romance; Chris felt that it would be better to wait until the show opened before further complicating Jana's life. Jana was relieved to have the impending affair put off for as long as possible. She was so involved with the show that she was not sure of her true feelings for Chris and just how far they would take her.

The summer of 1967 was also a time of opportunity for Kay. Revues were very much the rage. Many of these small-scaled shows—usually consisting of six performers and a lone piano going through their paces in some dingy firetrap—started Off-Off-Broadway. Producers whose conservative tastes had been put to rout by the advent of *Hair* went scurrying to the lofts, warehouses and saloons scattered throughout the city in search of possible prospects. They endured held curtains, hard seats and usually abominable displays of non-talent. Occasionally there was an exception, and *Raspberries* was one of those exceptions.

Early in July Kay decided she was never going to get anywhere in design if she continued to work at Eames Costume House. After leaving she landed a plum freelance position as a seamstress for a chic East Side boutique. She would only have to work half the time for the same salary, thus giving her the freedom to try to establish herself as a costume designer.

Armed with portfolio and panache, Kay set out to find her play. Most of her forays proved disappointing. Many of the Off-Broadway calls took her to a variety of grubby makeshift theatres that were breeding grounds for self-indulgence.

Then in a loft on Fourteenth Street Kay watched a rehearsal in progress of the musical revue entitled *Raspberries.* Six performers, a three-piece band and an energetic director were hard at work creating a fast-paced revue that satirized sex, politics, and life in New York City. Later she spoke to the director, who told her that not only did they not have a designer, but that what very little money they had to spend on costumes was coming out of his own pocket.

Kay liked the director and the cast. Following her instincts, she agreed to do the show, which was scheduled to open in the middle of August.

After watching more rehearsals, Kay conferred with the director, made preliminary notes and then went home to work all night on designs that would be effective, efficient, and inexpensive.

Although she had not slept, by morning Kay was filled with the kind of exhilaration one experiences through lone creativity. She had never questioned her talent, even though she was often unsure of herself in other areas. She enjoyed her work and ultimately found it more satisfying than anything else in her life. Over black coffee and a dish of fresh fruit, Kay estimated the cost of the materials required for her production. While at Eames she had learned where to find the best buys in the city on materials and trimmings. She'd also hoarded some eye-catching odds and ends bound for the Costume House's incinerator—a papier-mâché breast plate, a pirate's hat decorated with ostrich plumes, a paste-pearl and rhinestone tiara, a yellow silk parasol with an ivory handle. She was able to work many of these items into her costume scheme.

The set-up of the revue was perfect. The opening number introduced the six actors as themselves. While putting on makeup and dressing for the show they complained in song about the state of the theatre. In particular they referred to the nudity, vulgar language, and coarse actions foisted upon them by their directors and producers in order to shock, startle and seduce the public. Kay decided to dress the cast all in black and build her character images from there, using only suggestive accessories such as hats, feather boas, capes, gloves, vests, petticoats and the like. These pieces would be placed on coat racks and hung from the ceiling. She envisioned them onstage throughout the production so that the costumes would provide a motley setting of sorts. The actors, if the director agreed, would change accessories onstage before the audience.

She tidied her sketches and signed each of them. She had designed more than half the numbers in the show. Then she phoned her director to set up a meeting for that afternoon.

The Labor Day weekend of 1967 found New York in the grip of an unprecedented heat wave. Crime was up and water was low, and air-conditioning units were breaking down faster than soap opera heroines.

Raina was in a foul mood. Her bedroom air-conditioner—the only one in the apartment—had burned out. She'd spent an uncomfortable night, lying on clammy sheets damp with her own perspiration. Had she not been between lovers, she would have spent the night in someone else's apartment, but pride had kept her from calling any of her previous boyfriends. She had taken a cold shower, but within minutes she was as damp and sticky as if she hadn't showered at all.

Kay and Jana were in the living room attempting to get a fresh breeze from the floor fan they had placed in front of the terrace doors, but the sun was too hot and the air was too still. Jana was studying new scenes for her show, which was continuing in previews. Once again the opening date had been set back. Now it was September tenth. Kay was reading scripts submitted to her from a handful of Off-Broadway producers who had admired her work in *Raspberries*. That show had been optioned by a producer and there was talk of moving it to a West Side nightclub.

They both glanced up as Raina entered. Raina sniffed irritably. "Hasn't that goddam air-conditioning man shown up yet?" They shook their heads. "He said first thing in the morning. It's one o'clock," she growled.

Neither Jana nor Kay commented. Raina had become very difficult to live with because of her own increasing dissatisfaction with her contract and her inability to get out of *Bare Essentials*. After her breakup with Bradley Gerard, Raina had a brief fling with a local newscaster, but had dropped him as soon as he'd gotten her a few brief interviews on television. Once she'd exploited him to the limits of his contacts, she saw no point in continuing the relationship.

Jana and Kay could overhear Raina in the kitchen making a loud, demanding phone call to the air-conditioning repair service. She let go with a string of oaths that made even Kay blush. Then she slammed down the receiver and returned to the living room carrying a cup of coffee and a bag of miniature donuts.

"The son-of-a-bitch told me he'd be here before the

day's out. Damn, I've got to leave for the theatre by six-thirty. Will either of you be in?"

Jana said, "I'll be at rehearsal myself."

Kay added, "I have a meeting with a producer."

Raina viciously stabbed a donut into her coffee cup and ate it. Kay asked, "What are you trying to do? Lose your figure?"

"That's exactly what I'm trying to do. If I can't get out of the contract any other way, I'll put on so much weight they'll have to fire me."

"Raina, you can't do that," cried Jana. "You've only get a few more months to go."

"I cannot stand doing that show for that length of time. Can't you understand? I'm sick of it!" She slammed down her coffee cup.

Some coffee spilled over and stained the rug. "I'm sorry," Raina muttered.

Kay shot out of her seat and strode to Raina. *"You're* sick of it!" she said through clenched teeth. "It's always what *you're* sick of. Well I want to tell you how sick I am of your incessant complaining. That tacky little bare-assed show has made you a celebrity. Why, you're the envy of every young actress on Broadway. Nobody forced you to accept the part or to sign that contract, Raina. You committed yourself. *You* did!"

"Go on, Kay," said Raina coolly. "You've started. You might as well finish."

"Damn right I'm going to finish! You talk about other rôles, more demanding parts. Let me tell you something, Miss Pendleton. You couldn't begin to handle them. I think your attitude is abominable, your reasoning lousy and your manners unendurable. What a contrast you and Jana make. She's down there busting her butt trying to do anything she can to make the show a hit. Learning new lines, learning new dances. Why, she does more work in a day than you do in a week down at the Village Barn with your tits hanging out. And while we're on the subject of your tits hanging out, it's not our fault that you don't have a relationship going or that your air-conditioner broke down, or any of the thousand and one other things that you take out on us. You've become a horror to live with."

Raina, controlling her temper, regarded Jana calmly. "Do you agree with our astute friend?" she asked.

Jana hesitated, then said carefully, "Yes, I do. I knew there were many things you were not, Raina, but I always thought you were a trouper. I don't always approve of you, but I love you very much, just as Kay does. You've no right to take our affection for you and abuse it. You seem to think that nobody has any problems but you. I assume that's the way you were brought up. But things are different here in the big city. If you just bothered to look around you, you'd see that everybody has to do things they don't particularly want to do. I'm disappointed in you. I thought you had more style. I don't care if you don't like the show. As Kay said, you accepted the part and it's done very well for you. Besides, you *owe* something to your fellow performers, to the crew people, the director, the producers, and most of all to your audiences. You're being paid to perform, to perform the best you know how. I know that you've been walking through the part."

"How do you know that?" Raina interrupted sharply.

Jana brushed aside a strand of hair that was sticking to her forehead. "Everybody in theatre knows what's going on with the shows. Reports get around. Don't do this to yourself. Don't make producers afraid to hire you."

Raina angrily bit into another donut. "And who fed you these reports? Your precious little boyfriend, Chris Callahan?" Jana smarted. "He's just jealous because he tried out for the show and wasn't hired."

"I'm glad he wasn't," Jana replied unthinkingly, "I wouldn't want Chris romping about the stage in the nude. He's too good a person for that."

Raina threw back her head and laughed. "You little hypocrite. Yes, hypocrite! Chris is too good to be in a nude show, you're too good. Who the hell do you think you are, Mary and Joseph? Hah! That's good. Joseph didn't sleep with Mary either."

Kay threw down her script. "Now you're hitting below the belt, Raina. How dare you judge Jana's sex life by your own? Why, I admire her decision to wait a while before hopping into bed with Chris."

"Who are you to admire anything? Aside from your fling with that coward in Canada, and a dalliance with the number you picked up off the street, what the hell experience have you had? You don't even know the first goddam thing about men!" Raina sputtered.

"My values are not your values, Raina. I don't screw to get somewhere." Raina drew back as if she had been slapped. She gasped and lowered her eyes. "You damn dope," Kay added more gently, "the pathetic thing is you don't even have to do that. You can make it on your own. Lord knows, you're on your way already. Just as Jana and I are. You have looks, you have talent, you have money." She grinned ruefully. "All you lack is morals."

Raina lifted her head and replied evenly. "Well if you don't like my morals, Kay, you can just move out of this apartment." She snapped her head to Jana. "You too, Miss Goody Goody Gumdrop."

It was Jana's turn to raise her voice. "You'd better quit while you're ahead, Raina. You've no right to call Fred a coward. I can't believe you mean that. I think he's doing the brave thing by opposing the war. And as for either Kay or I moving, let me remind you of something. *All* of our names are on the lease. If you're unhappy here, you move. I don't give a damn that your father's influence got this apartment; you've used up all our gratitude. We've made this apartment a home, Kay and I. We've spent hours of hard labor planting and painting, sewing and fixing, and we're proud of our efforts, even if you're not."

Raina bit down on her lower lip but said nothing. Jana went on. "Kay's right. Our morals are not the same. I would never criticize yours . . . if they made you happy, but they don't. You're taking our your unhappiness on us. There are two things I admire in a human being, Raina. It's not intelligence or beauty, certainly not family background or money. The only two worthwhile things are kindness and talent. You have the latter and you used to have the former. What's happening to you? I'd like to think that you need us." She paused and added in a softer voice, "Just as we need you."

At that, Raina burst into tears and ran from the living room. Jana started to go after her, but Kay restrained her. "Let her alone for a bit. This storm has been brewing for quite awhile. Give her some time to sort things out."

"I don't like to be harsh, Kay, but I've just reached the end of my rope with her temper tantrums."

"You weren't harsh. Neither was I. We may have put things a little roughly, but they had to be said. We're all under a tremendous amount of pressure and what with this heat and all, some kind of blow-up was bound to happen. I only hope Raina takes it to heart."

The young women went back to their reading. A short time later they realized they were sitting in semi-darkness. They looked up simultaneously. The sky had suddenly grown black and a sharp breeze whipped the gauzy curtains on the terrace doors into a frenzy. They rushed out to the terrace, and the breath of welcome wind touched their flesh and whispered rain.

"The heat wave is going to break!" cried Kay.

"Thank God," said Jana. "I was beginning to feel as nasty as Raina."

They were aware of movement behind them. They turned and saw Raina's hand poking around the door frame rattling a bag of donuts. She stepped out looking embarrassed and ashamed. "I didn't have an olive branch," she said contritely. "Please forgive me, both of you. I've been a terrible bitch."

They rushed to Raina and embraced her. The sky opened up and suddenly it began raining. The girls, enjoying the cooling drops of moisture against their skin, held onto one another and basked in their reconciliation.

A short time later they were sharing the donuts over heavily creamed and sugared coffee. "To hell with our diets," offered Kay. "We're here, we're together, . . . and we're working!"

Chapter Twelve

Kay emerged from the subway station at Seventy-second Street and Broadway. The rain had turned the weather milder and she was wearing a stylish trenchcoat she had made herself. As usual she carried a huge leather bag stuffed with sketching materials, fabric swatches, makeup, several paperbacks—she had recently become addicted to gothics and went through them like tissues —and a three-page contract that gave her her very own Off-Broadway show.

She felt confident that she had made a good choice in signing on as costume designer of a new rock musical entitled *Hallelujah*. It was set in New York's lower East Side and concerned a free-wheeling young street musician who discovers he has the gift of healing. The hero then sets out to cure the afflicted among the poor and the minorities. Once his success becomes known, he is oppressed by a hostile society.

The book of the musical had immediately appealed to Kay. In her opinion, it illustrated the conflict of values between the burgeoning "counter-culture" of the day and the "Establishment." Despite its heavy message, she found the dialogue warm and amusing. She was also completely taken by the rock score, which had been written by two young newcomers to the theatre scene. Meetings with the director, set designer, lighting man and others connected with the production had further confirmed her opinion that she had picked a winner.

She swung her bag back and forth as she headed

toward the Red Apple supermarket. Both Jana and Raina were working that evening and she had invited Alex to dinner. It would just be the two of them. Kay hurried through the supermarket selecting items for a plain and healthful meal for her and her hard-working new lover. Alex was now employed as a stunt man for a TV police series that was being filmed in New York City. Despite a certain amount of danger connected with the job, Alex enjoyed the robust work and the high salary.

Turning down Seventy-fourth Street, Kay hummed the musical theme from the new show. She was immensely happy. She was pleased with the success of her friends, her plants were thriving, and her affair with Alex was warm and satisfying. The only sadness she experienced came from confused feelings concerning Fred Spangler. They still wrote to one another at least once a month, but the letters were no longer declarations of love. Rather they had gradually become letters of friendship, and despite her disappointment Kay was glad that they remained in touch.

As she reached her building she checked for the mail and found that neither Raina nor Jana had picked it up. While in the elevator she began flipping through the various envelopes. There was a letter from her father, she noticed with surprise. Her parents almost never wrote.

After scanning the notes left to her on the kitchen blackboard by her roommates, Kay unpacked the groceries, opened a can of Tab and sat down at the kitchen table to read her father's letter. It was a single page written on notebook paper. Her eyes quickly took in his words.

"Mom is sick . . . heart condition . . . must come home. . . ."

"Now why in the hell didn't he call?" muttered Kay. She poured her Tab into a glass, uncharacteristically added a shot of vodka, and drank nearly half of it. The liquor eased her anxieties. She picked up the kitchen phone and, surprised that she could still remember it, dialed her home number.

The phone was answered after six rings. "Terry, this is Kay . . . Kay . . . I'm fine. How are you? . . . Look, is pop there? . . . Why didn't you call me about mom? You could have called collect. When did all this happen? How serious is it? . . . Of course, it's complicated by high blood pressure! . . . Pop, pop, I can't come home right now. I've just signed a contract for my first Off-Broadway show. . . . What? What do you mean, come home and take care of things? I have a life of my own. . . . So get a nurse. . . . Dammit, you *can too* afford it. You know you can. Pop, I'm not coming home. As soon as this show's up, I'll fly down and see mom, but don't get the idea that I would even consider staying. . . . It is *not* my place. What do you think I'm working so hard for—to wind up as my parents' cook and housekeeper? Pop, you don't seem to realize, I'm going to be designing an Off-Broadway show. I'm twenty years old, I've been in New York thirteen months, and I've got my own Off-Broadway show."

She pressed her forehead against the wall. "Pop, look, I'm sorry we can't see eye-to-eye on this, but bickering about it long-distance won't help anything. Just give mom my love, and tell her I'm glad she's feeling better. As soon as I possibly can I'll fly down for a weekend."

After some awkward and mutually hostile farewells were exchanged, Kay slammed down the phone and pounded her head against the wall. "Lord, they must be from another planet!" Finally the tears came. She blew her nose on a paper towel and finished her drink. "Damn, I wish Raina or Jana were here."

After a good cry, but still very upset, Kay began cleaning the greens for the salad. When she had finished that, she marinated the steaks, then put the asparagus to soak in salty water. The kitchen clock read four-fifteen and Alex wasn't due until six or so. She straightened up the living room, cleaned off the table on the terrace, placed charcoal in the barbeque.

The telephone rang and Kay braced herself, thinking it was a call back from her father. "Oh, Alex, I was just thinking about you," she said with relief. . . . "No, six-thirty will be fine. But don't be any later. There's something I want to discuss with you . . . No, nothing to do with us . . . Wine? Bring red. We're having steak . . . O.K., see you later."

As Kay began cleaning the asparagus, she kept a running conversation with herself. "Dammit, I'm doing the right thing. This is my big chance. Oh dear, I sound like something out of an MGM musical. Anyway, I'm not going to go home and slop the hogs, that's for sure." Kay mixed herself another drink, then filled the tub with hot water and added fragrant bath salts. As she soaked she reread her contract several times over. Her mind told her that she was doing the right thing, but it took a little longer to convince her heart.

After each performance of *Bare Essentials* the cast was expected to greet their audience as they were leaving the theatre. This was not in itself an unusual occurrence, except that in the case of this particular production the cast members were completely nude. In the beginning Raina had difficulty with this segment of the show. Even though she had no inhibitions about being nude on stage, the close proximity of the audience made her nervous. In particular, she was afraid that somebody might touch her that she didn't want to touch her. After the show had been in performance several weeks, these fears were allayed. The audiences were in general more self-conscious than the performers. Eventually the entire charade bcame a source of amusement to Raina and she found that she actually looked forward to the display.

The actors had been instructed to vary their positions throughout the auditorium. On one particular night, Raina was closest to the exit door. She usually wasn't aware of individual people. They were just a blur of forms and faces, handshakes and comments.

"Aren't you afraid you'll catch a cold?" Raina's eyes

focused on a good looking man in his mid-thirties with dark hair and smooth features. He took her hand and squeezed it warmly. "I enjoyed your performance very much." He dropped his voice, "I wish I could say the same for the rest of the show."

"Thank you," Raina responded.

"Do you have an agent at present?"

"No, I don't, but . . ."

"I'm Lucas Balaban." He pressed a card into her hand. "Perhaps you'll be so kind as to give me a call tomorrow. I'd like to discuss your future."

"Why yes, of course," Raina stammered. "I'll be glad to."

Raina turned the card over in her hand. The card was not printed, but richly embossed.

Raina knew of Lucas Balaban. He was one of the top theatrical agents in New York City. As she sat down at the dressing table to remove her makeup, she began to reflect. What if she had been walking through the part that night? What if he had seen her on one of her frequent off-nights? No card and no interest in her career would have been forthcoming. She silently thanked Jana and Kay for their good advice. Raina felt like celebrating, but her generally negative attitude had alienated her fellow actors, she was heartily sick of all the lecherous men of her acquaintance, and Kay was involved with Alex while Jana would be tied up late at rehearsal. Raina faced an evening alone. After a quick shower and an application of street makeup, Raina set off across Sixth Avenue in search of a convivial bar.

The Hayloft was incongruously located in the basement of a red brick building on Christopher Street. Previously it had been a gay bar called Aunt Edna's. It now catered to straight Village singles. The decor was pseudo-rustic and the waitresses wore cowgirl outfits complete with fringed vests and ten-gallon hats. The bar was crowded but not jammed. The pink and orange lighting was designed to flatter the most city-pale face.

Raina spotted an empty stool toward the far end of the bar and went to claim it. She looked in the mirror opposite her and was pleased by her reflection. Without turning her head, Raina could feel that several people were already staring at her. The bartender, who resembled Tex Ritter both in appearance and costume, asked for her order. Raina closed her eyes and quickly tried to decide what she felt like having.

"Something sweet, I think. A vodka stinger on the rocks."

The drink arrived, and as she was sipping it a voice to her left said, "Haven't I seen you someplace before?"

Without looking Raina answered. "Haven't I heard that line somewhere before?"

"No, really," the voice persisted. "I have. I'm positive I have."

Raina turned and smiled at the young man. He was swarthy, Italian-looking, and very sexy. "Have you seen *Bare Essentials?*"

He started to shake his head, then the expression on his face changed to one of delighted surprise. "Hey, hey, that's where I've seen you. You're the girl on the poster. You're in the show. I haven't seen it yet, but I've seen you *everywhere.*"

"It's not a very good show."

"Are you still in it?" Raina nodded. "Then I'll have to catch it for you. Can I buy you another drink?" Raina looked down and was surprised to find she had already finished her stinger.

"Why not?"

The drink arrived and the young man asked, "Are you celebrating?"

"Yes, I guess I am."

"Is it personal or can you tell me what's the occasion? Your birthday?"

"Oh no, not my birthday. But I'm going to be leaving the show soon and I'm happy about that. Plus I just met an agent tonight who's interested in handling me. Lucas Balaban. He's very well known and has a great reputation."

"I don't know him."

Raina smiled and said not unkindly, "I take it you're not in show business."

"Nope, but I appreciate it. I really do appreciate it. I like to see shows. Did you see *Hair?*" Raina stifled a groan. "I thought it was terrific."

"I liked it too . . . the first time."

"How many times have you seen it?"

"I've lost track. It seems like every guy I ever went out with had a friend who had a friend who could get tickets for *Hair*. I've been sunshined out."

"Isn't your show something like *Hair?* I mean don't you all . . . strip?"

"That's all it is—a strip show."

Nervously licking his lips, the young man replied, "I'll have to catch you before you leave." Another round of drinks was ordered and this time Raina insisted on paying. They introduced themselves. Her drinking companion's name was Nick Bartolini, who worked as a telephone repairman.

"Yes, ma'am," Nick exclaimed eagerly. "I sure would like to see you in that show."

Raina, feeling the effects of the stingers, replied airly, "I'll give you my number and one night next week you'll be my guest."

Nick grinned crookedly. "Say now, that certainly is nice of you, Raina." He had made his remark with such an odd inflection that Raina turned to look at him. He laughed easily. "Yes, that certainly is nice. Hey, we're empty again." He waved his hand in the air. "Bartender. Two thirsty people down here."

"What's that you're drinking?" asked Raina, fascinated by the glass of varicolored liquids.

"A tequila sunrise. Want to try it?"

Raina sipped the drink. "Mmmm, that's good. Maybe I'll switch to that after I've finished my stinger."

Later, through a blur of alcohol, Raina asked, "Nick, would you like to see me home?"

He smiled that funny smile again as he slowly shook his head. "No, I don't think so, Raina. But I'll tell you what. I'll let you see me home."

"You're very sure of yourself," she replied. "What's that thing sparkling on your earlobe?"

Nick turned. "It's a fishhook. I like to catch fish." A gold-plated hook pierced his left earlobe; hanging from it were two small red feathers like large drops of blood.

Arm in arm they unsteadily made their way down Seventh Avenue toward Nick's apartment. It was a fourth floor walk-up. When Nick opened the door, Raina, even though she was drunk, was struck by the rank odor. He switched on the light and she looked around. It was a very small apartment consisting of one room, a pullman kitchen and a bath—and it was filthy, cluttered with piles of newspapers, dirty dishes and scattered clothes. Sheets were tacked over the windows and roaches skittered across the sink. Raina grimaced. "I can't stay. . . ."

The rest of her sentence was cut off by Nick's impassioned lips. Raina struggled and gasped for air as his teeth pressed hard against her unyielding mouth. Finally he released her. "Look," she said. "I can't stay here. You can come back with me if you want, or let's put it off until another time. It's just too. . . . How can you *live* like this?"

Nick stepped back against the door and, smiling, threw the bolt. "Don't be so shy, Raina. What have you got to be shy about? You dance around naked onstage. Come on, now dance around naked for me."

"I'm not staying here," snapped Raina and started for the door.

He grabbed her shoulders and slammed her against the wall. "You're not going anywhere!" he said harshly. "Do you like dancing in the nude, Raina? *Do you?*" His eyes were glowing with angry passion and tiny veins stood out on his forehead. Raina pulled away from him.

Her body was shaking and she was seething with outrage. "How—dare—you!" she said between clenched teeth. "Get out of my way, you animal!"

Nick drew back his hand and a stinging slap landed across Raina's cheek. She spun around and fell against the folding door of the kitchen. "You bastard!" she screamed. She ran at him and returned the slap with equal force. Nick grabbed her hands and tried to force her down to the floor. Raina brought her knee up into his stomach as hard as she could. The pain from the blow caused him to fall to his knees as he released her. She started across the room but he grabbed her by the ankle. "Slut!" he roared. "Slut! Slut!" His strong fingers dug into the flesh of her calf as he dragged her toward him. Raina's fingers clawed at the dirty covers of the bed but to no avail. She could not hold herself back. She grabbed hold of an empty bottle of liquor that was lying on the floor. Just as he was about to place his fingers around her throat, she hit him on the side of the face. He released her and she crawled away. He rolled over on the floor clutching his head and moaning. Blood ran down from his temple in a thin red ribbon.

"You bitch! You stinking bitch! You hurt me."

Raina eased along the wall, trying to get to the door. She glanced down and gasped. He was exposing himself, and he had an erection. He was smiling at her. The whites of his eyes were red and his pupils were dilated.

"Come on, puss," he said in a musical voice. "Dance for Nicky. Show him how you can dance."

He started coming toward her. "Nick, don't you dare come any nearer, or I'll scream down the walls and have the cops on you."

"Oh, she likes to scream," he said with an almost happy expression on his face.

Raina bumped against the dresser. The hard edge of the wood dug into her back. With her hands behind her she searched for something to throw at him and found a heavy glass ashtray. She pitched it across the room. It missed Nick's shoulder by inches, crashed to the wall and fell to the floor.

"Puss, puss . . ." For the first time Raina knew what it was to fear a man. *"Puss!"*

Nick was advancing and Raina's heart was beating

wildly. She frantically looked about for an escape route, rushed to the window and pulled down the dusty sheet covering it.

The windows were painted black.

"Here, puss, puss." He started to leap for her. Raina jumped aside and ran toward the bathroom door. Her trembling hands found the doorknob. She turned it and dashed inside, slammed it behind her and threw the bolt.

"Come on out, puss, come on out to daddy." Raina looked wildly around the bathroom and groaned in defeat. There was no window. "Come out, come out, wherever you are!" She could hear his fingernails scratching against the thin plywood door.

"Puss, puss," he crooned insanely and began beating at the door with his fists. The thin plywood began splintering. Raina's eyes fell upon a large bottle of ammonia on the floor near the edge of the bathtub. She grabbed the bottle and climbed up onto the sink, which was to the left of the door. Her feet slipped in the sink and she almost lost her balance, but caught herself on the towel rack. She began unscrewing the light bulb and leaned against the wall, watching in horror as the door continued to shatter. He was using his shoulders as a battering ram.

"Pusssss!" Nick bellowed. The center of the door split open with a sickening sound. Then she saw his clutching fingers reaching through to turn on the light. He clicked the switch several times, and when it didn't go on, he half groaned, half growled with satisfaction. Nick leaned back and began kicking at the middle panel of the door. Piece by piece it fell apart, landing on the tile floor of the bathroom. He could see inside now. The shower curtain was drawn. He assumed that Raina was cowering behind it. "Here, puss, puss," he breathed wetly. "Here, puss." Nick was inflamed with anticipation. How much fun it was going to be to rip down the shower curtain. The blood pulsed in his veins and his erection throbbed with perverse excitement. He savored each and every second, putting off the moment of pleasure for as long as possible. Finally he reached inside the doorframe, unlatched the door, and stepped inside.

"Here, puss, puss. . . ."

Raina brought the ammonia bottle down on his head with all the force she had. It broke and the burning liquid ran down over his forehead and into his eyes. Nick let out a shriek of agony and staggered forward. He grabbed the shower curtain and the plastic cloth ripped from the hooks as he fell into the tub. Raina jumped from her perch and ran into the main room. She heard the water running and glanced over her shoulder. She saw that Nick was rinsing the ammonia out of his eyes.

Raina broke several fingernails struggling with the bolt on the door. It was heavy and the fit was tight. She looked back and saw Nick emerging from the bathroom. He was trembling all over and his eyes were red and glowing. Her throat went dry as she began hitting the knob of the bolt with the palms of her hands. The pain was excruciating but the bolt moved. He was coming for her, his arms outstretched. The bolt gave way. Raina pulled upon the door and dashed through it just as Nick's hand reached for her. She ran down the steps not daring to look behind. He leaned over the bannister and screamed, "I'll kill you, you fucking bitch! I'll kill you!"

She ran past the doors of the other apartments. She wondered why no one had reacted to the commotion. Why no one had called the police. At last she reached the first floor and ran into the street. Clutching her chest she headed toward Seventh Avenue and hailed a cab. She climbed into the back seat and the driver asked: "Where to?"

"Home," she sobbed. "Please take me home."

Raina dug into her purse—crazily enough, it was still slung over her shoulder—to see if she had enough money to pay for the cab. She didn't notice Lucas Balaban's card fall to the floor, and because of her traumatic experience that night she would never remember to call him.

Jana's show, *The Games of War,* opened to universally bad reviews. The newspaper, magazine, radio and TV critics damned the production, attacking everything about it. They ripped apart the book, the music and lyrics, the directing, the sets, lighting and costumes, and all the actors . . . save for one.

Many critics singled Jana out as a young singer/dancer/actress to watch. While they ridiculed the role she had been given to play, they nonetheless felt that she transcended the silly situations, the banal lines and the virtually unsingable score. One particularly sarcastic critic wrote, *"The Games of War* is a frizzy, fuzzy, outgrowth of *Hair.* But all you opportunistic producers take note. Don't curse the darkness of your bad taste. Just get Jana Donatello to light up your stage. Or better still, won't somebody give this very talented young woman a decent part in a decent show?"

After the opening night curtain had been rung down, the first night audience, papered with friends of the producers, the writers, the technical staff and the actors, gamely applauded the performance and even managed to manufacture enough enthusiasm for a curtain call.

Kay, Alex, Raina and Chris had come. They smiled wanly at one another. "What can we do?" asked Raina. "We have to go backstage."

"What's so bad?" said Kay. "Jana was wonderful even though the show was a piece of junk."

They waited for the audience to shuffle out. Then the quartet made their way backstage. Raina, still somewhat shaken from her experience, wore heavy makeup and over-sized sunglasses to cover the bruises on her face. They were the result, she had told the others, of an accident in a cab. She had taken a brief leave of absence from her own show.

They eased their way through the crowd of well-wishers whose smiles were frozen on their faces and whose platitudes automatically popped out of their mouths like candy from a vending machine. They found Jana alone in her dressing room. Her eye make-up was streaked; she had been crying. She looked up and smiled bravely at her friends. "You don't have to tell me," she said choking. "I know, I could feel how terrible it was."

"It was," exclaimed Chris. "But you were smashing, really you were." Then he kissed her on both cheeks.

Raina embraced Jana. "Look, darling, you're going to survive this and come out smelling like roses. The critics are going to have to find something good to talk about, and you're going to be it. You wait and see."

Then Kay. "Jana, you were wonderful. Gwen Verdon couldn't have done any better than you with those dreadful lines and songs. Wipe your eyes and repair your makeup. We're going to the cast party, remember?"

"I can't," wailed Jana. "I can't."

Kay signaled the others that she wanted to be alone with Jana. When the door was closed, she knelt by Jana, who was sobbing quietly now, and said, "Look, baby, what more could you do? You worked your guts out for this show learning and relearning, and you gave it everything you've got. There had to be a few important people out there tonight besides the friends and friends of friends. Raina's right. The critics are going to have to find something good to write about. You're going to be it. You've got nothing at all to be ashamed of. *Nothing*. Now enough of this pep talk. Pull yourself together. Blow your nose and fix your face. We're going to celebrate tonight. We're going to celebrate you."

The cast party was held at Phebe's, the Off-Broadway equivalent of Sardi's. Everyone connected with the show was there. Smiling a little too broadly and drinking a little too quickly, they were hoping against hope that what they felt deep within them wasn't true. A few television sets had been scattered throughout the restaurant. One by one the television critics demolished their show. The producers ran from table to table loudly exclaiming that the television reviews didn't count, but everyone knew the die had been cast. The *Games of War* was going to come up a loser. At about one o'clock the morning papers started coming out. The party was over.

Alex and Kay had gone to bed and so had Raina, taking an ice pack with her to reduce facial swelling. Only Jana and Chris remained. They sat on the terrace, their feet propped up on the ledge, drinking champagne. The young couple, lost in thought, watched the stars as they appeared triumphantly in the dark sky as if intent upon paying homage to the moon. The entire city was overcast with a silver glow and in that bright argent light even the flesh of the beholder seemed rigid, metallic.

Jana raised her arm and caught the moon in her glass. It seemed to float on the sparkling champagne —a shimmering sail on a golden lake. "I love champagne. I love New York. I love being called 'a new, electric light in the theatre.'" She turned to Chris. "And I love you, Chris."

Chris took Jana's hand. "You surprise me. I've been waiting so long to hear you say it. And now that you have, I don't know how to react."

"You might tell me the same."

"I thought I had. I've thought it so often, I thought I must have said it. I love you, Jana."

"Now that's the best news I've heard all night, including my reviews."

"You're not so upset about the show?"

"What show? With reviews like that, I doubt if we'll have a second performance. I have a feeling that I'll be coming back to Joe Allen's sooner than expected."

"Oh no, you won't. Not with the personal praise you garnered from the critics. Why, they're a gold plated entree into any producer's or agent's office in the city."

"I guess I'll have to think about getting myself an agent. Contracts and things like that confuse me."

"How about Raina's agent?"

"You mean ex-agent, Bradley Gerard. No, I think not. That's just a little too incestuous."

"Well, I sure won't recommend my agent. He hasn't gotten me a job in more than a year. How about a little more champagne?"

"Mmm. That would be nice. I feel like a gigantic weight has been lifted from my shoulders."

"I can see why. You carried the whole damn show by yourself."

"Seriously, Chris, I didn't know what I was doing half of the time. You know, I was still memorizing lines just before I went on."

"You're amazing, Jana. A real phenomenon. I knew you could sing and I've worked with you enough on your scenes to know that you could act. But I didn't know you could dance so well."

"Well, I haven't had that much training, but I seem to be able to pick it up easily."

"Are you tired?" She nodded. "Do you want to go to bed?" She nodded again. "Alone?"

"No, not tonight. I don't want to be alone tonight."

Jana's bedroom was the smallest of the three, but it was the only one that opened onto the terrace. A double bed dominated the room. It was covered with a patchwork quilt Jana had bought at a secondhand shop. The headboard, a magnificent wooden sculpture of solid oak, had been found on one of Jana and Kay's midnight shopping forays.

They undressed in the light of the moon and sat down next to one another on the edge of the bed. Jana touched Chris's shoulder and felt him tremble.

"Chris, are you cold? Should I shut the terrace doors?"

"No, I'm not cold."

"Then what's wrong? You want to, don't you?"

"Yes, of course, Jana. It's just that. . . ."

"Don't be nervous, Chris," she murmured. "I'm nervous enough for both of us."

Chris managed a weak smile.

They lay down on the bed, their bodies touching. Chris began exploring Jana's body, but his fingers were like ice. Jana touched his arm and it was the same. It seemed as if all warmth had been drained from his body. "Is there anything I can do, Chris?" she asked hesitantly. "I'm inexperienced but willing."

"No, nothing, Jana. I'll—I'll do it all."

Chris rolled over on top of Jana. As he did, she automatically parted her legs. He began pushing forward but to no avail. He was totally flaccid and the more he tried the more he shrank. "Oh, damn!" he groaned. He began moving back and forth, hoping that the friction would cause him to grow erect, but nothing happened.

"Chris," said Jana gently. "Don't try to force it. We've had quite a bit of champagne to drink. Just relax and lie beside me. I like the feel of your body next to mine." Chris fell beside Jana.

"It's no good, Jana. It's just no good."

"Don't talk like that, Chris. We'll work it out. I may be inexperienced, but I'm patient."

"I wonder if you know how this is tearing me up. I was so sure that it would work for us. I do love you so." He broke off, practically sobbing.

"What is it, Chris? Is this more than a momentary problem?"

"I shouldn't have allowed this to happen. I should have just remained a friend." His voice grew more uncontrolled and Jana realized that he was crying. "I should not have involved you in my life, Jana. I'm a homosexual, and women just don't excite me. I've tried before and failed. And now I've failed again." He buried his face in his hands. "Please don't hate me."

In the silence that echoed through the room following this poignant outburst, Jana realized that she wasn't, after all, particularly shocked or surprised. Sad, yes, and disappointed, but not repelled. All the qualities she cherished in Chris—his sensitivity and compassion, high good humor and gentleness—had always struck her as being blessedly unlike the hard, so-called "virile"

attributes that drew Raina and Kay like magnets. So
Chris was gay. Did that have to mean that all that was
warm and nurturing in their relationship counted for
nothing?

He was her dear friend. She made comforting noises
and touched his shoulder. "I couldn't hate you, Chris.
But you should have told me."

"How could I? I wanted to love you so much."

"But we *do* love each other, Chris. We'll still be
friends," she said with soft intensity.

"I suppose I'd better go," he said disconsolately, and
reached for his clothes.

"Don't, Chris. Stay with me."

"I can't, Jana. I'm too ashamed."

"There's nothing to be ashamed of! You're a warm
and wonderful person. What you just told me doesn't
change my feelings for you. You must be proud of
yourself. Being gay doesn't make you any less of a
person. Are you sure you don't want to stay? I could
make some coffee."

"No, thanks. I really think I should leave."

Realizing that Chris was at least temporarily too un-
done to be assuaged, Jana slipped on her robe and
walked him to the front door. She kissed him on the
cheek saying, "Chris, we only have one life, and we
must live it in the way that makes us the happiest."

"Thanks, Jana. You deserve the best. I hope you get
it," said Chris, his face bleak and his voice expressionless. Then he hurried toward the elevator.

Jana climbed back into bed and pulled the sheet up
to her chin. Her teeth were chattering as if she were
very cold. Then she began crying. The ginger cat,
Farouk, was strolling on the terrace and heard her.
He entered the room and jumped up onto the bed.
Jana slid her arm around his great orange body. His
furry warmth gave her comfort and she was finally
able to fall asleep.

Chapter Thirteen

"That's it, Jana, baby. Hold it!" the photographer, Ben Fortuna, crooned. Jana was lying atop a pile of red cushions in an uncomfortable position beneath a battery of hot studio lights. Even though her face was stinging from the output of the high-powered fan, she smiled bravely at the camera as Ben cajoled her. "Now say the word—and love it. *Love it!*"

Her glistening red lips parted as she breathed a single word: "Vermilion."

The word of course did not register on the film, but it placed her mouth in the position the photographer wanted. Her upper lip curled back to reveal her white, even teeth. It was what Ben called the "tigress approach."

"Hold it. Hold it." Twenty shots later the photographer straightened up. "Take a break. Mandy, repowder Jana's forehead. It's shiny. And do something with her hair. It's been blown so much it's beginning to lose that studied casual look."

Relieved, Jana sat up, flexing and unflexing the muscles of her left arm. She asked the "go-fer" to bring her something to drink. A club soda with lemon was presented and she sipped it through the straw so that she would not mess her makeup. She glanced at the studio clock. It was past one-thirty. She hadn't had breakfast and she hadn't had lunch. And she was afraid her stomach would begin growling. But she hadn't dared eat before the shoot. Ben warned her that he needed her as gaunt as possible. The makeup man blotted the perspiration from her forehead, then brushed it with a pearlized powder. He redid her hair—combing, teasing and pulling it to achieve that impromptu look. Jana smiled gamely at the makeup man. "Don't ask me where I got the idea that modeling was glamorous."

"All the glamor's in the psycheck, sweetie," the man said as he applied yet another layer of eye shadow.

Out of the corners of her eyes, Jana could see Ben conferring with Clyde MacTavish, the American fashion designer whose product was the occasion for all the activity. They were photographing the advertisements for a new perfume created by MacTavish. He had named it Vermilion and it was a heady, sensual scent of tuberoses, oriental spices and musk. MacTavish had insisted upon an unknown model to promote his product; he didn't want to risk identification with any other company. He specified that he wanted the picture to suggest the all-American girl losing her innocence, or more succinctly, "an American college girl is kidnapped and finds passion in an opium den."

"All right, everybody, places!" Ben announced. "Are you ready, Jana baby?" Jana nodded. "Well, we're going to try something slightly different this time. Clyde wants it sexier."

"Shall I take off the dress?" Jana quipped.

"Not nude, sexy. Suggestive and sexy." Jana hobbled to the set-up and replaced herself on the red silk cushions. The material had been dyed to match the red label of the perfume bottle. The lights glanced off her shining black hair, enameled cheeks and glistening lips. The dress Jana was wearing had also been designed by MacTavish. It was made of a red sequined fabric with thin straps and a plunging décolletage. Jana wore a pair of red cinnabar earrings and necklace to match. Each bead had been hand-carved in the Orient to resemble stylized roses and then lacquered the featured shade of red. Ben turned to MacTavish, a slight man with a shock of color-treated hair and a flouncy manner.

"Clyde, I think the earrings are going to have to go if we're going to do as you suggest."

"Then get rid of them," the designer replied tersely.

Ben knelt beside Jana and held out his hands. "The earrings, baby. They're too much." She took them off and handed them to him.

"What about the necklace, Ben?"

"I want you to chew on that." She looked at him in surprise. "Yes, chew. Pretend they're an all-American treat. A string of great big reds." Jana looked more puzzled. He then whispered, "That's a drug."

Jana posed lying on her side, supporting her chin with her hand. She pulled the necklace through her teeth, hoping that Ben would tell her exactly what he wanted.

"Lower your lashes. That's it. Now bite down on them. Harder, they won't break. That's it. Turn your head a little more to the left. Perfect. Now hold it." There was a series of clicks as Ben continued shooting at slightly varying angles until he had completed the entire roll of film. "O.K., kids, that's a wrap." He went over to help Jana to her feet. "If you could see what I was seeing, you wouldn't complain about your stiff joints."

"You think it's going to turn out good?"

"*Good?* I'll just bet you that this'll be the hottest ad since Revlon's Fire and Ice, and that made a star out of Dorian Leigh, the model."

"I don't have to be a star, Ben. I just want to be a working actress."

Despite Jana's favorable personal reviews for *The Games of War,* success was not forthcoming. For six months Jana played the lead in a bus and truck company of *Cabaret* that traveled throughout the south and southwest. The work was exhausting, but it allowed her time to reassess her goals and to get over her pain and disappointment about Chris. They had remained good friends and Chris had become involved with Ben Fortuna, the photographer, an energetic young man of thirty with curly black hair and an extraordinary nose.

In profile he looked as if he might belong on a Roman coin. He had an easy manner and an infectious laugh that put the most nervous beginner and the most anxious client immediately at ease.

Eventually Ben turned out to be Jana's mentor in the Vermilion campaign. He had become friendly with Jana through Chris, and the three of them often went out together. Ben took some pictures of Jana for her portfolio and was struck by her fresh appeal in print. When his good friend Clyde MacTavish happened to mention at a cocktail party that he was looking for an unknown to launch the Vermilion campaign, Ben immediately thought of Jana. He showed the designer the photographs he had taken of her. Even though MacTavish had envisioned a redhead for the ad, he decided that Jana's dark hair and creamy complexion would beautifully set off the specially mixed red of his product.

At first Jana was completely uninterested in the project. But the more Ben and Chris spoke about it, the more the idea began to amuse her. And as Raina and Kay pointed out, the money was outrageous and could certainly keep her solvent for more than a year while she looked for theatre work. It was the last consideration that convinced Jana to finally take the assignment.

The session was pronounced a success and the photographer's studio quickly emptied except for Ben and Jana, who let their mutual exhaustion overtake them. They sprawled on a sofa facing the window of the Tudor City apartment. Jana was massaging her calves. "Ben, I wouldn't mind a cigarette."

"Since when did you start smoking?"

"I don't inhale, but I find it relaxes me."

"So how are the roommates?"

"We hardly see one another lately. Raina's out of town with Torrence Villere's new play. I guess they're in Philadelphia by now. And Kay's mother died. She went home for the funeral."

"That's sad, but I got the impression Kay had been expecting it."

"She had. But she'll deal with it just as she deals with everything. Kay's really a survivor."

"Not Raina? She seems to be the most resilient of all."

"I'm afraid Raina only *seems* in control. I worry about her a lot. I hope the show goes well. This is a big break for her. After being identified for so long with *Bare Essentials,* it was wonderful for her to get a new play by one of the country's leading playwrights. It's an honor."

"You sound a bit envious."

"I suppose I am, but I'm dealing with it."

"Tell you what. Why don't you and Chris and I go out tonight? It's Tuesday. His night off."

"I don't know, Ben. This session's left me a bit frazzled."

"So go home, take a nap. There's a new club open on West Eighty-sixth Street called the Grapevine. It's supposed to be a real mad place for singles."

Jana grinned. "Do I need to get shots, and bring my passport?"

"Neither. Just a pretty dress and a determination to have fun. Who knows, you might meet someone."

"Oh, it doesn't matter, as long as the three of us are together."

"You really mean that, don't you, Jana?" said Ben. "You really don't mind that Chris and I are lovers?"

"Why should I mind? It didn't work between Chris and me. You're happy. He's happy. And I'm very happy for both of you. You've nothing to be ashamed of. You're both terrific guys. Let me tell you something, Ben. I can't say I think much of the straight guys I've met here in New York. Why, I've even been thinking of having a sex change and becoming gay myself."

Ben laughed. "Hey, don't do that. We couldn't stand the competition."

The grave site was encompassed by a large horse-shoe bend in Route 78. Kay unconsciously counted the passing cars as the minister intoned his final words.

". . . earth to earth, ashes to ashes, dust to dust . . ."

". . . twenty-seven, twenty-eight . . ."

". . . insuring certain hope of the Resurrection to Eternal Life . . ."

". . . twenty-nine, thirty, thirty-one . . ."

". . . through our Lord, Jesus Christ, who shall change our vile body . . ."

The cemetery was located on the side of the hill that overlooked the steel mills and further on a collection of ugly gray buildings where Kay had been educated. She looked around the grounds. They were ill-kempt. Many of the monuments were grime-encrusted and the graves littered with rotting flowers. The trees were barren and stunted and stood out skeletally against the pale grey sky. It was a forlorn and melancholy scene, and Kay wondered why she felt so little sorrow.

". . . whereby He is able to subdue all things to Himself."

Kay's attention was drawn back to the ceremony. She stared at her mother's plot. It seemed like such a large opening for such a small life. She saw the minister signal her with his eyes as she joined her family. One by one, the Kincades walked to the edge of the grave, bent down and scooped up a handful of dirt, and threw it onto the lid of the coffin.

Two caretakers moved forward to lower the coffin. The relatives came together for a few brief moments to exchange tears and condolences. Everyone was expected back at the Kincade house for a reception. Kay informed her father that she would drive back in her rented car and wished to remain at the cemetery a little longer. He seemed nonplussed by her decision but set about herding the others into the waiting limousines.

After they had departed, Kay sat down on the ground and watched the caretakers fill in her mother's grave. She realized that the family would eventually have to put up a stone marker, but other than her name and the dates of her birth and her death, what was there to say? Kay smiled bitterly at her thoughts. It wasn't so many years ago that she had been a miniature of her mother. Ironically, Mrs. Kincade had not been heavy when she died, for the last months of her life she could barely eat at all.

Plucking at the dried grass on which she sat, Kay wondered idly if her father still expected her to stay in Bethlehem. Why did self-destructive people expect everyone else to behave in the same manner? Since her mother had become bedridden, a woman had been hired by her father to come in every day but Sunday to cook, clean, and see to the family's needs. Kay thought ruefully there was no reason why the woman couldn't continue to do so.

The ground was cold. She got up and brushed herself off. She walked to a knoll on the hill, leaned against a gnarled tree, and watched the caretakers finish their business. Little by little, the hole was filled up. Kay felt compelled to watch. It was as if her mother would not really be dead until her grave had been filled with dirt and padded down by the broad side of the shovels.

She had decided that she would stay on for one more day and that was all. Her new show—an all-black version of *Macbeth*—was slated for an Off-Broadway opening, and would not wait for her. And then there was Alex. . . .

The increasing number of injuries Alex sustained through his rôle as stuntman alarmed Kay. He'd torn a ligament in his knee, dislocated a shoulder, and then finally nearly severed the index finger from his right hand. He had become a one-man stunt team. It seemed to Kay that the chances Alex took for the TV police series was the acting out of his deep-rooted guilt for having survived the Vietnam war when so many hadn't. When she expressed her opinion to him, hoping that he might seek psychiatric counseling, he had scoffed at her ideas, saying, "You read too many of those self-analysis books. Don't give me hang-ups I don't have. Of course there's a certain amount of danger, but there is in every walk of life. I find them easier to take than mental abuse."

Despite his protestations, Kay didn't believe him. His fascination with stunts became more obsessive and the injuries more frequent. She knew that one day a miscalculation would take his life. As Alex became more enmeshed in his work, he waxed philosophical about his occupation. "The only truth there is is in doing a stunt. You can't fake it. It's either real or it's not."

Kay responded characteristically. "And I say you've got more balls than brains." Their time together was spent more with arguing than making love. Kay realized that their relationship was disintegrating and that she would have to be the one to either end or save it. Alex, who was able to face any physical danger, was not good at emotional confrontations. Kay had been on the threshold of forcing a show-down when her mother died and she'd had to return home. She intended to make her decision and take it back with her. But she wasn't sure what that decision was going to be.

More shaken by her mother's death than she was letting herself admit, Kay walked across the dead grass toward the main gate. She passed a group of people who had come to shed a tear and place a wreath on the grave of their loved one. She wondered whether she would ever come back and do the same for her mother. As she passed through the wrought iron gates, she encountered a group of children who were trick-or-treating. She had forgotten that it was Halloween. One ragged little girl was dressed as an Indian maiden. Two others were ghosts in gray sheets. And the fourth, a sturdily built boy taller than the others, wore the costume of a policeman made from a cheap shiny fabric decorated with gold-tone buttons.

Kay was reminded of Alex and the dreadful uniform he wore while performing his dangerous stunts.

"Trick-or-treat," he said in a demanding voice which was just beginning to change from childhood to adolescence. He drew a cap-gun and shot it several times in the air. The caps exploded and frightened a band of crows. They swooped and cawed, then turned and fled toward the horizon. The children fled, too, chanting in high, giggling voices:

"Trick-or-treat. Trick-or-treat. Trick-or-treat."

Kay watched the children romp across the fields, playing and shouting at one another. Then the older boy, the one wearing the uniform, tripped and fell over a grave stone. Kay shuddered with relief; she had made up her mind.

The lights of the Court Theatre in Philadelphia were blurred and ran together like watercolors. Huddled beneath the marquee, a large crowd dressed in an assortment of rainwear waited for the doors to open. The inclement weather had not kept the audience away. This night was an event that any serious-minded theatergoer would not want to miss. Pulitzer prize-winning playwright Torrence Villere's new play, *The Last Dance at the Blue Moon Cafe,* was in its out-of-town previews before heading to Broadway. The play, the first in five years for Villere, had finished a successful run in Boston where the critics were calling his new work the apex of his career.

Raina had a featured part rather than a starring role. She had not been chosen until the fourth callback. The problem had been her coloring. The part was that of a hot-blooded Cajun girl named Roux Caraquet. Villere, a native of Louisiana and a Cajun himself, had written yet another play that dealt with his heritage. The story concerned the struggle between Cajun tradition and modern technology. The Blue Moon Cafe, situated at the edge of a bayou where oil had been discovered, was slated for demolition. But not, the Cajuns insisted, before it was used one last time for *les danses rondes.* This was a matchmaking spring dance that once upon a time had been the only form of public entertainment allowed young people during Lent.

In her dressing room Raina finished her last minute touches to the makeup that would transform her into a young woman of Cajun descent. Her eyebrows had been thickened, her cheeks and lips colored a carmine red. She needed no body make-up or dark foundation. When she had not been rehearsing, she had acquired a tan. Her skin was now a rich shade of amber. The hairdresser helped her into a flowing black wig and her theatrical disguise was complete. Raina sized herself up in the mirror. She doubted that her own parents would recognize her, if indeed they ever saw the play.

"How does it feel, Raina?" asked the hairdresser, a young man of Spanish descent. "Is it too loose?"

Raina vigorously shook her head. "No, Manuel. It's just fine."

"Then I'll go check on the others. Good luck, Raina. Break both the legs."

No letters, no telegrams, not even a phone call from her parents. Raina brushed aside her personal hurt and spoke her opening lines to herself as she put on her costume.

It was a simple cotton dress—pink faded nearly to white. It had short, puffed sleeves and a low-cut bodice gathered beneath the bust. She wore no shoes. The effect was that of backwoods sensuality.

Raina stretched back on her divan and tried to empty her mind of everything except her role. After her devastating experience with Nick Bartolini, Raina had sought psychiatric help. She had desperately wanted to break her increasing dependence on drinking as an escape mechanism. She probably would never have gone home with Nick if she hadn't been high. She considered herself lucky to have had only a close flirtation with danger and wanted to alter the destructive course of her life.

The psychiatrist pointed out the obvious to Raina. Her irresponsible behavior was a desperate bid for her parents' attention. He further reminded her that she had indulged in such behavior since early childhood and it had made no difference whatsoever. Her parents remained shadowy figures in the background of her life. Wasn't it time to put childhood things away and get on with it? Raina liked the man's reasoning and his way of putting things. He'd said once that in a way people weren't as clever as laboratory rats. If you took a rat and put it in a maze containing a piece of cheese at the end of one of its corridors, the rat would eventually find it. If you then moved the cheese, the rat would change course and find the prize again. Human beings, on the other hand, were more stubborn than rats. If you moved the cheese on a human being, he would continue to return to the original place even though the cheese was no longer there.

Many times when Raina was tempted to have one drink too many, she would tell herself that "there ain't no cheese down that hole, girl." She was able to keep her habits under control, but she did not find the happiness she expected to find. She was puzzled by this disappointment and sought out the psychiatrist for an accounting. He told her that she had yet to learn the satisfaction that one derived from being good to one's self. Still Raina was unconvinced. Despite her new success in the theatre, something was wrong. She experienced a gnawing feeling of discontent. It was as if she had been the only one not invited to a gigantic party and somewhere it was going on without her. This nameless fear plagued her throughout rehearsals, and she had extreme difficulty dealing with it. Only after one of the cast members taught her to meditate had she felt able to seize control of her emotions and her rôle.

Places were called and Raina, refreshed and ready to perform, walked briskly to the place where she would be making her entrance. As she stood waiting in the wings, she silently prayed that Philadelphia would welcome *The Last Dance at the Blue Moon Cafe* with as much enthusiasm as Boston had.

Not only did Philadelphia approve Torrence Villere's new play, but the New York critics concurred. They opened on the night of November fourteenth, and after the reviews came out there were lines of ticket buyers stretching from the theatre to Broadway. Raina's personal reviews were excellent, ranging from "dynamic sensuality" to "a raw emotional force." Still Raina was discontent.

Dressed in a white lynx coat, Raina made her way through the crowds of shoppers on Fifth Avenue. The coat was a gift from her parents who had not yet seen her in the play. She stopped to admire the windows at Tiffany's featuring a collection of snowflakes fashioned out of diamonds. Then she lit a cigarette, pushed her sunglasses back on her head and decided, even though it was only the middle of November, to begin her Christmas shopping. She would start with gifts for Jana and Kay.

Raina was looking forward to spending Christmas with her two dear friends. Jana and Kay had elected not to go home; Raina hadn't even considered it. Her parents would be spending the holidays in Acapulco, and even if she had wanted to she wouldn't have been able to get time off from the play. Her roommates had planned an old-fashioned Christmas, including decorating a real tree with strings of cranberries and popcorn and preparing a traditional Christmas dinner. There would only be three placesettings unless, as Kay put it, "One of us gets lucky and finds a man in our Christmas stocking."

That didn't seem to be likely. Raina hadn't had an affair since that night with Nick. Kay had stopped seeing Alex, and although Jana was friends with Chris, there certainly wasn't any romance there. Still, none of them could complain. Their careers were flourishing, they were in New York City and they were together.

People stared at Raina but now she felt they were staring for the right reasons. The public had forgotten the *Bare Essentials* poster, and since she wore a black wig in her new role, she was hardly ever recognized. This pleased her. She made a mental note to ask her psychiatrist why she preferred to be admired for her beauty rather than her talent.

A mist of snowflakes swirled about Raina. Whether they were falling fresh from the dull gray sky or were being blown from various resting places, she could not tell. She pulled up the collar of her coat and crossed Fifth Avenue to Andre de Clermont's, a jewelry store which in the past several years had come to rival Tiffany's, Harry Winston's, and Van Cleef & Arpel's. The interior of the shop was both chic and inviting. It was completely done in shades of beige with laminated tortoise shell used as accents.

Raina strolled among the displays, searching for something both expensive and frivolous to buy her roommates for Christmas. She had seen a copy of Andre de Clermont's gift catalogue and had been intrigued by the many unusual pieces of jewelry and objets d'art offered.

In what was termed the "Mediterranean Collection" Raina's eyes fell upon a handmade silver cross from Greece that was encrusted with aquamarine. The piece was about three inches long and beautifully crafted. It would make a perfect gift for Jana—if the price were right. They had agreed not to spend more than fifty dollars on each other.

The saleswoman approached Raina. She matched the decor. Her hair, complexion and dress were also beige. "May I help you?" she asked pleasantly.

"Could you give me the price of the cross, the one with the aquamarine."

"That's a hundred and twenty-five dollars."

Raina decided that Jana needn't know the price. "I'll take it. Please have it gift-wrapped. But there's no hurry, I still have another present to pick out."

"Perhaps you'd like a cup of espresso while you're waiting."

"That would be lovely."

The saleswoman lead Raina to a small area partially enclosed by tropical plants. There was an arrangement of bamboo chairs of a Brighton Beach design and a gleaming copper espresso pot sitting on a stand. Raina sat down and lit a cigarette, while the saleswoman served her an excellent cup of coffee. As Raina sipped her espresso, she became aware that someone was staring at her. She looked up. A tall, elegantly-dressed man who looked as if he had stepped right off the cover of *Gentlemen's Quarterly* was smiling at her. His hair was steel grey and brushed back on either side of his head. His eyes were clear, blue-grey and inquiring, his nose thin and straight, his jaw-line perfectly squared. He was well over six feet tall and wore an impeccably tailored double-breasted suit of champagne-colored cashmere with a tie of deep vibrant red. Although the man had the look of a thoroughbred, Raina guessed he was a sales clerk. She mentally complimented Mr. de Clermont on his exquisite taste in hiring. Then she noticed the man's long and beautifully manicured hands. There were three rings on the left hand and two on the right. Four held jewels, one did not. Surely they did not allow the help to wear samples thought Raina as the man strode toward her.

"I hope you're enjoying your coffee," he said in a deep, faintly accented voice.

"I am, thank you. I think it's a lovely idea," said Raina, meaning the complimentary espresso. "It puts one in a better mood for shopping."

"Do you mind if I join you?" the man asked. Without waiting for a response, he sat down opposite her.

Raina shrugged. "I'm just a customer. I don't own the place." The man smiled enigmatically. "You see, I was shopping for my roommates. They're not easy to buy for. I've bought Jana's gift. A beautiful cross from Greece." The man nodded in approval. "But it's Kay's gift that's got me concerned."

"Why is that?"

"Well, she's so unlike anybody I've ever met. She's part bohemian, part haute couture."

"Perhaps an antique pin," suggested the man.

"That sounds like a good idea."

"We have some lovely art nouveau pieces which have just come in."

Raina smiled. "Then you do work here?"

"Yes, you could say that. Let me show them to you."

Raina followed him to a far corner of the store. "These pieces are all originals and in many cases are one of a kind." He removed several trays containing the fanciful pieces and put them on top of the display case. Raina looked over the trays. "I don't know. They're all so exquisite."

"How about this?" said the man, holding up a sensuously curved pin in the form of a mermaid. Its figure and hair were stylized in a series of sweeping curves. The mermaid's scales and tail were enameled in varying shades of green.

"You said she was half this and half that. What better gift than a mermaid—half fish, half woman."

"But how much does it cost?"

"Why—ah—it's exactly the same price as the cross."

"What? A hundred and twenty-five dollars? I can't believe it. You must be mistaken."

"I work here, you will remember."

"Then I'll take it."

The saleswoman stopped at the counter. "Oh, Monsieur de Clermont, I see you have helped the young lady."

"Yes, Estelle. She's decided to take this mermaid pin. Would you please wrap it for her? It's one hundred and twenty-five dollars."

The saleswoman hesitated for a brief moment. "I'll wrap it immediately, Monsieur, and make up the bill."

Raina turned to her "salesman," a smile of delight crossing her face. "You're Andre de Clermont?"

He grinned and bowed slightly. "Yes, I work here."

Raina inclined her head to one side. "Now, I know that mermaid must cost more than one hundred and twenty-five dollars."

He shrugged. "Our mark-up is extraordinary."

"I don't know how to thank you."

"You might be my guest for dinner, Miss . . ."

"Raina Pendleton. I'd love to, whenever you like."

"How about tonight?"

For what seemed an interminable amount of time

the two stared at one another. Raina could almost believe that for that brief piece of eternity, time stood still.

"I'm afraid I have to work tonight. But if a late supper would suit you?"

"It would," he said quickly.

"I have an idea. Have you seen Torrence Villere's new play, *The Last Dance at the Blue Moon Cafe?*" He shook his head. "Well then, why don't I arrange to have a ticket waiting for you at the box office."

"You're not coming?"

"I have a small part in the play," Raina replied modestly. "Then we could meet afterwards for supper."

"An actress!" he exclaimed. "How perfectly delightful. And do you have many of the lines?"

"Oh, a few," laughed Raina. "And I remember them *all.*"

As Raina was leaving the jewelry store she thought to herself, what a very nice man. I met him straight, without benefit of alcohol, and apparently he liked me that way.

It was what the gossip columnists loved to call a "whirlwind romance."

From the New York *Daily News:*

ANDRE DE CLERMONT'S NEWEST JEWEL

NEW YORK (AP) New York's most eligible bachelor, Andre de Clermont, owner of the fabulous Fifth Avenue store, is seen leaving the Morosco Theatre with his latest "good friend." She is Raina Pendleton, the much acclaimed young actress who has theatregoers cheering in Torrence Villere's new hit, *The Last Dance at the Blue Moon Cafe.* In case she looks familiar, New Yorkers, could you ever forget that Raina was the girl on the *Bare Essentials* poster? It became an instant collector's item. We wonder if Andre is planning on adding Raina to *his* collection. The jeweler is famous not only for his exquisite gems but for his past-tense romances with the most beautiful, social and talented young women in New York City. Not one of the ladies was able to steer Andre anywhere near an altar. So place your bets, ladies and gentlemen.

From the *National Star:*

DANCING TILL DAWN

(Pictured above) Cavorting at El Morocco are Andre de Clermont, Fifth Avenue jeweler, and Raina Pendleton, the Broadway actress, New York's newest most beautiful couple. To the left of the smiling twosome are Miss Pendleton's friends, Jana Donatello and Kay Kincade with their escorts.

From the New York *Post:*

CAUGHT IN THE ACT

NEW YORK (AP) A Plaza love nest turned into slug fest between Andre de Clermont and the *Post* staff photographer, Harry Denver. De Clermont's frequent battles with the press are notorious and reached an apex last night. The jeweler and his latest amour, Raina Pendleton the actress, checked into the hotel for the weekend taking adjoining rooms. Later, de Clermont apologized to the photographer and made a brief statement: "We came to the Plaza for privacy, hoping to avoid the press." Miss Pendleton was not available for comment.

• • •

Jana, her arms full of just-wrapped packages, walked into the living room. She was trailed by Farouk who could smell his gift from her—a half dozen jumbo shrimp—through the paper. "Now, Farouk, you'll have to wait until midnight when we all open our gifts."

Kay, who was standing on a ladder next to the tree, called down. "You're talking to the air. You might as well let him claw it open and enjoy."

"I suppose. What are you doing up there? Did a string of lights go out?"

"I decided to change the top ornament. I got to thinking an angel somehow wasn't appropriate. I was passing a cut-rate decoration store today so I stopped in and bought us a star. What do you think of it?" It was a five-point star made of gold-colored filigree.

"It's beautiful and you're right. It is much better."

"What time is it getting to be?"

"Last time I looked it was ten o'clock. Raina and Andre should be here soon."

"You don't mind his coming, do you?"

"Of course not. I like Andre. I know we planned Christmas Eve with just the three of us, but it seems like it isn't just the three of us anymore."

Kay put away the ladder while Jana arranged her presents under the tree. She succumbed to Farouk's persistence and unwrapped his present. The cat dove into the midst of the shrimp and flicked his tail appreciatively as he ate.

They changed clothes for the celebration. Jana wore a red satin minidress and Kay a pair of lounging pajamas in bright bottle green silk.

"I think everything's ready," said Jana. "The hors d'oeuvres are made, the champagne is chilling." She glanced at the base of the tree. "Farouk's got his shrimp. And we're all dressed. I really like the star, Kay. And it's so appropriate, particularly for Raina."

Kay put her arm around Jana's shoulder. "Well, we always knew it, didn't we? We're all stars, but some shine a little brighter than others."

The downstairs bell rang and Kay went to answer it. When she returned she said, "I declare, that poor old doorman sounds as if he was carried out of Shangri La. It's Andre. He's on his way up."

"Alone? I hope there's nothing wrong."

"What could be wrong with Andre de Clermont?"

Andre entered the apartment wearing a beaver coat and a bright smile. Melted snowflakes were twinkling on his eyelashes. "It's a perfect Christmas Eve. The snow is coming down like cats and dogs." Jana suppressed a smile and helped Andre off with his coat. "I sent the chauffeur on to the theatre to pick up Raina. It would be difficult for her to get a cab." As usual Andre kissed Jana on both cheeks. She stiffened. Andre was a bit too suave and wore too much cologne for her taste.

In the living room he repeated the Gallic gesture of affection with Kay, who seemed to enjoy it more than Jana. Andre complimented the tree, the apartment, and the young women themselves.

"Sit down, Andre," admonished Kay. "You're prancing about like one of Santa's reindeer."

He bowed and took Kay's hand. "I do apologize. You must excuse me. I'm a little . . . on the edge?" He looked directly into Jana's eyes as he spoke. "Is that correct?" He brushed a strand of hair away from Jana's face.

Jana felt herself blush. "It's 'on edge' . . . Andre."

He sat down in the center of the sofa and patted either side, indicating that the women should sit next to him. They glanced at one another, then sat down flanking him. "You see," Andre began, "I am going to ask Raina to marry me tonight."

"That's wonderful!" cried Kay.

"Yes, wonderful," added Jana with slightly less enthusiasm. "But," she began cautiously, "you've only known each other for a little over a month."

Andre affectionately squeezed Jana's arm. "Love always happens quickly," he pronounced.

"And you would know," ventured Jana.

Andre scowled. "Do not believe everything you read in the papers. It has only happened twice for me—my wife Suzanne and now Raina. As you know, Suzanne died shortly after the birth of my second son. It wasn't easy raising two boys without a mother. Somehow they managed to elude me. Neither wanted the life I had planned for them. They both rejected their heritage," he paused, "and me. They wanted to get away from New York and, I suppose, the business. They're in Berkeley."

"How old are they now?" asked Jana.

"Henri is sixteen and Louis is eighteen."

"They're not coming home for Christmas?" asked Kay.

Andre shrugged. "We are not in agreement. They have long hair, play the guitar, and are intent to change the world. My world, I am afraid. Still, I do not like all this publicity I get. Madcap bachelor and so forth. What am I supposed to do? Stay at home and polish my jewels?"

Kay suppressed a giggle. "No, of course not. But you have had quite a track record, Andre. Admit it."

"Yes, that's true, but do I deserve to be hounded unmercifully by the gossip mongers of the media? Take this last business at the Plaza. What do you think my sons thought of me? Acting like a drunken boxing player. Don't the press think of things like that?"

"I'm sure your sons understood," said Jana. "Young people are so much more sophisticated these days." He didn't respond. "They did understand, didn't they?"

"Neither of them mentioned it. But then, as I've said, we talk infrequently." Andre stood up, dug into his pockets and withdrew two narrow packages wrapped in silver. "I brought you each a present. Shall I put them under the tree?"

"I'll do it," said Kay taking the gifts and shaking them. I hope they can be measured in carats, she thought.

"Would you like to see what I'm going to give to Raina, that is, if she will accept me?" The girls gathered around the Frenchman. He produced a domed blue velvet box from his inside pocket. "I selected it from my shop," he grinned. "I get a discount."

He flipped open the lid and both young women gasped. "I did not think Raina would like the ordinary engagement ring," Andre explained. Inside was a platinum diamond ring. A domed mount was set with one hundred and fifty-eight round and baguette diamonds, which collectively weighed over twenty carats. They circled an emerald-cut diamond which weighed five carats.

"It's breathtaking," Jana said when she finally found her voice.

"I've never seen anything like it," said Kay. "Can I touch it?"

"Certainly. Try it on if you like."

"I wouldn't dare. You might have trouble getting it back." Kay held the ring up to the light. "It looks just like a fallen star, Andre. You ought to put it on the tree and make her hunt for it."

"What a charming idea. Do you have a piece of ribbon?"

"I'll get one," volunteered Jana.

Andre turned to Kay. "Kay, do you think it's too ostentatious?"

"For Raina? Good heavens no. She's ostentatious about the *right* things."

Jana returned with a length of silver ribbon. "Now where should I tie it?" wondered Andre.

"Oh, within reach," exclaimed Kay. "*Well* within reach."

Andre tied the ring on a lower branch. It shone more brightly than any ornament on the tree.

"She'll not miss that," said Kay. "Even if she's wearing sunglasses."

Farouk, who had finished his shrimp, eyed the bauble with interest. He walked over to it and took a swipe or two. His fascination with its sparkle quickly diminished when he discovered it was not something to eat.

"When did you plan on getting married?" Jana asked. "That is, if . . ."

"If the lady says yes," finished Andre. "Well, I've been thinking. Raina's contract is up in April. And if it is agreeable to her, I thought we might marry then, sail for Europe, tour the south of France, then visit my father at our family chateau in Vichy."

"A chateau in Vichy," said Kay wistfully.

"It sounds so wonderfully romantic," sighed Jana.

"I'm going to open a bottle of champagne," exclaimed Kay. "We'll drink a toast!"

Three glasses were poured and Kay proposed a toast. "Here's to your storybook romance!"

And let's hope it has a happy ending, Jana silently amended.

Chapter Fourteen

From the New York *Post:*

WEDDING BELLS FOR ANDRE AND RAINA

NEW YORK (AP) New York's most eligible bachelor has given up his bachelorhood. Broadway's most acclaimed young actress has left her play. Sunday afternoon, April ninth, at his townhouse on East Sixty-eighth Street, Andre de Clermont married his leading lady, Raina Pendleton. The brief ceremony and reception were attended by a small but glittering gathering of celebrities.

Miss Pendleton wore a wedding gown made from imported Chantilly lace decorated with seed pearls and tiny diamonds. The new Mrs. de Clermont is pictured above feeding wedding cake to her husband's two sons, from a previous marriage, Henri, sixteen and Louis, eighteen.

The couple plan to sail to France on the Cunard Line. They will tour the south of France, stopping off at Nice, Cannes, and St. Tropez. Later they will visit Mr. de Clermont's father, the Baron de Clermont at the family villa in Vichy.

(Story and more photographs on inside pages.)

The silver-grey touring car moved cautiously through the slow-moving people who filled the streets and sidewalks of Vichy. They had come from all over the world to the springs of Vichy to partake of the healing waters.

The majority were elderly, many were crippled or in wheelchairs, and they casually moved through the streets as if traffic didn't exist. Andre was impatient. He knocked on the glass partition and urged the chauffeur to go faster. The driver nodded and beeped his horn several times, but still the crowd did not part.

"Damn," muttered Andre. "I told him to take the other turn. That way we could have avoided all this and driven directly to the chateau."

"Be patient, darling," said Raina. "I'm as anxious as you are to see your father, but we can't run people down, can we?"

Andre kissed his new wife on the cheek. "You are right, Raina. We might as well, as you Americans say, relapse and enjoy it."

The car turned down a boulevard lined with plane trees. Raina, her face pressed against the closed windows of the air-conditioned car, observed the mobs with fascination. All the people seemed to wear the same expression of serenity, as if they had found what they had been looking for. Even the usually pained, blanched faces of those who were obviously ill were tempered with something like hope.

"Oh, Andre, you must bring me down here. I want to see everything and I want to go to the springs and take the waters."

Andre scowled. "They aren't exactly champagne, my dear."

"Oh, I know that. They're bitter aren't they and smell like rotten eggs? It doesn't matter. I'm a great believer in assimilation and when in Rome, or in Vichy in this instance, then one must do as the natives do."

Andre gazed adoringly at his young wife. She was outfitted in a broadbrimmed hat trimmed with lilacs the color of her dress. He was constantly surprised and delighted to find that his beautiful and talented wife was not nearly as worldly-wise as he had first thought. He had grown oh-so-tired of those sophisticates with whom he had frequently been linked. Nothing ever overwhelmed or even surprised them. And they tended to be difficult after a certain point.

"Oh, Andre, what's that up ahead?"

"The park."

"And that building?"

"A bandstand. The Municipal Band gives concerts there."

"Look, they seem to be giving one now. Oh, can I lower the window?"

"Of course, my dear."

Raina rolled down the window and was greeted by a burst of music. She stared through the pale green patches of vegetation fringing the park. In the distance was the bandstand with its slender columns and ornate canopies. The bewhiskered conductor was resplendent in a white uniform trimmed with bright red ribbons and brilliant gold braid. Under his baton, the band played with brassy enthusiasm. Hundreds of people were sitting on iron chairs that had been placed in concentric circles around the bandstand—nearly all the seats were occupied.

"What a delightful welcome," exclaimed Raina. "We must come down here."

"Well I . . ."

"What's the matter?" teased Raina. "Are the de Clermonts too high and mighty for such vulgar entertainments?"

"There's always a time for the first," replied Andre, typically muddling American expressions.

As the limousine passed the park, he pointed out two of the springs for which Vichy was famous. The Chomel and the Grande Grille. The famous Celestine Spring was close to town. "We have other diversions in Vichy besides bandstands and springs," said Andre. "There's also a handful of very nice casinos."

"Oh, I've never gambled," said Raina. "But now that I'm rich, I must learn, mustn't I?"

"Not necessarily. What you must learn is not to lose. That is the major rule of life, whether you are rich or poor, whether you are in business or are gambling."

He took her hand. "You see, I gambled and I won you. Aren't I the smart pants?"

Raina stroked her husband's thigh. "Smart pants is the perfect nickname for you," she laughed. "As a matter of fact, I think that's what I'll call you." Andre looked nervously toward the chauffeur and Raina amended, "When we're alone, of course."

The Chateau de Clermont was perched on a hill that dominated the countryside. Its battlements and fortifications recalled a history of conquests, of battles against the English, of religious wars. A small village clung to the side of the hill and the weather vanes of some of the little houses reached almost to the level of the chateau's terrace. Below were fields and meadows and hedgerows. Raina turned to her husband, her eyes wide and shining.

"Andre, you didn't tell me . . . I never expected . . . It's like something out of a fairytale."

He smiled. "I'm afraid some of it isn't so pretty up close. Certain sections are very neglected. Those parts date from medieval times. Papa simply will not spend money to restore and redecorate." He shrugged his shoulders. "Perhaps he's right. After all, he lives alone with only the servants for company. Is he to redecorate for the servants? Hah! But now that you're here it might be something to think about. Particularly when there are children."

Raina turned from her husband to keep him from seeing her startled expression. Surely they would not live at the chateau for any length of time. No, she must have misunderstood him. After all, his business was in New York, as was hers. She was an actress. She could not imagine herself finding contentment stalking the corridors of a crumbling building.

The chateau loomed into view, its great towers crowned with cupolas. As the limousine climbed the hill dozens of servants began to appear, shouting and waving and running along the arcades.

"Who are all those people?" Raina asked innocently.

"Why, they're the servants."

Raina swallowed and sat back in the seat. The gates of the great bastion suddenly opened and they drove through a huge archway into the courtyard. People came running from every corner of the chateau. Raina estimated there must be more than thirty men and women, all stocky, big bosomed or barrel chested, with reddish-brown, weatherworn and smiling faces. Waving hands, rags and brooms, they descended upon the limousine and surrounded it.

"These are all servants?" asked Raina meekly.

Andre did not reply. He had already emerged from the car and beckoned to her to follow. Slowly, smiling and nodding, they passed along the line of welcoming servants.

Raina was overwhelmed. This was one of those rare times in her life when she felt ill at ease. She had never stopped to consider exactly how wealthy Andre was. By Harrisburg standards her family was rich, but this was something far beyond her imaginings. This was grandeur. This was tradition. No wonder so many of Andre's less than charitable friends inferred by look, manner or word that she was marrying him for his money. As Andre introduced her to each of the servants, she wondered how he could possibly remember all their names. Raina, who had had only two years of highschool French, was literally at a loss for words. She had to make do with simple "bonjours" all around.

Raina tugged at Andre's sleeve. "Where's your father?" she whispered.

"He's probably in the library," he replied matter-of-factly.

As he swept her through the gallery, Andre explained, "Now, I've told you, Raina, my papa's a bit —well—eccentric."

"You mean he's senile?"

"Oh no, nothing like that. Even though the stroke confined him to a wheelchair, his mind is as alert as ever." They hurried past sixteenth century Flemish tapestries which Raina could only admire but briefly.

At the end of the corridor was a set of tall oak doors, the grain and fittings attesting to their age. "Now," Andre whispered, "he's going to want to make the cross examination of you." She looked at him inquiringly. "Because, of course, he thinks you married me for the money."

"Just like that?"

"Just like that." Andre kissed her quickly on the lips. "And he'll probably have me take leave of the room on some pretext or other so that he can talk to you alone. Do not be afraid of him, Raina. He hates people who are afraid of him."

"But my French . . ."

"Papa is quite proud of his English and will be happy to employ it." Andre rapped lightly on the door. There was a gruff sound from the other side. They stepped into the library.

The room was immense and filled with Louis Treize ebony and copper bookcases which covered three entire walls. On the far wall, separating the windows and the fireplace, were two sixteenth century limoges enamel portraits of Catherine de Medici and Henry II. The room was dark, the windows heavily draped with deep blue brocade. It took Raina several moments before she saw her father-in-law. He was seated behind a Louis Quinze mahogany desk, absorbed in an open leather-bound book and using an onyx magnifying glass as his guide. Raina and Andre walked forward but he gave no indication of acknowledging their presence. They stood awkwardly for a few moments until he evidently came to the end of a chapter or paragraph. Then he slammed the book shut and looked up. The desk light illuminated his face. Raina caught her breath. He looked so much like his son. It was as if a perverse Hollywood makeup artist had taken Andre and aged him a quarter of a century. He was still a handsome, vital man despite his years and state of health. The Baron looked directly at his son and said gruffly, "I understand that you have brought me another daughter-in-law." His speech was measured and his tones were hard and metallic.

Andre nodded eagerly. "Papa, I want you to meet my wife, Raina."

There was a long pause as if the Baron were deciding something. Then he snapped his head toward Raina and coolly appraised her. She just as coolly appraised him back. It was as if she had seen her husband age before her very eyes. The same steel grey hair, the same blue-grey eyes, the same square jaw. It was uncanny and not a little unsettling.

Raina, making a concession to the old man's age and infirmity, spoke first. "I'm happy to be here . . ." She paused, not knowing how to address him.

"Baron," he replied. "Yes, I'm sure that you are." Then he commanded his son. "Andre, go and tell the cook that I wish fish for our supper. Then go to the cellars and select an appropriate wine and have it chilled."

"Very well, Papa." Andre smiled weakly at Raina and backed out of the room.

Once the doors were closed Raina, without waiting to be asked, sat down opposite her father-in-law. She crossed her legs and, again without invitation, lit a cigarette. The Baron scowled but said nothing. Raina flicked an ash toward a silver tray and said, "Well, Baron, since you are convinced that I have married your son for his money, I'm surprised you haven't offered to buy me off."

The Baron ignored the remark. "I was reading a book . . . on genealogy. *Our* genealogy. It would appear that our male ancestors all had something in common. They were attracted to beautiful but weak women."

"Weak in what way?"

"Physically weak. They would bear one, perhaps two children and then expire of related complications. This was so with Suzanne, my son's last wife. You are beautiful, but you do not look weak."

Raina stubbed out her cigarette. "I have the consti-
tution of a horse."

The old man chuckled. "Yes, yes, of a horse. You
would not give my son weak children. My son's sons
are weak. They care nothing for the business. They care
nothing for the tradition. They care only for themselves.
I want for you to give Andre a son, one that will carry
on the business and the barony. You will do that." It
was more of an order than a conclusion. "You have
the high breasts, the proud look. You will produce
great squalling sons, grasping and tenacious, perhaps
like yourself."

"Do you also read palms, Baron?"

The old man smiled before he could stop himself.
"Not palms, my dear, breasts." He rolled his wheelchair around the edge of his desk until he was so close
to Raina that she could smell the brandy on his breath.

Raina cupped her breasts in her hands. "You see
sons in these?" she asked half-mockingly. The Baron's
lips were dry. He ran his pink pointed tongue over
them until they glistened, his eyes never leaving that
which she was holding.

"Of course, if I were afforded a better view . . ." He
reached out until his long fingers—Andre's!—touched
the thin fabric covering her breasts. Smiling, Raina tilted
back her head. Deftly he worked the buttons loose
and the bodice of her dress parted. As usual, Raina
wore no bra. The Baron sucked in his breath as he
gazed upon her full, perfectly-formed breasts. The au-
reoles stood out in harsh relief against the smooth contours of her flesh. Using his forefinger he touched each
nipple in turn. Then he drew an imaginary circle around
each one. It was as if he were decorating them with a
long forgotten fertility rite. Reaching behind him he
swung his desk lamp around so that the light illuminated
the objects of his intense interest. "Perfect, perfect," he
crooned. "Most assuredly your first-born will be a boy
and a true de Clermont." He pulled back abruptly and
returned to the other side of the desk. Raina refastened
her dress.

"You seem satisfied with yourself, Baron."

"I am always happy when I am right. My wife, the mother of my son, married me for money and position. I satisfied her greed, but she detested me for it. Her hatred became a source of satisfaction to me. She died while giving birth to Andre and later I actually found myself missing her hatred. I'd found her rage amusing." He touched his fingertips to his temples. "But that doesn't matter. Nothing matters; even if you do not remain married to my son for the promised lifetime, you must give him a son who will rightfully inherit the title of Baron de Clermont."

"What makes you think that our marriage isn't forever, Baron? Do you have a private cup of tea leaves somewhere?"

"*Cela ne fait rien.* Just give me a grandson who can see the flaw in a jewel and not believe that love is for free."

He held out his hand to Raina. "Come . . . Raina. We shall join my son. Would you mind pushing the chair? An old man has only so much strength in his fingers and I am afraid that I have expended mine."

"Not at all," smiled Raina.

"You're not offended by me?"

"On the contrary," Raina laughed. "I think I like you very much."

Andre was waiting for them in the outer hall. He was pleased to see that Raina was pushing his father's wheelchair and that they were laughing. Guilo, a servant, appeared and announced that it was time for the Baron to take his whirlpool bath. The old man grimaced. "I must endure it. It keeps my legs—and other vital parts—from atrophying. Andre, why don't you take Raina up to your room and let her refresh herself, then take her on a tour of the grounds. The house can wait. You do not want to miss the beautiful afternoon sun. I will see you both in the library at exactly five-thirty. We will have a cocktail, maybe even two, before we dine."

Andre led Raina to the main entrance hall, which

she had not seen before. A great stone staircase rose triumphantly from the marble floor only to disappear into the shadows of the vaulted ceiling. A huge canvas attributed to Fragonard hung above a seventeenth century Italian ivory marquetry table and was flanked by Louis Quatorze tôle sconces that had been rewired for electricity. On their way up the staircase Raina asked, "Do you always do what your father asks?"

"When I am in his home I do. How did you get on with the Baron?"

"At first I thought he was ready to eat me alive, but now I think he likes me. Yes, and in time I believe he will even accept me into the family."

Andre's room was characterized by rich patterns, colors and textures. Natural wood boiserie with Cordova leather panels warmed the large area and set off the marble chimneypiece medallion that depicted Louis XIV. The huge canopy bed was draped in royal blue velvet and trimmed with seventeenth century embroidery. A huge Savonnerie rug brilliant in shades of brown, blue and rose covered most of the exquisite parquet floor.

"It's lovely," murmured Raina. "That bed must have belonged to Sleeping Beauty."

Andre laughed. "I assure you, my dear, that I don't intend to let you sleep in it. Come, let's both have a quick bath to get rid of the dust of the journey. Then we'll tour the gardens before the sun sets."

Raina went to the windows and looked at a parterred rose garden below. The roses, spectacular splashes of red against the verdant green, bloomed brightly on the intricately trimmed bushes.

"Andre, do let's hurry and bathe. I want to see the roses."

The summer breeze caught the delicate scent of the roses and guided the two toward the ornamental gardens like a welcoming hand. Raina stopped to sniff each variety and comment on their beauty.

"There are some strains that are peculiar to this part

of the country," explained Andre. "Would you like to see the de Clermont rose?"

"I'd love to." He took her hand and led her through the garden maze to the middle of the parterre.

The de Clermont rose bloomed in a cluster of bushes that were fuller and greener than all the others. The blooms were the size of a man's fist and the color of the petals graduated from a deep red in the center to a light creamy pink at the tips. Their scent, too, was stronger than the others.

"They're extraordinary, Andre. I've never seen roses like them. But why are none seen in the States? Surely your father couldn't be so miserly as to deny them to the rest of the world."

He smiled. "It's been attempted. But the roses do not transport. They grow only in this soil and bloom only in this sunshine."

"But *you* thrived in the States," Raina teased.

"Ah, but I had to keep returning to the chateau to revivify myself. Can you understand that?"

"I understand what you're saying, Andre. And I believe that for you it's true. It isn't for me. I can't imagine anything more *un*revivifying than returning to Harrisburg, Pennsylvania," Raina reflected sadly, momentarily dwelling upon the lack of any such sustenance from her home or family.

"Would you like a de Clermont rose?"

Andre's question restored her to the present and dispelled the loneliness she felt at thinking of her parents. After all, here she was—with her husband, who loved her.

"Yes, very much," she replied.

Andre retrieved a gold pen knife from his pocket, cut a rose in half bloom, trimmed it of its thorns, and handed it to his wife. Raina carefully tucked the rose between her breasts. "Andre, make love to me," she begged with sudden urgency.

"All right. Shall we go then?"

"No, here. I want to do it here."

Andre frowned but felt his excitement mount.

"The hedges are high. The servants couldn't see," she persisted.

"I don't suppose it would matter anyhow. They've seen plenty in their time." He wrapped his arms around her and felt her heart beating as rapidly as his own. The scent of the rose as it was crushed against her flesh intoxicated him, and slowly he pulled her down to the ground. Raina lay back on the soft grass, her hair spreading outward like fallen sunbeams. Without speaking, Andre reached for the front of her dress, retracing the path the Baron's fingers had traveled but a short time ago. One by one he fumbled with the buttons until he could push aside the lilac fabric to reveal her shapely shoulders and breasts. As his hand touched her warm, soft flesh a tingle of expectation raced through him.

Raina reached up and lovingly caressed his face. Andre raised his head and looked at her. Her eyes slowly opening and closing told him of her need. Suddenly she pulled herself up toward him, her lips hungrily covering his with a warm, damp pressure, and he could feel the tip of her tongue flicking back and forth. He opened his mouth wide and slid his lips over hers, stiffening his tongue and pushing it inside. Her tongue curled around his as he slid the skirt of her dress up over her hips and took her buttocks in his hands. He pulled her hard against him until the breath was forced from her lungs.

"Don't tarry, darling," she gasped.

Andre nodded wordlessly. In the time it took him to tear off his shirt his desire for her had become a thick, choking sensation in his throat, and yet still he hesitated. He gazed downward, his eyes devouring her body. Raina's skin was dusky, glazed amber by the sun. Hers was softer than the flesh of any woman he could remember. The curved mounds of her breasts were firm and resilient—beautifully shaped crests tipped by the bright carmine of her nipples. His eyes darted back and forth over her form and his body trembled with lust.

"Hurry, darling," Raina urged. "Please hurry. I'm ready for you."

Andre bent over her and trailed his lips down her silky skin from her throat to one of her breasts. The tip of his tongue flicked across the bud of her nipple and a soft cry escaped Raina's lips. He let it slide into his mouth and gently sucked on it.

Raina's breath hissed out through her teeth as his lips and tongue slowly moved down her flat stomach until his chin brushed against her inner thighs. He lifted his head, letting his moist breath caress the lower part of her stomach. He put his hands on her thighs and held her fast as he stimulated her with hard, quick touches of his tongue.

"Please, darling, *please!*" Raina pleaded.

Andre sat up and looked at her. Her face was flushed and drawn with passion. Her lips were parted and moist and her eyes flashed with anticipation. He quickly peeled off his trousers. Unable to resist any longer, Raina reached for him and guided him into her. A wave of sensation roared through her body as they were joined. She wiggled her hips as she arched her back to accommodate him. Andre gripped her waist and rocked his hips, slowly floating on a blissful cloud of sensual enjoyment as he felt her enfold him. They moved together, increasing the pace of their love-making as they hurried toward a mutual climax.

From the vantage point of his bedroom terrace, the Baron watched his son and daughter-in-law cavorting below in the rose garden. He smiled in remembrance of past but not forgotten pleasures. His rheumy eyes filled with tears which coursed down his wrinkled cheeks. "She will give him a son." A random breeze picked up his words and carried them across the hills where they were offered up as an incantation to those gods who remembered and smiled upon the old man.

Part Three

Chapter Fifteen

A bulky woman in black shuffled down the hall toward apartment 15A. Her legs were muscular and knotted with varicose veins. Her shoes, a pair of heavy brogans, had been bought in a thrift shop for a dollar-fifty. They slapped loosely against her broad feet; to accommodate her corns, the sides of the shoes had been cut out with a razor blade. She cradled a load of mail in her arm. A battered purse dangled from her thick wrist and a brass key glinted in her calloused fingers.

She could hear the cat on the other side of the door purring like a small outboard motor. "I'm comin', Farouk. Just give me a minute—to—uh—work this—uh—ol' key." The door opened and the great ginger cat pressed affectionately against her legs. "Bet you're hungry for your breakfast. Well, I'm sorry I'm late but I took myself over to Central Park for the protest."

Securely locking the door behind her, the woman made her way directly to the kitchen. There she plugged in a pot of coffee she had prepared for percolating the day before. Then she went to the cabinet to select a can of cat food for Farouk.

"Let's see . . . Super Supper? Liver and Egg in Gravy? How about Tasty Treat?" As she was opening the can she kept up an ongoing conversation with herself. "They make this stuff sound better than what we humans get to eat." She sniffed the contents of the opened can and murmured to the cat, "Hmmm, not bad, Farouk. You'll enjoy this." She emptied the entire tin into a clean dish and placed it on the floor.

Then she refilled the cat's water bowl. "I guess you're gettin' a bit lonesome for company. Well, Miss Jana's due back soon, and Miss Kay, too."

On the dining room table she arranged the letters, circulars and magazines into three separate piles. The pile for Raina was the smallest since she hadn't lived in the apartment for several years. She ran her finger across the table and frowned at the dust. "I'd better do some good work in here today. Though I don't know why; they never use it."

Eight months earlier Jana and Kay had redecorated the dining room. They had repainted the walls a vibrant Chinese red and the woodwork white. The newly purchased furniture—a dining room table, six chairs and sideboard—were Chinese Chippendale and had been lacquered a dazzling white. A chandelier of the same design and color hung from the center of the ceiling and an oriental rug dominated by reds and purples covered the floor. It was, to the maid's way of thinking, "not a decent place to eat."

While waiting for the coffee to perk she spritzed all the plants and tested them for dryness. When she returned to the kitchen the cat was sitting on a stool cleaning his whiskers.

"Well you look just as contented as a you-know-what." She poured herself a cup of coffee, adding three heaping teaspoons of sugar. Then taking a *News* she had found in a trash bin, she went into the living room to relax before starting work. The date of the paper was September 12, 1972 and the headline read: "Nixon Defends Vietnam Policy." Then lower and in smaller letters: "Protest Set for Central Park."

"Ol' Nixon wouldn't be so sure of his pol-i-cy if he had boys instead of girls. Yes sir, if he'd had a son or two over there in those Chinky jungles, he wouldn't be so high falutin' sure of his pol-i-cy."

Birdie O'Connell was fifty years of age, worn out, and lonely. She had been "in service" for thirty-five years and had raised seven children. All of them were married and had moved away, with the exception of her youngest boy, Joseph. In 1968 Joseph had been summoned to the Vietnam war. Since the time of Joseph's induction Birdie spent her time cleaning other people's apartments and watching other people's lives. Never a great reader, she began scanning the newspapers, laboriously putting the words into sentences, so that she could keep up with the war. Each day the news was more discouraging.

She got up from the bentwood rocker—one of Kay's "finds"—and went to the large carved oak bar that sat next to the Steinway baby grand in the newly redecorated living room.

Even though no one was at home, Birdie looked around her with a considerable amount of stealth. Then she added a heavy dollop of scotch to her coffee. She sauntered back to her place of rest and, using the remote control, she switched on the television set. The soundless pictures kept her company while she sipped the scotch-laced coffee.

The flickering images of the people reminded her of the anti-war protest she had attended in Central Park earlier that day. The protesters had been solemn in their vigil. The police had roamed among the young people and stopped to listen to the speeches, occasionally joining the respectful applause of the others. Birdie O'Connell felt clumsy and out of place among so many fresh faced and colorfully attired youngsters. But she read their posters and listened to their rhetoric and she understood their simple message . . . end the war and bring back our boys.

"Oh Lord, bring back Birdie's boy," she cried, then drained the cup. It was time to go to work.

Farouk went for cover when Birdie started to vacuum. He hated the noise and usually stayed in the closet until she was finished. Birdie was a slow but careful worker. She did not just do the "walkways" but vacuumed every corner, each windowsill and under the beds. When she finished, Birdie started on the individual rooms. Raina's room was first. Since it had been closed for a long time

Birdie opened the windows to allow the fresh air inside, then she began waxing the furniture.

"Wonder when Miss Raina's going to come home. Poor thing. Having to live among all those Frenchies."

The American newspapers had carried accounts of the celebrated divorce proceedings between Raina and Andre de Clermont. The final settlement was undisclosed, but it was rumored to be in excess of one million dollars. Andre had been given custody of his son. One ascerbic columnist hinted that Raina had sold her son for a prodigious amount of money, while others reported that she was brokenhearted over the court's decision. In any case, Raina was returning to New York to resume her career. Nobody knew exactly when, but Kay and Jana were determined to keep things ready for her.

Birdie opened Raina's closets which were still jammed with clothing. She removed the moth balls and left the doors open so that the garments might be refreshed by the air. After cleaning Raina's bath, she moved on to Kay's room. Because of Kay's penchant for clutter and collecting things it was the most difficult of the three bedrooms to put right. Birdie started on the framed posters that lined the walls. They represented Kay's work in the New York theatre to date, starting with *Raspberries* and ending with a mystery entitled *Make Mine Murder*. Kay had designed five Broadway plays, and each one of them had flopped. Three of the five never made it into New York. Characteristically Kay referred to herself as "Queen of the Broadway Flops" and pressed on. She was currently in Philadelphia with another play that was making its bid for Broadway.

Birdie carefully cleaned Kay's dresser top, which was littered with cosmetics and framed pictures of her various friends. The largest frame contained an enlargement of a snapshot of a young man whose smiling face had always appealed to Birdie. It was a picture of Fred Spangler taken several years earlier with a friend in Montreal. Perhaps Birdie would have felt differently about the young man had she known that he had for-

saken his country rather than fight a war in which he
didn't believe. Perhaps not.

Birdie started on Jana's room next. She attacked her
work with fresh enthusiasm because she liked Jana best
of the three. The muscles in her arms stood out as she
polished the oak headboard until it gleamed brightly
enough to pass her own rigid standards. She washed the
windows on the French doors leading to the terrace both
inside and out. She not only cleaned the floor and
fixtures in Jana's bathroom, but the wall tiles as well.
While changing the sheets, Birdie wondered anew why
a nice young woman like Jana Donatello had not yet
married. Jana was pretty enough for any man and her
manner suggested that she would make a good wife
and mother. Birdie was looking forward to the young
woman's return home. Jana always took time to talk
to her. She seemed sincere and truly interested in the
old woman's problems. Birdie made a mental note to
buy some fresh daisies from the little old man who sat
near the Seventy-second Street subway and put them
in Jana's room the day of her return.

Jana rushed from the stage of the Detroit Civic
Auditorium to a dresser who awaited her behind a folding screen. She had a sixteen-second change between a
chorus number and a solo for the automobile industrial. The screen had been erected at Jana's insistence
since the change was very nearly total. She disliked
displaying herself in front of the stagehands and members of the cast. The other female members of the industrial were not so concerned; they changed in full
view of anyone who happened to be backstage. But
Jana was unbending and before she would go on the
opening night, she got what she wanted.

The dresser, a middle-aged woman named Maggie,
helped Jana out of her brief silver costume, quickly
patted her dry with a towel, then helped her into a tight-
fitting gown that was very nearly transparent. The
material had been embroidered with rhinestones and
mother of pearl, bits of lacework had been sewn in

strategic places and the bottom was edged in uneven tufts of white turkey feathers. Maggie zipped Jana up as the young woman moved the material so that the decorations were where they should be. Maggie draped a white feather boa over Jana's arms, then worked on her hair with a teasing comb until the cue was given.

Jana sang the title song of the industrial presentation entitled "Driving it Home." The entire production was lavish and employed some of the best talents in show business. It ran for only a week, but it was a tax deductible expense. The purpose of the show was to ballyhoo the new cars coming out of Detroit. The song had a slow insinuating rock beat and double entendre lyrics. The lines ostensibly referred to parts of an automobile, but worked as well for parts of the female anatomy.

Jana's appearance created quite a sensation with the audience. And when the music and the song started, they began to applaud the cumulative effect. Gigantic slides of different parts of the newly designed cars were flashed behind Jana as she sang. At the beginning of the second verse she was joined by a chorus of eight men and eight women. The tempo of the musical number became a pulsating, forceful beat that underscored the risqué lyrics.

After the curtain calls, Jana rushed to the main dressing room she shared with three other women and struggled out of the dress. She disliked doing the industrial and everything it stood for, but her finances were in such a state that she had to do something. And rather than go back to waiting tables, she had taken the first job offered her. The other three entered, congratulated her on her good work, and then began talking among themselves about their newly acquired boyfriends among the male cast members. Jana put on her robe and pinned up her hair. She intended to take a good long shower to wash away the perspiration, the makeup and all memories of Detroit.

There was a knock at the door, and since she was nearest, she answered it.

He had his hat in one hand and a box of violets in the other. His dark hair was marked by a jagged streak of white over each ear. His eyes were dark and deep-set beneath full, winged eyebrows. "Miss Donatello?" She nodded. "I'm Sam Benedict."

He looked to be in his late thirties, possibly older. But time had not imprinted any telltale signs upon his face. "I want to compliment you on your performance." He thrust the box at her and grinned self-consciously. "My card's inside. I own a Cadillac dealership in Rockland County, New York. The program notes said you were from New York, too. And I was wondering whether you would be interested in appearing in my television commercial."

"A commercial for Cadillacs?"

"Well, yes. The salary, I'm sure, would be to your liking."

"I don't think so, Mr. . . ."

"Benedict," he repeated.

"I'm an actress, not a television saleswoman."

"After enjoying you on stage, I would say you could do just about anything. Look, why don't we discuss it over a drink. I'm staying at the Excelsior Inn. They have a nice bar there." Jana frowned. He hurriedly added, "Or anyplace you say."

Jana didn't want to go. She had no interest in doing the commercial, but she hadn't yet learned how to say no to people.

"I have to shower and change."

"I don't mind waiting."

"The Inn's just across the road, isn't it? I'll meet you there in a half an hour."

He smiled profusely. "I'll be looking forward to it, Miss Donatello." Then he hurried away.

Jana opened the box. "How lovely. Violets in the winter." She was impressed by his originality. Any other man of his ilk, she reasoned, would have brought orchids.

"An admirer?" asked one of the girls.

"Some businessman who wants me to do a TV commercial for his New York-based Cadillac company. It's only a local thing."

"Only a local thing?" jeered another girl. "Why, they play those things so often that if you get the right bucks you can make yourself a nice fat roll."

"Still," protested Jana, "to hustle for *cars*."

"What do you think you're doing here, honey?"

"No one in New York can see me here," Jana replied sharply. "I'm an actress, not a car salesman."

"Honey, do anything to pay the rent."

Sam Benedict was standing at the bar when Jana entered. She was wearing a dress of periwinkle blue and had pinned the violets to her waist. Sam had been struck by Jana's sensuality onstage, now he was struck by her innocence. Jana saw Sam, smiled warmly, then hastened toward him.

"Am I late, Mr. Benedict?"

"Not at all, Miss Donatello. You're right on time."

She studied his face. His expression suggested a healthy degree of self-confidence but also a certain modesty. He took her arm and guided her to a table some distance from the bar and the entertainment—a cocktail lounge pianist and singer who was as untalented as he was over-amplified. After signaling the waitress, he sat down opposite her. "What will you have to drink, Miss Donatello?"

"I'll have a scotch and soda to celebrate the end of a very gruelling assignment. By the way, thank you for the violets. They happen to be my favorite flower." The drinks arrived with surprising efficiency. "Tell me about your commercial, Mr. Benedict."

Sam relaxed and went into his sales pitch. "I want this to be a classier commercial than your usual local advertisement. Believe me, it won't be anything like 'learn computers in your spare time' or 'greatest polka hits.' Not that our budget can be extravagant. If you agree to do it and represent us, I've been toying with the idea of getting the rights to the song you sang tonight. You could be filmed lying across a highly polished Cadillac. Your dress couldn't be anywhere as revealing as the one you wore tonight—I'm afraid it wouldn't pass the censors."

Jana smiled. "I wouldn't think of appearing on TV in that gown. Mr. Benedict, the only way you're going to get a quality commercial is to pay union scale. I don't mean just me, but the musicians, cameramen, director and so forth. Otherwise you're going to get something like the 'learn meditation in your spare time' type."

"I realize that. But the only way I would go for that kind of money is if I could get you under contract."

"Why me in particular, Mr. Benedict? There must be hundreds of young women out there who could sell your product. Frankly I'm not at all keen on being a Cadillac saleswoman. I'm an actress, Mr. Benedict."

"So you say. Well, Miss Donatello, I think you're also a bit of a snob. I play an excellent game of tennis, but while I'm waiting to win the Forest Hills finals I've got to make a living. A very good living, I might add. I'm the largest Cadillac distributor in New York, Connecticut and Massachusetts."

Jana was smarting. She did not like anyone defining her values. "Mr. Benedict, I don't think I'm a snob just because I don't want to lounge across a car in a scanty costume."

"I won't try to convince you. You have my card, and if you change your mind give me a call. Let's consider the case closed for now." Before Jana could protest, he signaled the waitress for another round of drinks. "Tell me about yourself. Where do you come from, how long have you been in New York, and what shows have you done?"

"I thought you read the program."

He managed to keep his smile. "Program notes are so cut and dried. I'd rather hear you tell it."

"What's the point, Mr. Benedict? I've already told you I'm not going to do your commercial."

"Perhaps the commercial wasn't the only reason I asked you for a drink."

"I thought not."

"I wanted to get to know you."

"You have me at a disadvantage, Mr. Benedict. You've read my program notes, but I know nothing about you except that you own a Cadillac showroom. Tell me, are you married?"

He frowned. "Yes, I am, but . . ."

Jana stood up. "I must be going, Mr. Benedict. I thank you for a most enlightening evening." She unpinned the violets and dropped them on the table. "Here, they're still fresh and the evening's still young. Perhaps you'll get lucky."

As Jana walked down the boulevard toward the hotel where the cast was garrisoned she wondered why she had been so rude to Sam Benedict. She had managed passes before—crude ones and subtle ones—from all kinds of men. But she had never gotten that angry before. "The hell with it. Tomorrow it's back to New York City. I'll be home with my own friends and I'll forget all about this whole incident." Still she wondered, if he hadn't been married, would she have stayed?

Kay stood backstage at the Biltmore Theatre in Philadelphia chewing on a cuticle as the third act curtain of her new show was lowered. The actors, forcing bright smiles, hurried into position for the curtain calls. The curtain was quickly raised to catch whatever scattered applause was forthcoming. There was not enough to warrant a second call.

The play was titled *Rumpled Sheets* and was purported to be a comedy. There were rumors that the producers were using the show as a tax write-off, and from what was going on onstage, that would seem to be true.

The assistant stage manager, a friendly young man named Eric Grainger, patted Kay on the back. "I'm sure glad we're not on stage. I've heard more applause at a funeral."

"Funerals are funnier," replied Kay bitterly. "Lord, why did I get involved in this project? Sex comedies of this kind have been out for years. It would have been better if the producers had just revived *The Moon Is Blue* or *Up in Mabel's Room*. I should have known a comedy with the opening lines 'It was the best of times, it was the worst of times' was somehow all wrong." Kay pressed her face against Eric's chest. "Oh Lord, Eric. This will be my sixth flop. You know how superstitious theatre people are. Everybody'll start believing I'm a bad omen. They'll be afraid to hire me. I'll become the Martin Beck of costume designers." She grinned crookedly. "That theatre hasn't housed a hit in years and years. Just one godawful flop after another."

"I think your costumes are really fine, Kay."

"Thanks, Eric, but who's going to see them? We'll never make it into New York."

"Forget it, Kay. Don't tear yourself apart." Eric gathered together his courage. "Look, why don't we go out tonight, have a few drinks and forget this fiasco?"

Before Kay could answer the seven actors filed off the stage. Each of them looked as stunned as if they had all just witnessed a terrible accident. Kay and Eric patted them on the arms, smiled weakly and murmured meaningless little phrases, but they came out sounding more like condolences. After the actors had descended the spiral staircase to the dressing rooms below, Eric turned back to Kay. "What do you say? We'll party a little and get this out of our systems."

Kay considered the young man. Eric's proposition was tempting and, as she noticed for the first time, he was not bad looking. He had a slight space between his front two teeth, but he had beautiful blond hair and sparkling green eyes. His skin tone was high, like that of an adolescent, and he was physically fit. Kay shook her head. "I'm sorry, Eric. I wouldn't be good company and I don't want to bring you down."

"You wouldn't bring me down. You're a permanent up, Kay."

"Thanks, but I think I'm going to pick up a bottle

of scotch, go back to the hotel and drink myself into a stupor."

He smiled gamely. "Well, if you change your mind, I'm only a floor away."

Kay nodded her appreciation. "I must be doing something wrong. Six shows, six flops. Talent ain't enough, kid. I've got to get me some taste."

"Call me. I've got taste."

"The script didn't seem *that* bad, but it's so hard to tell. And the actors are all pros. Daisy's a name. Why do you suppose she got involved in this piece of drek?"

"We've all got to work, Kay. We can't sit around on our butts waiting for plays with award-winning potential to come along. Anyway, I think you can learn from the bad as well as the good."

Kay kissed Eric on the cheek. He blushed and looked like he had gotten an instant sunburn. "We'll get together when I'm in a better mood, Eric. I promise you."

Returning to her room, Kay kicked off her shoes and flopped onto the bed with a bottle of scotch cradled in her arm. She dialed room service. "This is 602. Send up two buckets of ice and lots of club soda. Say about three or four bottles—quarts. And a tray of hors d'oeuvres—snacks—you know—something fattening . . . What have you got? . . . Mmmm, I'll have the shrimp puffs, a wedge of cheddar cheese and lots of crackers." She hung up. "I haven't had a goddam cracker in years!" Kay opened the bottle and took a long drink. "Gaaah! That's good stuff. One a day, that's all I ever have. One a day. Before this night's over, I intend to be up to May 8th, 1999." She balanced the bottle on her stomach and waited for her order to arrive. "I'll never get famous doing flops. I've got to stop grabbing at every show I can get my hands on. Oh damn, Fred, where are you tonight?" She reached for the phone. No. I can't call him after all this time, she thought. When did I talk to him last? Two or maybe three Christmases ago.

A short time later a bell boy arrived with a large tray.

Kay signed the check and tipped him, then she attacked the cheddar cheese and crackers with gusto. She paused long enough to mix herself a stiff drink, cutting it just slightly with ice and soda. Kay tried calling Jana in New York but got the service. "No, no thanks. No message." She leafed through her phone book for Fred's number in Montreal and tested herself before looking at the page. "One, five one four, three seven four seven six seven eight. I'll be damned. I had it right after all this time." She glanced at the travel alarm. It was past eleven. "No, it's too late. Fred's an early to bed, early to rise guy."

Kay returned to the scotch and snacks. At this point in her life an occasional binge didn't hurt her waistline. She had maintained her present weight of one hundred and sixteen for the past four years. She stirred her scotch with her finger and drank nearly half a glass. Then she stripped out of her clothes and put on a flowing caftan of a sheer blue fabric featuring a rococo design handpainted in gilt. Glass in hand, she whirled around the room humming a sprightly waltz. She stopped next to the phone and with a sharp intake of air picked up the receiver. "Oh, Fred, I want to call you and I want you to tell me it's all right. That I'm all right." Sighing she placed the receiver back in its cradle. "How can you tell me? You and I don't know each other anymore. Perhaps that's as it should be."

She sat down in a chair and stared out the window. It was raining. A soft, easy rain; the kind that brought with it a feeling of melancholy. She stared at the mottled pane and a series of wavering images appeared; faces in place of her own reflection. They were the faces of people she had known and loved during her lifetime: family, friends, and the few young men she had known intimately. Each in turn was washed away by the rain until only Fred's image remained. Kay reached out to touch his face, and he, too, disappeared. Without realizing it, Kay had the phone in her hand. Then she found herself dialing. Three rings before a vaguely familiar voice answered.

"Fred?" she said with controlled casualness. "Oh Fred, it's Kay, Kay Kincade . . . I'm fine. Actually I'm not so fine. That's why I'm calling . . . Sure, sure I can hold on . . . Oh you're back . . . Yes, it has been a long time . . . You sent me a letter? Well, I'm not in New York. I'm calling from Philadelphia. That's why I wanted to talk to you . . . An announcement? What kind of announcement?" Kay reached for her drink and pressed it against her cheek. "Oh, I see. Well—uh —congratulations, Fred . . . No, no, no, it wasn't important. Really, it wasn't. It's just important that you be happy, you hear . . . She's French. Well, that figures doesn't it . . . No, I only meant with you being there in Montreal and all . . . Look, Fred, there's a whole lot of people at my door. I'm supposed to be going out on the town tonight. We just opened a new show . . . Oh, yes, it's fabulous. Sure to run forever. All my best. And we'll be in touch . . . Yes, love you too."

Kay dabbed at her eyes with a cocktail napkin. "Now what in the hell did I think anyway. That he was going to be lying beside the phone gasping my name? Of course he got married. He's the marrying kind." She got up, went to freshen her drink and caught sight of herself in the mirror. "I think it's time to reinvent myself." She slammed down the drink and rushed into the bathroom where she brushed her teeth, freshened her makeup and tousled her hair. Then she added the green feather boa that Raina had given her, and on her way out of her hotel room grabbed the bottle of scotch.

Kay rapped lightly on Eric's door so that if he were asleep she would not wake him. The door opened almost immediately and Eric, barefoot and wearing just a pair of jeans, smiled broadly. His delight was obvious and his welcome genuine. Again he had startled Kay into an awareness of his warmth and appeal. "Kay, you changed your mind. This is great. Come in, come in!"

"Eric, I hope you don't mind. I felt I had to make a human connection."

"Well, I'm human, all right," he grinned. "I've argued the point often."

"My mood isn't any better," confessed Kay. "In fact, I'd say it's gotten a good deal worse."

"I've been told I'm a great mood changer."

"I brought some scotch. I've been trying to drink by myself. I don't know how Lillian Roth did it—I'll not cry tomorrow, I'll cry tonight."

"Want me to make you a drink?"

"Only if you'll have one with me. You got ice and mix?"

"Uh huh, I ordered it, hoping you'd drop by. I don't think the ice has melted yet."

Eric quickly mixed two drinks and motioned to Kay to sit down. The bed was the only piece of furniture besides the dresser—Eric's room was a good deal smaller and less expensive than Kay's. He sat down beside her and watched her as she sipped her drink. She looked as if she was about to burst into tears.

Eric was moved by her obvious unhappiness and, taking a chance, began bluntly: "Kay, I'm going to be straight with you. I think you're being self-indulgent about the play and—and whatever else is bothering you. You've got the long end of the stick: you're beautiful, you're talented, you're together, and you're desirable. What more do you want?"

Kay set her drink aside. "Right now I'd settle for just the last." Her eyes glistened with the tears that were ready to fall.

Eric took Kay in his arms and held her tight. She pressed her face against his shoulder and let her stored up sorrow and frustration burst forth. He stroked her hair and murmured soothing words until her tears were dry and she could cry no more. Then he reached for a tissue and dried her eyes. Kay looked at him gratefully. "Eric, could I stay the night with you?"

"Yes. I want you to."

"Will you forgive me if—just for tonight—I happen to call you Fred?"

He kissed the tip of her nose. "You can call me anything you like for as long as you like."

Eric again took her in his arms, enveloping her in a

warm and comforting embrace. They kissed, tentatively at first, then with quickened urgency and desire. Drawing off her long and flowing robe to reveal the ripe, womanly body beneath it, Eric gently urged Kay to lie back on the bed. Flesh met flesh, and Kay's earlier depression vanished in a rising tide of passion. Eric was a masterful and knowing lover, who seemed to sense instinctively that tonight the most important thing in the world to Kay was to have her womanhood reaffirmed.

Eric already knew that he loved Kay, and was determined to convince her by his lovemaking that she could love him, too. He caressed her slowly—firmly kneading and relaxing her shoulders—then let his hands slide down her throat to encompass her lush breasts, softly slipping the nipples between his fingers before bringing the pressure of his lips to bear upon them. He couldn't seem to get enough of her as he moved his powerful but gentle arms around her waist and clasped his hands to the small of her back, pulling her tightly against him. Trembling, he lifted himself enough to push off his jeans.

They explored each other's bodies with greedy delight, and by the time Eric entered her Kay was oblivious to everything but her desire to satisfy him and be satisfied in return. In the wake of their shuddering and heady climax, as they sat in bed contentedly sipping scotch and smoking cigarettes, she smilingly realized that not once in their lovemaking had it crossed her mind to call him Fred. Eric had returned her, at least for the length of this blissful interlude, to the present.

The silver Bentley pulled into Orly Airport on the outskirts of Paris. The chauffeur, a large man with brutal features, opened the door for his passenger. Raina stared at him dully. He reached out his hand to help her but she ignored it and climbed out by herself. Straining her eyes through the swirling snow, she saw a bright blur of neon—Air France.

"We're here, then?" she asked.

"Oui, Baroness."

"Speak English!" she snapped, her voice as cold and hard as ice.

Raina pulled the collar of the black sable coat around her face and walked toward the entrance. The chauffeur followed very closely behind. He acted somewhat like a keeper, which in a way he was. Gathered inside the glass entrance was a group of reporters and photographers. They were ill-tempered at having been kept waiting for more than an hour. Raina saw them in time to don her sunglasses. As she pushed open the doors they rushed toward her shouting their questions. Flashbulbs momentarily blinded her. She felt the chauffeur's arm guide her toward the ticket counter. Raina placed both of her hands on the countertop and asked breathlessly, "Has the plane left for New York yet?"

The reservation clerk responded in English. "No, Baroness. There was a delay. You are here in time." Raina pushed her ticket toward him. "And your luggage?"

"The chauffeur will see to that." Raina turned to him. "Keep those jackals away from me!"

The chauffeur stepped between Raina and the newsmen. His bulk was impressive. They backed away from the counter and Raina. "The Baroness has no statement. Please do not disturb her."

Raina ordered the chauffeur: "Check my luggage, Emile. Then bring the claim checks to Gate Twelve." As she turned, she encountered another barrage of flashbulbs. People stopped and stared and began chattering with one another as Raina made her way down the corridor. They no doubt recognized her from the enormous amount of publicity that had already filled the media. The photographers and newsmen darted around her like scavenger dogs. The popping bulbs continued exploding in her face, and the questions were as sharp and pointed as arrows. She knew enough French to understand their meanings.

"Why did you abandon your child?"

"There were rumors of adultery."

"Was it a settlement or a pay-off?"

It would be the same when she arrived in New York and Raina hoped that she would be able to keep up her strength. No one would be at Kennedy to protect her. She hadn't even let Jana or Kay know exactly when she was arriving. Why subject them to the brutal publicity?

Raina neared a bar. She wanted desperately to go inside and have a drink, but not with the newsmen around. That's all she'd need. Yet another picture of her. This time poised on a barstool downing a vodka and soda. She licked her lips and pushed on.

When she arrived at Gate 12 she was relieved to find that the flight was boarding. Now where in the hell was the chauffeur? She saw him casually walking toward her, holding the claim checks in his hand as if they were a gift. She snatched them from him. He touched his cap in mock respect. Without a word, Raina turned and walked toward the boarding gate.

Raina had a window seat in the first class section of the Boeing 707. The stewardess was flustered. Obviously she recognized Raina, but her sympathies seemed to be with the young woman. As she took Raina's coat to hang it up, Raina whispered, "Please, could I have a drink? I know we're not supposed to be served until we're in flight, but I really could use it."

"Of course, madam. What would you like?"

"A vodka double, with soda. And I really do appreciate it." Raina kept her face hidden in a French fashion magazine until the drink arrived. She sipped it slowly, knowing that she would have to make it last. Once the plane was airborne she would order another.

Raina endured the welcome speech by the captain and the safety demonstrations by the stewardesses. Her stewardess brought Raina another drink even before she had asked for it. Raina nodded in gratitude and stared at the glass. She hoped that the alcohol would blot out the past, but painful memories faded in and out of her consciousness like images on a motion picture screen.

*　　*　　*

Raina had not intended to get pregnant. She felt that she was much too young to be burdened with the bearing and raising of a child. But Andre had had other ideas. He was impatient to have a son. He planned to raise the boy the same way that he had been raised and was determined that his son would become the rightful heir to the de Clermont jewelry empire. This time he did not intend to let a foolish woman turn his boy into a fop the way Suzanne had spoiled his other two sons —sons he had never understood or even loved.

"You made me stop taking the pill because you said you were worried about my health. I counted on you, Andre. And you failed me on purpose!"

"Why do you think I married you—when we could simply have remained lovers—if not to have a child, a son?"

"I thought you loved me."

He smiled enigmatically.

"I'm too young to be tied down with children, Andre. Why, we've barely begun to know one another."

"Get dressed, Raina. Papa does not like to be kept waiting for dinner."

Raina began to realize that she was less a wife than a vessel for the oncoming child.

After a six-week cycle of illness had passed, more disillusionment awaited Raina. Andre refused to have sex with her. He believed that if he did so he might harm the baby. Raina was shocked. "That's superstition, Andre. You can't be serious. Couples have sex right up to the eighth month."

Andre replied coolly. "I shall move to another bedroom in the chateau."

"What am I? Just a human incubator for this child?"

He struck her face. "You will follow my orders. You're to take care of yourself. You're not to engage in any activity that's strenuous. You're to eat good food and get the proper amount of rest. You will stay here at the chateau, for that is where my son will be born."

Raina was distraught. She didn't want to be attended by the local doctor, even though he had successfully delivered Andre's other two sons. She wanted to be back in New York City and have her friends Jana and Kay nearby when the event took place.

But out of love and a need for love returned, she adhered to her husband's wishes. She tried to make allowances for him. After all, they had been brought up in different cultures. And he wanted to be sure he had a healthy child. Even so, in addition to the life growing inside of her, she had a terrible sense of foreboding.

Once Raina had become pregnant, Andre had returned to his work. A private helicopter transported him to Paris. From there he flew to Amsterdam, Rome and Monte Carlo, where there were other de Clermont jewelry stores, each run by a male cousin. He traveled back and forth across the Atlantic to New York then on to Phoenix and Los Angeles where other shops were located. Raina begged to be taken on these trips, but he was adamant in his refusal.

"Raina, you are in a most delicate condition. The flight could be dangerous to our son. And what if there should be an accident?"

"Then I would be dead," Raina replied bitterly.

But when Andre returned, he would be all concern and generosity. He brought her books in English and extravagant gifts of perfume, jewelry and maternity clothes purchased on the Champs Élysées in Paris. But he no longer made love to her.

The days and weeks plodded by. Raina attempted to keep herself busy by reading or strolling in the gardens. She had no conversations with anyone except her father-in-law, and then only at meals. Dr. Foucault from Vichy visited her at regular periods and, using stock English phrases, complimented her health and that of the oncoming child's. The baby was going to be small, for at four months Raina had only a barely rounded stomach to show for her trouble, and that was discreetly covered by a flow of lace or embroidery. The doctor encouraged Raina to eat more and to continue her walks. It was on one of these walks that Raina met Gabriel.

She had never seen him before. Apparently he was one of the gardener's sons, all of whom worked the grounds of the estate. He looked very young—perhaps not yet twenty. And like the other peasants, he was stocky and his complexion ruddy from working outdoors. She had seen him in the distance cleaning a fountain. He was bare except for a hat of straw and a pair of wet trousers. His body was thickly muscled and burnished by the sun. Raina, lowering the parasol that she carried to protect herself from the strong summer rays, walked toward the fountain. She uttered a cry of surprise as if she had come upon him unawares. The young man smiled. His teeth were large, even and very white.

"Bonjour," said Raina, aware that her greeting was out of place.

The young man had stopped work and was eating his lunch. He bit into a sausage, swallowed the piece nearly whole and replied, "Good day, Baroness." His expression was mischievous, as if he had secrets to share.

"You speak English?" she questioned, not daring to hope.

"Yes, Baroness. I worked at one of the casinos. I learned English there."

"Your name?"

"Gabriel, Baroness."

"Please don't keep referring to me as 'Baroness' at every turn. It makes me feel like a relic."

"Yes, Bar . . . madam."

"Well I don't want to interrupt your lunch." Gabriel smiled and bit into another sausage. Its hot garlicky scent wafted toward Raina and made her feel slightly nauseated. She brought the parasol around, blocking the young man from her view, and hurried across a bridge that spanned a small pond. The bridge was made of metal cast in the form of branches. Raina paused in the center and looked back. Gabriel was watching her as he continued to eat.

Throughout the night Raina thought of the young

man. The next day her heart was beating rapidly as she prepared for her afternoon walk. He was not at the fountain, which now gushed fresh, clear water from the mouths of mythical fish. Raina leaned against the edge. She was nearly hyperventilating with disappointment. She didn't dare ask any of the other servants of his whereabouts. She crossed the bridge. On the other side of the pond there was a slope where the vineyards began. The earth was dark red, the color of dried blood, and the sweetness of ripening grapes permeated the sultry air. The grapes were used for the baron's private stock—Chateau de Clermont—a light fruity wine that Raina found a bit saccharine for her taste. As she neared she became aware of the sound of garden shears. Snip . . . snip . . . snip. Gabriel was trimming dead leaves from the vines. He seemed happy but not surprised to see her.

Raina told herself that the affair began in innocence. It had culminated out of her own desperate loneliness and frustration. But with its sexual release, it brought a damning end to her marriage and her loss of her child.

"Baroness, your supper." The stewardess was standing in the aisle holding a tray of food. Raina accepted it and ordered another drink. The meal consisted of a filet mignon, endive salad, small roasted potatoes, assorted cheeses, bread sticks and a pot of chocolate mousse. Raina picked at the salad, ate a breadstick, and when the drink arrived she said, "I'm afraid I'm not hungry." The stewardess nodded and took away the tray.

Raina's need for human communication was so great that she found herself seeking out Gabriel's company each day. At first they spoke idly of inconsequential matters. He asked her to tell him about the United States—New York in particular—and she was happy to comply, in so doing reliving some of her warm memories. Then one afternoon after exchanging a few words with Raina, Gabriel disappeared into a large shed used for the storage of tools and wine presses. Just before entering, he cast a backward glance, and Raina knew that the inevitable culmination of their time spent together was at hand. She began walking toward the shed. In retrospect she knew that nothing on earth—marriage vows, pending motherhood, or a sense of morality—could have stopped her.

Gabriel was standing near several cloth bags containing the dead leaves from the grape vines. Motes of dust floating in shafts of sunlight gave the visual impression that he was inside an angular cage.

Their love-making was fierce and traumatic in its intensity, but this initial encounter did not burn away their desire for one another. The next day Raina and Gabriel met in the shed, and every day following for the rest of the month. They continued their affair until that afternoon when Raina was summoned to the Baron's library.

As she walked down the corridor, Raina noticed the complete absence of servants. There was always some young woman polishing or some old man sweeping. It gave her an uneasy feeling. Before she reached the doors they opened and the local priest emerged. He officiated at the small church located on the de Clermont property, which was attended by the servants and the inhabitants of the small village surrounding the chateau.

"Bonjour, Père Beauchemin," greeted Raina.

The priest dipped his bald head and muttered, "Bonjour, Baroness." Then he thrust his hands into his sleeves and scurried away.

Raina stood at the partially open doors wondering whether she should knock. "Come in, Raina." It was her father-in-law's voice. It was unusually deep, as if he were suffering from a sore throat. She entered. The Baron, as usual, was sitting behind his desk. Standing next to him was Andre. Raina was startled. Her husband wasn't due back for another week. She ran to him with outstretched arms, "Andre! How wonderful. . . ." She was stopped by the expression on his face. Hate? Disgust? Perhaps a mixture of both. "What's wrong, Andre? What's happened?"

Andre turned his back to Raina. The Baron spoke. "We are aware of your liaison with young Gabriel. There's no denying it. We have the information on the best authority."

Raina's mind raced. Gabriel wouldn't have told. He would be placing himself in jeopardy. But . . . who? Of course, it had to have been the priest. Gabriel had confessed to the priest and then the information had been passed on to the Baron.

"Have you nothing to say?" asked the Baron.

Raina stood defiantly before him. "I don't deny it. But then I don't deny my loneliness, nor my husband's refusal to share my bed. What in the hell do you expect me to do? There's no one here to talk to, no one to love or to love me. Andre! *Andre!* Look at me!"

He looked at her. His eyes were narrow slits. "You've dishonored your vows."

"What about the priest's vows?" snapped Raina. "You don't scorn him and he's supposed to be holy. A man of God. I—am—only human."

"I could kill you, Raina."

"Then do it, Andre. Go ahead." She smiled. "No, you wouldn't touch me. Not because you're afraid of harming me, but because of the baby. What if I tripped myself down a flight of stairs or rolled down a hillside?"

"Shut up, Raina," said the Baron. "You don't have much longer in confinement. You're not to leave the chateau during this final period. You can take your . . . walks in the courtyard. I've engaged Dr. Foucault to stay here. He will be able to attend you."

"Doctor or keeper?" retaliated Raina.

"That depends upon you, my dear."

"What have you done to Gabriel? Have you dismissed him, or worse?"

"That is no concern of yours. But let us just say that your errant lover is gone from the grounds and from the area. From now on you will dine alone. Neither Andre nor I have any wish to see you. Dr. Foucault will relay your needs to me. If they are within reason, I will see that they are attended to. You will have everything you wish to be well and comfortable until the birth of my grandson."

Raina was incredulous. "You mean to keep me here like more of a prisoner than I've already been. You'll not. I'll leave. I'll go back to the States and have my child."

The Baron winced, closed his eyes and spoke as if pronouncing a sentence. "You will not be allowed to leave the chateau until afterward. Then, I assure you, you can go anywhere you wish."

Raina slammed her fists on the desk. "This is not a fascist country. You can't make me stay here against my will."

"I am the Baron de Clermont. This is a small community and I am the power supreme." He smiled. "Dictator if you like."

"But after my child is born?"

"Then there will be plenty of time to assess the situation. You look tired, Raina. Why don't you go to your room and lie down? When Dr. Foucault arrives, I'll ask him if he would recommend vitamin shots."

The baby was not due until October twentieth, but on the night of September thirtieth, Raina, eating dinner alone in her room, was seized by a sudden convulsion. Grabbing the tablecloth she fell to her knees. Her dinner tray and lamp fell crashing to the floor. Then her water broke and Raina screamed. Her personal maid, a pudgy little woman named Marie with arms the color and size of smoked hams, heard the commotion and rushed inside.

"Dr. Foucault," Raina gasped. "Get Dr. Foucault!"

Dr. Foucault, a portly man with a huge tangle of white hair, checked Raina's pulse. "He is ahead of time, Baroness."

Raina, through her pain, tartly spit out: "You're all so sure it's going to be a boy. I hope to hell it's a girl!" The doctor ignored her remark.

"You will probably experience these pains at two

hour intervals to start and then they will get closer together. I'll have Marie remain in the room with you. I
am just across the hall and will be here when I'm
needed."

"You're not going to give me something for the pain?"

"That would be unwise at this point."

Raina gritted her teeth. "I hope it's a girl!"

The doctor stood up. He gazed upon her with a
flicker of compassion and shook his head sadly. "It's
not what you want, my dear . . . it never has been."

Raina remained in labor throughout the night. She
screamed her pain and terrible loneliness. Occasionally
in her agony she would call out for her husband, but
Andre remained in the library waiting out the birth of
his child with his father. Dr. Foucault sat calmly in his
room smoking cigarettes and reading Voltaire until a
short time past dawn Marie informed him that the
labor pains were coming every five minutes. He stubbed
out his cigarette and went to attend his patient.

As soon as he entered Raina's room, she cried,
"Something—for—the—pain. *Please!*" He pretended
he hadn't heard her. The doctor had been given specific
instructions by the Baron—no drugs.

At five after nine, Raina delivered a child . . . a boy.

The child was taken to another room where it was
cleaned and wrapped in soft flannel blankets embroidered with the de Clermont crest. The doctor ordered Marie to take it downstairs to present the child
to its father and grandfather.

"But," protested Marie, "the Baroness wants her son.
She's calling for him."

"She'll never see him," the doctor replied tersely.
"Now do as you're told."

Raina stubbed out her cigarette as the approach to
Kennedy was announced. She was exhausted. Troubled
by half dreams, she had not been able to sleep. She
wondered if she would ever be able to sleep again.

*   *   *

Kay and Jana were having a rare evening together at home. They sat wrapped in comfortable robes sharing a bowl of freshly made popcorn in front of the TV set. On top of the set a great mass of orange fur was enjoying the generated warmth.

The women were watching the late movie on Channel 2, an MGM epic of the forties entitled *Green Dolphin Street* starring Lana Turner and Van Heflin. They were completely immersed in the poignant melodrama, and when the telephone rang they promptly ignored it.

"The service will pick it up," said Jana.

"What would it be at this hour except bad news," observed Kay.

After seven rings Kay cursed. "Dammit, what are we paying for anyway? Why didn't they pick up?" There were two more rings.

"I can't stand it anymore." She grabbed the receiver. "Hello . . . What? *What!* . . . Where are you? Jana, it's Raina! She's at Kennedy."

Jana jumped up, spilling the popcorn. Farouk dove from the TV set and sniffed his way through the snowy puffs.

"No, we're both in. Here's Jana. She wants to talk with you."

"Oh, Raina, is it really you? Oh, what if we hadn't answered the phone? We were letting the service pick up and of course . . . oh yes, hurry, *hurry!* We're here." She turned to Kay. "She'll be here within the hour. We've got to straighten up the place. Do we have any champagne?" Kay nodded. "We must chill it. All of it."

"What will we say to her?" Kay asked quietly. "After all she's been through."

"We'll say nothing. She'll tell us what she wants to tell us and only when she's ready. Oh, what's important is that she's back, she's finally come home. Oh Lord, I'm crying. Farouk! Get out of the popcorn! Thank God Birdie's readied her room."

"I'll call down to the new doorman. He doesn't know her."

"Oh goodness, look at us. We've gone slob. We can't let Raina see us like this."

"You take your shower first, Jana. I'll clear up the popcorn. God, how are we going to act? She's a baroness now with a million-dollar settlement."

"Kay, we must act as if nothing has changed. It's important that we don't descend upon her with loads of questions like the reporters must have. Raina's home! Oh, I can't believe it. I simply *can't* believe it."

One hour and twenty minutes later the apartment was in order. Candles were burning and on the FM receiver a soft rock station was playing. A bottle of champagne was chilling in a bucket of ice and a tray of hors d'oeuvres had been prepared. Jana and Kay, now freshly bathed and smartly dressed, glanced from the clock to one another.

The buzzer sounded. Kay was informed by the doorman that Miss Pendleton had arrived. The women couldn't wait in the apartment. They opened the door and ran to the elevator. The doors opened and Raina stepped out. She saw her friends and rushed into their arms. Having locked the front door, the doorman had helped Raina with her luggage. Jana and Kay each picked up several bags and carried them into the apartment. Kay had a tip ready for the doorman.

"We have champagne, Raina," said Jana. "Would you like some?"

"Yes. I've had a few drinks on the plane but perhaps it will help me sleep tonight. God, do I need sleep."

"You look fabulous," said Kay. "Perhaps a bit thin, but you'll photograph better, won't she, Jana?"

"You just need some rest. That's all," Jana said. "Traveling's exhausting."

The champagne was poured. Raina sipped hers and saw that the other two were waiting, their glasses poised. "Oh, I forgot to make a toast. It's—it's been so long since I had any wishes to make." She began to cry. It was an internal howl which racked her body with harsh spasms. Jana and Kay hugged her and held her tight. When Raina stopped crying, she apologized.

"I'm sorry. Now I must really look a mess." She smiled crookedly. "I am a mess, and I don't know if I'm going to be able to put the pieces back together."

"Of course you will, Raina," said Jana. "You have to give yourself time, though."

"We're here for you, Raina," added Kay. "We always will be."

"You know," Raina began, "I've always been an irresponsible, careless person. When I fell in love with Andre and he asked me to marry him, I thought that he'd come along just in time, that my white knight had rescued me before I had the chance to become so jaded that there was no return." Then she told them everything, leaving out nothing, including her affair with Gabriel. Her voice broke as she spoke about her baby. "For a time I didn't know whether he was dead or alive. They never let me see him. I was informed of the impending divorce almost immediately after he was born."

"I don't see how they could do that," exclaimed Jana. "They couldn't. They simply couldn't."

"They had the power," replied Raina bleakly. "I never understood power before. It's a terrible thing. I was surprised by the 'generous' settlement they offered me. They told me that they would not bring up the adultery bit if I would agree to give up my son." She wiped her eyes. "I don't even know what they named him. Well, I spoke to my lawyer, who was probably in cahoots with them. He told me if they brought in adultery, I wouldn't have a chance to get my baby anyway. At the time it seemed like the best way out. Now I see I shouldn't have accepted the money. The press called it a payoff. And I'm sure that's what the Baron planned."

"Of course you should have taken the money," said Kay. "You certainly earned it."

Raina laughed bitterly. "By selling my own flesh and blood?"

"Can't you get a lawyer here in the States and reopen the case?" asked Jana.

Raina shook her head. "After the publicity I've gathered about myself—the million dollar settlement, giving up my son, and of course the leaked hints of adultery—there's not a judge or jury in the country who would be sympathetic to me. I've just got to learn to live with it. I came back because I had no place else to go. I don't want to burden either of you with my problems. I'll go through the motions of being alive."

"Raina," Jana said gently, "you mustn't let yourself despair. Even the kind of horrible pain you're feeling now eases eventually. You musn't give up on reclaiming your son, and you musn't give up on your work. You have a brilliant career to rebuild, and that will be your salvation."

Raina looked at her with brimming eyes. She almost wept again, but from gratitude this time, not grief. How often in the past ghastly months had she longed for this kind of compassion and support! "I will never be able to tell you two," she said evenly, "how very much you mean to me."

In a silence suffused with the warmth of their friendship, the three women slowly sipped their champagne. After a while, Raina looked up and said, "God, it's good to be back. I have absolutely no idea what *you've* been up to all that time I spent rotting away in de Clermont's dungeon. Fill me in."

"I guess my big news is that Fred got married," Kay said woefully.

Jana laughed ruefully. "I'm still a virgin," she confessed.

"To hell with men," said Raina. "What about your careers?"

"Well, I've done six shows," grunted Kay. "All flops."

Jana sighed. "I haven't had a decent acting job in ages."

Raina looked first at Jana, then Kay. "My dear friends, it seems as if we're all at a low point in our lives. It's right that we should be together. We'll get

what we want. I know it. We're all of us born sur-
vivors."

The three women stood up, refilled their glasses and
clinked them together. As they drank they wrapped
their arms around one another. It was a mutual gesture
of affection that they had expressed so many times in
the past. Only this time they did not jump up and
down. This time their feet were planted firmly on the
ground.

Chapter Sixteen

From the New York *Daily News* (Leisure Section, Sunday, February 12, 1974):

ENOUGH ROPE FOR A NEW SOAP?

A new bubble is emerging from the soap dish. Michael Bandy, president of MBS, has announced plans for an hour-long afternoon soap. This is to be a first for Municipal Broadcasting System, which has heretofore not ventured into the soap sweepstakes.

Bandy states that the new show, "Intimate Strangers" will be set in Manhattan. The major characters will live in the same apartment building and their lives will intermingle. Those characters include a divorcée trying to make it on her own, an intern with a drug problem, a bisexual decorator, a spinster of middle years who's considering plastic surgery to snare a man, a pregnant (and unmarried) secretary, a couple of swinging singles who are living together, a kept woman who "fools around" with every male attached or unattached in the building, and a black couple who are fighting for their space in a predominantly white world.

This heady brew does not sound like your typical soap opera. But MBS is counting on its success and has spent an unprecedented amount of money on publicity. They promise to give the viewers lively location shots done in and around

New York City in hopes of relieving the static quality of most soap operas. The publicity release informs us that "Intimate Strangers" intends to explore human nature honestly and deal openly with the issues of the day, including sex (premarital and otherwise), job discrimination, and drug abuse.

A huge cast of major and minor characters have been lured from New York theatres. Bandy promises that they will not portray "bland, one-dimensional characters" but will be "people of substance, with weaknesses as well as strengths." Bandy, whose manipulative talents have taken viewers away from the holy triumvirate of NBC, CBS and ABC, considers "Intimate Strangers" his "baby." And he will personally oversee the production. Bandy says he intends to breathe "real life" into washed out afternoon drama. Will the ratings soar? Will the strangers indeed become intimate? Will Bandy manage to cross the waters on this new bar of soap? *Caaan't wait* to find out!

The MBS studios were located on West Sixty-fourth Street. This was where the interiors of "Intimate Strangers" was taped. It was an invigorating walk for Jana and she took it five mornings a week. Her hair had been rolled around huge curlers and was covered by a brightly colored scarf. Her face was completely devoid of makeup. That would be taken care of later by the studio makeup man. Jana walked briskly down Seventy-fourth Street toward Broadway. She stopped at the crossing, withdrew a script from her bag and while waiting for the light to change checked her lines once again. Then she crossed the street, her lips moving silently as she repeated her lines for the morning's work. Several people cast sidelong glances at the young woman. Some were struck by the fresh beauty of her face, others were amused by the sight of a pretty young woman conversing with herself—a phenomenon usually reserved for bag ladies. Jana was oblivious to her "audience." All was right with her world. She was steadily employed and she loved her work.

Jana had been cast as the pivotal character in "Intimate Strangers." She played the part of a young divorcee named Melissa Holgate, who, after her divorce, moved from the security of suburban life to the perils of Manhattan. Lissa, as she was called, wanted to be a writer. She found a job at a woman's magazine and, like everyone else in New York City, struggled to make ends meet as she made her mark. She wrote short stories on the side and had high hopes of selling them. She was the type of person people were drawn to and confided in, which was both a joy and a problem for Melissa. It also gave the writers of the soap opera a considerable amount of leverage for introducing new characters. Being a beautiful young female alone in the big city, Lissa was pursued by men at almost every turn—the married and unmarried males in her apartment building, her business associates and a profusion of lecherous publishers who would run her stories but at what price? Additionally Melissa's mother was dying of cancer and her macho ex-husband kept showing up at her doorstep hoping that she'd be desperate enough to go to bed with him.

When "Intimate Strangers" debuted it drew 30.1 percent of the viewing public. Despite the high ratings, Michael Bandy was not satisfied with the initial success of his show and new revelations concerning drugs, sex, and explosive issues were hurried into the script. Within a few weeks of its premiere "Intimate Strangers" had become one of the most controversial shows on television and Bandy intended to keep it that way.

Jana reached the huge plain building of grey brick which housed the MBS offices and studios at exactly eight o'clock; as usual she was on time. The elderly guard grinned as she displayed her employee's card to him.

"No need to do that, Miss Donatello. I've known you by sight for some time now. The show's going right well, ain't it?"

"Seems to be, Jed."

"My wife says it's the best of the soaps."

"Well, on behalf of the rest of the cast, please give her our thanks."

The guard watched Jana as she walked purposefully toward the studio used for "dry rehearsals." He could not help but wonder about her. Why did no young man wait for her when her work was done?

She entered the room, which was already filled with smoke and permeated with odors of take-out breakfasts—bagels and cream cheese, sugary donuts, and ham and egg sandwiches. She brightly greeted those actors who had already arrived and blew a kiss to Kerry Lambert, the director, who was talking animatedly with the three writers of the show. She got a cup of coffee from the percolator and sat down at the table where the preliminary reading of that day's show would take place.

The actors were expected to know their lines, but many were dilatory. They argued that there was no point in memorization since there were always changes. There were, but Jana believed that knowing her scenes as thoroughly as possible made the changes easier to handle.

A few more actors arrived. Noticeably late was the handsome young actor who had been engaged to play the part of Melissa's ex-husband. The part of Ken Holgate was written as a self-centered, chauvinistic man of limited intelligence and sensitivity. To Jana's way of thinking, Damien Caputo, the actor playing the part, had been type cast.

The director sat down next to Jana. "Jana, darling, we're changing the thrust of the scene. There'll be quite a few dialogue changes and I'm afraid they're mostly yours. Can you handle it?"

"Don't I always?" Jana replied affably.

"That's my girl." He kissed her on the forehead, looked around the table and noted Damien's absence. "Now, where in the hell is that guy?" He glanced at his wrist watch. "It's already eight-fifteen. Damn it, if he doesn't start getting to rehearsal on time, I'll have the boys write him out. How would you feel about shooting your ex-husband?"

Jana grinned. "On or off the screen?"

Lambert stood up and spoke to the ensemble. "Well, gang, I suppose we'd better get down to business. There have been a few dialogue changes. The major ones come in Jana and Damien's scene so you needn't be too concerned. But keep your pencils poised."

They reached the point in the script where Jana's husband was required but he still hadn't arrived. The director exploded. "Damn him. This is a very difficult scene. How the hell does he expect to play it if he doesn't rehearse it?" He turned to his secretary. "Sally, try calling Damien, will you?"

"I have been, Mr. Lambert, but I keep getting his answering machine."

At that moment, Damien Caputo, the tardy young actor, entered the studio. Obviously he'd had a hard night. His handsome face was sallow and his usually bright blue eyes were dull and lusterless. The director told the cast to take a short break, then he ushered the actor into another room. Jana and the others were relieved that the director had decided to dress down Caputo in private. A short time later the two men emerged. Caputo was visibly shaken. The director announced, "Everybody but Jana leave the set. I want to work on their scene." The actors dutifully obeyed his orders.

Lambert led his actors through the set that depicted Jana's living room and foyer. It was a difficult scene, and explosive by afternoon television standards. Melissa Holgate had just arrived home from the hospital. She was having difficulty coping with her feelings concerning her mother's terminal illness. Her ex-husband arrived. He had been drinking and was intent upon getting his former wife into bed. The scene foreshadowed later developments where Melissa is raped by her ex-husband and takes him to trial.

"All right, Jana," instructed Lambert, "you've just

made yourself a cup of coffee. Take it from the point where you're carrying it from the kitchen into the living room and the door bell rings."

MELISSA: Yes, who is it? (Inaudible mumble from the other side of the door.) *Who is it?*

KEN: Lissa, it's me. Ken. Let me in.

MELISSA: Ken, please, not now. I don't want to see you.
(He begins banging on the door.)
Ken, stop that. I'll call the super.

KEN: Please, Lissa, I've got to see you.

MELISSA: (Resigned, unlocks the door and opens it.) You turned up at a bad time, Ken.

The scene continued for several minutes, then the director interrupted: "Damien, you're playing this thing like a zombie. And don't give me that crap about saving yourself for performance. I want to see something now. Jana, you're doing just fine. Start it over. And Damien, stay out of Jana's key light."

The scene was blocked and run several more times before Lambert was satisfied. After a few last-minute instructions Lambert left for another part of the sound stage to dry block another scene that did not include Jana. The young "divorcees" were left alone.

Jana suggested, "Let's run through it again on our own."

"Nah, it's going to be OK. Jesus, what a crock."

"Meaning?"

"All this soap suds junk. I feel like I'm in kindergarten again."

"That's because you act like it."

"You don't approve of me, do you, Jana?"

"No, I don't, Damien. You're a good actor, but you don't take your work seriously. Let me give you a little advice. If you don't clean up your act, Kerry is going to instruct the writers to write you out of the script."

"He wouldn't do that. I'm important. I get lots of fan mail. Women love me. Housewives love me."

"They should try working with you," Jana replied tartly.

Damien smiled and closed his fingers around Jana's wrist. "After the taping, why don't the two of us go out on the town? I know a terrific bar over on Amsterdam. It's dark, intimate, and they make the best Harvey Wallbangers in town."

Jana pulled free. "You're just a little thick, aren't you, Damien? Apparently I haven't made myself clear. I will not go out with you now or at any time in the future. It may come as a shock, but you hold absolutely no interest for me, socially or sexually."

Despite her comments, Damien slid his arm around Jana's shoulders, letting his hand drop and brush against her breast.

Jana stepped back. She was fuming. She narrowed her eyes and spoke softly, evenly: "If you ever touch me again, Damien, I'll write you out of the script myself. I'll bring charges against you at AFTRA. Now why don't you just go stick your head in a Harvey Wallbanger and stay out of my way."

Damien, embarrassed, left the set. Someone began applauding. Jana spun around to face her director.

"Marvelous, my dear. Marvelous. We'll have to see if we can work that scene into the script."

Jana managed a smile. "Really, Kerry, I don't know how much longer I can go on working with Damien. He's just impossible, both as an actor and as a person."

"Well, my dear, I've just spoken to our writers. I truly believe that out of something bad, something good always emerges. I told them I want to get rid of our young Lothario as quickly as possible. And they've come up with a brilliant idea. We're going to switch endings. In the scene where Ken rapes Melissa, she's now going to kill him in self defense."

Jana giggled. "Oh, that's beautiful, just beautiful."

"How about joining me in the cafeteria for a quick bite before we start taping?"

"I'd love to, Kerry."

Despite the problems Damien created, the taping went smoothly and at three o'clock Jana, tired but exhilarated, was ready to leave the studio. Still wearing the "glamorous" face and full flamboyant hair style the makeup man had given her, Jana walked toward Columbus Circle. She ran some errands, and still not wanting to return to the apartment, decided to go for a walk in the park. The following day was Saturday and the pressure of learning her next script could wait until Sunday.

At the entrance to the park Jana purchased a frozen yogurt. Someone behind her said, "I don't know which looks more appetizing, you or the ice cream." She swung around and found herself facing Sam Benedict, the Cadillac dealer from Rockland County she had met in Detroit.

Recovering her composure Jana managed to smile. "Well, hello, Sam Benedict. What are you doing in New York City?"

He looked younger than Jana remembered. Thinner, too.

"I drove down for the Automobile Show over at the Coliseum."

"Yes, of course. I noticed it was going on. Care to go for a walk in the park? I was just about to take one myself."

"I'd like that, Miss Donatello."

"Please call me Jana. I'm happy to see you again. I behaved rudely in Detroit and I want to apologize."

"No apology required."

They made their way through the street musicians, peddlers and panhandlers down tree-lined walkways dappled with sunlight resembling strewn golden coins. They walked in silence for several minutes. Then Sam asked, "Are you just coming from work?"

"How did you guess?"

"I happen to know the MBS studios are near here."

"Then you know about the show?"

"My ex-wife is a fan of yours."

"Your ex-wife? You're divorced?"

"Yes. We were in the process of being divorced when I met you."

"I'm really very sorry, on both counts—my misunderstanding you and the breakup of your marriage."

"Don't be. Susan and I are much better friends now. We like ourselves a lot better to boot."

"Do you have children?"

"No, I'm thankful to say, we don't. And you, Jana, you're still single."

Jana laughed. "How do you know, Sam?"

"Your cover story in TV Guide." Jana was pleased that he had read it. "You must be very happy. You've got a good part in a good show."

"You've seen it?"

Sam smiled. "I confess. I have watched it. I have a TV set in my office, and every afternoon if I can get away from the business I tune in to *Intimate Strangers*. I guess you might even say I'm hooked on it. What happened today?"

As they walked, Jana brought Sam up to date with the happenings on the soap opera. He listened intently and when she finished, he said, "That ex-husband of yours certainly gives you a lot of trouble."

"I have a secret to share," said Jana. "Promise that you won't tell anyone, not even your ex-wife."

"It's a promise. What happens?"

"Ken tries to rape me and while protecting my virtue I accidentally kill him. I *think* it's an accident anyway. Then later I'll be put on trial. Very dramatic stuff."

"I hope you're acquitted. It wouldn't do to have you behind bars."

"Oh, I will be. Hmmmm. The writers didn't tell me how I'm going to do it. A gun, a hammer, a meat cleaver? Ooooh, I hope it isn't too messy. You see, they just decided today to kill off Damien, the actor who plays my husband."

"He's a very handsome man."

"He's terrible to work with. That's why they decided

to get rid of him. I'm sorry to see someone lose his job, but if anybody deserves it, he does."

"No . . . romantic interests?"

"On the show or in my life?"

"What do you think?"

"I don't have time for romance, Sam. The show keeps me really busy."

"I'm sure it does. But I suspect that's not the real reason. You just haven't met anyone."

"That's a bit brutal, but the truth. I don't like most of the men I meet. I don't like the games and the role playing. My best male friends are gay. Why can't straight men be as considerate and thoughtful as gay men?"

"They're afraid to, I imagine. Afraid that their actions would be construed as weaknesses. At least that's what I read in *Psychology* Magazine."

Jana was amazed that the owner of a Cadillac dealership read a psychology magazine. Perhaps in Detroit she should have stayed around long enough to scratch his surface. She might have been surprised.

She asked, "What hapened to your marriage, Sam?"

"Nothing happened to it. I mean *nothing.*"

"Explain."

"I will if you give me a bite of that ice cream cone."

"It's yogurt. Here, it's good for you."

"I'll decide what's good for me, Jana. I had a wife who catered to me for five years. She never got it through her head that I don't like to be catered to. I suppose she was the kind of wife that a lot of guys would like. Susan is very pretty and a lot younger than I am."

"How old are you, Sam?"

"I'm forty-four, very healthy and I have great teeth."

"You didn't marry until thirty-nine?"

"That's right. I did the carefree bachelor bit. I really did it, and I got really sick of it."

A line of children on roller skates separated the couple.

"Hey, Sam, I wish I had my skates right now."

"Do you like to skate, Jana?"

"I love to but I haven't in years."

"Damn. I didn't think of bringing my skates with me. We could have taken a couple of turns." Jana looked at him in surprise. A suburban married type and Cadillac dealer, roller skating in Central Park. He was certainly something of an enigma. "Now, let's see, what was I talking about?"

"Your perfect wife."

"Oh, yes. It was like living in the Twilight Zone. Susan was twenty-five when we married. What can I say? She was an impeccable homemaker, she cooked up a storm and she made all of her clothes."

"It sounds ideal."

"You have no idea how boring it was. She claimed she couldn't have any children. I found out after the divorce that she had been lying: she was on the pill. She didn't want any children—she didn't want anything to interfere with our 'wedded bliss'. We didn't have friends. Never had relatives over. She didn't want to share me. She had absolutely no interests outside the house. She never read anything except housekeeping magazines. A couple of years ago I took up jogging because I was beginning to gain a lot of weight with the eating-sitting-around-watching-TV rut I was into. Do you think I could get her to get up and join me? Oh no. She couldn't bear to leave her model kitchen. I think she wanted me to get fat and middle-aged so that no one else would look at me."

Jana stopped and looked at her companion. "Are you making this up?"

Sam crossed his heart and shook his head. "Now how could I make something like this up? Well, I knew if I stayed married to Susan, I'd end up hating her. She's really not a bad person."

"How'd she take the divorce?"

"Not very well."

"And now?"

"She's adjusting. Of course I'm paying for her visits

to the psychiatrist three times a week. Not that I'm
complaining—I think it's making her a better person.
She's really trying."

"You still see each other?"

"Only as friends. Once in a while we go to a movie
together. Her psychiatrist thinks it's healthy." He
shrugged his shoulders. "And who am I to argue with
a guy who gets sixty bucks an hour?"

"Hey, we're at Seventy-second Street. Do you want
to walk me home? It's only a few blocks."

"I was planning on it. Are you busy tonight, Jana?"

Jana started to rattle off her usual list of priorities
when asked for a date but changed her mind. "Why
no, I'm not."

"I'm staying in town for the weekend. I wonder if
you'd like to have dinner with me."

"I'd love to. Say around eight?"

"What kind of food do you feel like having?"

"Do you like Szechuan?"

"I love oriental food, particularly when it's hot and
spicy."

"There's a very nice Chinese restaurant near me. We
could go there if you like."

"I'd like. Perhaps afterwards we could catch a nightclub act and go dancing."

"Let's see how dinner goes," Jana replied cautiously.
"I mean how late we're running. I've got a lot of lines
to learn over the weekend."

"Then we'll play it by ear."

"Well, here's where I live."

"This'll be easy to find—it looks like it must be a
landmark. I'll pick you up at eight."

"I'll be ready. I'm always on time."

Sam took Jana's hand and started to shake it. On
second thought he bent down and kissed her quickly
on the cheek.

Jana watched him as he disappeared among the people who were hurrying home from work. I like this
man, she said to herself. I *really like* this man.

Chapter Seventeen

Casting News
(From *Backstage,* March 3, 1974)

The new musical *Performance* due to open on Broadway in late spring is now casting. *Performance* is a musical about putting on a musical. Hank Heller will produce and direct. Steve Snow is writing the music and lyrics; Cal Ballantine, the book; Don Zalman, choreographer; Edward Shire, sets and lighting; and Kay Kincade, costumes. Needed are twelve women and twelve men. Age range 18–28. Must sing, dance and act. Must be physically attractive. Bring picture, résumé, up-tune ballad. Be prepared to do a thorough dance audition and a cold reading.

Thursday, March 12, Kay sat in the darkened auditorium of the Majestic Theater with producer-director Hank Heller and other members of the production team. Over six hundred Equity people had tried out at an earlier date and the non-Equity people were beyond counting. The prospective cast had been narrowed down to twenty-five actors of each sex who had been called back. Heller was making them go through their paces once again for further elimination. Kay as costume designer had no say in the final choice, but having a personal commitment to the musical she had elected to sit through the gruelling tryouts. *Performance* was the most exciting new show Kay had encountered in nearly a year's long search.

Kay listened as Heller conferred with choreographer Don Zalman. "This time, Don, I want you to really put them through the paces. Let's find out what kind of stuff they're made of as far as dancing goes. Since the main emphasis of the show is on dancing, I think you ought to have the final decision on who we cast." Heller was a small, balding man with thick glasses who resembled a tax accountant rather than a man of incredible theatrical genius.

"Good. I'll be looking for two things, Hank: that special quality that makes a dancer a performer, too, and stamina. But before I make my final choice I want to run them through a personal interview with me. I want to find out if any of them has sustained any old injuries." Zalman looked half as young as his forty years. He had a sharp, intelligent face and a taut, compact body.

"Couldn't we have a doctor examine them? You know actors don't always tell the truth."

"We might get into trouble with Equity on that one, Hank. They might name it as discrimination. I can't take that chance. Believe me, I'll be able to tell. With the rigors I'm going to put them through, no one with weak knees and screwed up cartilage will make it. Naturally, I'll warn them first what I'm about; I don't want anybody getting injured during this audition."

"Well, I suppose we ought to let them in and get started," Heller said with resignation. "Jesus, I hate auditions. I bet I hate them even more than the actors do. Let's send Jerry out for some coffee—we're going to need it." The director turned to Kay, who was sitting in the row in front of him. "Kay, would you like some coffee?"

"Love it, Hank."

He noticed her sketch pad. "You're not designing costumes already?"

"Since the opening sequence has the kids auditioning for the show, I thought I'd keep my eye out for any interesting audition clothes they were wearing themselves. It might give me some ideas. Remember that girl with the knitted pink leg warmers and the orange tights? I thought that was pretty startling."

"Startling it was. Too bad she didn't have any talent."

Eric Grainger sat on the edge of the stage waiting for the director's signal to start the callbacks. This was Eric's first job as stage manager. He credited Kay with getting him the opportunity to apply for the position. They were good friends, professional allies, and, as Eric knew, potentially much, much more. But their affair had cooled to a point. Despite Eric's understanding nature, Kay had withdrawn again—fearful of involvement, fearful of disappointment.

"All right, Eric," called Heller. "Let's begin."

Eric hurried offstage to where twenty-five young women were waiting. The hope and tension were so thick he could almost smell it. The women had already drawn numbers, one through twenty-five, which determined the order of their ordeal. Eric escorted number one to the center of the stage and announced her name, Daria Vasseux, to those in the auditorium who would be deciding her fate.

Heller stood up. "Relax, Daria. Tell me a little about yourself. Not what's on your résumé, but about yourself."

The young woman had enormous doe eyes and sleek black hair that reached almost to her waist. She grinned self-consciously. "I guess my name suits me. It's unusual, unique, and I think I am, too. I never worked at being different. You see, I grew up in a small town where being different was almost a sin. But I learned to like being different. It set me apart. It gave me dreams and ambitions I might never have had if I looked and acted like everybody else. My parents encouraged me to be myself. I took dancing and singing lessons and read everything I could about the famous people of the theatre. I feel like I belong here more than anywhere else." She giggled. "In the theatre I think being different is a plus."

Heller scribbled a few notes on the girl's résumé. He liked her charming egotism and her looks. He glanced at the notes he had made at her previous audition. "Sings very well. Voice range: two octave-belt F to C." And further down, "Dancing excellent." The comment was followed by five exclamation points. But, he wondered, would she be difficult to work with? "Daria, what's your least favorite color?"

"Green," she replied without hesitation.

"And if you had only one costume to wear in the show and it was decided that it must be green, how would you react?"

"I would pretend I'm wearing red," she grinned. "Red's my *favorite* color."

Heller liked that and nodded to the choreographer who bounded up onto the stage and asked a few pertinent questions concerning any injuries she might have gotten while performing. Daria replied that there were none. Don then put her through a rigorous dance set, and when she was finished she wasn't even breathing hard. The choreographer pulled on his right ear, signaling Heller that he was pleased and wanted her to stay.

"You wouldn't mind hanging around a little while longer, would you, Daria?" asked Heller.

The young woman could hardly contain her enthusiasm and thanked everybody profusely. The "go-fer" arrived with the coffee. Heller leaned over to Kay and asked, "What did you think?"

"She's be a dream to costume. What a body! And did you notice how she moves in her clothes? They don't dominate her, she dominates them."

"That's what I thought." Heller sighed. "Only twenty-four more to go, and then this afternoon the men."

"I'm looking forward to that," said Kay.

"So am I," grinned Heller.

The callbacks for the women ran overtime and lasted until one o'clock. Hank declared a lunch break and asked Kay and Don to accompany him to a nearby restaurant for a bite to eat and some conversation about the talents they had seen. Over salads, omelettes and white wine the men conversed and neither hesitated to ask Kay her opinion. Kay was flattered. She knew that finally she was in a winner's circle. All she had to do was please Hank Heller. She knew that he used his people over and over and that his projects were always innovative, always exciting, and always successful. Heller directed everything from plays and operas to films and TV. He was probably the most respected producer-director in the business. And he had won more awards than any other five directors combined.

"Well, Kay, we've eliminated six. Don discovered two girls with dance injuries that would be bound to give them trouble doing the vigorous choreography. There were three I just didn't cotton to. Call it instinct, whatever you like. Their personalities didn't appeal to me."

"And the sixth?" asked Kay.

"She's doing too many drugs," Heller replied solemnly. "She's probably not into anything heavier than grass, but she's doing a hell of a lot of it. You can tell by the way she speaks and her timing's off just an inch."

"I could hear it in her throat when she sang, too," said Don. "A slight huskiness creeps in. Eventually it will screw up the whole range."

Heller paid the check and Don hurried back to the theatre so that he could place a phone call before the afternoon session began. Heller and Kay strolled down Shubert Alley past the line of posters advertising hits of the day.

Two of Heller's productions were still running. Heller stopped and studied the huge poster advertising his two-year-old show *Love on the Thirty-third Floor,* a farce about office intrigues and politics. He frowned. "Damn it. David Halloran hasn't been in the show for three months. Why hasn't the replacement's name been pasted over?"

Kay spoke with admiration: "You really oversee every aspect of your productions, don't you, Hank?"

"You have to or you get less than perfect. I don't want to deal with less than perfect." He scrutinized Kay and asked bluntly, "Why did you involve yourself with so many flops, Kay?"

"I was too grasping, Hank. Desperate to have my name on a Broadway show."

He nodded with understanding. "I hope you've learned your lesson. One must proceed in one's career with a certain amount of taste."

"Why did you choose me as your costume designer?"

"The truth? Florrie Waxman wasn't available."

"Yes, I heard that, but why me? Most of the shows I did didn't even get into town."

"Well, I caught the ones that did." He grinned. "You might say I came out humming the costumes."

The twenty-five males who had been called back were already gathered in the offstage area awaiting the arrival of Hank Heller. Kay surveyed them appreciatively. They were a collection of vital young men with impressive talents and good looks, or else they wouldn't have gotten this far. Several of the hopefuls smiled at Kay. She returned their smiles impersonally, wondering why she couldn't generate any more enthusiasm for any of them. Surprisingly, she found her thoughts drifting more and more frequently to—Eric Grainger.

After the auditions Eric caught Kay before she left the theatre. "Have any plans, Kay?"

"I don't know, I'd just like to go somewhere and unwind, relax completely."

"Why don't you come back to my place? You haven't even seen my new apartment yet. It's not much, but it's all mine."

Much to Eric's delight and Kay's bewilderment, she readily—almost eagerly—agreed, quizzing him about his quarters as they left together.

"It's a railroad flat. You know, a string of rooms, each attached to one another like the vertebrae of an animal. I guess the only drawback is that the bathtub is in the kitchen."

"Why is that a drawback?" said Kay. "You can always eat while you're bathing."

"Well, I'll say one thing. When you've invited someone for dinner, you're sure as hell ready on time."

They walked up Eighth Avenue. Like so many exotic night-blooming flowers the assorted whores and pimps had begun to make their appearance. Kay insisted on stopping at a liquor store to get some wine as a housewarming present for Eric. She purchased a giant bottle of chilled Italian Soave. Together they headed toward Fiftieth Street and Ninth Avenue where Eric's apartment was located.

"You're sure convenient to the theatre," commented Kay.

"Yeah," Eric replied glumly.

"What's wrong? Isn't that a good thing? I mean, you don't have to take subways, or spend the money on taxi fares."

"It's not that, Kay. It's just I'm really worried."

"About what? *Performance?* I think the show's going to be fabulous."

"Oh, I know it is. I just hope I'm good enough to handle the job of stage manager."

"Now stop that kind of talk, Eric. You're just having a case of the 'inads.'" He looked at her quizzically. "The inadequacies. We all get it. Don't you think I'm scared working with Hank Heller for the first time? He's got a reputation as being the most demanding director on Broadway. Listen to me, Eric. That's a good thing. You know if we'd stuck to shows like Rumpled Stiltskin or whatever the hell it was . . ."

"*Rumpled Sheets.*"

"Oh yeah—I've almost succeeded in blotting it out of my mind forever. Then where would we be? This is a terrific chance for both of us. We'll both have to be on our toes. We'll have to reach and then reach further. But let me tell you something, that's the only way to get better—by reaching. Hank may be demanding, but you sure as hell know where you stand with him. There's no attitude, no indecision, no phoney theatrical stuff. So get rid of those 'inads.' Flush 'em out of your life. Stay busy and reach! You won't have time to think such thoughts. Just make sure you surround yourself with good people. That's Hank's secret. Remember that and remember that he chose *us*. By the way, how are you getting along with your assistant stage manager?"

"He's fine, enthusiastic. I guess we all are."

"I know I am. *Performance* just smells like a hit." Kay laughed. "I've already started composing my acceptance speech for the Tony Awards."

Eric slid his arm around Kay's waist and pulled her close to him. "You're terrific. You know that, don't you?"

"Yes, but I still like to hear it," she responded cheerfully.

"By the way, how are things with the roommates?"

Kay considered. "Moving right along as they say. Jana's happily tied up with her soap and she's been dating a real nice guy."

"No kidding. Who?"

"His name's Sam Benedict. He's forty-four, divorced, no children, lives in Rockland County and owns the biggest Cadillac business on the eastern seaboard, or something like that."

"He sounds kind of square."

"He's not though. Very self-educated and into absolutely everything—jogging, courses at the New School, and thirties' films."

"And Raina?"

"Well, Raina's another story. She's trying real hard. But what happened to her in France really took a chunk out of her heart."

"She's still going to a psychiatrist?"

"Yeah, and that's helping. He finally talked her into starting classes again, voice and dance. I think that's been real good for her. She was like a zombie for months—she wouldn't even go out of the apartment.

Hell, I don't blame her in a way. There are always reporters lurking around the entranceway. Did I tell you about that one guy from the *National Star?*" Eric shook his head. "He posed as a telephone repairman and actually got into the apartment. We had to call the cops and everything. We didn't find out until later that the son-of-a-bitch got a couple of pictures of her with one of those secret pocket cameras or something. So they published a big manufactured story and reproduced these pictures of Raina looking like death's sister. And there was that awful business with the baby . . . But as I said, she's doing pretty well now. It's taken a while, but I think in a couple of months she'll be ready to hit the audition circuit again."

"Too bad she couldn't have tried out for *Performance.*"

"I don't think it really would have been right for her. Raina's a real star if ever there was one. And the way the story line of *Performance* is set up with the chorus of twenty-four all acting out the story, the parts are too equal. Raina's personality and stage presence are too strong. She would have overwhelmed the others and upset the balance of the show."

"She's really that good?"

"She's really that good . . . she's everything the critics said she was in the Villere play. I don't know why the ones with all the talent have to be screwed up."

"You're not screwed up, Kay."

She grinned slyly. "No, but I'd like to be."

They entered Eric's building. "Prepare for a hike. I'm on the fifth floor and it's a walkup."

"Where's your romance? You should carry me."

"Not if you want any action later."

Kay noticed that despite the shoddy exterior of the building, the hallways were freshly painted, well-lit and clean. "Has this place been renovated?"

"No way. You know how landlords are in New York. Most of the tenants are in show biz. We all got together and cleaned up the halls and painted them.

We also replaced the twenty-five watt bulbs with hundreds. We formed a tenants organization and made the son-of-a-bitch put in a buzzer system. So far we haven't had any robberies, but I got a police lock and put gates on my back windows just to be safe."

They entered a large kitchen, the walls of which had been painted white and the ceiling shiny yellow. To one side the previously mentioned bathtub stood on a wooden platform. A pair of steps led up to it. At least a dozen plants hung from the ceiling, which had in its center a large skylight.

"Eric, it's charming. Where did you get all the interesting pieces of furniture?"

"After seeing your place I did a little 'midnight shopping' myself." Eric pointed to a small door next to the bathtub. "That's the john. If you have to wash your hands, I'm afraid you'll have to use the kitchen sink. Come on, let me show you the rest of the place. It goes on forever."

There were three more rooms in all, each leading off the other. The first room Eric used as an office and library. The next was the bedroom and the third and last was his living room.

"Eric, I think this is terrific, all this space. How much do you have to pay?"

"One hundred and thirty-two dollars and twenty-six cents."

"You were really lucky to find it."

"And a three-year lease to boot. Hell, *Performance* will still be running by the time my lease is up."

Kay took off her shawl. "Let's open the wine and take a bath together, shall we?"

Eric could only grin in response. They stripped out of their clothes and hung them over the backs of the kitchen chairs. Kay started the water in the tub while Eric poured the wine. He took the phone off the hook then handed a glass to Kay.

She asked, "You're not expecting any phone calls?"

"Nothing that can't wait."

"Let's drink our wine in the tub, shall we?"

The bathtub was a huge antique complete with claw feet and cracked porcelain. The couple sat down facing one another and sipped their wine.

"I think this is the biggest bathtub I've ever been in," remarked Kay. She closed her eyes and, despite herself, recalled New Hope and Fred.

"You're sure?"

"What? Sure of what?"

"Sure that it's the biggest," he joked with tentative bravado.

Kay smiled. "Yes." She leaned forward and kissed Eric on the tip of the nose. "You're very sweet, Eric. One of the sweetest people I've ever met."

Eric smiled sadly, "But not as sweet as Fred."

Kay bit down on her lip and shook her head. "I'm afraid I am still hung up on him, or at least the idea of him."

"You don't correspond now that he's married?"

"Just Christmas cards." She drained her glass. "Hey, how about some more wine?"

Eric reached for the bottle and filled both their glasses. "Will you let me make love to you later, Kay?"

"Do it now, Eric. Do it now," she whispered against his face. Her warm breath brushed his cheek, causing it to shine like a red candy apple.

Her words immediately stimulated him. He set down his wine glass and drew his hands beneath the water. There he began stroking her and gently manipulating the core of her femininity. Kay leaned back against the porcelain. Steam from the warm water rose like a drawn curtain between them. Eric's features became amorphous, hazy, as they disappeared, reappeared and disappeared again through the mist. It wasn't hard to imagine that he was Fred and that she was back in New Hope giving herself to the first man she had ever truly loved. But strangely enough, Kay's image of Fred began to dissipate, and she felt an enormous weight slip from her heart as she contemplated Eric as if for the first time.

As Eric titillated Kay with his fingers, he learned

forward and kissed the tip of one of her breasts. Kay reached out, urgently caressing his head and shoulders. Her hands combed through his hair and she curled swatches of it around her fingers. She bent her head down and began kissing him, running her lips over the side of his face and his ear.

"Let me do it," she said softly. "You lie back and stretch out your legs." Eric did as he was told. Kay raised herself to a crouching position over him and lowered herself into the water. He watched her face in fascination. She closed her eyes and parted her lips, which were glistening with dampness. Her eyelashes fluttered as she moved her hips from side to side driving him into her.

Eric wanted more than anything to erase Fred—his phantom rival—from Kay's mind, if only for the duration of their love-making. He lifted his hips and she gave a small, choked cry as he completely entered her. She stayed absolutely still, her eyes tightly closed, breathing through her parted lips. Then she let out the pent-up breath with a long, luxurious sigh and pressed herself downward. Eric stroked the tips of his fingers along the inside of her thighs and across her stomach, as he began moving upward with firm thrusts. The water around them slapped against the sides of the tub and its rhythmic sound added to the sensuality of the moment.

"Open your eyes, Kay. Look at me. Look at *me*."

Her eyes fluttered open and she smiled at him. "I know who I'm with, *Eric*."

She lifted his chin and began kissing him hotly on the lips, repeating his name over and over. Some of the bath water splashed over the edge of the tub as he responded passionately, pushing himself upward with unreserved movements. Kay responded eagerly. Eric gripped her waist in his large hands and began lifting her. The muscles covering his shoulders and arms stood out in hard relief as he plummeted into her. They kept their frenzied pace until Kay began emitting an intense groan of pleasure.

"Eric, *Eric,* I'm close. I'm so close," she whispered.

Eric closed his eyes and concentrated so that he could catch up with her. Soft, fluttery sounds escaped her lips like butterflies. Eric gritted his teeth as he raced to meet her head on.

"Don't stop, Eric. Please don't stop."

Nothing could have stopped him. He kept going and going until there was more water on the floor than there was in the tub. They broke apart, gasping and laughing, both with joy and at the ridiculousness of the situation.

"We'd better mop the floor, Eric," remarked Kay. "I don't want you to lose your three-year lease on this hundred and thirty-two dollar and twenty-six cent apartment . . . with its wonderful bathtub."

Chapter Eighteen

From the front page of *Variety*
July 12th, 1974:

SHAFNER'S NEW PLAY
SET FOR BROADWAY

Pulitzer prize-winning playwright Robert Shafner's new play, *Garden of Predators,* is being readied for a fall opening. The play had a successful production last year at Spoleto and it will be produced in New York under the auspices of Hank Heller. It has not been disclosed whether or not Mr. Heller will direct the piece. *Garden of Predators* is an allegory set on a mythical tropical island during the days of an internal revolution. The action is centered around the character Camilla Castellana, the daughter of an aristocratic family that has controlled the island's wealth for generations. She is in love with the young revolutionary Rosario and pledges to help the cause despite the danger to herself and her family. Once the revolution is started her lover and every member of her family are killed, and Camilla finds herself a political prisoner. Her beauty but not her will is destroyed by the new regime. Crippled and scarred, Camilla is left to wander the roads and beg her existence in a country that had once been her playground.

Noel Bannon of the New York *Times* called the

Spoleto production "explosive stuff." The public seemed to agree. The play was both extolled and denounced. A bomb was set off in the theatre by a group of Italian reactionaries. No one was injured and the culprits were caught and jailed.

Heller is quoted as saying: "It is a play for our times. The war may be over in Vietnam but the bloodshed in Southeast Asia has not been stopped. I expect *Garden of Predators* will be particularly meaningful to the American public."

The play is scheduled for a late October opening. No theatre has been set.

The article was circled in red and a note was scribbled in the margin. "Raina, I happen to know for certain that the part of Camilla has not been cast. In fact, Hank doesn't even have anyone under consideration. Why don't you give his office a call and set up an appointment? Love, Kay."

The newspaper had been left outside Raina's door and now, four hours later, it lay next to a glass of iced tea on the terrace of their apartment. Raina, glistening with Bain du Soleil, was stretched out on a beach lounge taking the hot July sun. She was wearing a black bikini and her freshly washed hair was wrapped in a towel. Somewhere a radio was playing and the music drifted through the still and humid air. Stretching her long legs, Raina contemplated the article. The play intrigued her, the part excited her, and Shafner had always been one of her favorite playwrights. But was she ready to once again step into the spotlight when she had spent such a long time seeking personal anonymity?

The words of Dr. David Carlyle, her psychiatrist for the past year, invaded her mind like the voice of childhood conscience. "It's time, Raina. It's time for you to get back to work."

Raina, her voice as thin as a little girl's, responded wearily, "Yes, I know, Dr. Carlyle. I promised."

"You promised yourself, Raina. Not me. Do it for yourself."

"Later," she sighed. "I'll do it later."

Raina reached for the newspaper but picked up the iced tea instead. She sat up and drank it down greedily. The cold liquid laced with artificial sweetener and mint momentarily distracted her. Distractions—that was what it was all about. If only she could keep herself distracted from the issue at hand. She switched on the small black and white portable TV that was sitting nearby. The Watergate Hearings came into focus. Raina turned off the audio and watched the Speaker of the House as he soundlessly questioned the key witness, John Dean. "Everyone cheats," Raina murmured. *"Everyone."*

Through the row of fica trees Raina saw the man she and her roommates had dubbed "the Peeper." He lived in the apartment building across the street and was leaning on his windowsill staring at her through a pair of high-powered binoculars. Raina made a fist and thrust her arm upwards in a crude gesture. Attempting to ignore his scrutiny, she turned over to lie on her stomach.

Summer sounds—a jumble of radio stations, screaming children and passing airplanes—droned in the distance.

She was so sick of people staring at her.

Dr. Carlyle: "Don't dwell on what is past, Raina."

She smiled as she imagined his super-calming voice. The money she had paid him probably accounted for the first floor of his townhouse.

. . . What has passed . . . what has passed. . . .

Returning to New York had been a nightmare. Raina had thought she was going to find sanctuary but she was badly mistaken. As soon as the press had found out where she lived, they began their siege. In the beginning she couldn't leave the apartment, not even for a stroll. She was badgered by reporters; unscrupulous photographers who seemed to appear from nowhere took unflattering pictures. Jana and Kay were supportive and did everything they could to keep the press at bay.

They monitored the phone calls, took care of her mail and saw to her personal wants and needs. Raina spent her days and nights brooding over the injustices that had been done to her. She slept little and ate less and her roommates became concerned about her physical as well as mental health. They urged her to seek professional help to get through this difficult period of her life. Raina steadfastly refused, believing that she was strong enough to cope with her own life.

Several weeks after her return Raina was desperate to get out of the apartment. She tucked her hair beneath a cloche hat and turned up the collar of her raincoat so that she looked, she thought, very anonymous. She slipped out of the apartment building and made her way to the Red Apple supermarket. She possessed a tremendous desire to do something as commonplace as marketing. Pushing a cart among the aisles crammed with food stuffs had a calming influence on Raina. She selected a good many things that she knew that they didn't need and possibly would never eat, but she was in a way enjoying herself. And then it happened.

She was searching among the boxes of cereal for something high in fiber and free of sugar when . . .

"Say cheese, Raina!" She turned and a flashbulb exploded in her face. "Thanks, Raina. How about another?" said the voice behind the glare.

Raina blinked and blinked again and began gasping for breath. "Don't, please, let me alone."

"Hey, how about one next to the babyfood?"

He came into focus. He was a short grubby-looking little man with nicotine stained teeth and a supercilious grin. "How about it? One by the babyfood?"

With all her strength Raina pushed the cart at him, hitting him squarely in the stomach. Then she turned and ran down the aisle, knocking over a stacked display of cleanser. As she pushed her way through the checkout line people shouted at her.

"Hey, lady, what's the matter with you?"

"Watch it!"

"Rude bitch!"

She was gasping for her breath when she reached the street. Raina ran all the way back to the apartment clutching her chest.

Sometime later when she was down in the lobby collecting mail she encountered a pretty woman with bright red hair who Raina assumed lived in the building. The woman began chatting with Raina in an outgoing friendly manner.

"Isn't this rain dreadful?" she remarked with a cheery smile.

"Oh, I don't mind it," Raina replied. "It's good for the plants on the terrace."

"Oh, you're one of the lucky ones. I wish I could have an apartment with a terrace."

"They're nice in the summer. You don't have to travel anywhere to get a tan."

"Oh, I don't anyway," the woman laughed. "I'm too fair to get in the sun. Fifteen minutes and I look like a broiled lobster. You look like you tan well though, for a blonde."

"Yes, I do. I guess I'm lucky." They walked toward the elevator. "Are you going up?" asked Raina.

"Oh yes," the young woman replied.

On an impulse Raina said, "Would you like to come in for a cup of tea?"

"Why that would be lovely. A nice way to pass a rainy afternoon."

Raina left her guest in the living room and went to the kitchen to put on the water. She called out, "I've got Earl Gray and orange spice. Which would you prefer?"

"Either," came the reply.

"And there are some lovely butter cookies. We'll have those."

When Raina returned to the living room the woman was walking around looking at the furnishings. "What a nice big bar you have," she commented. "And well stocked too."

"Yes, it is nice, isn't it? My roommates found it at an auction while I was . . . away."

The woman smiled and walked toward the terrace doors. "Nice terrace. This place must cost an awful lot."

"No, actually it's quite a buy. And of course there are three of us sharing it."

"Oh, yes, your roommates . . . Jana Donatello and Kay Kincade. That's right, isn't it?"

"Why yes. Have you met them?"

"How have things been going for you?"

Raina was puzzled by her question. "What do you mean?"

"I was wondering how you spend your time," the woman replied hastily, "what you usually do to occupy your rainy afternoons."

"There's the tea kettle. Why don't you come into the kitchen?" Raina poured hot water into a ceramic teapot that she had already prepared with premeasured tea. "I've been reading a lot—every play I've never read."

"You're thinking of going back into acting then?"

"How did you know I was an actress?"

The woman smiled the same automatic smile. "Well, I saw you in the Villere play."

"Oh, did you?" Raina was pleased. "Did you like it?"

She continued smiling. "Not my . . . cup of tea. I don't generally care for all that hot-Southern-love-among-the-swamp stuff. But I thought you were rather good."

"I'm sorry, I don't know your name. I'm Raina Pendleton. But then you already know that."

"Yes."

"And you're . . . ?"

"Ginny Wasserman."

"Nice to meet you, Ginny. Have you lived in the building long?"

"The tea must have steeped by now."

"Yes. I'll pour. Now, shall we have it here or in the living room?"

"Perhaps some place I haven't already seen."

"Fine. We'll go to the dining room. It's been redecorated and I think it's quite pretty." They sat down at the Chinese Chippendale table and sipped their tea. Raina was aware that Ginny was staring at her over the edge of her teacup, apparently waiting for her to make conversation. "Have a cookie, Ginny."

"When are you going to return to the theatre, Raina?"

"I don't know. I'm not ready yet."

"Still 'people shy'?"

Raina nodded unthinkingly. "I guess you might say that."

"What did you do with all that money?"

Raina, puzzled but not yet registering the truth, looked at her. "Why? I don't think that's any concern of yours."

"People want to know."

"It's none of their damn business."

"Are you in touch with your ex-husband? What about your child?"

"Look here," said Raina, "these are things I don't want to discuss with you or anyone."

"How did it feel to give up your own child for a million dollars?"

"Look, Ginny, I think you'd better be going. I . . ."

"Have some reading to do?" Her tone was sarcastic.

"You don't live in the building, do you?" Raina said with rising panic. "You'd better leave, Ginny, if that's your name." Raina noticed the woman's purse for the first time and realized that she had been carrying it with her as she had moved about the apartment. "There's a tape recorder in there." Raina grabbed for the purse. Ginny tried to pull away but it was too late. The women struggled. Raina tugged at the purse until she got it. She ran around the other side of the table, opened it up and found the cassette recorder. She flipped out the cassette tape, threw it on the floor and ground it under her heel.

"It doesn't matter," said Ginny. "I'll write whatever I want anyway."

"Get out! Get out of here!" Raina shoved the purse across the table to the reporter.

"You've broken my tape."

Raina went to the kitchen. She withdrew three dollars from the jar where they kept housekeeping money, crumpled them in her fist and threw them at the red-haired woman. "Take it!"

Smiling, Ginny knelt to the floor and picked up each dollar. Then slowly, deliberately, she walked out of the apartment.

After that Raina didn't go out at all. She waited for Jana or Kay or Birdie to bring up the mail. She ordered what she needed from local stores. They would deliver anything she wanted.

It was April. Another rainy day. Birdie called to say that a touch of flu was keeping her in bed and that she would not be in to clean that day. Raina was disappointed. She had been looking forward to having some company. She was waiting for her coffee to perk when Farouk rubbed against her legs wanting something to eat. She got a container of milk out of the refrigerator. She shook the carton. There wasn't enough milk for both Farouk and her coffee. She deferred to the cat and poured the remainder into his bowl. "I've got to order a few things from the store, Farouk. We're all out of milk." She opened the cabinet. "Let's see. We've got plenty of cat food. Enough to last you at least until the end of the week. I'd better get some eggs, and let's see, what else?"

Raina compiled a list, called the grocery store and placed her order along with a request that the delivery boy bring her a New York *Times*. Then she poured the black coffee back into the percolator. A quarter of an hour later the doorman told her that the delivery boy was on his way up. She opened the door, took the package and the paper and gave the young man a tip.

A little after three in the afternoon, Jana found Raina sitting on the kitchen floor with the newspaper spread across her lap.

"Raina, what's wrong? My God, what's wrong?" She dropped to her knees and pushed the newspaper away. Raina looked at her with dull eyes, then collapsed in her arms. Jana managed to get her into bed. Then she called Raina's physician, Dr. Dennison, and urged him to come to the apartment immediately. The doctor examined Raina and gave her an injection, then met with Jana.

"She'll proably sleep for at least twelve hours. But you'd better be with her when she wakes up."

"I'll be here."

"You've got to get Raina to see a psychiatrist, Miss Donatello. She should have gone months ago when she first got back from Europe, but now I think it's imperative. She's going to need a lot of help to get her through this latest shock. Raina's first psychiatrist helped her profoundly. Do you think you can talk her into going back to him?"

"I've tried," said Jana, "but I've had the feeling that Raina is too wounded and angry to *want* to get better. Besides, her old doctor isn't even practicing in New York anymore."

"Well, I'm going to give you the name of a man I recommend highly. His name's David Carlyle. It may be a matter of life and death that Raina get in touch with him."

A chill ran through Jana. "All right. I'll do everything in my power to persuade her."

After seeing the doctor out Jana went into the kitchen and gathered up the scattered newspaper. Once again she read the short column on the obituary page which stated that Andre de Clermont II had died at the age of five months of an undisclosed illness. Tears welled in Jana's eyes. Angrily she threw the newspaper across the floor. "The son-of-a-bitch didn't even call her!"

Raina swung her legs over the beach chaise and sat up. She'd had enough sun for today. She began fiddling with the television dial. Watergate disappeared and a diaper commercial took its place. A tot waddled toward the camera smiling and holding out its hands. Raina, wincing as if she had been hit in the stomach, ran inside the apartment. She rushed down the hallway to the kitchen and stood in the middle of the room holding onto herself trying to get her emotions under control. She clenched and unclenched her hands. She had to do something. She had to keep busy. She started mixing a milkshake in the blender as Dr. Dennison had recommended to help her build up her weight. She added whole milk, a couple of eggs, honey, wheat germ and a banana. Then she switched on the blender. The mixture flew all over the kitchen—she had forgotten to put on the lid. She quickly turned it off, but the gooey substance dripped from the wall and lay in puddles over the floor. She tore out a handful of paper towels and crouched to clean up the mess. Sobbing with a deep heartrending sound she fell to her knees.

At last Raina lifted her head. A hard glint of determination glowed in her eyes. "I'm going to get off my knees. I'm going to stop crying, and I'm going to stop feeling sorry for myself. I can't change my past, but dammit I can change my future!"

Raina went to the kitchen phone and dialed information. "Would you please give me the phone number of the Hank Heller Producing Agency?"

Chapter Nineteen

A fleet of limousines—silver Rolls Royces, black Bentleys and chocolate-brown Sevilles—formed a line three blocks long. They were waiting to discharge their glittering occupants at the Broadway Theatre. Floodlights crisscrossed the dark blue sky providing the only illumination of the heavens. The moon was hidden by a curtain of indigo clouds and the stars, perhaps out of deference to their human counterparts, had chosen not to come out.

A marquee identified the occasion in large bold letters—The Annual Tony Awards. Beneath, a circle of policemen aided by wooden barricades kept the urgent fans, autograph hounds and curiosity seekers at bay. News teams from all three major networks stood in separate groups, each intent upon getting a treasured word or two from the arriving personalities. On the periphery of the swelling mass were assorted denizens of the streets—pickpockets, hustlers, bums and bag ladies—all drawn to the commotion in hopes of obtaining a bit of money, freely given or otherwise.

Inside the theatre women wearing pinched faces and linty black dresses trimmed with white collars and cuffs scurried up and down the aisles delivering ticketholders to their seats. The bigger the star the better the seat. All of the nominees and top theatre, film and television personalities were seated on the first floor in the center of the auditorium. Those with lesser clout were given the side seats on the main floor. Those of even lesser importance were relegated to the mezzanine and balcony. Wearing rented tuxedoes and marked-down gowns they leaned forward in their balcony seats and gaped adoringly at each new arrival. Even though they were strictly forbidden, a few had brought with them tape recorders and infrared cameras.

Several musicians of the thirty-six piece orchestra made their way through the tangle of music stands to their seats. Despite the enormous salaries they were getting for that evening's work, many complained about the huge amount of music they were required to play. Their grumblings were commonplace. Broadway musicians owed no alliegance to any show or any star, only to their unions. They found their seats and made themselves as comfortable as possible in their crowded quarters. Some began tuning up their instruments, others gazed dispassionately at the proceedings.

The auditorium was now three-quarters full and the remainder of the expected people were arriving in a steady stream. The general mood was ebullient. The crowd had gathered together once again to pay tribute to their very own.

Outside, a dark blue Cadillac limousine pulled up to the curb. The automobile was from the floor of Sam Benedict's showroom. The driver, not in uniform, was Sam's younger nephew Mitch. He was obviously enjoying himself. An attendant stationed at curbside opened the back door and Jana and Sam emerged. In his tuxedo, newly purchased for the occasion, Sam Benedict looked like a matinee idol, and many members of the crowd speculated on just which play they had seen him in and what *was* his name anyway. Jana was dressed in an ankle length gown of flame red. It was made of a stretch jersey and had a scoop neck and long tight sleeves. The dress was ashimmer with hand-sewn pailettes. The round spangles were varied in diameter and ranged from reddish pink to deep scarlet. She was recognized by all of the television news teams and by most of the females in the gathered mob. Those who did not know either her or Sam cheered them just for the sheer spectacle of their appearance.

Jana waved and offered a brilliant smile to the throng. Sam took her arm and she pulled up the hem of her tight skirt as they strode toward the entrance of the theatre. The TV cameras recorded their arrival and the newscasters identified her for the viewing audience. "You afternoon television viewers will recognize Melissa Holgate, star of that sensational and front-running soap, *Intimate Strangers,* which airs on another network. In real life, the beautiful lady is known as Jana Donatello. Ms. Donatello started out in theatre herself before the advent of the successful afternoon drama. Miss Donatello's escort is man-about-town Sam Benedict. The character of Melissa Holgate is soon to be married on television. We can't help wondering if real life is going to imitate art for Jana and her handsome man," bubbled an enthusiastic newswoman with a mop of bleached blonde hair.

Several limousines later Kay, with Eric as her escort, stepped onto the pavement from their rented Mercedes. Eric looked uncomfortable in his tuxedo. Kay on the other hand looked very glamorous in a sea green chiffon gown. It was as revealing as it was simple. It had a halter top and was totally backless. Kay's bright auburn hair was arranged into an upsweep with curls and intertwined green ribbons dangling down the back of her neck. Out of the corner of her mouth Kay whispered, "For God's sakes, Eric, smile. You look like you're about to faint."

"Everybody's looking at us."

"Why of course. That's what they came here for." Head high, Kay marched forward. Ignoring the crowd that probably wouldn't know who she was, she offered her most dazzling smile to the television cameras. The blonde newswoman thrust a microphone toward Kay saying, "Miss Kay Kincade, ladies and gentlemen. Kay designed the wonderful costumes for the bright revival of that twenties musical *Hotcha!* Kay, this will be your second Tony nomination, won't it?"

Kay, surprised that the newswoman knew who she was, was nearly at a loss for words. "Why, yes. My second nomination. I'm afraid I didn't win for *Performance.*"

"Well you're certainly in the running tonight. Good luck to you, Kay!"

"Thank you," Kay replied and grabbed Eric's arm. Once inside the theatre she whispered, "Since when did they become interested in costume design?"

"Well, Kay, you have had an awful lot of publicity, 'youngest designer' and all of that. And don't forget the spread in *People* Magazine."

"I'm still surprised." She nodded to a few people she knew by sight. To Eric, "Let's find our seats. I'm so nervous." They waited for an usher to become available and then were led down the aisle toward their seats. "Oh look, Eric, there's Jana and Sam. They got here first. Oh, I hope Raina's not late."

"We're all sitting together?"

"Uh huh. You'll never believe what strings I had to pull to make that happen."

Kay had asked Hank Heller to use his influence so that the three roommates and their escorts could sit together. Heller not only did that but got them six of the best seats in the house, seats usually reserved for theatrical royalty. They were in the twelfth row off the aisle in the center of the auditorium.

Before taking their seats Kay and Eric saw Hank Heller sitting several rows down. Kay kissed him and thanked him for the tickets. "Good luck tonight, Kay," he said. "You deserved the last Tony. I hope to hell you get it tonight."

"I hope Raina gets it more. And you too for your direction."

Heller glanced around. "Raina's not here yet?"

"They were about a block behind us. It's like a supermarket opening out there. We'd better take our seats. We'll see you at the party afterwards?"

"Certainly. Win or lose, I'll be there."

A white Rolls Royce Corniche was easing its way towards the Broadway Theatre. Inside were Raina and Robert Shafner, the author of the play for which she was nominated as best actress. Robert was a man in his mid-forties with a high, intelligent brow, curly grey hair and an angular face. He wore tinted glasses to ward off the bright lights that irritated his eyes. He could feel the tension in Raina's hand which he was holding.

"Be calm, my darling. We're almost there and soon it will be over with. We'll be safely inside, past the fans and TV people."

"God, Robert, what if they stop me and want to ask me something. My throat's so dry I don't think I could respond."

"Then I shall speak for you," he replied with an easy smile. "After all, I'm known for my flowery prose."

"I can't remember having been so nervous in my life."

"You're not alone, Raina."

Impulsively she kissed him on the cheek. "Oh dear, now look what I've done. I've gotten lipstick on you."

"No matter. I have a handkerchief."

"I hope Jana and Kay are there."

"You look lovely."

"Oh, Robert, aren't you even a little bit nervous?"

"Of course I am, my dear. I haven't had a financial success on Broadway in years. We've just barely paid back the backers. If *Garden of Predators* wins the Tony for the best play it'll make the box office ring."

"That's not the only reason you want to win."

"No, it's not. I'd just like to be told that after three flops in a row I'm on the right track again."

"Robert, they were only financial flops, not artistic ones. The reviews were good."

"It doesn't work with me unless the people come. Thank God they're coming now."

The uniformed chauffeur eased the Corniche to the front of the theatre. Raina sucked in her breath as the door was opened.

"Come on, love," said Robert. "Our public awaits us." Then he winked. Raina relaxed and let him help her out.

The crowd gasped as Raina emerged. She looked every inch a star. Her silver-gold hair was pulled tightly back from her face and arranged at the nape of her neck in a huge chignon. Her face, always beautiful, had taken on a radiance with maturity. She smiled tentatively at the gathering and in an almost careless gesture she removed the floor length white ruffled organdy cape from her shoulders. Her gown was manmade fabric of shimmering white lamé which clung to the sensuous curves of her body like a second skin. The gown had a high collar but a thin V-opening plunged to a point just short of her navel and was held together by an immense diamond pin which had been a gift from the playwright.

The flashbulbs began bursting. Raina experienced a momentary panic. She reached out and grabbed Robert's hand and he steadied her. She glided across the red carpet toward the entrance of the theatre, which was suddenly blocked by a newscaster who gushed in honey tones, "It's two of our evening's stars, ladies and gentlemen. Robert Shafner, our foremost living playwright and author of *Garden of Predators,* and his leading lady, Raina Pendleton. Both are up for Tonys. Robert for writing his wonderful play and Raina for acting in it. Would the two of you say something to our television audience?"

Robert took the lead. "We *both* hope to win." He pulled Raina along so that she would not be trapped by the reporter.

"There they go," the newscaster went on. "One of New York's most beautiful couples."

At the entrance to the theatre Raina was prevailed upon to sign several autographs. She did so quickly, then she and Robert disappeared inside.

"Round one," Robert whispered.

"I can't believe I'm still standing. Now if I can only get through the ceremonies. Oh, Robert, I hope I don't win. I can't remember a word of my speech. It was terrible anyway."

"It'll come back to you, Raina. And if you can't remember it, just say thank you. Look, the rest of our party's already here. We'd better join them."

Raina immediately felt better when she saw Jana's and Kay's glowing faces. As Raina made her way down the aisle there was a smattering of sedate applause and a whisper of "good lucks" from well-wishers. She smiled and nodded, not really aware of anyone in particular. The group had barely had time to do more than exchange greetings when the orchestra conductor appeared. He raised his baton and the ceremonies began.

Raina began to relax. With Robert's help she had made it through the beginning of the festivities. She hoped she would be able to handle the rest.

As the orchestra was playing the overture Jana scanned the audience. In all the time she had lived in New York she had never seen so many stars. It made her feel quite humble. Several rows in front of her she was able to pick out Lauren Bacall. And not far away, Angela Lansbury. She closed her eyes and savored the feeling. Never, never would she forget this evening. It would be a special part of her life as long as there was memory.

Kay barely heard the music. She was rehearsing her speech in her mind in case she had the luck to win. She didn't think she was going to. The costume designers she was up against were all older, established figureheads of the theatre. Kay was a newcomer. The Tony committee usually favored staying power rather than the emergence of an upstart. She glanced at Raina. She looked calm enough but Kay knew what must be going through her mind. More than anything Kay wanted Raina to win. Perhaps in winning she would be finally convinced of the respect and admiration that people felt for her. Raina had made remarkable progress since her terrible marriage and the devastating events that followed. And if anything she had come further than her own expectations. Reverting to a childhood gesture, Kay crossed her fingers and silently prayed that the Almighty would favor her good friend.

Unable to do deep breathing exercises to calm herself, Raina began counting backwards. She started with one hundred and by the time she reached seventy-four she felt better. Thank goodness for her friends and for Robert. Their support had been instrumental in helping her pull her life together. Now she believed that each day was worth experiencing and she no longer needed to erase them through the use of liquor or anything else. For the first time in her life Raina actually looked forward to her future without fear.

The theme of the Tony Awards was "Beginnings." Each host and hostess had been asked to share with the audience a short anecdote concerning the start of their theatrical careers. Some would be amusing, some poignant, and a few would be risqué.

The overture was finished, the gilt curtain parted, and the master and mistress of ceremonies were introduced by an offstage voice. "Ladies and gentlemen, Amelia and Ian Ballinger!" The lights came up on an elderly and distinguished looking couple poised at the top of a staircase. The Ballingers were a theatrical institution and everyone in the auditorium rose to give them a deserved standing ovation.

The couple, stately and dignified, descended the staircase to the awaiting microphones and started the proceedings by relating a sweet and romantic tale of how they met and married over fifty years ago after having been cast in the same play. They ended the story on a wry note.

Amelia: "The play didn't run."

Ian: "But we did."

The adorable musical comedy star Maggie Weston, with her gigantic smile and mercurochrome colored hair, was brought onstage. She announced that throughout the evening musical numbers from the four nominated musical shows would be presented. She was happy to present to them the title number from the first nominated musical, *Hotcha!*

Kay bit down on her lower lip and slid lower into her seat as the excerpt from the musical for which she was nominated began. In the darkness there came the tinkling sound of a jazz piano in 4/4 time. As the lights slowly came up the lone piano was joined by another and yet another. Finally the audience saw a chorus of ten couples at ten upright pianos. Each piano had been painted glossy white. The scheme of Kay's spectacular Roaring Twenties costumes combined black and white stripes with a bold spectrum of accent colors. The effect was startling, and the audience responded with cheers and great waves of thunderous applause.

As the evening progressed *Hotcha!* won best scenic design and best lighting for a musical. It was now time for the costume nominations. A young Broadway actor now making it in Hollywood read the nominations. "Tanya Corday for *Nite Life,* Emilio Macelli for *Tales of Manhattan,* Kay Kincade for *Hotcha!* and Goldie Farber for *Passion Flower.*" He smiled genially at the audience. "And the winner is . . . Kay Kincade for *Hotcha!*"

Jana squealed and Sam began whistling like a Brooklyn baseball fan. "It's you! It's you!" screamed Raina. "Oh, Kay, it's you!" Kay shot out of her seat and stumbled into the aisle. Then she ran to the stage as if she were afraid that if she didn't quickly show up they would give the award to somebody else. The actor kissed her on the cheek and handed her the treasured Antoinette Perry Award. Kay cradled it in her hand for a moment before acknowledging her audience and their applause. Her voice was hoarse with emotion when she spoke. "I wanted this award so very, very much, and I didn't dare to think I would get it. I want to thank all of you who voted for me and even those who didn't. I am in wonderful company. I want to thank everybody involved in *Hotcha!*—from the producers and the director to the wonderful kids in the chorus. They're all magnificent." Kay grinned mischievously. "And in case you're wondering about my dress, yes, I made it myself." Kay made her way back to her seat stopping to accept congratulations from different members of the audience. When she sat back down she appeared stunned. "I can't believe it," she muttered. "I just can't believe it."

The last awards of the evening were given to the best actor and actress in a straight play and in a musical, plus the best musical of the year, and the best play of the year. Despite the fact that it was a revival, Kay's show *Hotcha!* won best musical and its two leading performers garnered the other coveted awards. Best actor of the year award went to a young Englishman in the play *Show Me the Way Home,* which had been warmly embraced by critics and audiences alike. It was now time for the award for the best actress in a straight play and this award was to be presented by Ian Ballinger.

In a strong rich voice which was only just beginning to show the quaverings of old age, the esteemed actor read the nominations. "The talented ladies nominated are: Cornelia Leeson, *Show Me the Way Home;* Ette Ayer, *Grendel's Mother;* Barbara Faulk, *Loving Weapons;* and Raina Pendleton, *Garden of Predators.*" He smiled at the audience. "I'm glad I wasn't on the committee. I don't know how I would have made a choice. And the winner is . . . Raina Pendleton for *Garden of Predators!*"

Robert Shafner let out a very undignified war whoop and kissed Raina. "Go on, Raina. Go and get it. You earned it." He stood up and helped Raina to her feet. Raina looked at him through glassy eyes.

"Robert, I don't remember my speech."

"It doesn't matter. Just go and say thank you."

Raina walked slowly to the edge of the stage and ascended the stairs. Ian Ballinger embraced her, handed her the award and backed away to let her have her moment. The cheers and applause from the audience were louder than they had been for any award that evening. Raina clutched the award to her chest and stepped to the microphone. The crowd became still. She said in a voice husky with emotion, "This is the most wonderful thing that has ever happened to me. I was very fortunate to be cast in Robert Shafner's miraculous play, to have been directed with an iron hand and love by Hank Heller, and to be surrounded by a group of actors who gave me every support possible. As you know, *Garden of Predators* is about a revolution. Well, my life has been a revolution of sorts. A series of defeats and victories. I think my appreciation for this honor can best be expressed by the final lines of the play wherein the character I portray says 'And when they asked me what I did during the revolution I shall tell them . . . I survived.' "

Even though *Hotcha!* and *Garden of Predators* went on to win the bet musical and best play awards, those awards were anticlimactic for everyone who knew of Raina's troubled past. The Tony did not only signify the recognition of Raina's talent by her peers, it represented a kind of triumph of the human spirit. Raina Pendleton had survived the exploitation of her life by others and by herself.

Part Four

Chapter Twenty

Rockland County, New York

Birch Court was a densely wooded cul-de-sac located in an exclusive section of Rockland County, New York. Five driveways extended from the lane like fingers on a hand. These led to five homes each worth a fortune. The houses were completely different in architectural style and were just barely visible through the profusion of trees. The limbs of stately oaks, slender birches and frivolous maples appeared to support various sections of the buildings—an upper deck, a cupola, a pair of dormer windows. An imaginative passerby might possibly get the impression that Birch Court was a community of treehouses.

A mailbox painted a woodsy brown with black lettering read "Mr. and Mrs. Samuel Benedict." Below in smaller characters was printed "Jana Donatello." A clump of English ivy had entwined itself around the post and only a veteran postman would know that it was there. From the far end of the lane the owner of the mailbox jogged into view. He was wearing a red headband, a red sweatshirt, blue shorts and a pair of running shoes. Sam Benedict was in better physical condition than ever. His stomach was as flat as a college swimmer's and his legs could easily rival those of any tennis court hero. When he stopped at the mailbox he was barely out of breath. He flipped it open and withdrew a profusion of magazines, newspapers and letters. He tucked them under his arm and sprinted up the driveway to the house.

The house had been built in the nineteen-thirties and was designed to accommodate the steep slope that swelled upwards from the property. The house appeared to be a series of boxes and was covered with redwood shingles. The major rooms of the structure were on separate floors but were connected by wooden ramps. Sam climbed the ramp leading to the back deck. The house was overgrown with grapevines which offered natural shade. He entered the gallery of the huge kitchen. The floor was made of flagstones gathered from the property itself. A diverse selection of brass utensils hung from the ceiling and gleamed like a display of treasured spoils of war. Sam saw that Jana was up. She was standing next to the kitchen sink preparing grapefruit for breakfast. She hadn't heard him enter. He leaned against the counter and observed her. The expression on his face radiated love. Jana saw his reflection in the windowpane.

"Morning, darling. Did you enjoy your jogging?"

"I enjoyed it more because I knew my legs were bringing me home to you. Why are you up so early, honey? It's only eight o'clock."

"I know I should sleep in on Saturdays, but I can't. I'm too used to the weekly routine. Coffee's ready and I'm doing the grapefruit."

He ran his fingers through her hair, which was still slightly damp from a morning shower, and kissed her lightly on the cheek. "My dutiful wife."

Jana kissed him back. "I thought you didn't like being catered to."

"I don't unless it goes both ways. I'll make the eggs. Scrambled, O.K.?"

She nodded. "Oh, you picked up the mail. There looks like a lot of it."

"Mainly fan letters for you, my dear. Nothing for me except bills." He turned down the corners of his mouth in mock depression.

Jana kissed him again. "Poor baby, I'll write one to you."

"And what would you say?"

"Sweet icky things. I'm afraid it'd sound like a cheap Valentine's card."

"The cheaper the better." Sam grinned and patted Jana's stomach. "Feel anything yet?"

"It's only four months. A little too soon for kicking."

He ran his hand up from her stomach to her breasts which he stroked through the thin fabric of her housecoat. "Mmmm. I'd better get to the eggs before I change my mind about breakfast."

"Just make me one, Sam. And only one slice of toast."

"Is that all you're having? You're eating for two now."

"I'm going to have jam. I have a dreadful craving for raspberry jam."

Jana unfolded the New York *Times* and glanced at the headlines. "Sam, listen to this. President Ford has granted amnesty to the draft resisters. I think that's wonderful."

"It's about time."

"I thought that you felt different, having been in Korea and all. What changed your mind?"

"Since I met you I've discovered I'm a lover, not a fighter. Anyhow, I didn't believe in the Vietnam war any more than anybody else did. Sure I can't coerce you into two eggs?"

"Nope." Jana laughed. "Here comes Farouk. He heard you cracking eggs. For an old cat he's still got terrific hearing."

The huge orange cat entered the kitchen like a monarch. After surveying his subjects he favored Sam with a rub because Sam was cooking.

"Hello, big boy. Seems like the only thing that gets you up is food. I'll scramble one for you. Jana, if you'd told me a year ago that I'd be cooking for a cat, I'd have said you were completely out of your mind."

Jana scratched Farouk under the chin. "He's getting

old, Sam. The vet said we had to cook him special things. Cats are like people. When they get older certain foods aren't so easy to digest. Who knows what junk they put in those cans. I'd better get him his pill while he's still hungry." Jana stuck the prescribed digestive pill into a small piece of butter and put it on his plate. The cat swallowed it nearly whole.

"Shall we have our breakfast outside?" Sam asked.

"I'd love it. I'll get the trays."

After giving Farouk his portion of scrambled eggs, Sam and Jana carried their breakfasts into the garden, where a stone enclosure Sam had built created a secluded setting for table and chairs under the shade of a huge oak tree. As they ate they talked to one another. No newspapers, radios, TVs or paperback novels, just conversation.

"Have you heard from Raina or Kay?" Sam asked.

"Not for a while. But I owe them both letters. I'm going to write them after breakfast. We must decide what to do with the apartment. It's a shame to keep it empty when people are so desperate for space in the city."

"Have you kept Birdie on?"

"Just once a week to dust and water the plants. We've been waiting to see what Kay is going to do. Raina doesn't want the apartment, we don't need it, and Kay might stay on in Los Angeles."

"You got it at a great price when it went co-op."

"I know, and since the three of us had the money it seemed a shame to let it pass us by. Sam, I've had an idea and I think one that the others will approve. I was thinking that we should offer the apartment to three young women starting out in the theatre . . . each group could have it for a four-year period. I've spoken to a woman at Equity and they'd be willing to arrange the whole thing. The apartment was lucky for us. Maybe it would be lucky for others. Besides, it's a lovely place to live, and the only expense would be the cost of the maintenance. God knows that's not very high, not by today's standards."

"I think that's a very sweet idea, Jana. Almost like the three of you establishing your own scholarship."

Jana spread a prodigious amount of raspberry jam on her toast and took a bite. "I'll definitely write Kay and Raina this morning. I've got to write letters anyhow. I'm behind in answering my fan mail."

Sam sipped his coffee. "How do the fans feel about Melissa Holgate having a baby?"

"They love it despite the, shall we say, seamy circumstances. Raped by an ex-husband whom she kills with a marble ashtray, put on trial, then acquitted . . . only to discover that his attack has made her pregnant."

Sam grinned. "I imagine they're eating it up."

"The ratings have never been so high."

"How are you going to manage to have the baby on TV?"

"Well naturally they won't be showing much. While I'm really having my own baby the soap's going to focus on the myriad problems of Melissa's neighbors."

"I'm always amazed."

"By what, Sam?"

"By the way the writers manage to juggle life's little problems so deftly. Too bad real life can't be planned as easily as that."

"We're lucky, Sam." She reached across the table and touched his hand. "We have each other."

"Life is so much easier when you find somebody."

"I don't suppose we'll ever want for anything. It's all within our grasp." Jana laughed. "Aren't we being just a little self-satisfied?"

"We'd better be careful and not make the gods jealous of us, although they have every right to be."

He paused and added a little dourly, "If only your mother would come around."

Jana sighed. "Mother's opinion has nothing to do with our marriage or you, Sam. She's soured on life and has been for as long as I can remember. Since she won't allow herself any happiness, how could she enjoy the happiness of others? Ostensibly, she disapproves of our marriage because you've already been married and divorced. But if that hadn't been the case she would have found other reasons. She's like that, Sam. I don't pretend to understand her, but I will not allow her distorted opinions of life to infect my incredible happiness. Neither should you." She brightened. "Besides, your parents like me."

"They love you."

"Well that sort of evens things out, doesn't it?"

"You should hear mom talk about you. She always refers to you as 'my talented and beautiful soon-to-be-a-mother daughter-in-law.'"

Jana laughed. "Estelle is terrific. And so's your dad."

"He carries that autographed picture you gave him everywhere. I'm sure his card playing cronies get tired of him showing it around."

"Why don't you ask them over for dinner tonight, Sam?"

"Are you sure you feel up to it?"

"Of course. I'll do something slimming, simple, and healthy. Perhaps chicken and fresh vegetables in the wok. Call her before you start to work in the yard. She likes to hear from her handsome soon-to-be-a-father son."

"I'll do it if you promise to take a nap this afternoon."

"I promise." She lowered her eyelashes. "Perhaps later you'll join me."

Jana rinsed the dishes and put them into the dishwasher. Then she carried the mail into the den, which also served as an office. She sat down at a late Federal mahogany desk that she and Sam had bought at an auction in up-state New York. She sorted the mail into three piles: bills, personal letters and fan mail. She attacked a huge pile of fan mail first. Most were requests for autographed pictures, which had been already signed and waited in eight-by-ten manila folders. Some of the letters required short personal notes to which Jana amiably replied. She worked at her fan mail for more than two hours without stopping. At the end of the time she had finished that week's chore. Next week there would be another raft of correspondence to deal with, but that was all part of being a soap opera heroine.

She wrote a brief "duty letter" to her mother. The letter was as strained and impersonal as her mother's were to her. Jana had not mentioned the impending birth of her child and did not mention it in this letter. She signed the letter "as ever, Jana."

"As ever what?" she mused. Then Jana wrote letters to Raina and Kay telling them of her happiness with Sam, her work and the coming baby. She also stated her proposal concerning the apartment and asked for their opinions. She closed by inviting them to visit and reaffirmed her love for each of them.

Farouk jumped up on the desk and made himself a nest in the pile of fan letters. He curled into a ball of orange fur and went to sleep. "I think you've got the right idea, Farouk. I'm tired too. But that's to be expected."

Jana stretched, turned out the lamp and glanced out the window. Sam was hard at work and rivulets of sweat poured from his body. His muscles strained as he shoveled dirt into a wheelbarrow. From that distance Jana thought that he looked more like a teenager than a man of forty-five.

Jana climbed the stairs to the master bedroom. Once inside, she closed the shutters against the bright noonday sun. The room was large enough to accommodate sleeping, breakfast and sitting areas. Sam and Jana's "finds" at country auctions accounted for most of the furniture and decorative pieces. The bed was a fourposter of heavy polished oak. It was covered with a quilt of a "Jacob's Ladder" design.

Jana took off her housecoat and slipped between the soft percale sheets. She wrapped her arms around Sam's pillow, which made her feel safe and comfortable. "Sam," she whispered to the pillow. "My sweet Sam." Then she drifted into a deep and contented sleep.

Some time later Sam, having showered, stood at the

foot of the bed watching Jana as she slept. After drying himself with a towel he slid beneath the sheets. He gently removed the pillow from Jana's arms and placed himself where it had been. Jana stirred as she felt the heat of his body warm her own. Her eyes still closed, she reached out and touched his face with her fore-finger. Sam parted his lips and sucked her finger inside his mouth. Jana caught her breath and opened her eyes. "Sam, what a lovely surprise."

Sam responded by taking each of her fingers in turn into his mouth. Jana moved close to him and savored the contours of his hard body. It remained wonderfully the same for her—a total sensuality honed by Sam's tenderness and love. In the beginning his patience in love-making had dispelled whatever fears she might have had. They still made love as passionately and with as much care as they had that very first night of their honeymoon.

They embraced one another. Sam watched the tiny pulse throbbing beneath Jana's left eye, each beat making her eyelashes flutter involuntarily. Every time they made love he felt as if he had entered a world he had never been in before. He had never experienced such rapture with any other woman. Sometimes when Sam was away from Jana thoughts of her invaded his mind and nearly made his heart break with joyful thanksgiving. Then he'd stop whatever he was doing and rush to be with her. A weight would lift from his innermost heart and he would need to make love to her to reaffirm the goodness of his life. He would sometimes undress her where she stood, kissing her hands, her arms, her shoulders, her breasts as he gazed at her with un-blinking eyes. He had never been able to tell Jana the way he felt. His love mingled elation and despair and was beyond words.

Sam clasped Jana like a man drowning until finally a turbulent ecstasy engulfed him and pulled him into a whirl of exquisite pleasure.

They lay facing each other, their lips touching,

breathing in and out of each other's mouths. Suddenly Jana jerked her body.

"What's wrong?"

"Sam, I felt him move. I'm sure I did."

Sam slipped his hand down between their bodies and caressed Jana's stomach. He felt the slightest movement beneath his palm and he began laughing.

"I do believe the little son-of-a-gun is jealous."

Chapter Twenty-one

Acapulco, Mexico

Raina and Robert Shafner's Tony Awards for *Garden of Predators* were serving as bookends. They held the slim volumes of Shafner's twelve published plays. The playwright himself was now at work on his thirteenth play, *Tarnished Thrones,* which dealt with the corruption of power in high places.

Robert paused in his typing and looked through the open louvers. From his vantage point he could see the swimming pool glistening under the Acapulco sun, and his wife lounging on the patio reading scripts.

He forced his attention back to his work. He scanned what he had written, then leaned back in his chair and smiled with satisfaction. Never before had a play come so easily. Was it his contented marriage that brought his characters to life, or had he become so experienced in plot construction and language that his labor was considerably less than it had been at the beginning of his career? It was not a dilemma to worry about but rather one to enjoy.

Unable to concentrate on his work any longer, Robert switched off the typewriter. He went to the doorway and watched Raina as she oiled her body. There had been a time when he thought he would never find happiness with a woman again. After his first wife died of cancer, he'd retreated from the world content to express his emotions through his writing. At first he had been afraid of his love for Raina; afraid that it might somehow rob him of his talent. How wrong he had been.

Unable to resist making contact with her, he called, "Some life you have. You're getting a sun tan while I'm typing my fingers to the bone." Raina looked up and laughed.

"Not bloody likely on that electric typewriter, my darling. Come join me. It's nearly time for lunch anyway."

"Be with you in a minute." Robert placed what he had written that morning into a drawer, then went to join his wife. He bent down and kissed her on the top of her head.

"Is that the best you can do?"

"You're greasy everywhere else."

"Not everywhere," she smiled. "How's it going?"

"Quite well. It makes me rather nervous."

"Why is that?"

"I'm not used to things coming so easily."

"Are you satisfied with it?"

"Yes, I think it's damn good."

"Then stop worrying."

"How are the scripts?"

Raina groaned. "Absolutely ghastly. You just wouldn't believe some of the things agents are sending me."

Robert grinned slyly. "Not to worry, my dear. My new play is almost finished. I thought you knew that I was writing it expressly for you."

"Well, I was hoping," Raina admitted.

"I've been corresponding with Hank. He wants to produce it, and perhaps direct it as well if his schedule permits."

"When are you going to let me read your play, Robert?"

"Soon as I polish it up a bit; perhaps by the end of the week."

"Aren't you at least going to give me a hint as to what it's about?"

"It's a parable about corruption and you play a cool, blond and very corruptible woman."

Raina laughed. "No fair. That sounds like type casting." She stood up. "I'd like something cool to drink. How about you, darling?"

"Perhaps an iced coffee."

Raina sprinted across the patio to the arched loggia that housed an enormous living/dining area, open to the landscape on both sides. Ceiling fans circulated the breezes that wafted through the arches. She pushed open the louvered doors leading to the kitchen and pantry and went about preparing the iced coffee.

As she returned through the hall Raina noticed the mail lying on a side table. She picked out Jana's letter and carried it back with her to the pool.

"What have you got there?" asked Robert.

"A letter from Jana. I'll read it aloud." He listened to his wife as she read the missive in the dramatic manner of a true actress. He watched her face as she repeated Jana's feelings about her coming child. Robert was happy to notice that Raina did not falter, nor did her expression grow cloudy. Her psychiatrist had helped her to come to terms with her past. When she finished Raina exclaimed, "Oh, she sounds so happy!"

"She deserves to be."

"What did you think of her suggestion about the apartment?"

"I think it sounds like a fine idea. After all, we don't need it. We have our own."

"Of course it all depends on Kay and on whether or not she decides to stay on the coast or return to New York City. By the way, darling, when are we going back?"

"Well, if the play goes as smoothly as it has been, we should be returning late in August." Robert got up and stripped down to his walking shorts. "Come on, Raina, let's take a couple of laps around the pool before lunch."

Laughing, Raina ran to the poolside. "I'll bet I can beat you." She dove neatly, barely stirring the water.

"Hey, that's no fair. You didn't wait for the starting whistle." Robert also ran to the edge of the pool and dove in. He was an expert swimmer and caught up with Raina before she reached the middle of the pool. He cut through the water with the fitness and grace of an olympic swimmer. He stuck out his tongue at Raina as he passed her and reached the edge of the pool first. "You smoke too much, my dear."

"I know," she gasped. "I'm going to cut down. I promise you."

When Raina reached him, Robert wrapped his arms around her waist. "Mmmm." He kissed her and pulled her underwater. They both came up gasping for air. "I'll tell you what, Raina. I'll race you back."

"Only if you promise to let me win."

Robert held back, taking lazy strokes and barely kicking his feet. Triumphant, Raina pulled herself out of the pool and strutted back and forth claiming her victory and laughing. "I won, I won! But now I must have a prize. I know—you must promise to read me something from your new play tonight."

"You're terrible. You make me let you win and then you blackmail me."

"Please, Robert."

"All right, all right," Robert said with amused exasperation. "You win. I'll read selected passages right after dinner."

The setting sun streaked the Mexican sky with incredible colors, making it resemble a brightly colored Oriental shawl. The moon was just barely visible. It appeared to float toward earth like a great silver disc scattering shards of light in its wake.

Raina and Robert were sitting in the living room savoring their brandy as they enjoyed the visual richness of the oncoming night. They were dressed casually in bright, loose-fitting resort wear. Neither wore shoes. Robert turned up the lamp and placed the box containing his manuscript in his lap. He smiled at his adoring wife. "My first audience." He reached out and touched her hair, which was as soft as a skein of silk. "I'll read you bits and pieces from the scenes I think are the best."

Raina sat at her husband's feet listening to his words. She was totally immersed in the story and his presentation of it. She sat transfixed for more than an hour and was completely overwhelmed. "It's a truly wonderful, wonderful play, Robert. I can't tell you how moved I am," she breathed when he'd finished.

"My gift to you, Raina, for making me so terribly happy."

Raina blinked her glistening eyes. "I can't tell you, Robert. I feel so lucky."

"No, my darling. I'm the lucky one." He took her hand. "Shall we go up to bed?" Raina nodded and leaned her head against his shoulder. As they walked up the staircase she said softly, "It's awful not to be loved. It makes you wild and destructive. But now I *am* loved, now I know I truly am."

Chapter Twenty-two

Los Angeles, California

The largest soundstage at Supreme Pictures had been converted into a disco decorated in a pseudo-western manner. Giant phallic cacti made of lucite sat in front of the manufactured sunset projected on the cyclorama. A giant bar, horseshoe-shaped and completely mirrored, stood in the center of the set. The fifteen million dollar musical extravaganza was aimed at the disco-oriented youth market. It was entitled *Hot Sunset* and starred the successful male singing group, The Lone Stars.

The five young men, dressed in mock western garb, had begun their careers in homosexual clubs in Greenwich Village. A smart promoter signed them to a contract, and they became a phenomenal success with eight gold records to their credit. They were riding high on the back of success when Bernie Katz, the boy wonder of Hollywood, signed them for a film. A script was tailored to meet their talents. Katz intended to release the film under the biggest barrage of hype since *Grease*. As Katz put it, "Give it enough publicity and a pretty package and I can sell anything!"

Hot Sunset was Kay's first Hollywood assignment. She decided to visit the set on the last day of shooting. She was looking very Hollywood—wearing giant sunglasses and two narrow braids that framed her carefully made up face. She was svelte as ever in her status

jeans and she wore a discreet selection of fine gold
bracelets. Her T-shirt, decorated extensively with se-
quins and bearing the logo of *Hot Sunset,* was a gift
from Bernie Katz.

After being admitted to the soundstage, Kay milled
around with the extras and the technicians, who were
all waiting for the stars—The Lone Stars—to reappear
so that shooting could continue. It seemed that two of
the group had run out of energy. They retired to their
dressing rooms to renew themselves by snorting coke
and washing down uppers with Southern Comfort.

Kay had not visited the set often, but had spent her
time in pursuit of other contracts. She had been signed
for two more pictures and was now looking for an
apartment to rent. Kay was presently staying at the exclusive Beverly-Wilshire as Bernie Katz's guest. "Kaylove, my people go first class. Don't worry. It's all
deductible."

Kay spotted Bernie. Sitting amid the debris of empty
food containers, he was holding court for a group of
young male extras. Katz was grossly fat and had a
flamboyant personality. He had a penchant for junk
food and young men. His blond hair had been recently
curled and his cherubic face was all but hidden behind
huge glasses with pink frames. As usual he wore a
staggering amount of heavy gold jewelry and a caftan
which was unsuccessful at hiding his bloated body.

Kay and Bernie had met at Studio 54 in New York
City. She liked him immediately and felt an empathy
for him, perhaps because their tastes at one time or
another had been similar. By the time he had come to
New York to see The Lone Stars and decided to sign
them for a film, the twenty-four-year-old multimil-
lionaire had already parlayed family money into several blockbusting films of the mid-seventies.

He saw Kay's show *Hotcha!* and was extremely impressed with her designs. After fifteen minutes of Kay's
company he asked her if she'd do the costumes for The
Lone Stars' film. Kay immediately agreed and later,

when the script was written and contracts were signed, she flew to the coast to design *Hot Sunset*.

The obese entrepreneur saw Kay. He shrieked across the soundstage, "Kaylove, I'm over here!" Bernie always assumed that people were looking for him.

Kay made her way through the crowd and endured a wet kiss on each cheek from Bernie. "But how divoon," he gurgled "dropping in for the last roundup. Do you want something to eat, drink or sniff?"

Kay shook her head. "How's it going, Bernie?"

"If we can just keep the Lone Stars high enough we might just finish this thing." He threw a fleshy arm around her. "Come, there's coffee and the most delicious little donuts not far from here." Bernie led her through the extras, cutting a wide swath as he went, kissing and pinching everyone within reaching distance. "How do you stay so thin? I haven't lost a pound. Not even an ounce for that matter. Thinking of having my jaws wired together, but that would put me out of business. Sexy-looking cast, don't you think?"

"Very," agreed Kay. "Where did you find them all?"

"The girls came from central casting. The boys from my casting couch." He emitted a high pitched giggle. "What's next on your agenda? You follow up those leads I gave you?"

"Yes, Bernie, thanks. I've signed contracts for two more movies."

"Which ones, Kaylove?"

"One O'clock Romance and *Riff-Raff."*

"Hope you're getting the star treatment. After all, you're one of my people."

"The money's terrific. I'm looking for an apartment now."

"Going to stay on this mad coast are you?"

"There's more work out here. It's as simple as that."

Bernie's giggles were cut off by the sight of the donuts. "Ah, here we are . . . glazed and gooey. Sounds as if I'm describing myself. You want a donut, Kay?"

"No, thanks, Bernie. Just coffee. I used to have a weight problem."

"Hah. I used to have a thin problem."

Kay gasped and nearly dropped her coffee cup. "Bernie, that guy up there."

"Yes, Kaylove. Which one?"

"Him." She pointed a shaking finger toward a muscular man with short cropped hair and a neatly trimmed beard. He was standing atop some scaffolding adjusting a kleig light. "Do you see him? The one with the neat beard and plaid shirt?"

"He's one of the lighting assistants. Straight as an arrow, but I hired him anyway. One mustn't be chauvinistic. Do you want to meet him?"

"I think I already have. What's his name?"

"I don't remember, but I think he's from somewhere in Canada. Dan Goldstein recommended him. Seems that he's done a lot of documentaries. Dreary stuff. Indian burial rites, mating elks and the like. You want me to call him down?"

"No, no. I'll manage things in my own time," Kay murmured.

"Well, let me go light a fire under the director's ass. Surely those snowheads are ready to perform by now. This waiting around is costing a fortune, but," he smiled, "it's deductible."

Kay watched Bernie giggle through the crowd dispensing words and gropes as he went. He was the boss, the king, the little emperor of the set. No one questioned his authority to do anything, and no one made fun of him the way they had during his childhood days in Texas. *No one.*

Kay turned her attention back to the man on the scaffold. He was moving from light to light marking time. It *was* Fred. She was sure of it. Older, thinner, and wearing his hair shorter. But there was no mistaking that physique. Her head was spinning.

The Lone Stars, eyes sparkling and made up with desert tans, were brought back on the set to continue the final number. They exemplified the now macho look: some wore earrings, their hair was cropped short and they sported a variety of mustaches, everything from Zapatas to handlebars. These were set off by rococo sideburns, goatees or beards. Kay had costumed them in the same color scheme the set designer had used for his set. It was a campy take-off on the Trucolor process popular in the forties. Dominating the spectrum were orange, brown and blue tints. Their costumes, done in sepia tones, were very tight and revealing. After a preliminary session by the director, The Lone Stars took their positions on top of the bar where the last shot had ended.

"Scene 96, Take 12!"

Music was brought up to accompany the young men's singing. The actual track would be dubbed in later for clarity and emphasis. The choreography was simple and pelvic-oriented. Kay noted that it was a good thing that the song would be dubbed later. The Lone Stars weren't in good voice.

"I love my body, my body loves me.

Baby, won't you love my bod-bod-bod-ee too?"

"Lord," Kay muttered. "And they *pay* people to write lyrics like that." She eased herself around so that she could get a better view of Fred. Carefully stepping over the cables, she got herself into position so that she could see his profile. There was no doubt about his nose—it was the same pugnacious projection. And he still had the longest lashes she had ever seen on a man. Kay suddenly felt her anger rising. What was he doing here? He was supposed to be in Montreal with his little French pastry.

As Kay stared at Fred a crucial point in the scene was reached wherein the five men were to jump from the bar. The filming was stopped so that the men could be wired, helping them with their extraordinary leap. Kay pressed her hand over her mouth to keep from crying out—Fred was coming down the scaffolding. She was incapable of moving and had no idea how she was going to respond to him.

He jumped to the floor beside her, smiled absently and said, "Hi, how ya doin'?" He started to walk away, stopped and turned. "Hey, don't I know you

from somewhere? Of course I do . . . You're Kay
Kincade!"

"Of course I am!"

He picked her up and swung her around. "You look
terrific. I'm Fred Spangler. Remember me? New Hope?
The Playhouse?" Kay nodded. "I knew you'd done
the costumes, but I didn't think I'd run into you."

"Maybe you didn't look very hard."

Fred flushed with embarrassment. "I didn't think
. . . well, I thought you might not want to see me. It's
been a long time."

"Thirteen years, give or take a heartbeat."

"You really look different. Thirteen years have
changed you a lot."

"You look different too, Fred."

"Better or worse?"

"I can't tell yet."

"You're a real classy lady now. I mean, you look like
you're hanging onto the steering wheel, and what's
more you're liking it."

"Yes. Yes, I do. Is your wife with you, Fred?"

"We were divorced a couple of years ago. She didn't
dig my work. Wouldn't come with me on locations.
Look, Kay, I'm sorry I got married, but I was lonely
up there. No family, no friends. In the beginning, I
was lucky to have enough work to allow me to eat. The
Canadians didn't exactly embrace us with open arms,
you know. We were up there taking their jobs. At first
I did some scab work, then later I did pretty good
stuff. When the amnesty was announced, I thought I'd
try L.A. I've been following your career. You're doing
real well. A Tony. God, what I wouldn't give for one
of those." He paused and lowered his voice. "We
made such good love together."

"Did we? You want to 'recapture the rapture' or
something like that?" He'd hurt her so badly that Kay
felt her life depended on maintaining a cool and brittle
pose, even though she was giddy with the sight of him.

Before Fred could reply, Harry, the lighting designer,
put his hand on his shoulder. "Man, we're going to

close down for the rest of the day. One of The Lone Stars took too many uppers and he's speeding faster than sound."

"Thanks, Harry. That's fine with me."

Impetuously, Kay caught Fred's arm. "Come on, Fred. Let's go back to my hotel and have a drink." He nodded, but his expression unnerved her. Were his eyes gleaming with passion or triumph?

They drove Kay's rented car back to her hotel. Kay's emotions were confused. *What am I doing? I was too easy. I should have hidden my feelings. I'm making a mistake. Well, at least I'll have him one more time. I'll be able to find out if it was as good as I remember. . . .*

In the elegant lobby of the Beverly-Wilshire Kay stopped to collect her mail. She smiled at Fred. "Credit cards do catch up with one." As they were riding up in the elevator, she leafed through the envelopes and smiled to herself when she recognized Jana's handwriting on one of them.

As they entered the room Fred looked enviously at Kay's Tony Award, which was sitting on the bar. "I take it with me everywhere," she said. "Now how about fixing us a drink? There ought to be enough ice there. They refill the bucket every time you turn around."

"It's a classy place."

Kay shrugged. "It goes with the job, Fred. I'll have a scotch on the rocks. Would you like lunch?" He shook his head. "Music?"

"No, let's talk, Kay. We need to talk."

"About what?" replied Kay blithely. "Us? Well you can't pick it up again like you pick up a book you never finished."

"Sure you can. You just skim over the already read pages."

Kay laughed, but it was hollow. "Fred, you reached inside of me and turned me inside out. I never got over you. I don't have much pride, do I, admitting that to you? And all these years I've imagined that I was still in love with you."

"And are you, Kay?"

"I don't know. Thirteen years! Thirteen long years."

Fred took Kay's drink from her trembling hand. He wrapped his arms around her and held her tight. "Come on, Kay, let's not waste another second."

Kay hesitated and in that brief moment she knew the answer to the question that had haunted her for most of her adult life.

Epilogue

Jana found a parking place on West End Avenue and walked several blocks to the apartment. A wave of nostalgia washed over her as she passed all the familiar buildings. Seventy-fourth Street looked somewhat spiffier—the co-op boom was transforming the neighborhood. She stopped and smiled at the gargoyles above the entranceway. One of their noses was chipped. She wondered how that could have happened. The doorman had his back to her and was staring toward the River.

"Timothy?" she ventured. The doorman turned around.

"Ma'am?"

"I'm sorry. I thought you were Timothy."

"Timothy's gone, Ma'am."

"Retired?"

"Dead."

"I'm so sorry." The new doorman shrugged. "I'm Jana Donatello. I still have an apartment here."

"Oh yes, Miss Donatello. Miss Pendleton is already upstairs. She's expecting you."

The lobby had been freshly painted and the shabby furniture had been replaced. It made Jana feel happy to see that her building had been properly looked after.

Raina opened the door. For a split moment her eyes fell upon Jana's stomach. She blinked then broke into a smile. "You look wonderful." She embraced her.

"It's so good to see you," Jana murmured. They went inside. "Why the place looks marvelous."

"Birdie's kept it up beautifully. Even the plants are in good shape."

Jana looked around the living room. "It looks great. But not lived in."

"You're right. It's a sin for it to go unused. Your plan to turn it over to the 'younger generation' was a stroke of genius. Kay should be here soon. She called. She's staying at the St. Moritz."

"Not here?"

"She said the studio was picking up the tab and she was going to take advantage of it. I've been looking around to see if there was anything I wanted to take, but I didn't find a thing. How about you?"

"I don't think so. It seems that everything belongs here." Jana laughed. "God, look at that chest. Why I remember Kay and I struggling to carry it in off the street one cold winter night." The women sat down on the couch.

"I'm glad we're doing this," said Raina. "It's like paying back all the good luck the three of us have had."

"That's how I feel. I wonder what's keeping Kay."

"Cross-town traffic I imagine. What time are the girls arriving?"

"Five o'clock. They've been personally recommended by Betsy Westoff at Equity. She assured me that they're talented, serious and very good friends."

Raina threw back her head and laughed. "Now *that* does sound familiar."

The doorbell rang. "That's Kay," said Raina jumping up from the couch. "It's got to be."

Both women ran to the door. Kay stood in the entrance. Before letting out a yell, the three women embraced and hurried inside.

"I've brought cold champagne in case there wasn't anything in the house," said Kay.

"Lord, when didn't we have champagne at the crucial times of our lives?" said Raina.

"I'll get the glasses," said Jana.

Kay wandered around the apartment for a few moments, then came back into the living room. "It seems like I must have lived here in another life."

"You like the Coast then?" asked Jana.

"I like some things about it. There's a lot of work there. Oh, did I write you that I ran into Fred?" she added with obviously affected nonchalance.

"Tell, tell!" demanded the other two.

Kay smiled sadly. "There's nothing to tell. I was hanging onto a dream, and dreams are only valid when they hold a promise for the future."

"Then it didn't work out?" ventured Jana.

Kay shook her head. "No, but at least now I'm free of that handsome spectre of my youth. Fred came to my hotel room in Los Angeles, but when he tried to make love to me, I knew in my heart that everything was really all over between us—and had been for a long, long time." Kay smiled sheepishly. "As soon as he left, I realized what a fool I'd been for so many years. How long I'd let myself hold on to a fantasy of things past while the guy who was *really* right for me, who was *really* my other half, waited patiently on the sidelines, loving me dearly and taking all the nonsense I had to dish out."

"You're talking about Eric, aren't you, Kay?" Jana asked with knowing excitement. "Have you told him how you feel? Are you going to see him while you're in New York?"

"Yes and yes and yes," Kay almost crowed. "I'm meeting him at his apartment on Central Park South as soon as we're finished here. He's come a long way from that railroad flat on Ninth Avenue, but he's waiting for me still. I feel as if I'm going to be reunited with my life." Her voice broke with emotion, but she quickly recovered herself and flashed her old grin. "Come on," she said. "Let's have a drink."

The three women lifted their glasses. Raina said, "I offer a toast to *us*. We did it, my dear friends. We *really* did it."

"I hope this apartment is as lucky for the next three girls," said Jana.

"It will be if they've got the right stuff," said Raina.

They chattered nonstop for more than an hour, telling each other of the important plans they were making for the future as well as the trivial events of their daily lives. Their speeches overlapped and often they found themselves all talking at the same time as they reminisced with unabashed sentimentality. They heard the bell ring and Kay held up her hands. "It can't be five o'clock already?"

Raina looked at her watch. "We've talked our way through two bottles of champagne."

"I'll get the door," offered Jana, "since I've spoken to the girls before."

Jana entered the living room with three young women trailing behind her. Raina and Kay rose to greet the arrivals. The older women introduced themselves to the nervous newcomers. They were Noelle Adams, a petite brunette with a perfectly oval face and enormous green eyes; Tessa Thompson, a gangly redhead with milk-white skin and a profusion of freckles; and Valerie Franklin, a classic blonde with startling cheekbones and a sensuous mouth. They were as unlike in manner and appearance as Jana, Raina and Kay. Noelle was sedate, Valerie gregarious and Tessa shy. They were also ambitious, desperate for success in the theatre, and very close friends.

After a while the girls began to talk openly. They were from different parts of Maine and had met while working at a summer theatre in Ogunquit. Valerie wanted to be an actress, Noelle a musical comedy star and Tessa was determined to be a successful playwright. Jana, Raina and Kay recognized their younger counterparts. They saw themselves as they had been at that precious, optimistic and impossible stage of their lives.

While the young girls toured the apartment, Jana, Raina and Kay retired to the terrace with their nearly empty glasses of champagne.

"I think they're perfect," said Raina.

"Perfectly green," said Kay. "Just like we were."

"Then it's settled?" asked Jana. The other women nodded. "I'll take care of the business matters, the signing of the agreement and so forth."

They inclined their heads toward the open terrace door and listened. The girls were shouting to one another as they surveyed the apartment. They couldn't make out the words, but it didn't matter. The tone was eager, happy and just a little bit frightened—a high fidelity record of their own not-so-distant past. It was a bittersweet moment, and one to be savored for the rest of their lives.

"Were we ever so callow?" wondered Kay. Jana and Raina smiled their unspoken answer . . . *you know we were.* "I think that by holding onto the apartment we were holding onto our youth." Kay hoisted her glass. "I for one would like to say that . . ." her voice caught in her throat, ". . . that I wouldn't have missed either of you for the world. Here's to the life we've shared and will *continue* sharing."

"Always forward," agreed Jana.

"We're women now," added Raina. "We have responsibilities and new dreams to pursue."

The afternoon was slowly melting into twilight and the city was beginning to turn on its lights. They hugged each other tightly, none of them daring to speak.

At last Kay broke the silence: "Remember when we were driving into New York City for the first time? I said I could almost see our names spelled out in the lights. Well, there they are. Bigger and brighter than any of us ever dreamed. Can you see them?"

"Yes, yes," the others whispered.

They turned their glasses upside down on a table and, arm in arm, hurried inside to keep an appointment with their future.

Dear Reader:

Would you take a few moments to fill out this questionnaire and mail it to:

Richard Gallen Books/Questionnaire
8-10 West 36th St., New York, N.Y. 10018

1. What rating would you give *Star Quality*?
   ☐ excellent ☐ very good ☐ fair ☐ poor

2. What prompted you to buy this book? ☐ title
   ☐ front cover ☐ back cover ☐ friend's recommendation ☐ other (please specify) _____

3. Check off the elements you liked best:
   ☐ hero ☐ heroine ☐ other characters ☐ story
   ☐ setting ☐ ending ☐ love scenes

4. Were the love scenes ☐ too explicit
   ☐ not explicit enough ☐ just right

5. Any additional comments about the book?
   _____

6. Would you recommend this book to friends?
   ☐ yes ☐ no

7. Have you read other Richard Gallen
   romances? ☐ yes ☐ no

8. Do you plan to buy other Richard Gallen
   romances? ☐ yes ☐ no

9. What kind of romances do you enjoy reading?
   ☐ historical romance ☐ contemporary romance
   ☐ Regency romance ☐ light modern romance
   ☐ Gothic romance

10. Please check your general age group:
    ☐ under 25 ☐ 25-35 ☐ 35-45 ☐ 45-55 ☐ over 55

11. If you would like to receive a romance
    newsletter please fill in your name and
    address:
    _____
    _____
    _____

Romance & Adventure

New and exciting romantic fiction—passionate and strong-willed characters with deep feelings making crucial decisions in every situation imaginable—each more thrilling than the last.

Read these dramatic and colorful novels—from Pocket Books/Richard Gallen Publications

___83331	THE MOONKISSED Barbara Faith	$2.50
___83445	THIS RAGING FLOWER Lynn Erickson	$2.50
___83682	BRIDE OF THE BAJA Jocelyn Wilde	$2.50
___41266	PILLARS OF HEAVEN Leila Lyons	$2.50
___41294	WINGS OF MORNING Dee Stuart	$2.50
___83683	THIS GOLDEN RAPTURE Paula Moore	$2.50
___41295	THE FIRE BRIDE Julia Wherlock	$2.50
___41463	HEATHER SONG Nicole Norman	$2.75

POCKET BOOKS/RICHARD GALLEN PUBLICATIONS
Department RG
1230 Avenue of the Americas
New York, N.Y. 10020

Please send me the books I have checked above. I am enclosing $_____
(please add 50¢ to cover postage and handling for each order, N.Y.S. and N.Y.C.
residents please add appropriate sales tax). Send check or money order—no
cash or C.O.D.s please. Allow up to six weeks for delivery.

NAME_____

ADDRESS_____

CITY_____ STATE/ZIP_____